PENGUIN BOOKS

DANGEROUS GAMES

'A rattlingly good tale of romance, political and commercial intrigue, violence, sex, blackmail, murder ... An unfailing pleasure to read ... There is a sort of erotic gaiety, an irresponsible, buccaneering joy which makes her one of the most enjoyable writers in a highly competitive field' – *Sunday Telegraph*

'The cleverest, best written and most enjoyable novel I read' – Auberon Waugh in the *Sunday Telegraph* Books of the Year

'Transcends its genre ... This is a case where it would be puritanical to pretend that anything so readable isn't any good' – Brendan O'Keefe in the *Observer*

'A cracking good diplomatic thriller' – Jilly Cooper in the *Sunday Times* Pick of the Year

'Susan Crosland uses her inside knowledge of the political world to good effect throughout this carefully plotted story. And it is not just the wheeling and the dealing that sound authentic. She gets the atmosphere right' – Maureen Freely in the *Literary Review*

'Glitzy but intelligent novel' – *Daily Express*

ABOUT THE AUTHOR

Born in Baltimore, Maryland, the daughter of a Pulitzer Prize winning newspaperman, Susan Crosland began her own career in journalism when she came to London. She first wrote for the *Sunday Express* and quickly became known for her vivid and penetrating profiles of the rich and powerful. Two selections of her *Sunday Times* profiles have been published as books: *Behind the Image* (under the name Susan Barnes) and *Looking Out, Looking In*. For thirteen years she was married to Anthony Crosland, senior cabinet minister and the British Foreign Secretary at the time of his sudden death. Her unusual biography, *Tony Crosland*, was a bestseller. Her first novel, *Ruling Passions*, was a bestseller in 1990.

SUSAN CROSLAND

DANGEROUS GAMES

PENGUIN BOOKS

PENGUIN BOOKS

Published by the Penguin Group
Penguin Books Ltd, 27 Wrights Lane, London W8 5TZ, England
Penguin Books USA Inc., 375 Hudson Street, New York, New York 10014, USA
Penguin Books Australia Ltd, Ringwood, Victoria, Australia
Penguin Books Canada Ltd, 10 Alcorn Avenue, Toronto, Ontario, Canada M4V 3B2
Penguin Books (NZ) Ltd, 182–190 Wairau Road, Auckland 10, New Zealand

Penguin Books Ltd, Registered Offices: Harmondsworth, Middlesex, England

First published in Great Britain by George Weidenfeld & Nicolson 1991
Published in Penguin Books 1992
5 7 9 10 8 6 4

Printed in England by Clays Ltd, St Ives plc

For Sheila and Ellen-Craig

I

'OK, so everyone who's anyone opens the *News* and turns straight to the op-ed page to see what Hugo Carroll has to say on the latest Capitol Hill scandal. Hugo the fearless. Hugo the scourge. Hugo the sage. Hugo the supreme political columnist who'd better fucking well be on your side or you've had it. But the thing Hugo can't forgive is that I'm now as famous as he is. You really can't stand that, can you, Hugo.'

She saw in his light eyes what he intended as she stood three feet from him, challenging him. His fists were clenched at his side. He wanted to hit her, and she sensed he wanted to hit her in the solar plexus. But she didn't move. Standing there, slender in the narrow, white silk dress, no ornaments except a Tiffany cluster of diamonds fastened in each ear, silently she defied him to hit her.

They faced each other in the big centre hall of the Georgetown house, its front door closed behind them. He could have hit her without anybody else knowing, so long as he was careful what damage he did. In the eight years they'd been married, Hugo had never hit Georgie. He'd never hit any woman. That wasn't his scene.

Sometimes Georgie liked to goad the born-and-bred Virginia gentleman in him, to see how far she could push him before one day, perhaps, he would turn brute and lash out at her. Tonight was the second time she'd seen in his eyes that it was in his mind. The first time had been a few months earlier when, like tonight, a furious row had begun in the back of the Lincoln Continental.

This time the row had been even more savage. It had started as soon as they got into the car after Imogene Randall's dinner for the Secretary of State. Hugo leaned forward to close the glass partition and, if their voices carried through it, the back of Whitmore's cap and his broad-shouldered driver's uniform gave no hint he might be overhearing them. Whitmore had been Hugo's driver for ten years, not counting when Hugo had been working abroad. Whitmore knew nearly as much about Hugo as Georgie did.

'When the Secretary of State interrupts the dinner conversation to ask me what I think of the White House rifts, believe it or not he wants *my* opinion, not yours,' Hugo said in a tight voice. 'You really do believe you should pronounce on every subject under the sun, don't you.' It was a statement, not a question.

'God you're prickly,' said Georgie. 'It's like living with a porcupine.'

'Hardly that,' he replied angrily. 'You could scarcely be described as "living with me" – unless you count weekends and the odd weeknight when you deign to take the shuttle to Washington for a dinner so grand even the great Georgie can't stay away. And I might remind you,' he added, taking a different line of attack as people do when incensed, '*I'm* the one who got you the invitations in the first

2

place. You'd still be working in a news-room if it weren't for me.'

People remarked that even their names sounded good together: 'Hugo and Georgie' – or 'Georgie and Hugo', depending on which of this lustrous couple currently had an edge on the other.

Ranking among top journalists is not always easy to define. In any case, Hugo Carroll and Georgie Chase (in private life as well as professionally she used her own name) liked to present themselves as above such petty considerations. Each was the best, and together they were the best. Either alone was a number one catch for the Washington hostess or New York host involved in the influence trade. If you got both halves of this formidable couple at your party, your stock as a power broker rose a further eight notches.

At these prized gatherings of media, politicians, lobbyists, the rich and assorted hangers-on, neither Georgie nor Hugo ever took back seat to the other. From the outset they were seen as a team who took high risks and brought them off, he in his career, she in hers. To have a successful marriage as well was enough to turn the knife of jealousy in the hearts of all but the most saintly colleagues and friends, not to mention enemies.

'One of these days, baby, you're going to push my patience too far,' he said in the same cutting voice. She'd seen his gripped hands loosen. The rage which had nearly overwhelmed his upbringing was now

3

under control, turned to icy hatred. Not that he often hated her. Just sometimes.

'It's not your goddamn fame – the world's most "brilliant", "feared", "powerful" magazine editor – that I hate.' The quotes came out hard-edged. 'It's the self-importance you've taken on.'

'You're projecting, Hugo.'

She spoke as if she were talking to a slightly dim child. Nothing maddened him more than that, she knew.

'It's *your* self-importance, Hugo, that can't stand my being as successful as you.'

'Jesus. Six visits to that New York shrink whose feet are licked by any of your friends who can't bear to have a single thought of their own – which, let us be frank, means most of them – and you can't open your trap without parroting his garbage. *Projecting.*'

He almost spat the word with the rasp of the dirt-farmers he remembered on the steps of country stores in his childhood as they sent the stream of tobacco juice in a quick straight shot at the spittoon. He'd been repelled and fascinated by the crudeness of the dirt-farmers. They represented everything his own polished family was not.

'*Projecting*,' he repeated sarcastically. 'These days any criticism of you must be "psychologically interpreted" as someone else's defect which they're trying to put on you. You – the great Georgie, every man and woman's dream of Venus and Mammon and, we mustn't be unduly modest, God rolled into one – you are now above all criticism. Anyone who dares to suggest you've become a pain in the ass is merely "projecting".'

'I'm perfectly capable of taking criticism if it's rational,' she retorted, 'if it comes from someone who isn't motivated simply by spite. Ask Ralph Kernon.'

'Fuck Ralph Kernon. I wish he'd never taken it into his pea-head to make you editor of his precious weekly. King Kernon and Queen Georgie. What a pair of clowns.'

'Dear, dear,' she said, resuming the condescending tone guaranteed to drive him up the wall. 'Hugo isn't himself tonight.'

She saw his hands clench again into fists.

This time he knew he would hit her unless she got out of the way. 'I don't suppose you'd care to go up to bed while I have a quiet drink,' he said coldly, and without giving her a chance to answer he turned his back and strode through the living-room's open door.

Despite air-conditioners for the hot summer months, doors in most Southerners' homes remained open, a habit inherited from all those generations whose lives were dominated from June to September by the craving for a breath of cool air. Draughts were created, not avoided. But tonight Hugo jerked the living-room door shut behind him.

With steely nonchalance, Georgie ignored the door slammed in her face. 'Don't let blokes control your feelings.' That's how she had kept control of where she was going. At thirty-two she was at the top. And she had got there by her refusal to let others hurt her: if you let people tamper with your emotions, you got bogged down. She knew her control meant she missed

5

out on intense inner experience. She didn't care. It mattered more to miss out on the pain which others would inflict if you didn't say to hell with them.

'To hell with Hugo,' she muttered to the empty hall. Languidly, almost sashaying in her white silk dress, she went up the wide stairs which curved back on themselves to the bedroom floor above.

2

Hugo strode across the room to the Hepplewhite secretary-bookcase beside the french window overlooking the back garden. At thirty-eight there was still a boyishness about his appearance – slim build, six feet tall, skin lined only at the corners of his very light blue eyes, and the straight brown hair brushed back with the front bits invariably freeing themselves to fall across his forehead, giving a casual effect at odds with the formal cast of his features.

It amused him to ignore Hepplewhite's original intention, instead using the elegant enclosed bookcase as the perfect drinks cabinet. Even in his fury tonight a bit of him noticed the inlay of honeysuckle embellishing the delicately carved doors he opened to take out a bottle of Scotch, a British soda syphon from Georgie's favourite shop, and a chunky crystal glass. He'd skip going to the kitchen for ice. He needed to calm down.

The rest of the furniture was a mix of antique and expensive modern, early Victorian console tables below a pair of heavily carved Sheraton mirrors, thick glass Italian coffee-table, deep sofas covered in a supple mocha hide, overstuffed chairs in chequered pale blue and coffee-coloured silk. Chic and comfortable. Floor-length pale blue silk curtains remained open to let in the night air which in the first week of June was still fresh in Washington.

Like many eighteenth-century houses in Georgetown, its back garden was enclosed by a wall made of the same brick as the house – that pinkish brick carried as ballast in English schooners which, once safely in Chesapeake Bay, had made for Baltimore or Annapolis. When the bricks had been unloaded, the holds were filled with Maryland's tobacco leaf for the journey back to England. Sometimes the schooners sailed slightly farther south to Norfolk, Virginia, where in the wooden sheds behind the Custom House the tobacco was waiting in bales. From those days until 1865, when that most tragic of all wars was ended by General Lee's surrender in Appomattox Court House, the Carrolls had lived the well-born Southerner's life of leisure, courtesy of tobacco planted and picked by slaves. From the once grand houses, only the Hepplewhite secretary-bookcase and the pair of Sheraton console mirrors had come to Hugo.

Everything else from that indolent past had long since been sold or lost or passed on to one or another of an extended family. Hugo's great-grandparents had not quite gone under after the Civil War. But with slave labour finished, the tobacco leaf was abandoned. Most of the Carrolls moved from the country into Richmond.

By the time Hugo was born, the family abounded with lawyers and doctors, plus the occasional banker. Two of his uncles were congressmen in Washington, both fairly undistinguished. At the University, as Thomas Jefferson's dramatically beautiful red and white University of Virginia was known, a number of

8

his fellow undergraduates were from a background like Hugo's. But unlike most of them, after graduation Hugo took off from Virginia. He wanted to make his name in the big world outside.

Yet he placed a high value on the background that produced him. He liked the relaxed attitude of his Richmond relatives, their pleasure in the creature comforts as well as what his mother called 'the things of the mind'. Occasionally Hugo thought about the violence that lay somewhere beneath those exquisite Virginia manners. One of his uncles had shot himself. Another had shot his wife as she was packing lunch for their boating afternoon on the Eastern Shore with their small children, and then he'd turned the gun on himself. Afterwards Hugo's mother had said: 'The War still takes its toll.' In Virginia 'the War' meant the Civil War. 'Defeat left deep tensions,' she said more than once.

His manners and soft-accented voice could give the impression that Hugo was laid-back, but he was deeply ambitious. He was capable of sustained hard work. He took chances and sometimes cut corners in a way that his Virginia forebears might or might not have approved. Hugo had balls.

His first job was as a reporter on the *Washington Post*. When the White House press corps was united in the view that the President had ridden out the latest political storm, Hugo had ferreted out the truth behind the front. When his piece appeared on the *Post*'s front page, it was denied by the White House. But in less than a week, he was vindicated. He never looked back.

In journalism, as in most trades, two-faced scheming could take you to the top. But Hugo's route was a different one. The two-faced role was not for him. He was a man of his word. Politicians knew they couldn't hoodwink him, and those who still were rash enough to try always regretted it.

When the *News* poached him, he moved to its main office in New York. After the senior reporter on national affairs had a coronary, Hugo was appointed to replace him. Then Hugo met the proprietor's daughter and they fell in love. They intended to marry.

Unfortunately, he hadn't fully realized that his fiancée expected the rich woman's prerogative of bossing others around. Even in bed she tended to be dictatorial. He was a skilful and considerate lover: he liked giving her pleasure. But something about the brisk manner of her demands began to grate: 'No, I prefer it done *this* way,' directing his hand in the peremptory fashion of a set-in-her-ways medical consultant.

Before the knot could be tied, the engagement was called off. Her father was sorry. He liked Hugo. 'But these things happen,' he said, not allowing his disappointment at losing Hugo as a son-in-law to interfere with his proprietorial interest in keeping Hugo in a star spot on the *News*. Later that year Hugo was given the plum job of London bureau chief.

Unlike many American correspondents, he understood how the British politician ticks. And he would burst out laughing when the English mocked Americans' preoccupation with the dollar. 'For pure, unsentimental materialism,' he wrote, 'no American can match the English gent.'

It was a warm English summer evening when MV *Aureole* left Charing Cross pier at seven. The *Aureole* had been hired for sixty guests of Britain's best-known newspaper editor, Ben Franwell, rough, right wing, amiable when he felt like it, not overly concerned with scruples, a man you didn't cross if you could avoid it. Holding forth on the *Aureole*'s foredeck, Franwell said to Hugo: 'People say power corrupts, money corrupts. I'll tell you what corrupts: friendship.'

Except for the head of the US Senate Armed Forces Committee, who was sensibly combining pleasure with business while in London, and a famous film producer with his popsy, and the New York stockbroker whose reputation hung in the balance as a Congressional investigation into insider-dealing entered its sixth week, Hugo was the only American among Ben Franwell's party.

The rest were natives, and if Hugo didn't know them already, he knew most of their faces: Cabinet ministers, newspaper proprietors, publishers, the Prime Minister's favourite ad man, financial kings, star television presenters, political editors and gossip diarists whose faces looked out at you from newsstands every day, plus some spouses, assorted 'partners' and what are called good-time girls or sex objects, according to whether they are currently doing well or badly in their quest for the easy life.

By now Hugo had been the *News* bureau chief for

nearly two years. Franwell's guests who didn't already know Hugo Carroll were given the impression they certainly should be familiar with his reputation. Most British influence-wielders had a copy of the *News* among the required daily newspapers in their offices. They could gauge their international standing by whether Hugo Carroll wrote about them or didn't bother. He was the American journalist every British politician was eager to see – which in turn opened doors for him to those houses where politics, the media and money come together. And of course it didn't hurt that he was unattached. Unattached successful men – and unattached successful women, so long as they are glamorous and know how to capitalize on the package they have to offer – are given a wide choice of social life in London.

Sipping their champagne as the *Aureole* moved downstream beneath Southwark Bridge's looming central arch, several of Franwell's guests looked down at the force of the tidal water. Under Southwark Bridge only a few summers later, another launch would go under the bows of a giant sand dredger, and fifty-one carefree party-goers would be sucked into the cold deep and carried many miles before the tidal force would let go of their bodies. But Franwell's guests were uninterrupted in making contacts, making an impression, trading power gossip. Few took notice of the river banks gliding past, where Victorian warehouses still resisted the spread of sleek condominiums for City executives, and Hawksmoor's steeples glinted in the long day's sun.

An hour later, just past Greenwich, the *Aureole*

docked at the pier of a fashionable restaurant. Under a striped canopy in the garden, a banquet was spread. Each round table with starched cloth and sparkling silverware and glass was laid for ten. Hugo found himself placed beside the Defence Secretary's wife. On his other side a singularly striking young woman had already taken her seat. She was dressed in citric yellow, which happened to be his favourite colour. But he forgot her clothes when he looked at the black hair cut like a Japanese doll and saw her eyes were a hazel which appeared golden. Taking a quick glance at her place card, he read: 'Georgie Chase'.

Hugo spoke first to the woman he already knew. Then he turned to introduce himself to Georgie Chase.

'I already know who you are,' she said. 'I asked when I saw you on the *Aureole*'s foredeck. I'm a journalist too. But not as grand as you are. One day I shall be.' She was then twenty-three years old. Hugo was twenty-nine.

They both burst out laughing.

3

Georgie Chase had a hole in her sense of identity. It had been there since she was nine. Before that, she had known exactly who she was: a bright and happy youngest child in a comfortably off American family. And she was Daddy's darling.

As a child she wouldn't have defined her family as Middle America, but that's what it was. The 580-acre grain and dairy farm outside Lincoln, Nebraska had belonged to the Chases since the turn of the century. It lay in gently rolling pastures increasingly taken over by bankers and industrialists who liked the swank of a house in the country, but wanted to commute easily to their offices.

Georgie was named for her father. His father had always lived in the rambling white clapboard farmhouse, and took great satisfaction in running the farm. Soon after old Mr Chase's death, George Chase quit his job as a vice-president of Lincoln Canning Company; he'd realized he wanted to go back to the farm with his family. George had never much enjoyed being a businessman.

'How would you feel about it, Jane darling?' he asked his wife. He adored his wife. 'The farm is large enough, just, to produce a good living without my having to work my guts out. I'd have more time with you and the girls. And you'd have at least as much social life on your doorstep as in town.'

'It's OK with me,' said Jane Chase. 'All I ask is that nobody expects me to milk a cow.'

At least she looked like a pretty milkmaid with her blonde hair and pink and white skin and china-blue eyes. Like her husband, she was good-humoured and rather idle. Helping to run the farm would have bored her. But using the serenely sprawling house as a base for her social life had distinct charms. It was much smarter to live in the country than in town.

Georgie's family life was relaxed and warm and stable. She was nearly five when they moved to the farm, and her two sisters were already in high school. When she got home from kindergarten, the first person she always looked for was her father. The best part of each afternoon was hanging around with him in the barns while he supervised the milking.

After her sisters went away to college, Georgie had the special pleasures of an only child doted on by her parents. True, it was only her father who did the doting, but her mother's cheerful nature made her uncritical of Georgie. Georgie knew the deep happiness of a child surrounded by what she saw as unblemished love.

Two days after her ninth birthday, when she got home from school her mother called her out on the veranda. 'Come sit beside me on the swing, Georgie.'

One of Georgie's favourite places was the three-seater settee suspended from green-painted supports. Her legs were just long enough for her feet to touch the wide wooden floor-boards of the veranda, and if she gave a push with her feet she could make the swing go back and forth sometimes three, sometimes four times before she had to give another little shove.

'I have something to tell you, dear,' her mother said.

Georgie pushed again with her feet, and side by side she and her mother swung gently back and forth.

'You seemed to enjoy yourself,' her mother said, 'whenever you've gone with Daddy and me to have lunch next door. Last Sunday I watched you walking hand in hand with Francis when you went down to the duckpond.' Francis Naylor was the industrialist who owned the big estate half a mile away.

'That was because he took my hand,' said Georgie.

Jane Chase reapproached the subject. 'Daddy and I,' she said, 'love each other. We always will. But you know, Georgie, it isn't easy for two people to live a lifetime together. It was different when people didn't live so long. But today – you know this from many of your friends – couples often find after twenty years that they are not good for each other any longer.'

'But you and Daddy aren't like that. And you and Daddy are good for me,' said Georgie.

'I know, dear. And you are good for us,' said her mother. 'But if Daddy and I went on living together, we would quarrel, and you would find we were not good for you then. If Daddy and I lived apart, you would still see both of us. It's just that you would have two homes instead of one. Lots of people would give anything to have two homes.'

'But I don't want two homes,' said Georgie. Her neck had become stiff and it hurt all down her back.

The swing was coming to a stop. If she shoved with her foot and the swing got going again, maybe it would be just like before and the pain down her back would go away. She pushed against the floor-boards. She liked the way the veranda's boards felt different from those inside the house; it must have something to do with the space between the veranda and the ground. She and her mother swung back and forth.

'Well, Georgie, your father and I have agreed it would be best to live separately. You and I will move in with Francis. But you and Daddy can visit each other as much as you like.'

Not long after their marriage, Jane and Francis Naylor decided to move to London where he would become executive director of the firm's British branch. During the three weeks of palaver involved in the move, Georgie stayed at the farm with her father. When the time came to say goodbye, George Chase's eyes filled with tears, and when they started down his face he turned away.

Georgie didn't cry. 'It's OK, Dad. Mom says I can come back to the farm for vacations. And we can write to each other.'

As she said it, her small face expressionless, she became aware of a feeling inside her which was different from a real feeling. It was the opposite to a real feeling. She thought of the space under the veranda, but that didn't describe it either. It was as if there was a hole somewhere inside her. She'd never noticed it before.

*

Six months after she'd begun her London life in the handsome house just off Wimbledon Common, Georgie was in her bedroom writing a letter to her father when her mother came to the room. Jane put her arms around Georgie.

'I must tell you something, dear,' Jane said. 'Your father died yesterday. He had cancer. He was lucky it wasn't drawn out the way it often is. He didn't suffer.'

Georgie didn't cry. She sat motionless. He'd gone away. Just like that. He hadn't even said goodbye. She'd never know whether he had suffered or not. She'd never be able to explain to him how much she loved him. The pain was so terrible she pushed it away. But she could feel the hole inside her.

Francis Naylor was a pleasant enough stepfather. He and Jane spent their happiest moments at the card-table, and their skill at bridge, with Naylor's money and business connections, soon brought them to the notice of London's smart, upper-class society. Not long after they'd been taken as guests to the St James's Bridge Club in London they were proposed for membership, which they accepted with alacrity. And when Francis Naylor was put up for the Reform Club no member of the committee blackballed him as might have happened had he been an Englishman; no one had a grudge against Francis.

Like the English children she now knew, Georgie saw more of the housekeeper whose bedroom adjoined hers than she did of her mother. When she was eleven she was sent away to boarding-school.

Georgie didn't take it personally being dispatched from home: all the other privileged girls at her school had been decanted from their families. During the first week, one or two girls cried at night, but Georgie didn't feel much of anything.

She made plenty of new friends. She was clever. She was charming to look at – slim, her mother's pink and white skin, hazel eyes that were golden in certain lights and contrasted with the dark, nearly black hair she'd inherited from her father, which fell in long waves.

Soon after her twelfth birthday she used her paper-scissors to cut off seven or eight inches of her hair, a couple of inches at a time, until all the waves were strewn on the carpet and only a short, straight bob remained above her ear lobes. Though she'd never heard of the exquisite actress who had briefly been a 1920s' cult figure, Georgie had seen a black and white photograph of Louise Brooks in a Sunday supplement, and she liked the long fringe and short bob. She couldn't manage the back, but another girl cut it for her in an uneven sloping line. In the end the housemistress decided the best way out of this situation was to send Georgie to a proper hairdresser who evened up the fringe and the sides where they were chopped off above the ear lobes, shingling the hair at the back so the pretty point of the nape became pronounced and enticing. It often made men wonder how sexually aware this schoolgirl was.

Georgie wasn't obsessively competitive. She was amused by the intense rivalry – positive hatred – which croquet roused in male guests at a country-house weekend; she couldn't have cared less whether she won or lost at croquet. But when she was interested in something – most of her studies, gymnastics, tennis – she wanted to be best at it.

'None of us was in the least surprised that she should have won a scholarship to Oxford,' her head-mistress wrote to Georgie's mother.

The first thing Georgie noticed at Oxford was that the competition was infinitely stiffer than at school: she'd have to make more effort if others were to sit up and take notice. That applied to social life even more than to her work. She had girlfriends (non-sexual) and boyfriends (sometimes sexual, other times not). She was amusing and not quite like other people. While she enjoyed social life, if there was nothing to do she was content with her own company and would either read or day-dream.

Several times she fell in love. But her capacity for love was restricted by an emotional detachment. She didn't regret this: it gave her an armour against being hurt. But it also gave her a tendency to see people as vehicles. If they disappointed her she discarded them.

One of her suitors was eminently suitable. 'I know, I know: it would suit my mother down to the ground,' Georgie said to Patsy Fawcett. Soon after she and Patsy met at Oxford, they were each other's best friend. 'But what he really wants is for me to be first and foremost his wife. When he says he wouldn't mind if I had a career, he's only kidding himself. So he'll have to go.'

For Georgie wanted to drive a chariot of her own, and she guessed its gilt would be brighter on the other side of the Atlantic, probably in New York. She wanted to be a journalist.

She'd always liked Britain, by which she really meant London. A huge choice of national newspapers and glossy magazines was there. At any one time, a dozen female stars shimmered in journalism's firmament. Yet British journalism was still essentially a man's world. Anyone who doubted that had only to look around a news-room. And a woman editor, even of a tabloid, was still beyond the horizon.

New York seemed to her the ideal place, not for the sake of living in that hard fast lane, but because New York offered the greatest choice of glossy magazines. Most of all, Georgie wanted to be editor of a magazine where she could hold power politics – politician politics, media politics, money politics, literary politics, social politics, fashion politics, the whole bloody shebang – in her hand.

'I want to be the person who makes the puppets dance,' she said to Patsy Fawcett.

Since her father's death, Georgie had thought of returning to America only in terms of a career. She never felt homesick for Nebraska. If sometimes, inadvertently, an image of the farm came to mind, it had a picture-frame around it like a snapshot from long ago.

Patsy Fawcett was raised in a family security which Georgie hadn't known since early childhood. Patsy's father was a Recorder of the Crown Court. She'd been treasured by her parents even before her mother learned she could have no more children. Whenever

Judge Fawcett was asked by one of his bewigged colleagues if he'd thought of sending his daughter to a girls' boarding-school, invariably he replied: 'I detested being sent away from home when I was nine. My wife detested being sent to Cheltenham. We find no compelling reason to inflict this strange English custom on our own child.'

Instead Patsy went to London's top girls' day-school which happened to be a twenty-minute bus ride from the Fawcetts' home in Kensington. She had to be bright, of course, to get into St Paul's. And between the ages of nine and thirteen, Antonia, as she then was, excelled both at studies and at games. All hell broke loose, however, soon after Antonia's thirteenth birthday.

Judge Fawcett could remember the day vividly: it was during one of Britain's cherished sunny Julys, and the three of them were having Sunday lunch at the teak table on the big balcony overlooking the back garden. Sunlight filtered through the overhanging oak tree and glinted on Antonia's curtain of honey-coloured hair, turning it a deep gold. The hell began when Antonia announced that henceforth she was to be known as Patsy. The judge and his wife looked at one another.

'But Antonia is such a beautiful name, dear,' Mrs Fawcett said to her daughter.

'It doesn't suit me.'

Again her parents glanced at one another. They would have to proceed with care.

'If you want to change your name,' said the judge affably, 'mightn't it be better to brood on the thing before taking your final decision? Americans commonly use the word "patsy" to mean fall guy.'

'I don't care. Anyhow, no one is ever going to confuse me with a fall guy.'

The judge noticed his daughter's green eyes had turned aquamarine, defiant as they reflected the cloudless sky. He suppressed a sigh. Her eyes softened when she turned to her mother.

'I'm sorry about the towels, Mummy. Perhaps I can pick the stitches out of the A.'

Mrs Fawcett, whose daily hours were more than sufficiently occupied, had made a special trip to Harrods to choose a pair of peppermint-green Turkish towels and have them monogrammed 'AF' in time for Antonia's birthday.

Patsy remained good at studies and games, but two other interests suffused her when she woke in her bedroom each morning. One was the awareness of her body as she stretched her legs apart and lifted her arms so the backs of her hands could lie on the shiny, honey-coloured hair spread out on her pillow. (She had considered calling herself Honey but had decided that sounded too American.) The other, closely related, was the excitement of thinking about a fifth-former from St Paul's boys' school. Twice a week when Patsy left her own school soon after four, he was standing near a plane-tree on the green. They had coffee together in Hammersmith Road before she caught the tube home.

Overnight, it seemed to the judge, his home life became dominated by Patsy's desire for this acne-faced youth. Every conversation in the Fawcett family included a fresh challenge from Patsy. Why couldn't she go out on weekday evenings? Why did she have to be home on Saturday night before anybody else? Why couldn't she and this (in the judge's view) frightful youth take their overfilled mugs of coffee up to her room? What was wrong with smoking pot in her room? Each of the next four years was pretty good hell, if you asked the judge.

At least when Patsy was at Oxford she was outside her parents' responsibility, which all three found a relief. 'Out of sight out of mind' actually did work, Mrs Fawcett was surprised to discover. Even so, she sometimes worried about her daughter's impulsive nature. Glad that Patsy didn't appear to be promiscuous, she was uneasy about the intensity with which Patsy loved.

How long Patsy remained in love was unpredictable. Sometimes it was a year or two, other times a month at the most. When she was the one to get bored or fall for somebody else, she was not always thoughtful of the rejected one's feelings. When she was the one rejected, she was really down. 'You shouldn't let blokes control your feelings. To hell with him,' Georgie would say to Patsy.

Georgie tried to teach Patsy her own technique: 'Put on a front: pretend you couldn't care less that he dumped you. You'll find the front has an effect on your insides and you do care less.'

'But it doesn't work with me,' Patsy wailed.

'That's because you don't properly detach yourself. It may not work one hundred per cent straight away, but it will. Just keep saying to yourself: "I'm not going to let that prick control my feelings."'

Shortly after leaving Oxford, Georgie and Patsy decided to rent a London flat together. Notting Hill Gate was an obvious place to start looking for something they could afford – in a converted house still shabby rather than done up. The area was popular with London's young intelligentsia, and it was convenient for reaching their offices by tube – Georgie to *Harper's*, Patsy to Jonathan Cape.

Notting Hill had the added attraction of being not far from the Fawcetts' home. Often when Patsy went to see her parents, she took Georgie with her. 'Your family is everything mine's not,' Georgie said without resentment. It was a simple statement of fact. Had she been asked if she felt envious, she would have said, 'No.' She had lived so long without family commitment that she imagined she'd never want the emotional responsibility of a close family life. Yet it always seemed to her like a special occasion when she visited the Fawcetts. Not only did she respect them: she came to love them more than she'd loved any older person since she was nine.

'They never touch each other in front of other people,' she said to Patsy, 'yet they always give the sense of being a total couple. I don't know any other couple like them.'

At the same time that Georgie began to climb the ladder at *Harper's*, Patsy used more time than perhaps a junior editor at Cape should have done drawing in a large plain-leaf notebook, sketching comic scenes with comic people as she imagined them from the manuscripts she was editing.

'Authors take their subjects so bloody seriously,

when most of them are utterly absurd,' she said to Georgie.

Georgie burst out laughing at Patsy's sketches. 'You ought to enrol in an evening class and get some proper training,' she told her. But Patsy was too occupied by being in love to leave enough time for that.

'Well, one thing is absolutely certain,' she said on the morning after she dumped the man she had adored for eighteen months. 'However much in love I am the next time, Georgie, I'm not going to marry until I've stayed in love for three years.'

She had gone out several times with MPs and found each of them a real turn-off. 'You think they're going to be exciting and glamorous. They turn out to be pompous pigs.'

Then she met Ian Lonsdale. His irony and self-sufficiency attracted her instantly. She liked his air of knowing where he was going without a great song and dance about it. The slight limp made him more intriguing, not less.

His father had been in the colonial service, and Ian was five when his parents died of malaria in Rhodesia. He was raised by his grandparents in their comfortable house in Derbyshire.

The accident had happened during his final year at school. Ian was driving and, unusually for the driver, was the only one of the youths who was badly hurt. Lying in a hospital bed for the next ten months, he was glad no one else could be blamed. If you had to be broken up, it was better that you were responsible for it. He'd never shirked responsibility.

Despite the fifth operation on his leg, it was never quite right. It barred him from athletics in which he'd previously excelled. Perhaps that's why sexual prowess became so important to him at Oxford. Or perhaps it was simply the old id. Whatever the reason, the fact of being in love with a girl did not in the least deter him from screwing around with other girls.

If his limp had any effect on women, it made him more attractive. With his dark hair and long grey eyes and commanding height he was handsome, and women get suspicious when a man is too handsome. A little imperfection reassures them.

After Oxford Ian started his own software business in the Midlands. He was confident, competent and lucky. The business snowballed.

He was twenty-five when he made his first attempt to become a Member of Parliament. Four years later, having earned his spurs fighting a hopeless seat, he was given the chance to fight a safe one. His party lost its majority at the general election, but Ian became MP for Shurston. Within months his reputation in the House began to rise. Then he met Patsy.

As soon as he saw the honey-coloured curtain of hair, the green eyes and pert expression, he could scarcely keep his hands from reaching out and touching her. Soon after he first got her into bed, he discovered he was in love in a way he had never been before.

'I couldn't bear it,' she said one night when, both of them wet with sweat, she was lying on her side with one arm thrown across his chest, 'if you did this with somebody else.'

Ian said nothing.

'I've never been attracted to two men at the same time. I can't imagine I ever could be,' she said.

He remained silent.

She propped herself on an elbow so she could look down into his face. With one hand he fingered her hair where it was still damp as it lay on her shoulders. The corners of his mouth smiled when he touched the tips of the dark lashes which fringed the green eyes. He loved the relaxed innocence of her expression after its absorbed concentration when she was reaching her climax.

'You say you've never before wanted to marry anyone,' she said. 'Does that mean you won't want . . .' She hesitated. Each knew what was in her mind.

'I'll go and wash,' he said. 'Shall we have a nightcap before I take you back to Notting Hill? We needn't get dressed yet, but let's go into the drawing-room and have a talk.'

'If it's to be a serious talk, I suppose I'd better have some clothes on,' she said.

Both were dressed when they sat down beside one another on his sofa, two whisky-and-sodas on the coffee-table. He came straight to the point. 'You may perfectly well conclude I want it both ways.'

I know what's fucking coming, Patsy said to herself.

Ian had the manner of many Englishmen of his upbringing. If compelled to discuss his deeper feelings, he preferred to do so as if he were discussing a business deal. But the seeming chilliness was misleading: he was by no means unemotional.

'You say you've never been sexually attracted to two people at the same time. I hope to God you're never again attracted to any man but me, Patsy. I'll try to keep that from happening.' He paused only briefly before going on in a self-mocking manner: 'It would be easy for me to tell you that for the rest of my days on this earth I shall never never have some totally inconsequential adventure. Nothing seems less likely at the moment, I must say. But I don't like the idea of having to write out a hundred per cent guarantee.'

Patsy felt the blood rush to her face, but she sipped her whisky-and-soda. She fucking well wasn't going to let him see the tears she felt pricking her eyes. This was meant to be a grown-up conversation, for Christ's sake. She composed her face in her calm, grown-up expression.

'What I *can* guarantee,' he said, 'is that if ever, out of childishness or male vanity or God knows what idiotic weakness of character, I had a brief fling, it wouldn't affect us in any way. And it wouldn't happen in a way that could affect your pride. Or vanity. Whatever one wants to call it. Ever.'

He knew she didn't want to hear any of this. Yet he was convinced he had to get something established if they were to avoid doom. For it was impossible for him to imagine a lifetime of fidelity. He would have added that occasional casual screwing on his part might make his love for her even stronger, but that seemed too disgraceful a line of argument, even though it might be true.

'Do you know how cold you sound?' she said. 'It

29

makes me sick. I may just have to leave the room for a few minutes while I vomit. What you're saying is that as I'm monogamous and you are not, therefore I should be above such shoddy feelings as jealousy when you goat around with little slags. And as far as I can make out,' she added, in what was a slightly separate point, 'any bird who applies to be an MP's secretary is looking for a husband or an easy lay.'

Ian turned and looked at her profile. He could see only one green eye, but he sensed the cold white sparks shooting out from both her eyes. The corners of his mouth turned up again. He was perfectly capable of seeing how offensive she found his proposition.

'Let's forget it,' he said. 'It was an asinine thing for me to raise.'

Barely four months after they'd first met, Patsy married Ian Lonsdale. She didn't want the conventional six little children as bridesmaids and pages. Instead, her only attendant was Georgie.

The wedding was held in London's fashionable St George's Church in Hanover Square. The Fawcetts had chosen the Hyde Park Hotel for the reception, but it took longer for the wedding party and guests to get there than they expected. Grosvenor Square and all streets leading from it had been cordoned off by police, with ambulances waiting. Sniffer dogs searched beneath parked cars while the bomb squad systematically dissected the twisted rubble of what had been a gleaming BMW.

For at the same moment that St George's organist

had pulled out all his stops for the triumphant wedding march, three pounds of Semtex went off beneath the BMW parked a few streets away, killing a man and woman who happened to be walking by.

4

Because she went out so much, others imagined Georgie was always gregarious. In fact she still liked to have time to herself during the few hours she might be home in an evening or at the weekend. Patsy's marriage meant Georgie had to find someone else to share the rent in a flat too big for one person. She groaned at the thought.

Then one evening when Ian was at the House, she and Patsy were dining out together and Patsy said: 'You know that basement flat in Mummy and Daddy's house? It's got only one bedroom. The tenant is moving back to France in a fortnight. Why don't you move in there? Even though it has a separate entrance from the rest of the house, it wouldn't have worked for me to live that close to my family. But it would be different with you.'

Still in their forties, the judge and his wife both led lives considerably more demanding than Georgie's. Occasionally she had a drink or a meal with them, or she might bump into one of them outside the house, but most of the time they went their separate ways. While Georgie had never sought a family base after her own was swept away, she liked the feeling of living downstairs in the Fawcetts' house.

Often she went straight from work to a literary party, awful as most of them proved to be, one conceited writer swaggering in front of another, agents and publishers vying in aggressive charm. She began an affair with an eminent literary critic who didn't allow his marriage to inconvenience him unduly. Then she added an eminent political journalist to her bow. He wrote a famous diary for Ben Franwell's newspaper, the *Rampart*, and he was the person who took her to Franwell's party on the *Aureole*. When he pointed out the new Home Secretary in a tête-à-tête with Hugo Carroll on the foredeck, Georgie determined to find an opportunity to meet Hugo before the evening was over.

It was not just that he was extremely attractive. Equally to the point, he had more connections than either of her current boyfriends. The one she was with on the *Aureole* was a big cheese among Britain's media and politicians, but unknown in America. When she discovered she would be seated beside Hugo Carroll at dinner, it was as if a key piece in the jigsaw puzzle was suddenly found. Now she had to put it in place.

His good manners meant he divided his time during dinner between his two table partners. But whenever he was talking with the Defence Secretary's wife, a piece of his brain was thinking about the girl in the citric-yellow dress who sat on his other side. Her jaunty boldness was at odds with her delicate face and the hair cut like a Japanese doll.

At the dinner's end, when Ben Franwell and his sixty guests strolled back along the pier where the *Aureole* waited, Hugo and Georgie were still talking together. Franwell came up to them.

'Hugo, do you know the coming man in the

opposition party?' he said with ponderous geniality. The evening had gone well and he was in an expansive mood.

Georgie began to laugh. The MP that Franwell was introducing to Hugo was Ian Lonsdale, and beside him stood Patsy. Patsy gave Georgie a conspiratorial wink; they'd spent part of the pre-dinner boat ride gossiping over the champagne. But neither Patsy nor Ian had met Hugo before. Politician and journalist instantly fell into shop-talk.

'For three weeks we've been reading that the new Home Secretary is the next thing to God,' Ian said. 'Your column yesterday is the only one to point out the depths of his shallowness.'

Hugo laughed. 'He was just telling me before dinner tonight that I've grossly misunderstood him.'

'Grossly understood him.'

'I know.'

Patsy said to Georgie in a low voice: 'Your political diarist admirer seems pissed off. I bumped into him a minute ago and all he said was: "Where the bloody hell has Georgie got to?"'

'It's a good question,' Georgie replied, looking at Hugo as he talked with Ian. 'Ask me again in a few days' time.'

Then the *Rampart*'s political diarist spotted her, and she boarded the *Aureole* with him. Not until the ropes were being secured to Charing Cross pier and the passengers were crowded together to disembark did she see Hugo again. Even before she turned around, she knew the person pressing against her in the throng was Hugo Carroll.

'We kept getting separated,' he said. 'I'll have to do something about that.' If he suspected that the man standing just on her other side might be a boyfriend, he ignored it. 'I'll ring you at *Harper's*.'

Each time her office phone rang the next day, Georgie picked it up expectantly. Each time she was disappointed.

It never occurred to her to ring Hugo at the *News* bureau. While half the women she knew made formal approaches to the man, it didn't fit in with her idea of herself: she preferred not to show she gave a damn. 'To hell with him,' she said towards the end of the afternoon, trying to practise what she'd preached to Patsy, and having little success.

She was short-tempered over her dinner with the eminent literary critic. The fact that she was having an affair with him as well as the *Rampart*'s political diarist didn't mean he could make assumptions: any idea he had of getting her into bed that evening got short shrift. 'I've got my period,' she said in the abrupt tone of someone who wants no argument about ways to get round this condition.

Halfway through the next morning when her office telephone rang for the umpteenth time, she picked it up impatiently. For a moment the person at the other end didn't speak, and she felt the blood rush into her face: she knew it was him.

'It's Hugo Carroll,' he said in his laid-back voice. 'We met at Ben Franwell's party.'

She burst out laughing. 'So we did.'

'I was trying to remember what you said about your career. That it would one day be as "grand" as

35

mine? If you ever go out for a non-grand evening, would you like to have dinner next week?'

On Monday evening she went home from *Harper's* to change before she met him. Zipping up the citric-yellow dress, she smiled: he'd asked her if she would wear it again. 'You may rightly regard it as none of my business what you wear,' he'd said, laughing, 'but it's my favourite colour.'

Looking at him across their table at Launceston Place, a single candle flickering between them, she knew it was not just what Hugo Carroll could do for her career that made her want him: she wanted him for himself. As they talked, her eyes examined every inch of his face – the light-blue eyes contrasting with the straight brown hair brushed back, the sensual mouth at odds with the formal cast of his features. When he poured out more claret from the bottle on the table, her eyes followed his hand. It was a handsome hand, well-made, confident. She imagined it touching her, and immediately she felt her stomach tighten low down.

He took her home in a taxi, telling the driver to go first to the house in Kensington, then on to Belgravia which is where his own flat was. While the driver waited, he saw her to the basement door.

When they met again two evenings later, after dinner he gave the taxi-driver the Kensington address only. Georgie said nothing, but her stomach tightened, and by the time she was putting her key in the lock, she felt sick. It wasn't the sick feeling that has to do with nausea: it was the tension of sexual desire.

Once inside the flat, he reached around her to

close the door and then he stood facing her. He stretched out his arms either side of her shoulders, his hands flat against the door, fencing her in as she stood with her back against the door. He leaned his face over hers. After a moment's hesitation she tipped back her head, and his mouth closed over hers. For a long time they stood like that, Georgie with her arms hanging at her sides, Hugo's arms fencing her in against the door, their bodies not touching as they explored each other's mouth. The space he kept between their bodies while they kissed began to feel like a solid barrier. With every minute her desire grew for the barrier to be smashed. When at last he lowered his arms and began unbuttoning her blouse as she still stood with her back against the door, her breasts were so erect they hurt. When he had finished undressing her, she touched him for the first time. Then neither of them could stop touching the other, and as the hall was carpeted they lay down where they were, just inside the front door. Neither spoke, and only the sound of their breathing when it turned into short, hoarse panting broke the silence of the hall until Hugo gave a low shout that swelled louder until it stopped. Then he began kissing her mouth again.

It was not until their third evening together that he discovered the trick guaranteed to make Georgie come. She had experienced orgasm with a previous lover, and it had been a fantastic sense of physical achievement and release, but as soon as it was completed, she had the same feeling men often do: it was a physical pleasure completed without any emotional closeness afterwards. As soon as the act was finished, she began thinking about what she had to do the next day. Instead of wanting to go on lying there beside him, enjoying the intimacy and post-coital tenderness, she would almost immediately go off to the bathroom and wash herself.

With Hugo it was different. It was her first experience of being totally in love. Whereas previously she had thought nothing of conducting two affairs at the same time, now the idea became repugnant to her.

'What is so fantastic,' she said one day to Patsy, 'is that he has everything I want. I'm not faced with the choice between someone leading the kind of life I like, and someone I like for himself. Hugo has got it all.'

He felt precisely the same about Georgie. By nature he was monogamous, and he gave his love in its entirety to this ravishing girl whose undisguised ambition appealed to him. He knew she wanted a career where she could drive a chariot of her own. There were doors in America that he was ideally placed to open for her. He was glad and proud to do so: he wanted to help her make her name. Theirs would be the dream partnership.

In February, on her twenty-fourth birthday, eight months after they'd met on the *Aureole*, they were married in Kensington Registry Office. The only people present at their marriage were Patsy and Ian Lonsdale, Judge Fawcett and his wife, and Georgie's mother and stepfather. The reception for eighty friends of Hugo and Georgie was held in the Fawcetts' home in Kensington.

'Georgie dear,' the judge had said after Patsy first raised the matter with her parents, 'nothing would give us greater pleasure. But don't you think it might hurt your mother's feelings if you held your reception in someone else's home?'

'They live in Wimbledon,' Georgie said in an expressionless voice, her face closed. 'It's too far away.'

Patsy caught her mother's eye. Half the guests lived south of the Thames and would find it just as easy to drive to Wimbledon as to drive to Kensington. But the judge and his wife tactfully took Georgie's explanation at face value, though Mrs Fawcett worded it somewhat differently when she wrote to Georgie's mother, asking this woman she'd never met if the Fawcetts could have the joy and honour of holding Georgie's reception in their home, 'which happens to be so close to Kensington Registry Office'.

That spring, when his assignment as London bureau chief came to its natural end, Hugo was appointed chief political editor of the *News*. He and Georgie flew Concorde to New York and spent a week unwinding in the Hamptons at the cottage (a ten-bedroom affair set in twenty acres overlooking Long Island Sound) of the New York senator who was a friend of Hugo.

'How do you feel being back in the land of your birth?' asked Hugo, as he and Georgie swam side by side in a leisurely crawl towards their host's raft moored fifty yards offshore.

'Nothing sentimental,' she replied. 'But the water

feels fine. No ghastly shocks to the system when you first go in.' She had never understood why Britain's beaches were surrounded by water that froze your ass off, despite the Gulf Stream's efforts to warm things up.

'Wait till we dive into the hurly-burly,' Hugo replied, laughing. 'You'll get one or two shocks then.' So far, the fast lanes of New York and Washington existed only in Georgie's dreams. He had abundant experience of how the *bonhomie* pervading a rich man's 'cottage' in the Hamptons disappears – *pffft* – in the soul-searing competition of Manhattan and Capitol Hill.

Georgie kicked the water harder so she pulled ahead, her skin gleaming in the morning sun. Switching to a relaxed breast-stroke so he could watch her, Hugo found the rhythmical movement of her wet, slender arms produced sudden desire. He thought of the previous afternoon when they had returned to their bedroom for an hour. Now, as Georgie put her hands up on the wooden raft and gracefully levered herself aboard it, her black, cropped hair glistening as the water ran off it – like water off a bird's feathers, Hugo thought – he changed back to a fast crawl. By the time he reached the raft, he knew what he wanted to do with Georgie.

'How visible are we from the house?' he said, as he pulled himself up beside her and she watched the well-made hands that gave her so much pleasure reach for the front fastening on her bikini top.

'Fairly,' she replied. 'Does it matter?' It amused her to egg him on to little outbreaks of incorrect social behaviour which went against his upbringing.

'Not much,' he said. Somewhat to his surprise, the born-and-bred gentleman found a distinct *frisson* in the thought that what they did next might be a live video in a round frame for anyone who decided to take a look through the telescope mounted on the veranda of the distant house. An intent half-smile flickered across Hugo's face as, to start with, he undid the clasp of the bikini top.

5

In Washington's fashionable Georgetown area they found a good row-house, what the British call a terrace house. Once again Whitmore, at the wheel of the Lincoln, became an essential adjunct to Hugo as part of the deal with the *News*.

Hugo introduced Georgie to the *Washington Post* feature editor, and a job offer followed. Quickly *Post* readers were looking for her byline. She was a sharp observer, witty, irreverent. And being Hugo's wife opened all the capital's doors that mattered.

He took her to her first White House reception towards the end of their first year in Washington. 'It's far more important for you to get on with the First Lady than flirt with the President,' he told her while they waited for the officers at the Pennsylvania Avenue entrance gates to finish security.

Georgie got on immediately with the First Lady. Four months later when they were invited to a White House dinner for the British Prime Minister, Georgie went not just as Hugo's wife but in her own right too: Hugo Carroll and Georgie Chase. She had become one of the two top feature writers in town.

Eight months later she received the offer from *Bazaar* in New York. Its proprietor wasn't satisfied with *Bazaar* being the market leader among predominantly fashion-orientated glossies. He wanted to introduce a harder edge to its features. And he wanted some sharp political input: 'Any self-important journalist can churn out sage thoughts on weighty matters. I want our readers to laugh, be shocked, and at the same time know they've learned something. It's got to be pithy, sceptical, close to libel but not so close we get sued.'

He emphasized that if Georgie accepted the post of executive features editor, he couldn't guarantee what the future held, but he believed *Bazaar*'s present editor wouldn't be in that chair much longer.

All that weekend Georgie and Hugo talked it over: it meant they'd need a small apartment in Manhattan, dividing their time between the two cities, separated during most of the work week.

'I hate the idea of being apart for four nights,' Hugo told her.

'Well, they say that weekend marriages stay hotter than full-time ones,' she replied.

'I'll try to persuade my cock of that when he starts complaining during the week,' said Hugo.

Both could see she should go for it.

On the first night in her 57th Street apartment, the traffic woke her early, but instead of minding it she tingled with excitement. On most weekends she would return to the Georgetown house, but Hugo came to New York the first weekend. 'I must put my personal mark on your nice new sheets,' he said, laughing with pleasure as he pulled her down on the bed beside him.

They wanted to have children one day, ideally two. But when? No time looked likely to be the ideal time. Georgie's work days at *Bazaar* lasted a good ten

43

hours, if you counted lunch at Lutece and the Four Seasons as work, which rightly she did, and didn't count the evening drinks parties and dinners which were rarely less than three times a week. Occasionally Hugo took the Trump Shuttle to New York to join her on a weeknight, and she took the shuttle to Washington for a dinner that really mattered – which meant it could be useful for her career. This was less coldly calculating than some might imagine, for while Georgie had a basic emotional detachment, she was not a chilly person. She was a woman whose career was as much a part of her make-up as it is for an ambitious man. For Hugo the line between work and play was pretty fuzzy. For Georgie the line had become non-existent: everything should provide a contact for something else. If social life was not useful, she'd as soon be by herself.

'I get on well enough with thousands of people in New York and Washington,' she wrote to Patsy, 'but my only real true friend in America is Hugo. Isn't it lucky to feel that way about a husband and also have it good in bed?'

She and Hugo had neither the time for infidelity nor the inclination. Theirs was one of the really successful marriages, and they had no desire to muck around with it. They could live apart during the week because they were confident of their relationship.

Initially in her task of producing hard-edged yet seductive features, Georgie telephoned Hugo any number of times a week for leads on politicians she was pin-pointing. He never let her down. Gradually she built up such a network of information that she could call on him less. Meanwhile *Bazaar*'s readership rose steadily and – the point of the exercise – a wider range of advertisers began buying space.

When, through uncharacteristic carelessness, she became pregnant, she and Hugo agreed this was probably as good a moment as any. Also, each of them was immensely moved by Georgie's pregnancy. 'I didn't know I'd feel like this,' she said, holding his hand against her belly.

But she didn't let her pregnancy interfere with her work/socializing schedule. When she began ballooning in her sixth month, she had her bobbed hair cropped into a midshipman's crew cut, and her maternity clothes were designed like a sailor's blouse with the big flat collar and V-neck and little black tie. The effect was charming and made people smile. She was in her office at *Bazaar* up to ten days before she went into labour. Six weeks after Sarah was born, Georgie was back at her desk.

She'd moved into a larger apartment so there'd be a room for Sarah and a good enough extra bedroom to satisfy the responsible young woman hired to look after her. At weekends Georgie took Sarah to Washington, and those two days were some of the happiest she knew. From the moment his daughter was born, Hugo had felt a fierce love for her, and the three of them lived a 'proper family life' for those two days in the Georgetown house. 'It's like playing house,' Georgie said to Hugo as they sat down to the dinner she cooked after they put Sarah to bed.

Then *Bazaar*'s editor resigned – or was sacked, depending on how you interpreted the proprietor's carefully worded press statement. Georgie was promoted to be number one. *Bazaar*'s readers and advertisers increased further.

Two years later, Jamie was born. That was that. Georgie's childbearing was done. Now when she flew to Washington with the children for the weekend with Hugo, she took the nanny with her. Sometimes Sarah and Jamie and the nanny stayed on in the Georgetown house with Hugo, and Georgie returned to her Manhattan apartment alone.

'I wish you'd sometimes wear colours again, Georgie,' Hugo said. 'I dreamed about you the other night – wearing that citric yellow. I woke up yearning for you in yellow. You were wearing it the night we met on that Thames riverboat. Remember?'

Following Jamie's birth, instead of having even the mildest post-partum depression, Georgie had changed her style of dressing: in the cold months she now wore black, in the hot months white. She was the first to acknowledge that using black and white as a trademark was an affectation. 'Of course it is. But since I feel like it, why not?' she said.

Jamie's first birthday fell on a Wednesday but they celebrated it at Sunday lunch in the Georgetown house. Georgie knew Jamie was less than totally absorbed by having completed a full year on this earth, but Sarah was old enough to take the calendar seriously. In a way, his birthday celebration was conducted for Sarah's satisfaction. She had just helped him blow out his candle when the telephone rang in the next room. Hugo went to take it, and in a minute was back.

'It's for you, Georgie. It's Ralph Kernon. As he's phoned himself, you'd better prise yourself away from the birthday cake.'

Kernon's empire included one of America's three top weeklies. A notoriously efficient man, he saw no point in using energy in preambles. Georgie had said little more than hello into the telephone before Kernon's hoarse voice rapped out the short series of assertions and rhetorical questions which character- ized his conversation.

'Several thoughts have just come together in my mind. It's time a top news weekly had a woman editor. What woman journalist is cool enough to take on the job? She'd have to have roots in America. OK, you can say being Brits didn't keep Tina Brown and Anna Wintour from becoming editors of Ameri- can magazines.'

Georgie said nothing.

'They both used being British to their advantage: it gave them an arm's-length insight,' he stated, and then immediately went on to qualify his assertion. 'But they only needed insight into cosmopolitan trends, social phenomena. *World* has to have an editor with some instinct for three and a quarter million readers across the whole damn country. How can you expect a Limey to understand anything about America beyond the Hudson?'

It didn't occur to Kernon to allow even a token pause to follow this question. He went straight on:

'At least three million of our readers belong to Middle America. If you're to keep them identifying with *World*, the editor has to 've had a certain kind of experience in the States – brought up in the family of a suburban Chicago stockbroker, or maybe a Missouri farmer, or a Texas lawyer – has to 've been inoculated with some gut understanding of what I call real Americans. The editor has to know the audience. The trick is to have each piece be comprehensible and informal for the non-expert – *and* respectable for the expert. I know your work. I'm told you were born and bred in Lincoln, Nebraska. I want to know about that.'

The hoarse voice abruptly stopped.

After his second sentence, Georgie had sat down on the nearest chair, one hand holding the telephone while the other cupped her face to shut out all distraction.

When the line suddenly was silent, she didn't need to be prompted that it was her turn to speak without preamble. In a split second she decided how best to maximize her American childhood – sounding forthcoming but skipping details which would draw undue attention to how young she'd been. And she'd skip the American stuff she'd absorbed since coming back as Hugo's wife: Kernon would know that already.

'My grandfather had a small farm outside Lincoln. But we lived in town. My father worked for Lincoln Canning. My sisters were a lot older than me. They were going to high school at the time my grandfather died. When that happened, we went back to the farm.'

She paused. It seemed an awfully long monologue. As Kernon said damn all, she knew she was meant to go on.

'My father ran the farm. It was grain and dairy – 580 acres. He and I were very close to each other. When I'd get home from school I'd go down to the barns with him for the milking. Then my mother went off with the industrialist who lived on the big place nearby. She got custody of me. My stepfather's company had a British office. When he was sent to London to run it, he and my mother took me with them. That's why the rest of my education was in England. But it's not chance that I wanted to marry an American. That's what I am.'

Georgie stopped speaking.

Kernon made a sound that sounded like 'hurm'.

Georgie said nothing.

'Did you come back often to see your father?'

'My father died of cancer soon after my mother took me to London.'

'Hurm.'

It was unusual for Kernon's conversation to have so many pauses in it.

Georgie said nothing.

'*World* also needs an editor who has an international gut feeling. England is one of the few countries that can speak the same language as us, even though they speak it funny. I noticed when I met you, you don't have any particular accent. That could be your general attitude. Mainstream Americans have to be able to identify with *World*. But at the same time, they themselves have so many different attitudes – at each others' throats over everything under the sun: abortion, dope, spraying goddamn apples. An editor who could *think* without any particular accent would be good at stirring the whole goddamn melting pot. And you've got another plus: with your outsider's eye, you'd pick out what's really interesting, bizarre, in this country. How'd you feel about being *World*'s first woman editor?'

In Manhattan, twenty-two floors above Madison Avenue, *World* was carved up into little cubicles like most corporate offices. 'You might as well be working in a file cabinet,' was the usual grouse. How many partitioned walls did you have? Did you get a window? Tiles or carpet? Only the editor hadn't to thrust for a bigger and better cubicle: all she had to do was make sure no one pushed her from her throne.

Within weeks of Georgie's arrival at *World*, the editor's office and the top editorial staff were transformed. The editor's office had never been a 'file cabinet': it was always a proper room with a wall of windows looking down on an endless traffic jam. But the red Turkey carpet and beige walls which had served as backdrop for Georgie's two predecessors were now replaced by a black pile carpet and walls covered in wildly expensive white metallic paper.

As for the editor's immediate staff, these were five people of her own choice. Even the PA, who had risen from secretary to become number one dogsbody for the past nine years, was replaced. Not often did Georgie wish to be unkind. Nor was she a bully. But she was smart and tough. She knew that staff already in place always claimed the previous editor was better and that the new editor was, well, not quite one of us. So she cleared them out.

She brought in three people she had worked with on the *Washington Post* and *Bazaar*, and she raided *Time* and *Newsweek* for two others. She gave them departmental responsibility and pay to match. They gave her loyalty.

They learned quickly that while she delegated to them, she was a hands-on editor: no story or picture was published in *World* without being approved by Georgie. If she rejected something, the rejection was final: if you couldn't accept it, you went elsewhere. Anyway, there wasn't time to argue: ninety-six glossy pages had to capture the readers' attention every single week. They had to capture other media's attention. And they certainly had to capture the attention of advertisers who were paramount to the financial viability of a mass-readership publication. An editor with a high profile was an added ingredient for success.

Initially there was scepticism among other news weeklies: would a woman editor change the balance in *World*, tilting it towards 'frothy' subjects? But that didn't happen. Georgie operated by osmosis. Between Hugo's and her own connections, she was already rubbing shoulders with those select politicians who made things happen, and gossiping with the media reporters who were just as essential to the process. No one knew better than Georgie that politicians and the media are locked together in a love–hate relationship: each needs the other.

At the start of her rule at *World*, Hugo was generous with advice – not only helping her with political contacts, but keeping an eye on how she handled the material: 'You let that senator get away with murder, Georgie. *World* quoted him on five different subjects and let his opponent answer only two. That might be OK if the senator had a good case. But he's a bum.' They spoke on the telephone at least once a day.

But when her stardom began to match his own, he became less generous with offering her contacts. Sometimes he seemed to relish criticizing *World*.

Georgie would bristle. But once she got over her initial irritation and realized Hugo was right, instantly she forgot her resentment of his rebuke. She wasn't interested in hugging grievances: she was interested in success. This made her a fast learner. She kept getting better at her job.

Ralph Kernon seldom interfered directly in editorial decisions, but if he was particularly displeased he let her know. 'You got a man's balls, Georgie,' Kernon would say. 'Women always take things personally. You don't.' Inwardly she bridled at his assumption that women approach everything emotionally.

She was certain her head would always rule her heart.

In keeping with her new status, she moved to a spacious apartment in Gracie Square where old money remained as new people moved in. Overlooking the East River in the mid-80s, it was a few blocks from the Mayor's home at Gracie Mansion. There was more room for Sarah and Jamie and the nanny, a bigger bedroom for Hugo to share if he came to New York, and a spectacular living-room for entertaining. An interior designer handled most of the furnishing and decorating, though Georgie was consulted once a week until her apartment was completed. Her salary combined with Hugo's, plus the perks that went with their jobs, meant money was the least of their problems, not that they seemed to have problems of any kind. Both preferred to invest in bricks and mortar which they could enjoy now, rather than stash money away in stocks and shares. They knew they were riding a crest, and they shared a preference for making the most of it today, this minute.

No one, except Georgie in her determined dreams, had imagined how quickly she would increase *World*'s already enormous circulation. It had always been in international offices and hotels; now it was also on the chic coffee-table of every American who was anyone in the power game. By the end of her second year as *World*'s editor, people in New York were as likely to say 'Georgie and Hugo' as 'Hugo and Georgie'. All this had happened in the nine years since they'd met at Ben Franwell's party on the *Aureole*.

Of course Hugo was immensely proud of Georgie. Yet increasingly he found it grated when the new order was used in Washington: 'Georgie and Hugo'. He'd overheard it, twice, during the evening which ended with that first ugly row when his wife had seen in his eyes that he wanted to hit her.

The second time he had nearly hit her was after Imogene Randall's dinner for the Secretary of State where various people had said, as if it was the most natural thing in the world: 'Georgie and Hugo'.

Afterwards, when he'd shut himself in the

living-room and poured a Scotch and soda, he sprawled on one of the mocha hide sofas, his drink in his left hand, his eyes looking into the middle distance, half-seeing his Hepplewhite secretary-bookcase standing by the garden window. After fifteen or so minutes, he decided he had calmed down enough to go up to his and Georgie's bedroom. He thought he'd relaxed.

Had he glanced down at the sofa where his right hand rested, he would have seen it clenched in a tight fist.

6

'Bastards,' Hugo muttered. He tore off the Associated Press news bulletin which had glided from the fax machine in his Georgetown study. It was three days since the ferocious row in the front hall. Georgie had returned to New York early the following morning, and since then they'd spoken only once on the telephone.

This Friday, instead of going into the office, Hugo was writing his column at home. As the *News* was a morning paper, it was produced as late as possible in the afternoon and evening. But if he wrote a 'think piece' instead of comment on that day's news, he could get it out of the way earlier. The nanny was bringing the children on a train due in the afternoon, and Georgie would follow on the evening shuttle after *World* went off to the printers.

The big desk in his study held the keyboard, screen, laser printer and the modem which sent his copy over the telephone. The fax machine stood on a table. The shiny sheet which his office had faxed him was in his hand. He read it again.

'British MP killed by car bomb. When leaving his Chelsea home in London to drive to his constituency, Mr John Marsden, MP for Lansdowne South, was killed instantly as he opened the door of his car parked in front of his house. His five-year-old daughter, standing with Mrs Marsden just inside the front gate, was injured by the explosion and has been taken to St Thomas's Hospital with head and leg wounds. Her condition is described as serious. A member of the House of Commons committee on industry, Mr Marsden has often questioned recent government policy which encourages joint ventures with new industry in Northern Ireland. Scotland Yard cannot yet say when the bomb was planted, but it is believed to have been activated by remote control when Mr Marsden was leaving his home after returning there for a family lunch on his daughter's birthday. The IRA has claimed responsibility.'

Hugo thought of Sarah. When the children were at the Manhattan apartment with Georgie during the week – Sarah had started at the nursery school favoured by New York career women – he sometimes missed Sarah even more than he missed Georgie. Hugo loved Jamie too, but Jamie was still not much more than a baby, really. Sarah was a little girl of five. Also, though he would not readily have acknowledged it, he'd felt a special love for Sarah since the day she was born.

'Bastards.'

He crumpled the fax sheet in his fist, wishing it was an IRA masked face, and flung it in the wastebasket. Returning to his keyboard and screen, he stored his half-finished piece about the ongoing White House crisis: that would have to wait for another day.

He started afresh.

'Americans of Irish descent are fiercely proud of their forebears. Many have ties on both sides of the disputed border which separates the Republic of Ireland from tormented Northern Ireland.

'On St Patrick's Day these Americans revel in Irish nationalist sentiment. But when the parade is over, they furl the green, white and orange flag and put it back in the cupboard for another year. During the other 364 days they see themselves as Americans. That's what this country is about.

'And yet. Some of these same citizens can be deceived and cajoled by those Irish-Americans who, misguided or twisted, continue to support the savage sectarian killings in Northern Ireland. IRA masked squads make no distinction between soldier and civilian as they shoot, club and burn. They are terrorists, no more, no less.

'And like most terrorists, they need others to fund them. Colonel Gadaffi of Libya has been happy to oblige them. That should surprise no one: the Colonel enjoys brutishness.

'But what about decent citizens of Massachusetts? When Senator Patrick J. Rourke's favourite constituents in South Boston hand over a large slice of their wages to Noraid, the American support group of the IRA, how do they think their money will be used? To fight some romantic battle "for the cause of Irish nationalism"? Or to arm psychopaths who get a kick out of the furtive plot, the civilian trapped, the torture, the car bomb? Does Senator Rourke himself grasp the enormity of the crimes made possible by his own assistance, knowingly or unknowingly, to Noraid?

'Proudly the IRA claimed responsibility for blowing

57

up another British MP as he left his home in London. John Marsden had argued against the recent government policy to create more jobs in Northern Ireland for Catholic workers. Mr Marsden took a pessimistic view, which some would describe as realistic: he maintained that any British intention to improve life in Northern Ireland was doomed to fail.

'Is that why the IRA murdered him? If so, its hypocrisy knows no bounds. For the last thing the IRA itself wants to see is productive cooperation between the British government and Northern Ireland's Catholics. A more likely reason for the murder is the IRA policy of sowing confusion and fear.

'Mr Marsden had returned to his Chelsea home for a family lunch to celebrate his daughter's fifth birthday. When he got into his car afterwards, the bomb was detonated. His small daughter lies in hospital with head and leg injuries from the explosion that killed her father before her eyes.

'This may give gratification to Noraid's twisted activists. But is it really how Irish-Americans intend their contributions to be used? Are they proud today?'

He knew he'd soon be getting a telephone call from the *News* lawyers, in a flap that he was skirting too close to libelling Senator Patrick Rourke. But Hugo would not bow to their twitchy concern, for he had chosen his words with care: nowhere had he actually said that Pat Rourke himself endorsed the IRA's terrorism against civilians.

'One of these days we'll have to buy a helicopter,'

Georgie said, laughing. Neither she nor Hugo had referred to their ferocious row earlier in the week. She had put it out of her mind.

From the Georgetown house to the Eastern Shore of Maryland took at least an hour and a half, and Saturday morning traffic made it slower. Hugo was at the wheel of the Volvo station-wagon they used for the weekends they went to the Shore, twice a month at the most. Georgie was beside him, with the children and the young English nanny in the back. It was Hugo who had insisted on buying a rather run-down place called Rycroft Lodge. Previously used as a shooting-lodge, the Rycroft daughters sold it to Hugo after their father reluctantly renounced his passion for bourbon and duck shooting. Georgie had thought Hugo was mad.

'If we have to go to the country for weekends – and personally I'd rather stay in town, New York, Washington, take your pick – why can't we get a hut at Quogue? It wouldn't be so bloody hot,' she had said more than once.

They couldn't pay Long Island prices for their third home, Hugo had replied doggedly.

'I keep telling you, I don't even want a third home. It's just more suitcase-packing,' Georgie would remind him.

Well, it was good for them as a family to have some outdoor place to get away from it all, he said. And it was good for Sarah and Jamie to have somewhere that Carroll relations could come for visits. As Georgie declined to visit what remained of her family connections in Nebraska, and not often did they stay with Hugo's family in Richmond, the children should have a sense of roots somewhere, he said.

He was aware that his determination to buy Rycroft Lodge had to do with nostalgia for the simpler pleasures of his childhood. He could still remember the excitement of the trips to his uncle's shooting-lodge, the long drive up to Annapolis to reach the Bay Bridge, not long built, which made the Shore suddenly accessible.

In recent years, ambitious young aides in Washington offices moved at weekends to the sand beaches on the Atlantic Ocean side of this long tongue starting in Delaware and running south beside Maryland and Virginia. But the old families still lived on the Bay side of the peninsula, on the narrow back-rivers where time stood still. At the necks formed by the tidal streams were the old mansions. Duck blinds stood among the scrub.

The watermen who earned their living from the Bay dropped nets which spread and sank to the riverbeds, and markers of coloured glass balls, bound with scraps of net, floated on the water's surface. Hugo loved the jewel-like glow of these floats – yellow, red, blue, green, sparkling as they bobbed in their net prisons above the shellfish trapped below.

His uncle's house had stood on the other side from Rycroft Lodge, farther up the twisting inlet. To reach it from Rycroft Lodge would have taken minutes by water, but an hour by car, a day or more by wagon in Colonial times. Boats had always been essential for neighbours as well as the oystermen and crabbers.

When the Volvo reached the Bay Bridge toll-gate, Sarah opened her window to pay. 'You can pay next time, Jamie.'

Five minutes later they reached the bridge's low crest. 'Well, here we go into God's forsaken land,' said Georgie as they began the four-mile gradual decline to the eastern side, the Shore in all its flatness spread before them. She turned to look at the three passengers behind her. 'Still, if anyone back there has an emotional problem, there's much to be said for the Eastern Shore – not even the teensiest weensiest mound to break the monotony. Nothing to stir you up. Soothing, you could say.'

It was true. There was nothing in this tidewater terrain to agitate emotions; if you were unhappy, its horizontality could be restful.

'Tidewater natives find it satisfying rather than dull,' Hugo said a little stiffly.

Having rolled down her window to smell the briny water flowing beneath the bridge, Georgie was now concentrating on holding her seatbelt away from her already sticky white shirt. 'Ridiculous country,' she grumbled, largely to herself. 'You open the bloody window for a bloody moment and you're poached alive. Satisfyingly poached, of course.'

When the bridge's gentle slope levelled off, she closed the window again so the air-conditioning could function properly. Through the dusty glass her eyes followed the shabby clapboard houses which stood desultorily alongside the highway, elderly blacks the colour of charcoal sitting on the steps or in rocking-chairs on the small front porches. She supposed it was all that sun that made them blacker than most black journalists who worked for her.

'Will Mr Pierce have brought the dogs over?' asked Sarah.

'He said he would,' Hugo answered.

A native Shoreman, Martin Pierce lived on the next place, beyond a bend in the river. He looked after the fifteen acres of cornfield, lawn, shore, scrub that went with Rycroft Lodge. When Hugo and Georgie decided to buy a pair of Doberman pups from the local breeder, it was agreed that Pierce would train them and look after them. Two large wire pens were built for the dogs, one on Pierce's place, the other at Rycroft Lodge.

The breeder was surprised when Georgie specified she wanted the Dobermans to be entirely black. But when a litter produced two males without the usual brown markings, instead of being a problem for the breeder it meant an instant sale. Buyers' quirks could come in handy.

Just after eleven, Hugo drove between the two big posts, painted white, where the narrow dirt road began, winding through a cornfield, past a couple of farm buildings, past the large wire pen, ending at the gravel forecourt of the unpretentious house. Its white clapboard reflected the nearly white sun burning through the fine mist of an empty sky.

'Where are the dogs?' asked Sarah. 'They weren't in the cage.'

'Pen,' said Georgie. 'It sounds cheerier. They don't have such a bad life. Lots of people would envy it. Pierce must be exercising them.'

Inside the house, Sarah and Jamie ran straight through to the big hall used as an enormous reception room, where glass double doors in one long wall opened on to a quartz terrace. The lawn, its spring emerald not too faded this early in June, ran down to a wooden pier extending over the water. The narrow river meandered quietly, without drama, moving so steadily and so nearly on the same plane as the flat land that the sense of placidity was unbroken. Off to the right a ragged clump of straight little poplars ambled down to the coarse-sand shore strewn with broken clam shells. Even the poplars common to the Shore made no real impact on the overall horizontality; they existed simply as a boundary between Rycroft Lodge and Pierce's place.

'There they are.' Sarah began running towards the three figures that had just appeared from the strip of woods.

'*Stop running, Sarah!* Stay where you are,' Georgie shouted, herself running to catch up with her daughter who had stopped in her tracks.

'I've told you,' Georgie said, taking the small hand, 'never run at them. Never run away from them. It can overexcite them. That's how accidents happen.'

Together, sweating in the sultry heat, they walked towards Pierce and the two Dobermans approaching, ebony coats gleaming, each heavy black leather collar coupled to a thick black plaited leash gripped by Pierce. The dogs bounded on their hind legs, barking with what appeared to be pleasure, straining at the leash as Pierce stopped a few feet away from Georgie and Sarah.

'Sure glad to see you, ma'm. How'ya doing, Sarah?'

Sarah put out a hand to one black blunt muzzle. 'Good morning, Hannibal,' she said. 'What big white teeth you have.' The other dog thrust its muzzle at her hand. 'Good morning, Othello. What a long pink tongue you have.'

Georgie laughed. 'Come on, Sarah. I'll take them, Mr Pierce. Hugo's up at the house. I know he'd like to see you.'

She and Sarah strolled down to the pier, each holding a leather leash as the dogs pranced before them. Sarah's cornflower-blue cotton sun-dress had darkened with sweat. Georgie's white top stuck to her.

'It's ninety bloody degrees, and the summer's only begun,' she muttered as they took off their sandals and went down the lopsided steps to the strip of sand running just below the level of the lawn. The water was muggy. 'Like tepid soup,' said Georgie as they waded a few steps and climbed on to the pier which extended some thirty yards to a boat-house. The dogs shook the water off their black feet, nails like talons glistening.

'I like looking through the cracks of the planks and seeing the water below,' Sarah said.

Georgie unfastened the leashes from the dogs' collars. She picked up two clam shells bleached white that were lying on the pier. She walked back to where the pier began and, standing there, flung the shells as far as she could on to the lawn. Flanking her the dogs whined, ears pricked, tail stubs quivering.

'*Get it*,' she said sharply.

They made a great leap over the strip of sand and hurtled towards the white shells. Pouncing, they tossed the shells in the air, two or three times, before finally each dog seized one and bore it back to the pier. Sarah clapped her hands. Georgie stroked the two panting muzzles.

'Why doesn't Jamie like them, Mama?'

'They are pretty big.'

'But they'd never hurt anybody unless that anybody was trying to hurt us, would they, Mama?'

'That's the idea. But Mr Pierce says never, never are you to take them for a walk without him or me or Daddy. You understand that, I know, Sarah.'

As they walked back to the house, the dogs trotting free ahead of them, they could see the small figure of Jamie sitting in one of the white cane chairs on the terrace, watching them.

The unbroken view of the sky added to the placidity of the flat terrain. The dogs' display of ferocity seemed only a charade. The heat pressed steadily down.

7

At six o'clock that evening six people were sitting on the terrace. Once or twice a hint of a breeze nudged the muggy air. Hugo's cousin and his wife, Hammond and Lottie Marshall, had come by car, as their own place was on the same side of the river as Rycroft Lodge. With them were their house guests.

Hammond Marshall was a US Congressman from Virginia. One of his house guests was Jock Liddon, the Washington lawyer who liked to think of himself as a puppetmaster, always on the look-out for senators and congressmen and members of the executive he could attach to his strings. Eminent journalists were to be cultivated whenever the opportunity arose.

Jock's business was big business: lobbying. Unlike those who look after a single industry, Jock was aggressively broking power. Supremely self-confident, he was one of the few lobbyists called upon to work in different areas. Maybe you wanted to get a contract with the Pentagon. Maybe the European Community needed a shot in the arm. Maybe your Korean deal for tobacco was in danger of being screwed up by the American tobacco lobby. Jock Liddon was the man to know.

At forty-seven his heavy-jowled face had a general well-fed smoothness, apart from the deepening grooves either side of the fleshy mouth. It wasn't a particularly large mouth, and the lips were curly. He seemed taller than five foot six inches, not so much because of the lifts on the short boots he normally wore, always highly polished, rain or shine, but because of his burliness. Broad-shouldered, barrel-chested, short black curls growing low on the nape of his neck, even when he was dressed in conventional chalk-stripe suit and Brooks Brothers shirt he carried a faint sense of menace. When they'd met at Washington parties, Georgie enjoyed looking at Jock, interested in how he appeared convivial and threatening at the same time. This evening he wore sneakers with his seersucker trousers and tieless blue shirt, top button undone, though the sneakers looked newer than you expected to see when you went out for drinks on the Shore.

With him was a young woman he introduced as his aide. Lisa Tabor was twenty-four. Her straight blonde hair fell to her shoulders. Out in Hammond's boat that morning she'd worn her hair in bunches, each bunch held with a rubber band, which made her look like a nubile fourteen-year-old until you got close. Then you saw her face was a mixture of peachskin innocence and an intelligent alertness which had about it an air of experience. As soon as she and Georgie were introduced, Georgie had a sense of being scrutinized. She didn't object to that. After all, she was a scrutinizer herself. Instantly she was curious about Lisa Tabor.

'How long have you worked for Mr Fixit?' Georgie asked as Lisa took the chair beside her.

'Two years. I started there as an intern the fall

after I came out of college.' Her eyes looked straight at you when she was talking with you, and it was hard to decide their colour. Blue? Grey? This evening they looked violet. But it was her mouth that Georgie found most intriguing: the upper lip was as full as the lower one, and Georgie had quite enough experience of make-up to know the mouth actually was shaped like that, not the result of skilfully applied lip pencil. She was a very pretty girl.

At *Bazaar*, Georgie had seen plenty of smart, tough, pretty girls. She wasn't intimidated by them or jealous, because she knew she was pretty, at least as tough, and sharper than they were. Still, Lisa looked as if her brains were in good order too.

'Interning, naturally, means you get the drudgery,' Lisa said. 'Getting congressmen's voting records. Putting it all on computer. Collating it.' The same-size lips parted in a laugh. 'Thank God that's behind me.'

Watching them from across the terrace, Hugo thought how arresting they looked together, Georgie's cropped black hair and simple white dress, cool in both senses, Lisa's fine pale hair skimming the bows which fastened the shoulder-straps of her lilac dress, the Dobermans lying in front of them, blunt muzzles on forepaws, watching the visitors with a steadiness which Lottie Marshall found irritating. She didn't much like dogs.

Hammond Marshall had already observed that the two little bows appeared to be all that held Lisa's dress together. Hugo wondered if she was wearing a bra. He wondered if later tonight Jock Liddon would untie those two little bows and Lisa's dress would fall straight down over her hips and on to the floor. He looked at the hands of the burly man sitting in the white chair beside him.

With one hand Jock was holding the tall glass where it was wrapped in a linen napkin, the glass's bare upper half frosted from crushed ice that reached its brim, three long sprigs of mint sticking up. It was a square hand with stumpy fingers, well-kept. You could tell the nails had been manicured by a professional. Glancing at Jock's other hand, Hugo wondered how often he had his nails done.

'You make a great mint julep, Hugo,' Jock said. 'I only drink them once or twice at the start of every goddamn summer. Then I take the oath and switch back to gin and tonic. That piece you wrote on Noraid got close to libelling Pat Rourke. He sure ain't going to thank you for it. You as good as said his Irish constituents had killed that British MP. And even though you didn't say Rourke himself as good as wired up that bomb, you sure put the idea in people's minds.'

Hugo shrugged. 'If he wants me to write a different kind of piece, all he has to do is disown IRA atrocities. But of course he never will – as long as he gets his cut from Noraid.'

Jock's molten brown eyes remained fixed on Hugo, but his face showed no expression. After a few moments, he looked away and took a swallow of his julep. Then he changed the subject.

'I was interested in that piece you ran ten days ago about the Senate's number one asshole in the sunny

South. Where'd you get your information about his cosy set-up with American Tobacco? One of my clients has a big *big*' – he drew out the word, nodding his head at the thought of how big it was – 'interest in tobacco for the Third World.' The self-mockery in his style of speaking made Jock amusing instead of insufferable.

'I was surprised myself,' Hugo said.

Neither of them commented on the fact that Hugo hadn't answered Jock's question. Jock knew journalists get that kind of information about a senator by keeping clam about who told them. Still, you could always try. This was one hell of a strong mint julep. He'd always heard this ballsy Carroll was a Southern gent of the old school. Jesus, he must have poured five shots of Old Turkey into each glass.

'Speaking of the weed, as we're sitting out under an open sky does anybody mind if I light up?' said Jock. 'I'll go down and sit on your pier, Georgie, if you're worried about me polluting your space.'

Georgie laughed. 'Toss me one. I indulge from time to time.'

Leaning forward, he dug in a hip pocket. After taking a cigarette from the pack, he pulled back his arm to throw the pack to Georgie. The dogs leaped to their feet.

'*Stay*,' she said sharply. Everyone watched as the pack sailed over the open-jawed ebony heads and Georgie caught it in her hands. 'Lie down,' she told the dogs with a quiet intentness as Jock got up from his chair and sauntered across the terrace to her, taking out his gold Ronson as he walked, stepping around the dogs to light her cigarette and then his own as he took the empty chair on the other side of her.

As he's such an ace, Hugo said to himself, why didn't he throw his fucking lighter as well? Actually, he had nothing against Jock. It was just that Hugo found he was feeling irritable tonight. He picked up Jock's glass and took it over to him. 'You forgot this.' He looked down at Lisa. 'Lottie and Hammond want to compare notes on motor boats. Would you like to walk down to the pier with us?'

When they reached the edge of the terrace, Lisa kicked off her sandals. Something about her tanned bare feet on the coarse grass aroused a good memory from Hugo's childhood. He saw her dress was cut so low at the back that she definitely couldn't be wearing a bra.

Remaining on the terrace with Georgie, Jock eyed the Dobermans' bulging eyes fixed on him. 'Jesus, Georgie, don't you ever get claustrophobic with those Baskervilles hanging all over you?' he said, at the same time admiring the way the brass studs in the thick black collars went with the gold bracelets on Georgie's wrists. Black and gold. White and gold. He liked her style. But he wished to Christ the bastards would stop panting. They must weigh a couple of hundred pounds between them. Someone once told him dogs sweat through their tongues. 'How do you know they won't suddenly do their nut and go careering across the lawn and have raw Hugo for supper?'

His eyes had moved to the four figures climbing on to the pier. He bet his mother's tits Hugo Carroll was this very minute wondering how he could get his hands on Lisa's. Being married to a babe like Georgie had to have its downside.

Georgie laughed. 'They're pretty unlikely to eat Hugo: he helped train them. The man who owns the place the other side of the woods – Mr Pierce – did most of the training. He spent some time in the Quartermaster Corps. One of their jobs is called instruction of war dogs. He's a real pro. He taught me how to handle these two. Hugo has handled dogs all his life.'

'I thought Southern gents went in for foxhounds, not mankillers,' said Jock.

Her eyes met his. She found that dark, liquid brown harder to read than blue eyes. She always knew what Hugo was thinking. She had no idea what was in Jock's mind.

'Does Hugo keep things from you?' he said, sniffing at the mint leaves, now a little limp, before sucking more of the world's sweetest firewater through the crushed ice. 'In the line of work, I mean. Like who tells him what about the Pentagon's real intentions on Israel's arms trade. We simple lobbyists are usually pretty open about what we're doing. You journalists are much cagier.'

Georgie looked away. Across the lawn she saw the four figures emerge from the boat-house. Watching them, she answered Jock. 'He used to tell me everything – who was really responsible for denying the general his other star, what the President said during their five minutes alone beside the rhododendrons, how much of it probably was a try-on, how much was refreshing candour, how much was a slip which somebody would come to regret. When I was writing features for the *Washington Post*, Hugo always gave me background stuff. When I was putting the hard edge on *Bazaar*, he still gave me help when I needed it with politicians.'

She paused.

'It's only since I've been editing *World* that we've been in competition – covering the same stories at the same time. That's bound to make it harder for him to help me now.'

'Yeah,' Jock said.

He noticed how she'd said it uncritically. For his benefit? he wondered. Or because she really didn't mind if Hugo grudged her his help these days?

At that moment Georgie's ebony attendants jumped to their feet and stood motionless as they watched the four figures returning across the grass. Jock looked at the black stubs between the wide hindquarters. Though he had trained himself to keep his expression impassive, his lower lip now tightened in distaste.

'Who cropped their tails?' he asked.

'You think I did, don't you?'

'That's what you power women are meant to go in for – tails, nuts, cocks. Cut 'em off, crush 'em, eat 'em up.'

Georgie burst out laughing. 'If you want to know, Hugo and Pierce cropped their tails while I was engaged in old-fashioned female activities like childbirth. That was three years ago – when Jamie was born. The dogs and Jamie are almost the same age.'

'Umm.' Jock had lost interest in the dogs, and he certainly wasn't interested in Jamie. 'We're going to be taking off in a few minutes, Georgie. Lottie's lined up dinner with a World Bank adviser whose shooting-lodge is half an hour from here. She says he's just up my street, whatever that may mean.'

'A dark street, perhaps, where you can hit him over the head before he's seen you coming?'

'I like that English "perhaps". It's got more style than "maybe". Lottie says you know this guy. Why aren't you and Hugo coming?'

'We thought about it. But this weekend is a short one anyhow, and we like to have some time together. Did you know the secret of a successful marriage is to live apart during the week? It makes you appreciate each other.'

'Yeah, yeah. Listen, Georgie, I've got a coupla big *big*' – he gave the nod – 'clients in New York. Why don't I phone you when I'm there and we have a drink. Maybe I could put you on to a couple of things that would come in handy for *World*. Or maybe we could just have the drink for fun, though something in here' – he tapped the black curls – 'tells me you never do anything just for fun. Neither do I.'

Ignoring Georgie's quizzical smile he added: 'That's why you and I are going to get on so well. You'll see.'

8

In their seersucker suits, each with his briefcase, both men looked at Lisa Tabor, one having to make do with her reflection in the mirror glass that lined the elevator walls. Lisa stared at the closed brass doors. At floor nine they opened to disgorge one of her fellow passengers, at twelve to disgorge the other.

She remembered the first time she took the mirrored elevator to Suite 1600, when the reflected Lisa in her little suit, smart but not overtly sexy, had rapidly recombed her hair where it fell forward on to her right cheek-bone. This Lisa gave her reflection the minimum checkout: beige linen jacket with its navy grosgrain trim, short, neat matching crease-proof skirt, cream silk tank top, navy sling-back pumps, legs so tanned it didn't matter they were bare. Not that she'd changed all that conspicuously in those two years. But this Lisa was more savvy. This Lisa knew her way around the labyrinth of Washington lobbying. Well, some way around it. The brass doors parted.

From the outset, floor sixteen said to you: Anybody with an office on this floor has made it in a big *big* way. Standing opposite the elevator in the role of welcome committee was a reproduction Sheraton table with an enormous basket of fresh flowers. The marmalade-coloured walls had been rag-rolled by

Washington's leading decorator. The pale blue carpet felt two inches thick. Lisa walked twenty feet down the corridor covered wall-to-wall in the stuff before reaching suite 1600. Beside its door was a small gleaming brass plaque: J. M. Liddon International. You couldn't count on Jock always being showy: he could turn around and be discreet as hell. This small brass plaque was saying: Leave it to me.

'Hi Dawn.'

'Hi Lisa.'

Dawn looked like an advertisement for the up-market receptionist: immaculate coiffure, chic suit, no jewellery except large pearl clips in her ears. Her clearly defined territory in the big magnolia-white reception room was set well back from the entrance door, so if you were with the boss and wanted to ignore her, you had an empty expanse of thick coral-coloured pile to circumvent her magnolia-white desk. She swivelled to the switchboard that made her territory L-shaped. 'Liddon International good *mor*-ning . . . I'm *sor*-ry, Mr Liddon's secretary is in a *mee*-ting. May I have her call you? . . . Thank you very *muh*-uch.' She unplugged the call.

'What's the meeting?' asked Lisa.

'She's gone to the can. How'ya doing? I feel a tension in the air. The big white chief is already in his office, and not repeat *not* taking calls from lil ol' me, and *not* to be interrupted. Ooops.' She picked up the red phone on her desk. 'Yes, Mr Liddon.' Under its perfect make-up, her face showed nothing. 'I'll tell her, Mr Liddon. I know she's here.' Dawn replaced the red telephone. 'He says there's no one answering in your office, and when you come in will I tell you to get your tail around to him pronto.'

Lisa blew a kiss to Dawn. 'I'll dump my gear first.'

The coral carpet rolled onwards into a waiting-room where the mood changed. Two genuine Georgian mahogany tables stood against damask-covered walls of Williamstown blue (Wedgwood blue, the English would have called it). Above each table was a hand-coloured hunting print in black mount and gold-leaf frame. Two settees covered in gold damask faced one another across a vast marble coffee-table. On the table, carefully laid out in a graduated sheaf between the Steuben bowl of peonies and a crystal ashtray, were the *News* and the *Wall Street Journal* along with several other morning newspapers published in Washington or New York or London. Three weeklies were fanned out with *World* on top. At nine o'clock the room was unoccupied, Lisa saw as she passed it and followed the coral carpet to a door which led to offices of varying size.

When you opened that door, you found the brass strip which ran across the doorway separated the plush coral on one side from a smart weave of coral sisal on the other. Lisa shared one of the rooms on the sisal side of the door with another aide, Margot. Though Lisa had rapidly moved up from a put-upon intern to a middle-level aide, the hierarchy of aides was not precisely defined. Besides Jock, who was president of his company, the only person with a proper title was his number two. For the two years that Lisa had been with J. M. Liddon International, the executive vice-president was Michael P.

O'Donovan. His office was at the other end of suite 1600, just before Jock's.

Margot was on Capitol Hill that morning to attend the National Committee on Abortion Reform. She knew every clause in every abortion amendment as well as a Supreme Court Justice does. ('Earning good money makes you concentrate,' said Jock, 'though they say first-hand experience also helps. How many abortions have you had, Margot?')

Lisa hung up her jacket and switched her answering machine to: 'Lisa Tabor is in a meeting. If you'd like to leave a message, she'll get back to you as soon as she can.' Dawn would give backup if needed. Dawn was a pal.

Stepping two doors along to the ladies' room, Lisa ran cold water over her hands and wrists, even though the air-conditioning rebuffed most of the heat already rising from K Street's pavement. She was careful that water didn't get on the moon-faced platinum watch with its lapis lazuli Arabic numerals, shining against her tanned skin, the only form of jewellery she wore. When she loosened the two tortoiseshell clips which held back the fine blonde hair, it fell straight against her throat, and as soon as she'd combed her hair she refastened it off her face. The thing about Washington's humid summer heat was to contrive to *look* cool. She glanced at her watch: 9.07.

Returning to her office to leave her handbag, she stepped confidently from sisal carpet to pile, and passing Dawn's back she saw the face in the mirror above the switchboard wink one eye. As she approached the other end of the suite, Michael O'Donovan emerged from his own office.

'Good morning, Michael.'

His narrow, cold face looked at her, and he pulled his door to in such a way that she heard the extra click of the lock fastening. Something in his manner suggested he was leaving his office after having been inside it for quite some time, and she wondered how long he had been there before anyone else arrived for work. Instead of answering, he nodded to her, his face expressionless.

At 9.10 she knocked on the bleached mahogany door at the end.

Silence.

She knocked again. 'It's Lisa.'

'Come on in,' a woman's gruff voice said impatiently.

Jancis had been Jock's personal secretary for seven years. These things take it out of you. She looked like a lean, chic, well-preserved woman of forty instead of one who'd just lately had her thirtieth birthday.

Sometimes Jancis was in her watchdog mood, guarding J. D. Liddon as if he were a national monument. Other times she didn't give a damn whether she phoned through to him at the perfect moment or the imperfect one. The only thing you could be certain of with Jancis was that you'd get the watchdog treatment if you acted as if you had easy access to Jock. Sure, she knew – who better? – that if you were female and clean and worked for Jock, you'd find his buffed-nailed hands all over you. Jancis could just picture it when she saw any of the junior female staff go into the inner sanctum and heard the click of the door being bolted by remote control. What Jancis wouldn't put up with was when somebody acted as if she had special rights; the girl would then find herself lucky if Jancis *ever* picked up the red phone to tell Jock she was there. And you'd need to have your head examined if you told Jancis your moon-faced platinum watch had been given to you by Jock.

'Lisa's here. I'll send her in.'

Jancis waved one hand of scarlet mandarin nails at the brass-studded navy baize door. Lisa opened it, stepped through and closed the door behind her. Click.

The Jacobean chair behind Jock's massive walnut desk was empty. Sprawled comfortably in Charles Eames's classic chair, he looked ready for business in his seersucker trousers and striped shirt, cuff-links fastened, tie in place, short boots of blond calfskin gleaming. He was in the Eames chair near the wall of plate-glass windows overlooking K Street. Placed strategically around the mushroom-coloured room were four more identical Eames chairs, their sculpted, soft black leather upholstery elegant and inviting above the graceful satin chrome swivel base, each with a capacious low table and crystal ashtray within easy reach. Lisa had seen this ultimate status symbol in several bosses' offices, but she'd never seen five Eames chairs together before, nor indeed had many other people unless they'd been in Brunei International Airport's VIP lounge where those hoping to have an audience with the Sultan waited for their luggage.

In Washington DC, most rooms as enormous as this would have had at least one sofa. But Jock liked to keep a space not just between himself and clients who came to see him in his office. He kept them separate from each other as well. This made it harder for them to gang up against him. If there's one thing you've got to guard against in the power game, it's other gangs, he would say. Gangs of arms dealers and heart-disease researchers, cotton producers and civil-liberties activists, salt-free food faddists and fertilizer merchants – each lobby was a gang.

'You name it, we've got it,' Jock said to Lisa. He reached out to the nearest crystal bowl to tip the ash off his cheroot. If he was smoking a cheroot instead of a cigarette before ten in the morning, you knew he was in a reflective mood. 'Brains, heart, brawn, crap, there's a gang lobbying for every one of them. And each gang knows there's only so much cake being baked over there.' He jerked a thumb over his shoulder in the direction of Capitol Hill. 'If you want a big slice, you gotta be pushy in a big *big* way. You gotta hand out a *lot* of moolah. And I'm here to show you how to do it. But don't try to gang up on me,' he said, addressing the four empty Eames chairs as if they were occupied by members of an oil cartel. 'C'mere a minute.'

Lisa looked at the empty Eames chair nearest Jock's.

'Here, I said. You're looking good. Lemme see what colour eyes you got this morning. Where'd you get that break-the-bank-of-Monte-Carlo watch you're wearing?'

He reached up from the low chair and pulled her on to his lap. 'I guessed right: blue shading into violet.' He shifted his legs so they were apart and she was sitting on only one of his chunky thighs. 'When your eyes go that colour it always gives me a hard-on. You may have noticed.' He reached for one of her hands. 'But nothing too dramatic this morning. The Israeli gang arrives at ten. I don't want my seersuckers creased.'

It was after six that evening when she got back to the group house. She had lived there for the past two years. The group house had dormer windows which made the third-floor rooms smaller than those down-stairs. The guy from Baltimore who worked in Senator Iglehart's office had the main room on the third floor, and Lisa had the other two. They shared a bathroom, and both were careful to leave it clean.

One of Lisa's rooms looked out on the yellow-painted clapboard house next door. Her other room looked out the front over the street where, instead of houses on the other side, a tall wire mesh fence hemmed in the woods of tall maples and oaks that covered a steep hillside. Somewhere on that hill, out of sight, was the old Chinese embassy of Chiang Kai-shek, whose name was just something in a history book so far as anyone in the group house was concerned.

Two girls and a guy were on the second floor. On the first floor, a cameraman who worked for local television lived in what had been intended as the dining-room when the house was built in the 1920s.

They all shared the living-room and the big side porch and the kitchen with its back porch overlooking the roughly tended back yard of dogwood and hibiscus. The porches and all the doors and windows were screened, and nobody in the group house bothered to remove the screens when the cold weather came. None of them could see the point in taking them down, putting them in the cellar, and six months later bringing them up and putting them back again.

Lisa sat drinking iced tea on the long bench in front of the green-painted wooden counter running the full width of the back porch. It was her favourite place in the group house. You could think your thoughts as if you were alone, even if somebody else was sitting out there drinking iced tea or iced coffee or a cold beer, because you'd be well spaced along the bench and all facing the back yard: you wouldn't be looking at each other.

Soon after she had got her job as intern with J. M. Liddon International, she'd seen the newspaper ad: '6th m/f wanted to share group house in Cleveland Park. 3 min. walk to Conn. Ave stores and subway 25 min. Capitol Hill.'

Like a lot of young office staff in Washington, she was on her own. Only a very few times did she return to northern Pennsylvania to visit her parents in hicksville, where Lisa and her brother had been born and raised. Mr Tabor was a dentist. Mrs Tabor was a slob. No one else would have thought of Mrs Tabor in that way – tidy in her tidy house – but that's how Lisa thought of her mother. 'Shouldn't you think about getting married?' seemed the only thing Mrs

Tabor had to say to her daughter after Lisa turned seventeen.

Lisa hated her family's house, but then she had hated the three houses that preceded it. They were all the same: neat front yard, neat back yard, settee and matching lounge chairs facing the television set in the fake fireplace, statutory number of straight chairs in the cramped dining-room, and on the upper floor a moderate-sized bedroom and two pinched ones. If Mrs Tabor had ever had imagination, she had long since tuned it out.

Lisa had imagination. She knew there was a glamorous world somewhere else, and she wanted to be part of it. And she knew there was just one person she could count on to get her there. Herself.

She won a scholarship to the University of Pennsylvania, but it covered only half the costs. Her father made up most of the difference, and Lisa got summer jobs to earn the rest. Her mother made little ritual sounds: 'Is it really necessary to spend money on four years of college education if you're going to get married right-away afterwards?' But Mrs Tabor was too much of a slob to pursue the argument. Lisa knew what she wanted at Penn: she wanted to get into those worlds which would be stepping-stones for her ambition.

She engaged in a detached way in the campus stuff you'd expect of a bright, attractive girl. She was always fussy about who was permitted to go to bed with her. It wasn't that she thought being in love with the guy was a requirement: but she wanted to feel he had something to offer that would be useful to her. She wanted to know what his father or mother did. If it was up-market and something that interested Lisa, she'd encourage the guy to ask her home for dinner with his parents. If they lived in New York or Washington, she made damn sure he asked her home.

What interested Lisa most were the media, advertising, public relations – and of course politics, which in a way is the sum of the other three. She decided to major in poli-sci. But she also took a lot of literature courses and the general course in art history. In her senior year she threw in the general course in music history. She didn't know exactly where she was going, but she intended to be well equipped to walk into those wonderful rooms on the other side of doors still closed to her.

And she knew where she was *not* going. She was not going back to hicksville. She was not going to fall in love with a clean-cut businessman who would expect his wife to be thrilled at playing perfect hostess when they entertained his section manager, and to be content driving the children to school in the second car. As Georgie recognized when she met Lisa on the Shore, they had some things in common.

Along with other matters Lisa learned at Penn, she was introduced to the pleasures of the orgasm. This she regarded as a highly agreeable bonus rather than the be-all and end-all of a relationship. She'd never yet sacked out with somebody really repulsive, and she hoped she'd never have to. But she had a clear idea of give and take. Few men have everything. If they had good bodies and sack talent and money and power, great. But she'd yet to meet one who did. Her priority was that he have power, with money coming next down the list. And she noticed that when power and money were all he had to offer you – he knew he was no Adonis or a big deal in the sack – he was more likely to help you in your career and give you a really nice present.

She glanced at her watch as she sipped her iced tea. Jock was picking her up at seven. They tended to dine together once a week, though there was no routine. After their weekend at the Shore, he'd gone to New York for two days, so there'd be a lot to talk about. She'd better go have a shower.

The chauffeur pulled up to the kerb. The doorman at the Willard stepped forward smartly to open the Cadillac's back door. 'Good evening, sir. Glad to see you back. Nice to see you, miss.'

Lisa was wearing a black linen skirt with a matching double-breasted jacket whose lapels crossed just where the curve of her breasts began. Unless she unbuttoned it, you wouldn't know whether she had a low-cut blouse underneath. The doorman bet she didn't. But she didn't look cheap like some of these chicks in their low-cut jackets and no blouse.

Jock was wearing a white linen suit, blue shirt, and pink tie. This evening the short boots with their built-up heels were made of white kid. Jock was observant enough of the Washington scene to know he'd never be mistaken for a gentleman. He looked like a Mississippi gambler. But then that's what he was – if you substituted Newark for Mississippi – and if you didn't like it, that was your hard luck.

They made a striking couple. At a nearby table, two elderly Philadelphia ladies with their double strands of real pearls were uncertain about the relationship between that tasteless creature with the curly black hair and the self-contained young woman. But the congressman who got up from his own table to come across to Jock's had a shrewd idea.

'How'ya doing, Jock? I'm meaning to phone you this week.'

'This is Lisa Tabor. She works for me. She's going far.'

'Great to see you, Lisa. How're we going to persuade my distinguished colleagues that animal fats are the finest thing a man can eat?'

Lisa laughed. 'Jock keeps saying: "A good lobbyist is defined by results." Give me three days, and I'll have the answer for you.'

The congressman clapped a hand on Jock's shoulder. 'You lucky dog. I'll call you tomorrow.'

Before they reached the soft-shelled crabs, Jock had left the table twice, ambling across the restaurant to speak to the White House aide he had spotted, glad-handing a senator and reminding him they had a date about the chemical fertilizer bill.

His conversation with Lisa was not about how beguiling she looked. Nor did it occur to her that he'd be remotely interested in the crazy mix-up at the group house the night before. What they talked about with total absorption was work.

'I'll tell Mike O'Donovan to let you sit in when the king of margarine comes to see him this week. You gotta learn everything about how they'll pitch their case if you want to see the way to make the same case for butter. There must be two foot thick of legislation on the subject – and that's after it's been boiled down.'

'Mike didn't like it once before when I asked to sit in on something. He said he was working at selling tobacco as mankind's greatest boon, and why should he give me information which would help the cancer lobby. Saying it in that hard Boston accent made it worse.'

Jock laughed. 'Mike gets like that from time to time. But deep in his Irish gut he knows you can play it both ways. You can work one ball off drafting legislative language for the tobacco kings, and you can work the other ball off doing the same thing for the cancer people. So long as you give each of them what they need, what have they got to complain about?'

Lisa's eyes, violet in the candlelight, were serious. 'Margot told me she lost the embryos-for-science account when they discovered J. D. Liddon was also acting for the right-to-life people.'

'Margot made a balls-up. I nearly kicked her out on her can. But if somebody makes a mistake and you give 'em a second chance, maybe they'll cut corners better than they ever would of done before they were shit scared for their job.'

He lit the cheroot clamped between his short, fleshy lips with their pronounced bow. 'Listen. There's a lot of garbage talked about how clients with opposing interests shouldn't give their business to the same consultant. "Canons of ethics" is what the lawyers call it. Most lobbyists are lawyers; they like to dress up a smart practice with Jesus words. Canons of ethics my ass. You're a hired gun. And you're hired to try and influence public policy. OK, so post-Watergate this place is crawling with laws and regulations. But there's nothing says you gotta go public about every goddamn thing you do.'

'But everyone seems to know who your clients are,' said Lisa.

'They only think they do. If some smarmy consultancy wants to list its glossy clients – Rolls-Royce, Ministry of Defence, Saudi armaments – on its stationery used for special purposes, I'm not against that. But I don't gotta do the same. I told you already, Lisa, we're not a bunch of fucking preachers.'

Holding his cheroot in one hand, a thin blue column of smoke rising from it, he put his other hand under the starched white tablecloth. His table was a corner one where the two green leather banquettes met. He sat on one banquette, Lisa on the adjoining one. Under the linen tablecloth, her knees were only inches away from him. He patted one knee in an abstract way, pushed her linen skirt higher, and jabbed his third finger up to see if she was wearing a girdle. As she was wearing only silky briefs, she winced. It was not so much that it hurt when his finger suddenly stubbed into her. What bothered her was her sense of propriety: they were at the Willard.

Having satisfied his curiosity, Jock put his hand back on the table and continued his tutorial to his young aide. 'There's no such thing as bad morals in lobbying. Anybody tells you that is lying. Legislation is a free-for-all. What counts is hard work. You got berks with the simple-minded notion it's all done in bed. OK. There's been that. But a hot night in bed won't commit legislation. That takes hard work.'

As the chauffeur drove the Cadillac back to Jock's apartment on P Street, Lisa thought with detachment of the different kind of hard work which still lay ahead for her that evening. It seldom took more than twenty minutes, though. Jock wasn't remotely interested in whether she was enjoying it, which made it easier to concentrate on the stuff that would get him off. His chauffeur would be waiting to drive her back to Cleveland Park afterwards.

Thirty-five minutes later she waved goodnight to the chauffeur. Inside the front door of the group house was a notice board with messages that one or another of them had taken.

'Lisa: Hugo Carroll phoned at 7.30. Can you phone him at the *News* tomorrow? 283-9876.'

9

Good little Americans are taught at their mother's knee that ambition is a virtue: 'If you try hard enough, you can be president when you grow up.'

The British prefer to cloak their personal ambition. Yet they too are as interested in advancing themselves as in serving their country.

Ian Lonsdale was aiming for the top. He was not one of those MPs who find nothing more exciting than shouting at the other side: he got bored by rhetoric and ranting. He preferred the approach of the famous Cabinet minister who said, 'Politics is the art of the possible.' Ian applied the same idea to other areas of his life. He was not prepared to sacrifice all other pleasures for politics.

When his party was returned to government, the Prime Minister appointed Ian to a second-rank post at the Board of Industry, Trade and Energy – the recently created huge conglomerate known as BITE. The clamour of the Greens made it logical to join the Department of Energy with the Department of Trade and Industry. Uniquely among the major departments, BITE's empire extended to the Province of Ulster. This too had a logic, but it required the most sensitive meshing with the Northern Ireland Office, where a senior BITE civil servant was now attached.

Within months of the new government's formation, it was rocked by a sex scandal more lurid than anyone could remember since the Profumo case. A senior Cabinet minister was photographed in the sack with a woman other than his wife and, as if that wasn't misfortune enough, a rent-boy sharing their bed. (The Prime Minister would never understand why Cabinet ministers could not put their libidos on the back burner when they took on high office.) In the reshuffle which followed, the BITE Secretary was made Home Secretary – and Ian was promoted to the Cabinet as the new head of BITE. At thirty-nine he held one of the most important posts in Britain.

'I'm so proud,' Patsy said when he came back from seeing the Prime Minister. 'But we won't have to be three-in-a-bed with a policeman, will we?'

'No,' said Ian, laughing as he poured them a celebration drink.

The matter of security had led to the most heated of many heated arguments when Whitehall was spawning BITE several years before. The then Prime Minister remained adamantly opposed to special security for the BITE Secretary.

'Half the point of BITE is to try and undermine the IRA's propaganda against the British government. We're trying to persuade Ulster's Catholic workers that we genuinely want to join hands with them in creating jobs and economic growth on both sides of the Irish Sea,' the Prime Minister had said. 'How then can we have the minister in charge of this enterprise going around like an armoured tank? We must *show* his role is entirely different from that of the Northern Ireland Secretary who the minority,

with some reason, see as there to police them.'
Coming from the Prime Minister, that had put an
end to the argument.

Thus, in his sensitive post, Ian had no more security
than the Chancellor of the Exchequer. As second in
the Cabinet hierarchy, the Chancellor, who was perhaps a little too vain, was sometimes piqued that he
didn't have a specially armoured Jaguar like those
used by the Foreign Secretary, the Home Secretary,
the Defence Secretary and the Northern Ireland Secretary. And it occasionally irritated him that while
his next-door neighbour at Number 10 Downing
Street had a round-the-clock policeman on the front
step, no policeman stood outside the Chancellor's
home at Number 11.

Ian, who was less vain, welcomed the lack of
security. It meant he had a personal freedom denied
to those colleagues who could go nowhere without a
detective with them.

Two years after Ian and Patsy had married, Sam was
born. Nina turned up two years after that. 'It doesn't
make a lot of difference what we call her,' Patsy said
to her mother, Mrs Fawcett's silence having made
plain she was dubious about Nina as a name for her
granddaughter. 'She's bound to change it anyhow,
Mummy.'

Patsy had found a house in Pimlico with a decent-
sized garden and five bedrooms. It was in the
division-bell area, less than ten minutes from the
House of Commons. This meant that some evenings
Ian could come home for dinner, and when the

special bell installed in their front hall began the racket which announced the House had 'divided', he had time to get back to the House and cast his vote.

A second priority in Patsy's search for the house had been that the children's and au pair's rooms be on a different floor from the marital bedroom and what she referred to as the 'sulk room'. Englishmen who slept apart from their wives referred to their own bedroom as their dressing-room, but as Ian slept there only when he and Patsy were having a row, her description was apt.

Their big bedroom was at the front of the house. On the same floor, beyond the 'sulk room' and over-looking the back garden, was a small room with a painter's easel, a large desk and two armchairs. This was Patsy's room. Here she wrote and illustrated the children's books which came out almost every two years and were bought eagerly by adults looking for something they would enjoy reading to their children – or which older children would want to read for themselves.

She'd written the first one to entertain Sam and Nina. She was good at telling stories that taught you something and also made you laugh, sometimes cry. Patsy's stories were unpredictable.

When the thought had firmly taken shape in her mind that she wanted a career alongside the wife-and-mother bit, she took a twice-a-week course in draftsmanship, as Georgie had previously advised her to do. Once she had that under her belt, Patsy took off as a children's book author and illustrator.

'Everything keeps going right in our lives. It's too

good to be true,' she said one night to Ian when they were talking in his study. She was in one of her thoughtful moods. 'God, fate, something or other always makes luck run out. How do we know that at this very minute there's not a black spot coming over the horizon, but still so far away we can't see it? Only when it's nearer will we be able to make it out, and as it gets bigger we'll realize it's coming towards us.'

'What a morbid thought,' Ian said, getting out of his chair to cross to hers and lift her to her feet. Putting his arms around her, he kissed her hair. 'I have a happier thought,' he said. 'Why don't we go upstairs and take our clothes off?'

Later, when he fell asleep, his body pressed against hers, one arm still around her, Patsy found her bad thoughts had been expunged. In their place she now put good ones, thinking how the conversation they'd had before they married – about Ian's chronic inability to be a hundred per cent faithful – had proved unnecessary. In their nine years together, there'd been no sign of his wanting to wander. And even if the idea appealed to him, she couldn't see how he would have time for a bit on the side. Actually, she didn't think about it a lot, though once or twice she wondered whether *if* it happened she wanted to know. Perhaps it would be better not to know. Then it wouldn't make any difference – *if* it happened, and she ardently hoped it wouldn't. She fell asleep.

Three nights later, she was in a different mood.

'Does anyone in Her Majesty's Government ever think of stuffing himself?' she said. 'Sorry. Him- or herself. For a moment I forgot that two women are allowed to sit at the Cabinet table with you twenty great men.'

'What's the matter with you tonight, Patsy? We've had a woman Prime Minister. Remember?'

'Stuff her too. Stuff all of you. Male or female. Tall or short. Smart or stupid. You're all so bloody pompous that it makes any normal human being want to kick you in the shins, if not higher.'

Ian began to laugh. He couldn't help it. Sometimes when Patsy lost her temper, it was a serious business. Tonight, standing there in his study wearing his cotton pyjama top which reached halfway down her bare thighs, she looked so childish in her unheralded rage that he couldn't take it to heart.

All that had provoked this outburst was his making a perfectly ordinary pleasantry when he'd got back from the ten-o'clock vote at the Commons. He'd gone up to their bedroom where she was reading, propped comfortably against the pillows, and she'd returned downstairs with him to his study where they were about to have a nightcap together. They liked to exchange gossip accumulated since he'd left home in the ministerial car that morning. But this evening, when she'd stumbled over the red ministerial box which he'd put on the floor just inside the study door, and he'd said: 'Careful, Patsy, the nation's future depends on those papers. I don't want to find them bruised when I start reading them later,' she'd blown her top.

'Why do you bother to come home?' she said, turning on her heel to stomp upstairs, stomping one bare foot rather gingerly. For in fact she'd caught its little toe on that bloody, bloody box, and it hurt like hell. She'd not be in the least surprised if she'd broken it.

Under the lamp on the bedside table nearest the door, she checked to see if the toe was hanging apart from the others the way it did when several years ago she'd caught it on a banister while running upstairs in her bare feet. It had had to be taped to the next toe, and she couldn't wear closed shoes for a month, her coral-lacquered toenails contrasting perkily with the surgical bandage. But tonight, she observed, it was lined up OK, the coral nails glistening in a neat curve.

Rubbing the toe, which had begun to hurt less, she continued to hate the red box. It symbolized the endless demands which high ministerial office made on private life. She'd been looking forward to tonight, as she always did to Ian's return from the Commons, to their having half an hour together before he opened that hateful red box to read the briefs before the next day's meetings began. She wished he'd come upstairs so she could tell him she was sorry. Why should he when she so patently was the one in the wrong? At that moment she heard his steps with their distinctive irregularity. The bedroom door opened.

'Has something happened that I should know about?' he said, standing in the doorway.

She was relieved – and touched – by his taking the responsibility to make peace. She got off the bed and put the flat of her hands against his chest. He'd taken his jacket off and she could feel the warmth of his skin through his shirt. She stood so that the pyjama top skimmed his shirt, yet her breasts weren't quite against him. Looking up at him – over six feet, he was a good half a foot taller than she was – she said: 'I'm very very very sorry. Actually, I nearly broke my toe on that bloody box. Suddenly it seemed symbolic. Could we start the tape again? I'd like to hear what you've been doing since you went away this morning.'

He leaned down and kissed her mouth. This time Patsy moved up against him, laughing softly as she turned languidly from side to side so her breasts rubbed against him.

He laughed too before taking her hand and starting back down the steps. They were halfway to the next floor when the telephone rang. Ian frowned and looked at his watch: it was coming up to eleven. At least it was the regular telephone. If it was the government line at this hour, it was likely to be even more of a pain.

'Go on down. I'll take it in the bedroom,' Patsy said, running up the stairs again. 'Are you home?'

'Only if you think it's necessary for me to take it.'

As the telephone began its fourth double-ring she picked it up. 'Hullo?'

'Is Ian there?' The voice had a soft lilt.

Patsy wasn't used to having an unfamiliar voice ask out of the blue for 'Ian' – as if the unknown person was claiming friendship. Generally strangers asked for Mr Lonsdale or for the Minister. Perhaps it's me who's become pompous, she thought wryly.

'This is his wife.'

'Oh. Mrs Lonsdale,' said the soft voice, the lilt going up as it accented the second syllable of the name.

She's Irish, Patsy thought. Something about the voice put her on her guard. She was aware she was standing absolutely still and felt all at once cold as she waited. She didn't know how she knew this velvet-voiced unknown woman was menacing, but she knew it.

'Could you give Ian a message when you see him? Could you tell him I'm sorry I couldn't make it? I wasn't able to ring him before. I'll say goodnight then.'

The telephone clicked in Patsy's hand.

She had a sense of looking at herself from the outside when she hung up the telephone and started down the stairs again, seeing her bare legs below Ian's pyjama top, watching her bare feet as they touched each step. She remembered that one of her toes with their glittery coral nails had hurt like hell after she'd stumbled over the red box, but now she couldn't feel it at all.

'Who was that?'

She saw he'd already unlocked the red box: it was open on the floor beside his armchair. He put down the brief he'd been reading when she came into the room. He'd left a whisky-and-soda on the table beside her chair facing his across the study fireplace. She took a sip before replying.

'She didn't say.'

She took another sip. Holding the glass just a few inches from her face and looking over the brim at

Ian, she said: 'She said to tell you she was sorry not to have been able to keep her engagement with you.'

His face was inscrutable. Laconically he said: 'I wonder how many bored strangers ring numbers late at night to deliver messages which are totally meaningless.'

She went on looking at him over her glass.

'It must be hard for strangers to find a name and number that match when the telephone isn't listed in the directory,' she said. She could hear a hard edge in her voice. 'I hate the Irish,' she added, though she'd never felt any particular emotion about them before.

'What does that mean?' asked Ian.

'It means the soft little voice delivering her soft little message was Irish,' said Patsy, aware again of the tight edge her own voice had taken on.

'OK. Perhaps this Irish voice didn't belong to a stranger,' he said smoothly. 'Perhaps it was one of the switchboard operators at BITE, the one I'm having a passionate affair with in the basement while my office does my work. I must have mentioned her to you a hundred times.'

The image produced a fleeting wan smile on Patsy's face. She took another sip of her whisky and put the glass back on her table. 'I'll leave you to get on with that stuff.' She gestured towards the red box. 'Gossip-time seems doomed tonight.'

He got up to kiss her lightly on her lips. 'I won't be too late,' he said. 'Actually, my day was rather boring anyhow. Did anything happen in yours that won't keep until tomorrow night?'

'I've forgotten,' said Patsy as she opened the study door and went out, closing it behind her.

On her way back upstairs, she realized what she'd only half noticed at the time: he hadn't actually denied anything.

10

At 12.30, Downing Street was crowded with Rovers and the four Jaguars specially armoured against land-mines. Most Thursday meetings of the Cabinet went on until one, but you never knew. Government drivers clustered in the street talking while they waited. Detectives stood alongside the Jaguars which belonged to Cabinet ministers most vulnerable to terrorism.

Just before one o'clock the door of Number Ten opened. Eighteen men and two women came down the steps and made for their cars, each carrying a red box except for the Foreign Secretary whose box was black. As the Chancellor of the Exchequer was lunching at home, he didn't need a car: he could walk through the inside door connecting Number Ten and Number Eleven.

Ian Lonsdale sauntered towards his Rover and handed his red box to his driver. 'I'll walk to lunch, Chris. And I'll walk back to the department afterwards. I need some exercise.'

'Yes, sir.'

Buckling his seat belt, Chris glanced at his card with Ian's engagements for that day: 'Private lunch.'

The bristling, black iron gates, erected by Margaret Thatcher to barricade Downing Street against terrorist attack, were opened to let the ministerial cars depart. Policemen touched their helmets as Ian walked through and turned south into Whitehall. Up ahead Big Ben's lapis lazuli blue hands stood at one o'clock exactly.

He cut across the corner of Parliament Square and strode into Victoria Street, his limp scarcely discernible. Ahead, on the other side, loomed BITE. Ian's eyes glanced up at the top floor, even though his ministerial rooms were at the back where you had the view over Westminster Hospital to the Thames and the south bank spread out beyond.

He might have been on his way to one of several restaurants favoured by MPs. Automatically he looked across the street for the first glimpse of the Roman Catholic cathedral standing calmly in its close; he liked the neo-Byzantine calm of its single campanile and the bold stripes of stone against the brick. He turned right and then right again into Stag Place. A minute later he rang the top-floor bell of a terrace house.

Its façade had been recently painted on the cheap and was already peeling. He glanced up at the two window-boxes of geraniums and petunias outside the top-floor windows.

'Yes?' The voice on the Entryphone gave nothing away.

'It's Ian.'

The lock buzzed as it was released. He heard it reclick as the door swung shut behind him and he started up the first flight of the pinched stairway, its beige carpet wearing through, not because it was all that old but because the landlord had spent as little as possible for a pleasant initial effect. There was one door on each floor. When he reached the top floor its door was already open. He closed it behind him.

The entrance hall was tiny, but the bedroom on the right was quite a good size. He saw it was empty. He went into the sitting room, and through the door leading from it he saw her standing at the kitchen sink. Shoulder-length auburn curls. Pink T-shirt. Pink trousers. Strappy high-heeled sandals. He heard the clatter of an ice tray. When she turned she had a chrome ice bucket in her hands. Her eyes challenged his.

'We'd better have a talk,' he said.

'What could be more delightful, Minister,' she said, handing him the chrome bucket.

Unhurriedly she opened a cupboard door and took out two glasses as he stood there holding the bucket, irritated and uneasy at her self-possession.

'After you,' she said, with a polite little smile which added to his unease.

In the sitting-room with its cheap beige carpet wearing through in two places, he put the bucket down beside the whisky bottle on a low bookcase. A painted earthenware pot held a polyanthus whose variegated green and white leaves cascaded over the paperbacks half-filling the shelves. One corner of Ian's mouth pulled up into a brief, bitter imitation of a smile at the fleeting memory of his pleasure – only a few weeks ago? – in watching Maureen's lithe fingers nip off the leaves which had reverted to all-over green. 'Otherwise, no more variegated ones will grow,' she'd said. She liked to play at domesticity.

He'd never asked in any detail about her secretarial

work. Nothing very fascinating, she'd said. She liked working freelance so she could arrange her own time, she'd said. Ian's manners did not extend to wanting to hold long conversations about Maureen's secretarial work, so her lack of interest in discussing it suited them both.

They'd met when he was addressing a ginger group which was open to the press. She'd come along with a journalist covering the meeting for the *Belfast Telegraph*. There was intense interest in Northern Ireland about whether he would invest £50 million to enable Belfast's motor-cycle factory to remain a going concern. Its three hundred employees were almost all from Belfast's Catholic minority. Ian could only touch on the subject in his speech, giving no hint of what his decision would be: 'You'll have to wait for that to be announced in the House of Commons.'

At the reception afterwards, Maureen Halloran introduced herself to Ian, explaining she'd come to hear him because of her own interest in Ulster, where she was born. Her eyes and his engaged directly, and after discovering she was now living ten minutes from Parliament Square, he said: 'Perhaps you'll have lunch with me one day and give me a first-hand impression of what it's like in Northern Ireland.'

Their first meeting had been at a French restaurant near Victoria Street, where no one thought it necessarily suspicious when politicians lunched with attractive members of the opposite sex. Maureen might have been a journalist, a constituency activist, a visiting cousin, whatever. Chris had the car waiting outside the restaurant when they left, and at Maureen's suggestion she was dropped off opposite Westminster Cathedral before Ian went on to the House of Commons for Prime Minister's Question Time.

On their second date they met at her flat just off Stag Place. He had taken the precaution of telling Chris he wanted some exercise and would not need the car. At 2.15 he used Maureen's pay-card telephone to ring the restaurant and apologize for having to miss his lunch booking because a meeting had run on longer than expected.

Subsequently he'd gone to Stag Place about once every two or three weeks. As ministers' telephone calls on government phones were monitored by their own private offices, he disliked ringing Maureen from his room at BITE, even though it was generally assumed his private line would not be monitored. He preferred ringing her when he went over to his room in the Commons, outside Whitehall civil servants' domain. Once Maureen left a message with his Commons secretary for Ian to ring Miss Halloran. ('Will he know what it's about?' his secretary had asked. 'Yes.')

Ian now came straight to the point: 'Why did you ring my home?'

She took a sip of her whisky and looked at him over her glass. He banished the image of Patsy looking at him in the same way.

'Why shouldn't I?' she said.

In the three months they'd known each other, she once had teasingly dared him to give her his home number 'to show that you trust me', and he had rattled it off, not imagining she would even remember it. In any case, it was taken as understood that she wouldn't ring him at home.

His long, grey eyes surveyed her. Maureen was probably nearly thirty, possibly a bit more. She always made him think of a cat when she lifted her arms above her head, bending them so that the backs of her hands rested against her auburn curls spread out on the pillow, and he could switch off the memory of Patsy doing the same thing. Sometimes he teased Maureen about her exceptional versatility: 'How is it that a well-brought-up Catholic girl should have so much carnal knowledge?' he would say, and she would laugh.

Her sexual entertainments were part of a general easy nature. After playing the Irish innocent who was to be ravished, or the Irish barmaid in black suspender belt and black stockings – there was no doubt that Maureen had a real gift for improvisation – she would happily slide off the bed after the great climax, and, with a skimpy negligée wrapped around her, go to the kitchen to get the delicatessen meal she'd bought.

They'd eat at a round table in the sitting-room, Ian half-dressed in his pin-stripe trousers and Jermyn Street shirt. He always opened a bottle of champagne if she'd put it on ice, or else a bottle of claret. He'd had Berry Bros. deliver crates of both to her. Quite often he had Berry Bros. deliver wine to a friend who was convalescing or was celebrating publication of a novel, so it was hardly surprising he did as much for someone who was unusually fetching and good-tempered and an *artiste suprême* in bed.

'You must know my wife doesn't know about you.'

'Doesn't she now. Oh dear.'

Maureen took another sip of her whisky, a faint, pussy-cat smile on her lips, an expression he couldn't read in her eyes. He felt as if there was a large stone in his stomach.

'I like you better in your other roles,' he said.

'Do you now.' It was a mockery, not a question.

Jesus. 'What's going on in your mind, Maureen?' he said, half-drawling the words so the question could be taken as light-hearted or serious.

She decided it was time to switch her own tone. 'Why haven't you rung me for nearly three weeks?'

'I've been tied up. My job is generally regarded as a demanding one, you may have heard.' He was now quite angry.

'Is it so demanding that you can't find five minutes to consider the livelihood of three hundred hardworking Irishmen whose only fault is that they're not fucking Protestants?'

'What the hell are you on about, Maureen?'

He could guess the answer easily enough, though he didn't know why she had a particular interest in his pending decision about whether to pump money into the Belfast motor-cycle factory.

She had put her glass down on the table, and she now made her stretching cat gesture as she lay back against the sofa cushions. She spread open her slim legs in the silky pink trousers, the high heels of her sandals sliding along the cheap carpet. Then she slowly let her right arm fall in a dancer's graceful curve until her hand was resting, its slender fingers spread, over her crotch. Half-lying in that position, her crotch had to be open under those pink trousers, he knew. Yet the last thing he had any interest in at this moment was sex. What he felt was a mix of emotions he hadn't previously experienced with a woman: anger, resentment, fear, all combined.

'Would you care to put your big cock inside me, Minister?' The pussy-cat smile was back on her face as she stroked her crotch. 'Or would you care to discuss those poor Irish lads that a loyal girl like Maureen must always remember,' she said, in a musical lilt, 'no matter how much she is enjoying her own little pastimes? Or would you care, perhaps, to talk about the lovely Patsy? You've never discussed her with me. Come to think of it, you've never discussed much of anything with me except what you'd like me to do with my body. If you think about it,' she said, and dropping her other hand to her left breast she used the tips of her fingers to begin stroking the nipple which now stood out against her pink T-shirt, 'if you think about it, Minister, you can see you've done nothing but use me. A lot of people would see me as a victim.'

What added to his anger and resentment and fear was that his cock had stiffened. He got to his feet and strode over to the sofa. Looking down at her, he took the hand that was still gracefully stroking her crotch and pulled her to her feet. There was more room on the carpet than on the sofa. He pulled her down with him.

Neither of them bothered to take off her T-shirt.

He did no more than undo his own trousers, and when he pulled hers down, he found she was wearing nothing under them. The whole thing was quick and rough. Afterwards, as he lay on his back on the carpet, she stood up and pulled on the pink trousers again. Then she returned to the sofa and leaned back against the cushions.

He watched her from under his partly closed eyelids. She gave a little half-yawn before she said in her soft lilt: 'As I was saying, Minister, would you like to discuss the jobs of those three hundred hard-working decent Irish lads? Or shall we talk about Patsy?'

He smashed into the table as he jumped to his feet, his post-coital dishevelment adding to his rage. With the flat of his hand he hit her across one side of her face. The blow pushed her head around so the other side of her face was buried in the sofa cushions. Instinctively she dropped her arms to protect her head from a second blow.

When it didn't come, she turned her head back again, looking at him over her bent arms. He could see the crimson handprint on the right side of her face.

'Why, Minister, what would your lady wife think about a fine English gentleman behaving like a drunken Irish peasant?' she said in the unhurried lilt, spreading her legs wide again.

Ian had his clothes back in place. Without glancing again at the pink-clad figure on the sofa, he turned on his heel. He heard his irregular steps as he went down to the front door. When it swung to behind him, he heard the click as the lock re-engaged. The thought crossed his mind that if he looked up at the window-boxes of geraniums and petunias he would see the auburn of Maureen's hair as she stood on the other side of the glass, watching him. Or maybe she was still spread out like a whoretrap on that fucking sofa.

Only when he reached Victoria Street did he glance at his watch. 2.10. He was surprised. Hours might have passed since Cabinet had ended and he'd walked through Downing Street's iron gates. He still had an hour and five minutes before his Permanent Secretary would come to his room at BITE to discuss the 3.30 meeting with the German Trade Minister. Ian stepped out of the glaring June sunlight into the first pub he saw.

At the bar he bought a large whisky and a sandwich and carried them to an empty table in the corner. Thank Christ there wouldn't be anyone here he was likely to know. The first thing he needed was to calm down. The next thing was to think where in hell he went from here.

I I

Jock Liddon was sitting in a Senate committee room. He preferred the back row where he was close to the door: 'Always keep your options open.' Also, from there he could identify most people seated in the rows between him and the focal point – the raised table at the front of the room.

Jock liked the room's grand formality. Its multicoloured marble columns and baroque arches reminded you that nineteenth-century senators wouldn't put up with the utilitarian crap built for their late twentieth-century counterparts.

The chairman, flanked by other committee members, sat at the raised table, like a judge. Sitting in the twelve rows of seats that filled the rest of the room were other senators, aides, lobbyists, media. Television cameras were at the sides.

Ostensibly addressing the chairman, Senator Chalmers Morley turned his body slightly to the right so the nearest camera, its red eye glowing, would get a good clean picture. He was a well-made man of middle height in a cream-coloured linen suit, his tie a black ribbon fastened into two long loops and two loose ends which dangled on to a sky-blue shirt, his face and hands the colour of butterscotch. He looked exactly like an actor playing the role of Senator Chalmers Morley, but then actors and politicians have much in common.

Jock's face was expressionless as he watched Morley's handsome profile with its chin lifted just enough to display its well-moulded strength of purpose.

'Yessuh,' the Senator replied to his inquisitor in his deep Texan bass. 'I am proud, suh, to say that my record is second to none in this mattuh.'

Jock panned across the committee members' faces he could see from where he sat, most of them wearing a serious frown as their owners juggled with their private feelings – the keen pleasure of seeing someone else squirm, the fear of one day finding their own short cuts and shortcomings on public display. His eyes returned to Morley's profile. At the end of the morning session Jock would be taking Senator Chalmers Morley to lunch, a date which the Senator had had to postpone twice. Jock needed Senator Morley. He needed him real bad.

American Star Oil was one of J. D. Liddon's clients. And a series of medium-sized oilfields had been discovered near the Hebrides west of Scotland. If the consortium led by Star Oil could get a licence for one of the fields, there'd be one helluva cut for anyone who helped make it happen. Jock wanted that cut. But Star Oil had a big *big* problem: how to get the green light turned on.

When fire had engulfed one of its North Sea production platforms, many people said OK, even the best-managed companies can have an accident. And Star Oil had played its cards well: within forty-eight hours it offered such large sums to the dead men's families that most of the bereaved chose to accept the money without the further misery of a drawn-out court claim. But two rigs collapsing in flames within three years, two hundred and ninety men given the choice of being fried alive in the burning oil which spread over the sea's surface or drowned in the waters beneath, that was more difficult for Star Oil's management to explain away. As its chairman had said to Jock: 'We live in terrible times. Terrible. You can't put things down to acts of God any more. Today everybody holds human beings responsible for every goddamn thing that goes wrong.'

The shade cast by the Hay-Adams' portico imparted a sense of privacy and withdrawal from the hard light of the midday sun which revealed the rest of Lafayette Square. Brass buttons shone on the doorman's black coat as he stepped forward, one spotless white glove touching his gleaming black hat in seeming deference, the other opening the back door of Jock's Cadillac. Senator Chalmers Morley got out first. Jock followed.

'An island of civility in a sea of power' was how the Hay-Adams liked to describe itself. It stood on the site occupied at the end of the nineteenth century by the adjoining homes of John Hay and Henry Adams. Unlike most political luminaries, Hay and Adams remained intimate friends, and a door was cut in the connecting wall between their homes. Then in 1927, these two famous houses were replaced by the Hay-Adams Hotel with its marble baths and accommodation for personal maids and chauffeurs. In 1980 it was restored afresh, and its lobby presented guests with the sense they were entering a grand English country house, the elaborate plasterwork of the arches and soaring ceiling painted a creamy yellow to contrast with the walnut-panelled walls.

'Ah'll just make a call before we go into lunch,' said Senator Morley, seating himself conspicuously at a Georgian writing-table standing beneath one of the huge seventeenth-century Medici tapestries adorning the lobby's walls. There wasn't the slightest need for him to make the call to his office, other than the demands of self-importance. He lifted a cream and gilt old-fashioned telephone from its cradle. The Hay-Adams was the only place he knew where you still actually dialled the number.

When he completed his unnecessary call, he rejoined Jock who had used his own time in the lobby to glad-hand the head of the *Washington Post* financial section, then a congressman on the Appropriations Committee, then the British Embassy's chief adviser on defence procurement. They were all on their way to the Adams Room.

Other dining-rooms in the Hay-Adams were more resplendent, but the Adams Room was the power brokers' favourite for breakfast and lunch. The interior designer had re-created 'old' Washington's blend of formal and informal – gold tapestry-covered walls and crystal chandeliers, white voile curtains gathered at windows overlooking the garden on three sides. Sunshine drenched the room. The tables, with their floor-length floral skirts topped by starched white cloths, were set so far apart that as well as ensuring private conversation, the spaciousness imparted a sense of leisure. In fact, work was taking place at each table. Every lunch in the Adams Room was put down on somebody's business expenses.

Jock and Morley needed several minutes to reach Jock's table beside one of the two marble fireplaces. If you engaged yourself in pressing the flesh of half the people present, it was bound to take you a while to get across the room. Jock's eyes and hands were no busier than the Senator's. 'Nice to see you,' said Morley, his mouth and eyes out of sync, big white teeth gleaming in a broad smile while his eyes had the flat look of someone calculating what he had to gain from this encounter.

The head waiter had long ago perfected his own technique for dealing with guests whose progress to their tables was slowed by their preoccupation with contacts, or 'access' as the power brokers preferred to call it; he would precede them until they made their first serious foray, when he would give a small bow of immense dignity and then gesture imperiously to a lesser waiter to take his place in attendance.

'What'll you have?' Jock asked when at last they were settled.

'I think I'd like a fine big bourbon after all that shit this morning,' replied Senator Morley.

Jock ordered a fine big bourbon for each of them. 'You did all right, Senator. If there's one thing that gets up my ass, it's when your colleagues go all holy as if *their* campaign manager's secretary never made a mistake adding up campaign contributions.'

Chalmers Morley looked morose. He wished that waiter would return with the bourbon. 'It grieves me,

Jock, when some upstart from Oklahoma thinks he's entitled to impugn *my* reputation. I don't mind so much for my sake. But Helen feels it.' Helen was the Senator's edgy wife. 'All her friends watch Senate cross-examinations on the box. Then they phone Helen to tell her how *outrageous* they think it is that I should be asked questions about money matters. But Helen knows they can't wait to phone each other and laugh at her discomfiture. Women can be so unkind to one another. Cunt-faced bitches.' On private occasions, Morley's conversational style was unpredictable, the old-fashioned gentleman stuff jostling with gutter slang.

Jock said nothing. He wondered if those two long loops of rolled black ribbon with the ends dangling halfway down the Senator's chest had been tied by the butterscotch hands that morning, or whether they were sewn in place permanently, with a clip fastening the tie under the collar at the back.

'Ahhh,' said the Senator, something like bliss flitting across the handsome face as the waiter set before him a large chunky glass filled to the brim with the mahogany nectar and ice. Then he banished his look of happy expectation. With a self-discipline which made him proud, he didn't touch the drink for a good half minute, looking at it with a carefully arranged unseeing expression as if the bourbon was entirely peripheral to his thoughts. When at last he picked it up, he held it for another few moments before drinking off a third of it in a single, slow swallow. Chalmers Morley didn't like to see people guzzle their drink; he preferred the more decorous process of appearing to take a mere sip while opening his throat so that a huge slug of firewater could slide down. Jock watched the performance deadpan.

By the time the waiter served their shad, Jock figured the bourbon had sufficiently relaxed the Senator. 'I see it like this,' he said. Jock liked getting into a subject without farting around. 'PACs and honoraria are useful, but you gotta have more to top 'em up.'

The Political Action Committee system in Washington allows senators and congressmen to accept a limited contribution to their election campaigns from any number of lobbies – guns, highway signs, salt-free butter, women's right to a rest, anything goes. You need a lot of dough to buy television time when you're running for office. If the senator takes the money and then fails to vote the way that particular lobby wants, he's less likely to get its contribution to his next election. But you never know. There's always tomorrow. The cardinal rule for lobbyists is: look for the possibility of putting it together another time. Keep access.

The shad is the Chesapeake Bay's most succulent delicacy, but it has more bones than any other fish. However deft the boning done in the Hay-Adams kitchen by the black men employed for that alone, Jock still had to remove one or two hair-fine bones from his mouth. 'Those goddamn guys in the kitchen must be blind from a hangover. I should've ordered lobster Thermidor.'

As he removed two more shad bones from his mouth, the Senator looked at the stumpy fingers, wondering how often Jock had them manicured.

'I'll tell you something, Senator,' Jock said. 'If you had a few more friends – big *big* friends – maybe in the oil industry, your campaign manager's secretary wouldn't gotten her accounts screwed up so the contributions went over the legal limit.'

'Only one contribution went over the limit, ol' boy.'

Jock ignored this. He knew the cotton lobby's next contribution to Senator Morley was curtailed pronto only because the shit had hit the fan. 'As I say, a coupla hundred PACs contributing to your campaign is peanuts. And listening sympathetically to all of 'em takes a lotta time.'

Jock grunted to himself at his own tasteful choice of 'listening sympathetically'. It was all the same to him whether he said Morley listened sympathetically or whether he said Morley had been bought by the cotton lobby and the soy bean lobby and the abortion lobby and would support any goddamn thing in their interest that came before the Senate.

'You wouldn't have to waste all that time,' Jock went on, 'if you had more big *big* friends like the ones I'm talking about. And they'd sure want you to be comfortable when you're flying round the world. They wouldn't want you in London and you didn't enjoy yourself.'

Jock allowed the Senator time to decipher the code words before asking: 'Do you wanna dessert? What about another bourbon?'

'Now that you mention it, I think I'll have a bourbon.'

Jock swivelled his head towards the waiter without

bothering to look at him, as if tossing the words over his shoulder: 'Another bourbon for the Senator. I'll keep him company. And coffee. And bring some cigars.'

The waiter removed the two dessert menus he'd just presented.

'I hear that slob who runs Apex Sugar wanted to come to your Senate office to give you his cheque.'

Morley's office was in Hart, the most luxurious of the three new Senate office buildings, where as a senior senator he had claimed one of its suites. On the whole, congressmen try to avoid accepting contributions on congressional premises.

Senator Morley's thoughts were briefly distracted by the reference to sugar. He thought of the pretty little Georgian silver box, curved to lie comfortably in his hip pocket. Helen had bought it in the Burlington Arcade in Piccadilly when she'd been on a three-day tour of London the previous summer. She'd intended it for the saccharin he sometimes used instead of sugar in his coffee; he also found it handy for his amphetamines and percodans which, fortunately, were easy to distinguish from one another. He could have used an upper at this moment, but he sternly put the thought from his mind.

'Some people just don't know how to behave, Jock. My staff had to say to this Apex president's office: "The Senator would be glad, of course, to hear your views, but not at the same time as you hand over a cheque."'

'Yeah. Well, some of these dickheads need to be reassured. If you actually tell him you support his group at the same minute he hands you the cheque, it keeps him happy. It means he can go back to his board and tell 'em he can guarantee they're getting something out of contributing to your campaign. But I agree, it's only a crud-bum who's gotta have these things spelled out.'

Both men selected a fat missile from the rich-smelling box offered by the waiter. Morley held his cigar between thumb and forefinger, sniffing its aroma. Jock left him to it, lighting his own. Then he came to the point.

'I've got an interest in American Star Oil, Senator. They're my clients.' His opaque brown eyes looked directly into the Senator's translucent blue ones. This was Jock playing his cards face up for the Senator to see. It was one of Jock's neatest techniques.

'One thing I appreciate is frankness,' said the Senator.

'Yeah. Well, frankly I'm worried about Star Oil missing a golden opportunity lying in the ocean west of Scotland. Why should the Brits have more confidence in their oil companies than the United States Senate has in Americans? You could almost say it's unpatriotic when some of our congressmen don't lift a finger to help American companies spread their investments.'

He paused, watching the Senator finally finish the foreplay and light his cigar. He wanted to give Morley a moment to register the 'unpatriotic' bit.

Then Jock went on: 'That asshole from Oklahoma is sending a coupla henchmen to London to dump on Star Oil's application to get a licence for one of those fields discovered near the Hebrides. I don't gotta tell you the senator's father-in-law already put in a bid for the consortium led by his own oil company. He figures the Brits will limit how many American companies they let buy in. To give Oklahoma Petroleum a better chance, he's gotta block the consortium led by Star Oil.'

Senator Morley's face gave nothing away. 'What's he going to use for his bad-mouth line?' he asked.

'Star Oil lost two rigs in the North Sea in three years,' Jock said bluntly, like a man coming clean, even though only an ostrich could have been unaware of what had taken place in the North Sea. The scenes of the burning oil enveloping the toppling rigs, survivors wrapped in bandages like mummies, intrusive interviews with new widows, all had been top of the pops on American television for three days running when the first rig exploded, five days the second time.

'Senator Asshole from Oklahoma is gonna say that until the final insurance claims are complete, Star Oil shouldn't get a licence to invest in any new fields. Christ, here you got not just the survivors of those fucking accidents; you got the families of those whose, uh, luck ran out – all of 'em happy as clams to accept Star Oil's sweet pay-off. The Brits hardly even thought about suing until the lawyers got at them.'

The Senator cleared his throat. 'Am I right in believing that all the men involved in the Star Oil rig disasters were British?'

'Yeah.'

'I believe, Jock, that British courts are not as well

designed for those who want to sue as are our American courts.'

'Well, sure, Senator. When it comes to suing, no place can match the Land of the Free. But that's not the point. The point is just because the British legal system is like a goddamn snail, the insurance claims haven't even been settled already. But that don't mean Star Oil copped out of all safety precautions. The investigation decided the charge of manslaughter couldn't be proved. What more does anybody want? Yet Senator Asshole from Oklahoma has never heard you're innocent until you're proved guilty. Somebody oughta send him to school.'

'You could almost say Star Oil's voluntary pay-offs, uh, pay-outs to the survivors was a lesson in good management,' said Senator Morley, who was rehearsing reasons why he might 'be sympathetic' to Star Oil's application to the British minister who would decide who got the licences. He couldn't stand that prick from Oklahoma who had tried to impugn *his*, Chalmers Morley's, integrity. And if Star Oil had thought it worth all those millions which he knew they'd spent buying off most of the survivors of those oil rig balls-ups, they would sure see that he and Helen travelled by Concorde and she could shop to her heart's content in London while he talked up their application. And it was clear that if he helped Star Oil, they'd guarantee him more PACs without him having to work his guts out listening sympathetically to all of them. The unwanted memory returned of his secretary landing him in the shit with her goddamn accounts. He wished to God he'd been able to fire her. But if he did that, next thing he knew she'd be blabbing to the press about other mistakes in his accounts. When he'd started in politics, you could rely on your secretary to keep her mouth shut. These days you couldn't trust anybody.

'With you being on the Senate Appropriations Committee,' Jock said, 'you'd be bound to carry weight with whoever you'd have to see in London. And we'd get a deal lined up for you to offer them in exchange. An MP on their Appropriations Select Committee is a good friend of mine. James Arden. He'd organize things for you. He knows better than anyone that important contacts can't be done on the cheap.'

Jock's face was without expression as he looked at the Senator through the two columns of smoke rising between them. No need to mention any other ways he could make the Senator's life more comfortable: a time and a place for everything.

Removing his cigar from his mouth to tip the fluffy ash into the cut-glass bowl the waiter had put between them, Senator Morley adopted the role of a statesman reflecting on where his patriotic duty lay. He returned his cigar to his lips, and his blue eyes gave Jock as sincere a look as Jock had ever received from mortal being.

'I'd like to be able to help you, Jock. You make a good case for Star Oil. Maybe we ought to parley again.'

'We don't want to leave it too long, Senator. By the time you blink, the Brits will be grabbing all those oilfields for themselves, with maybe one tossed to the consortium led by Oklahoma Petroleum. We gotta move fast.'

Senator Morley puffed on his cigar solemnly. 'Maybe the best thing, Jock, would be for you and someone from Star Oil to have a drink at my place early one evening. My house is in Bethesda. Usually I don't fly back to Texas until Fridays. Maybe there'd be some time later this week when I was going home before Helen and I go out to dinner. We could have a drink then. Have your secretary phone mine.'

'I'll do that, Senator. And there's another thing you might be thinking about. These oil fields near the Hebrides are within spitting distance of Northern Ireland. Star Oil is holding talks with British Refineries about a joint venture in Northern Ireland. The idea is to build an oil refinery there – providing Star Oil gets a field. BritRef is saying it can't put up more money – which we know they got. My executive vice-president, Michael O'Donovan, has already been back and forth a coupla times, trying to convince BritRef that they should quit hoarding their assets up their ass. A respected figure like you could do a lot to convince that Limey company to increase their input in a joint venture with Star Oil.'

'That sounds an excellent project. Excellent. We can discuss it further when you and – did you say it would be Star Oil's president? – come for a drink.'

'Yeah,' said Jock noncommittally. He hadn't yet told Star Oil's president that his services would be needed with Senator Chalmers Morley. 'Lemme give you a lift back to Capitol Hill, Senator.'

*

In his K Street office, Jock's meeting with a client and the client's team of lawyers came to an end at five o'clock. Jock pressed the buzzer on the table beside his Eames chair, and ten seconds later Jancis appeared. When she'd shown the visitors back down the thick coral carpet to the entrance door, she returned to Jock's office with the appointments book and notepad of messages.

His tie already loosened, he had moved to a chair by the window where a low table was spread with bound files. He was flicking through the one titled 'Star Oil'.

'Have you heard from Morley?' he said without looking up at Jancis who remained standing.

'We've arranged for Wednesday evening at six. At that time of day you should allow forty minutes to get to Bethesda.'

When she'd given him the other messages, Jock got out of his chair, lifting his arms with the elbows bent as he stretched his chest muscles – 'Uhhhh-mmmmmm.' He patted Jancis's bottom in its neat navy skirt, and ambled to his desk. Jancis went out the door, closing it behind her.

Jock picked up the green telephone and pressed three numbers. 'You alone, Mike?' he said. Michael O'Donovan was the only member of J. D. Liddon to whom such courtesy was shown. In fact it was precaution: Michael was the only member of Jock's staff who might have an important client in his room when Jock rang. The rest of the staff would be expected to go to the client's office or meet in a restaurant. 'Gimme ten minutes. Then come in my office. We oughta go through some things together.'

Replacing the green telephone, Jock picked up the red one. 'Jancis, I wanna talk with the editor of *World* in New York. Georgie Chase. Yeah. If she's available now, put me through. Otherwise find out when she will be.'

He had just finished a note to himself in the margin of page twenty in Star Oil's file when Jancis buzzed him. 'Georgie Chase can speak to you now.'

'OK.'

With his free hand Jock reached for the humidor on his desk and took out one of the unwrapped cigars, inserted it between his curly lips, and reached for the silver table lighter. An eagerness had appeared on the usually impassive face, and something in the molten brown eyes was similar to the eyes of the two Dobermans when they'd flanked Georgie on the pier, their tail stubs quivering as they'd waited for her to shout: '*Get it.*'

I2

That Wednesday Hugo wrote his piece at the office. He'd chosen a subject he could polish off safely by six without the risk of some evening news announcement compelling him to rewrite it. He had arranged to meet her for dinner.

The Washington bureau of the *News* was spread across the top two floors of one of the newer plush office buildings clustered near Franklin Square. Nearly fifty journalists were in one enormous room, heads of sections demarcated by waist-high partitions around their desks. The three grandest journalists each had an office furnished to his own taste, but the glass wall between them and the rest of the staff was transparent, and usually the doors were kept open. One of the glassed-off offices was Hugo's. It brought to mind a library in an English house – leather Chesterfield sofa, mahogany bookcases, an Edwardian roll-top desk as well as a modern flat-top with his computer.

The chief political editor of the *News* was bound to be based in its Washington bureau rather than the main office in New York. That suited Hugo. 'You think Capitol Hill is political. My God, it's nothing to the politics in our main office,' he'd said to Georgie when they first moved to Washington. He was adroit enough at office politics, but he disliked the self-centred amorality, each person obsessed with clambering over someone else's back. 'If you go to main office, you'll find a bunch of full-grown men in kindergarten,' he said.

The Washington bureau's atmosphere was altogether different. Journalists helped each other. They didn't switch their stories off their computer screen when another journalist appeared at their shoulder. Hugo consulted with lesser colleagues on congressional business, foreign affairs, any relevant national stuff, even arts and leisure. They consulted with him. 'If ever we don't help each other at the bureau, it's because the office manager isn't handling the office right,' he'd said to Georgie. For several years now the office manager had done well.

At the same time that the bureau practised internal camaraderie, it proclaimed to the world it was top of the heap. Visitors stepped off the elevator into a reception room large enough to house a dozen Puerto Rican families. The receptionist could afford to be particularly polite and friendly: she sat behind a sleek Art Deco-style piece of furniture which made you think of a small ocean liner. At one end of the marble floor, sumptuous dove-grey leather armchairs stood in a square around a magnificent glass table. Fanned out on the table were pristine copies of that day's international newspapers, while above them rose the dramatic striped fronds of an aechmea, its rich, red sensual core glowing like a pomegranate. The Washington bureau of the *News* stated to the world: we're powerful and rich and we like our comfort.

When Georgie first visited the bureau, she'd been

amazed by the glamour and amiable self-confidence which pervaded the whole place. 'You must get it straight,' Hugo had told her. 'Even the lowliest reporter on the *News* is somebody in this town. In London, unless you're a star, you're treated like a grunt.'

As the satin chrome doors of the elevator closed and it started its swoosh descent, he looked at his watch: 6.25. Outside the main entrance, Whitmore was waiting in the Lincoln. Hugo got in beside him.

When they approached the smart office buildings of K Street, Hugo looked at his watch: just past 6.30. She had said she'd come down and wait at the front door. He wondered what colour dress she'd be wearing.

Then he saw it was that green which made him think of a river, even though rivers rarely have the clean luminosity of eau-de-Nil silk. The dress was exactly right for the occasion – a simple silk shift that looked expensive as it skimmed her breasts and hips, making one aware of the supple body underneath without flaunting it. Fast-lane New Yorkers referred to Washington as a provincial town. Except for the Reagan years and a few of today's new rich who got it wrong, Washingtonians dressed conservatively – expensive and unflashy. Lisa's dress was sexy enough to make it close to the borderline, but it stayed on the right side. She was wearing her hair loose. As Whitmore pulled the car over to the curb, Hugo saw how her silky blonde hair seemed to reflect the pale green of the dress.

'I'll get it, Whitmore,' he said, opening his door and jumping out. 'Have you been here long?' he asked Lisa. He was astounded by how happy he was to see her.

'All of one and a half minutes,' she said, laughing, as she slid across the back seat so he could follow.

'We needn't stay long at Imogene's,' he said, 'but I promised her I'd drop by.'

'I'd like to meet her.'

Hugo knew that. He'd asked Lisa to dine this evening instead of yesterday, because yesterday's cocktail party had less clout than an Imogene party. Imogene Randall was one of Washington's few remaining great hostesses who were old family. Any week of the year, every power broker in Washington would rather be seen at an Imogene party than at the most dazzling splash laid on by new money. That Hugo should want to impress Lisa was an innocent enough vanity. In any case, he liked giving pleasure.

'We have time to go through the park, Whitmore, and it's nice this time of day,' he said.

'Even after two years in Washington I still love it when the driver turns into Rock Creek Park,' Lisa remarked when Whitmore headed up the canyon of poplar and pine trees, rough grass, water rushing pell-mell over a riverbed heaped with large grey stones whose jagged tops shimmered in the long day's sunshine. Joggers streaming with sweat, their thoughts abstracted by their exertions, appeared at intervals on the tow-path beside the creek. A few people were bicycling home from work, their office clothes in a bag strapped behind the saddle.

Whitmore left the park to exit for Georgetown, and a few minutes later pulled up behind a car which had hardly come to a halt when two bodyguards jumped out. From its rear door stepped a stocky, grizzle-haired man followed by a tall, willowy blonde.

'The Kissingers,' said Lisa as she watched them walk through the open wooden gate to Imogene Randall's eighteenth-century house.

Washed with chalky pink, the brick house was set back in a front garden dominated by an enormous magnolia tree, its waxy leaves glistening coolly despite June's heat, propped up in its old age by a deep-dug wooden brace. The front door at the top of the steps had shut behind the Kissingers by the time Lisa and Hugo reached it, and he rang the big brass bell.

The first thing Lisa noticed when the butler closed the door behind them was the sense of tranquillity in the centre hall, undisturbed by the distant hubbub of voices indicating that other guests had arrived at 6.30 sharp. Some would be going on to a second cocktail party before dinner, and all would be leaving their dinner parties soon after ten. Washingtonians did everything early by London standards.

Slightly awed by the stillness of the hall, Lisa noticed several inches of silk edging had come loose from one of a pair of Regency elbow chairs standing either side of a table against one wall. The faded yellow silk of their seat-covering complemented the deep blue of a matched pair of Wedgwood urns on the elegant Regency tea-table, its satinwood turned buttery gold by sun and age, its hinged leaf unfolded to stand upright against the wall. The urns looked wonderfully peaceful, as if they'd been there a long time. Hugo had been in houses like this all his life. Lisa had not. She took it all in.

Through the door on the left they went down a few stairs into a long library with one wall of windows looking out on the back garden. Some of the thirty guests already there stood in small groups; others sat on sofas clustered around a big coffee-table at each end of the room.

A fine-boned woman in dove-grey chiffon separated herself from a group. She had already conveyed to the Kissingers that the California senator was longing to talk with Henry about the fraught border-control problem with Mexico, and she moved unhurriedly, as if she had all the time in the world, to her next two guests.

'I was delighted when Hugo told me he'd be bringing you this evening,' Imogene said.

Elegant even in her teens, Imogene had always seemed ageless. Fair-skinned, slender, dignified, at sixty she appeared virtually unchanged since more than thirty years earlier she'd married the Senate's most distinguished Southern member and made an easy transition from North Carolina to Washington. When her husband died after twenty years of marriage, she withdrew into a year's mourning. Then she resumed her grand, high-powered social life. How she distributed her charms privately remained a mystery.

Nothing in Imogene's grey eyes indicated that she was sizing up Lisa. 'One of these days Georgie will find she has stayed away too long,' Imogene said to herself, not for the first time. Aloud she said in the low voice which forced you to concentrate in order to hear her: 'Hugo tells me you are working with Jock Liddon.'

Lisa noted the preposition: 'with' Jock Liddon. Anyone else she knew would have said 'for' him. She was tremendously impressed by Imogene's grace.

Imogene also had optic powers unknown to lesser souls. Without letting her eyes look away from Lisa and Hugo, she was able to see that Robert O. Robertson was just coming down the steps into the library. Congressman Robert O. Robertson might be an unadulterated bore, but as Speaker of the House of Representatives he was about the biggest shot on Capitol Hill.

'Oh Hugo,' Imogene said, 'will you introduce Miss Tabor to the Senator from Massachusetts? I particularly invited him so you and he could discuss Noraid,' she said sweetly. Imogene enjoyed stirring things up, so long as the guests did not actually throw their drinks at one another. With one long delicate hand she indicated a group standing around Senator Patrick Rourke, and almost simultaneously she turned her smooth-browed face towards the advancing Speaker, suggesting there was nobody, absolutely nobody in the world, that Imogene Randall wanted to see more than him.

A lot of journalists are embarrassed when they run into a person they've publicly castigated. But Hugo always welcomed the opportunity to confront them face to face: if Pat Rourke wanted to complain, let him do so to Hugo's face.

'Nice to meetcha, Lisa,' Senator Rourke said when Hugo introduced them. 'What're you doing with a dog like Hugo?'

'She's come to see what you hotshots get up to when you're not fund-raising,' Hugo said equably.

'Lisa,' said the Senator, 'could you just reach me a gin-and-tonic from that tray going past your shoulder? Here.' He handed her his empty glass which she swapped for a full one, helping herself to an orange juice. Hugo took an old-fashioned glass filled with ice and whisky so dark he didn't need to ask the waiter if it was bourbon.

After a long pull at his gin-and-tonic, Pat Rourke said: 'It's a funny thing, Hugo. When I was reading that piece you wrote last week when that British MP got blown up, for a minute I thought you were getting at me. I didn't like that, Hugo. And I didn't like what you said about my constituents.'

Hugo gave a wintry smile. 'I imagine the MP's family didn't like what your constituents have done to them.'

Pat Rourke's wide face, a faint blue tinging the flushed skin, appeared to be wholly absorbed in draining the last drop of gin from his glass. When it was plain that only the rattle of ice would reward further effort in that direction, he looked again at Hugo.

'You know me, Hugo. I'd never endorse anything like blowing up that MP. Why the hell did you want to drag in my name when you're writing about something like that? If I weren't such a nice guy, I'd accuse you of trying to smear me.'

'I've never smeared anyone in my life, Pat,' said Hugo evenly.

Rourke changed tack. 'Well, you shouldn't have said that about my Irish constituents. You can take it from me, Hugo: just because they support Noraid doesn't mean they approve of blowing up that Brit.'

'I'm glad to hear it. Yet somebody in Noraid must approve of how its funds are used by the IRA. Any ideas, Pat?'

'I've already told you. None of my constituents would have approved of blowing up that Brit.' Accustomed to playing it both ways, Rourke added: 'On the other hand, some of them could understand it.'

'On the other hand,' Hugo mimicked acidly. He despised the weasel line of the politician playing it both ways.

Immediately Pat Rourke set out to explain himself. 'If you had family in Belfast, Hugo, being crapped on every day by Protestant pricks unfit to lick the soles of their feet, and you knew it's only the British government makes it possible for those cunts to crap on your family, I think you'd understand how some of my constituents feel about the Brits.'

Lisa glanced sideways at Hugo's face. Though she had met him only that one time on the Shore ten days ago, she was unsurprised when she saw the faint flush that crept up his cheeks.

'Even British five-year-olds, Pat?' said Hugo drily. Then he steered Lisa away to another group.

After forty-five more minutes doing the rounds of Imogene's library, he was ready to have some time alone with Lisa. They found Imogene in the centre hall, saying goodbye to Speaker Robert O. Robertson, whose gravelly voice was still in full flow as he recounted a conversation he'd had in the Oval Office. 'And I said to the President,' he boomed, sweeping one arm wide in a magnificent gesture of mastery, 'Mr President . . .'

But Lisa couldn't take in what he had said to the President. Her eyes were fixed with fascinated horror on the Regency tea-table holding the pair of Wedgwood urns. Speaker Robert O. Robertson's waving hand had caught one edge of the hinged leaf standing against the wall, and the leaf was slowly folding down, pushing the irreplaceable porcelain twins forward. They were in midair when the leaf finished closing with a clonk, and in unison they at last collided with the polished wood floor, smashing into a hundred pieces.

The guests in the hall were speechless. The Speaker looked aghast. The butler stepped forward and stood erect and sombre, like someone at a mourning service for a high dignitary.

'These things happen every day,' Imogene said to the Speaker. 'You mustn't think another thing about it. James,' she said, turning languidly to the butler, 'have Queenie get a dustpan and clear those things up.' She turned her smooth-browed face to Hugo and Lisa. 'I'm so glad you both could make it. Do let's meet soon.'

In the Lincoln, Lisa was silent.

'Did you enjoy it?' Hugo asked.

'She's so cool,' Lisa said. 'If it had been my family's house, my mother would have thought the whole family disgraced if a piece of chair edging had come unstitched. Not that any of our chairs had silk edging to start with. Were those urns real old Wedgwood?'

'I'm afraid so.'

Lisa was silent again as her brain filed her observations of another world. This evening Hugo had opened its door for her. But she knew the door wouldn't open again automatically. She had much to do before that would happen.

When Whitmore stopped in front of the Willard, Lisa said nothing about having dined there the week before with Jock. Hugo's table was in a different corner of the restaurant, with the dual advantage of being conspicuous and yet far enough away from other tables.

Being conspicuous served three purposes tonight. As usual, it enabled politicians to spot him and come over to exchange political gossip. Equally it enabled him to see them without having to rubberneck. And tonight it also advertised that his dining *à deux* with a sexy lady was above-board. Had he been screwing her, he would have taken her somewhere less public. Wouldn't he?

Between placing their order and its being served, Hugo introduced Lisa to the White House press spokeswoman, then a California senator, and finally a long-time lobbyist, all of them having wandered over apparently to speak to Hugo but more than a little curious to meet the lady.

It was when Hugo and Lisa were at last getting into their own conversation that something made her glance across the dining-room. She looked straight into the flint-like face of Michael O'Donovan watching her. He nodded. Then he turned his eyes back to the file of papers he was reading as he ate his dinner alone.

'What's the matter?' asked Hugo, seeing the look of confusion on Lisa's face.

'I wish he wasn't here tonight.'

Hugo started to turn to see who she was talking about.

'Don't turn around, Hugo. It's Michael O'Donovan. He's the only person except Jock who really matters at J. D. Liddon.'

'Do you want to go over and speak to him?'

'No. He has a thing about his privacy. It's funny: he's Boston-Irish, but he couldn't be less like Senator Rourke. Michael went to Harvard. If he has any emotions buttoned up under his Brooks Brothers suit, I can't see them. He's creepy. Who else would come to the Willard for a working dinner by himself?'

'Maybe he thought you might be here and he could have the pleasure of looking at you while he eats his solitary meal,' Hugo said teasingly.

Lisa didn't reply. The thought of Michael keeping tabs on her didn't entertain her, even as a joke. She had no idea where she stood with him, nor did she really know anything about his relationship with Jock. Not until the waiter served the Crab Imperial could she shake off her awareness that Michael was across the room, and then she and Hugo got down to uninterrupted conversation.

Used to dates consisting of shop-talk laced with sexual innuendo – whether it was dinner with Jock or with friends her own age – she was surprised when Hugo asked about her family life. He didn't just say 'oh yeah' when she said she'd been brought up in a small town in northern Pennsylvania. He asked her: 'What was it like?'

At first she didn't answer. She looked down at her Crab Imperial and daintily took another mouthful, curtaining off her eyes from Hugo.

He was happy to wait; he knew she'd be looking up at him again, those violet eyes looking straight at him with their open candour. He'd watched them turn from blue-grey to violet when the waiter lit the candle on their table. While she went on looking down, he examined her face with total pleasure, the skin lightly tanned, smooth over the high cheekbones and firm, conveying a sense of healthy litheness. He bet she did some sort of regular exercise. Her big upper lip seemed to swell slightly as she put a forkful of crab in her mouth and withdrew the fork slowly; she hadn't actually sucked the creamy crab off the tines, yet something about the full upper lip, slightly turned out, made Hugo imagine it sucking.

Lisa was looking down because she was deciding how to answer. With a few people she met who would never know otherwise, she glamorized her upbringing. Most Americans couldn't care less where you came from, but some did, and Lisa liked to keep her options open. There'd been no point in doing that with Jock, who didn't give a shit about her background: what mattered to him was her performance today and tomorrow – in the sack, sure, but above all how she performed at keeping the clients coming to J. D. Liddon International for the best lobbying money could buy.

With Hugo, Lisa had to be careful. With just a couple of questions, he'd find her out if she pretended her family was up-market. She was a quick learner; but she knew she still lacked a feel for getting that sort of social lie right if she tried it with an insider.

And anyhow there were much more important lies she might need to use. Use. That's how Lisa thought of lies – as something you use, like a special tool for a craft. She couldn't have been more than fourteen when she decided it was a lot of garbage to think that telling lies was wrong. Right and wrong were flexible words, something her mother was too brain-dead to grasp.

But the trouble with lies was that you had to have a special card index file in your brain to keep track of them. Lisa had exceptional energy. Beginning with when she got up in time for forty minutes of exercises every morning, she organized each day to maximize her energies. Having to keep checking out her brain's file of lies used up energy, so she rarely told them unless she was confident they'd come in useful.

She looked up at Hugo, the violet eyes steady and direct. 'I hated it. I used to think: if anyone sells their body to get out of this boring place, I don't blame them.'

Her frankness touched him. 'Did you ever?'

'Sell my body? I didn't have to. Shall I tell you about hicksville? My father's a dentist. I've never heard him actually have a conversation with my mother. "Did you have a nice day, dear?" he would say every single evening when we sat down in that dead, dead dining-room. "So-so. What about yours?" she would say as she dished up the mashed potatoes. "It was all right. Mrs Jones came in with a sore gum. I told her: Mrs Jones, there's nothing the matter with your gum except you're not brushing your teeth right. You've got to brush *away* from the gum, I said." That's what my family was like.'

Hugo thought he had never seen anything so lovely as Lisa's face as she told him this bleak story. She looked down again and took another forkful of crab.

The waiter topped up their glasses from the bottle of Pouilly Fuissé standing in a cold tub.

'Did your mother ever yearn for anything different?'

'My mother *yearn*?' The violet eyes hardened with contempt. 'How can you yearn if you haven't any imagination? Long ago she let her brain turn into one of those balls of fluff you see under beds. Shall I tell you what she said to me on my seventeenth birthday? "Shouldn't you think about getting married?" That's about all she ever had to say to me afterwards. She always said it with a sniff.'

She didn't speak with bitterness. She was matter-of-fact. Her manner made the unkind words rather impressive.

Hugo reached towards the small bowl of roses that stood beneath the flickering candle. Revolving the bowl on the starched tablecloth so he could examine each rose, he chose a citric yellow one not yet fully open. Easing it out of the mesh holding it, he laid it beside Lisa's wineglass. He wanted to give her something.

She picked it up and smelled it. Then she held the rose so its moist petals touched her moist, same-size lips, her eyes smiling at him. She made him feel there was nothing he could ever give her that she'd value more than this yellow rose. Something about her innocence made her sexuality more pronounced. Beneath the white starched tablecloth Hugo felt himself harden.

13

Of course he knew Lisa was attracted to him. Yet he felt uneasy about plucking this innocent flower just for his own pleasure. After all, he was a married man: he could offer her nothing in return.

If he suspected she might have been less attracted had he been a nobody, he suppressed that thought. The gallantry instilled by his upbringing coloured how he saw her, how he imagined her feelings for him. It would not have occurred to Hugo that when someone held his position of power at the *News* all he needed to say to Lisa was: 'I want to screw you.'

Instead, after their third dinner together, he said: 'I'm on my own during the week. Would you like to see where I write when I don't go into the office?'

He thought about having Whitmore drop them off at the Georgetown house and not come back that night: Lisa could go home in a taxi. Yet a piece of Hugo knew she liked the luxury of a chauffeur-driven Lincoln being at hand. Also, he didn't want to make things obvious to Whitmore. So he told Whitmore to come back in an hour and wait to take Miss Tabor home. Saying 'an hour' seemed to Hugo to give the impression that everything was above-board. After all, he often asked friends back to the house for a drink.

He took her into the living-room. Getting the whisky from the Hepplewhite secretary-bookcase he said: 'This is one of the few things I have from my family's house of long ago.'

'It's so different,' she said, 'from the furniture in my family's house.'

He led her by the hand to one of the Sheraton console mirrors. He stood just behind her, both of them looking at her reflection in the mirror, this delicate flower in her simple sleeveless silk sheath dress, its tiny buttons, each fastened with a silken hoop, running from above her breasts and ending just below her hip bones. If the dress was unbuttoned and he slipped her arms out, it would drop to the floor. 'When some ancestor of mine was looking in this mirror two hundred years ago,' he said, 'I wonder if he saw before him anything as beautiful as what I'm seeing now.'

She enjoyed her beauty in the Sheraton mirror. She liked seeing Hugo's face looking over her shoulder, looking at her. When his hands appeared in the mirror, she watched them begin with the top button. When he got to the sixth one, he put his hand inside the silk. 'I knew it,' he said, when he found her breast bare. He withdrew his hand from under the silk, and he and Lisa watched in the mirror as he went on undoing the buttons. When he reached her waist, he slipped her arms from the sleeves so that the silk fell down and rested on her hips. 'I knew it,' he repeated. She liked the husky excitement in his voice. 'I knew they'd be beautiful.' They both looked at her in the mirror, Hugo's light blue eyes moist with desire and happiness. She lifted her arms with the elbows bent so her fingertips touched her face, framing it. Both of them watched him looking over her shoulder at this nymph-like creature standing half-naked before him. He knelt while he reached up under her skirt to pull off her panties. Then he stood again behind her, and his hands reappeared in the mirror. He unfastened more of the buttons of the silk dress still resting on her hips until suddenly, with a soft sibilance, it slipped to the floor. The nymph stood naked in the mirror, innocent and desiring, yielding to him alone.

Of course he knew there had been some man, several perhaps, before him. But when he asked Lisa about it, she always smiled softly, resting her fingertips on his arm for a moment when they were in a restaurant, touching his face with her fingertips when they were alone. 'It seems such a long time ago,' she would say. 'Whatever happened, happened. Yet it had no significance. It was as if it never happened at all. I've never felt like this before,' she would say. He believed her. Very occasionally an image of Jock's stumpy hands came to his mind's eye, but he could banish it.

The next time he took her back to the Georgetown house, they again made love in the living-room. Like the first night, he left her naked long enough to go upstairs and get several soft giant Turkish towels. However infatuated he was with Lisa, a piece of Hugo's mind still warned him that care had to be taken. He could throw the towels in the washing machine.

But as soon as he had dealt with the practical side of things – how to conceal what was happening from Georgie – he was totally engrossed again in the delights of Lisa. As he spread the Turkish towels on top of one another in the middle of the Persian carpet, they brought to his mind the floor coverings of an Eastern harem, and he drew his odalisque down beside him.

One evening he asked her whether she minded their staying downstairs in the living-room. 'I like it here,' she answered in a low voice that was both sensual and humble. 'It wouldn't seem right to go up to your wife's bedroom.' He loved her even more for that. At the same time, her saying it made him want one night to take her up to that bedroom.

He had stopped bothering to make any pretence with Whitmore. Neither of them alluded to the thing. Each took unspoken trust for granted.

That Hugo was betraying Georgie's trust rarely came to the front of his mind. He had almost persuaded himself he was as innocent as he imagined Lisa. It was Georgie's fault, he said to himself, that he had fallen in love with Lisa. If Georgie hadn't been hell-bent on her career, he would never have given in to his feelings for this fragile flower of a girl. Lisa aroused in him the urge to ravish her and the wish to protect her as well. The thought of her vulnerability moved him deeply. Georgie no longer needed any help from him: Georgie had grown tough and invulnerable.

Another reason why Hugo felt that this passion for Lisa was right – almost destined – was that it didn't seem to have affected his physical relations with his wife. The weekend after he and Lisa became lovers, he had wondered whether he'd have a problem with Georgie – whether he would find he was turned off

Georgie. But when she was undressing that evening, he pulled her down on their bed with an urgency which surprised them both. 'Wait a minute, can't you, while I throw off the counterpane before you put a great lake in the middle of it,' she'd said, laughing, making them both get off the bed while she threw the cover back, then pulling him down on top of her. He didn't want to do the things he'd done with Lisa before finally entering her, but after nine years' practice with Georgie he knew how to bring her fast to the point where she could start coming to her own climax almost as soon as he was inside her. It was as if Lisa had so stimulated his sexuality that desire for Georgie, lessened by the passage of time, had been refreshed and boosted as well.

But Hugo did not discuss any of this with Georgie. A key part of their marriage had been their physical interest only in each other, and he didn't want to jeopardize his marriage.

He had another reason not to tell his wife: he wanted to keep his secret for the pleasure of having a secret. Lisa was his secret garden.

After his dinner alone in a K Street restaurant where the service was fast, Michael O'Donovan returned to an office building almost empty except for the security guards on the ground floor. When he got off the mirror-lined elevator at the sixteenth floor, his sense of intent pleasure increased as he walked down the thick blue carpet to suite 1600. Something like a smile flickered briefly on his narrow face as he glanced at the small brass plaque with its discreet announcement that this was J. M. Liddon International. Michael was amused by the occasional touches of formality which veneered Jock's normal showy shamelessness.

Dropping his keys back in his pocket, Michael slipped his hand behind a painting hung near the door and pressed a light switch. When the heavy door had closed behind him, his intent pleasure increased: he liked the stillness of the deserted office. Turning to the right-hand corridor, he walked soundlessly down the thick coral pile which led ultimately to Jock's enclave. Passing his own secretary's office, Michael stopped at the next door, took out his bunch of keys again, and entered his own capacious room.

As number two, he was entitled to idiosyncrasies not permitted anyone else except Jock. It was accepted that Michael had an obsession with secrecy. Behind his comfortably furnished room, where he received visitors and did most of his work at a handsome, tooled leather-topped desk, was a smaller room. He now used another key to unlock its door.

This second room was entirely utilitarian. On its unadorned desk was a telephone which was billed directly to Michael. The fax and photocopy machines were never touched by his secretary except when he wanted fresh paper put in.

From his briefcase he took out a file he'd been reading over dinner. Its index tab was inscribed in his small neat handwriting: 'BITE Lonsdale'. Wordplay was one of Michael's few indulgences. He smiled thinly. Then he selected three pages and carried them to his photocopier.

14

'What's with the black and white, Georgie? Don't you ever wanna break out with some hot colour?'

They were having a drink at the Colony before Georgie went on to Ralph Kernon's dinner for the head of CBS. Before leaving her office she had replaced her white shirt with a low-necked, double-breasted white grosgrain jacket matching her narrow skirt. Her small breasts were rounded and high; severely tailored jackets which showed the top curve of the breasts suited her. She wore a single choker of pearls and big pearl earclips which contrasted with the nearly black hair. When she entered the bar where Jock was waiting, half the people in the room watched her, several nudging their companions, as she walked to his table in the corner.

Georgie grinned. 'I could say I do it because it saves time – wearing white from May to September, black the rest of the year. But of course that would be a lie. Why do you think I do it, even though it irritates people?'

Jock grunted. He was lighting a cigar.

'For effect,' he said, looking at her through the column of smoke as he drew on the cigar held between his thumb and forefinger. 'It says: "Look at me." Sure it irritates. It also commands respect: "I'm doing what I feel like doing. If you don't like it, get lost."'

Georgie sipped her Perrier.

'Why didn't you want a drink?'

Regarding social life as intended for the give and take of useful information, Jock asked personal questions as unhesitatingly as a policeman who has charged you with an offence.

Georgie laughed. She enjoyed his full-frontal approach. 'I'll have one when I get to my dinner party. I don't like drinking before then. It takes the edge off. Actually, I don't drink that much ever. I can't stand the sense that I'm not in control.'

'Of yourself? Or others?'

She looked at the stumpy hand holding the cigar to the fleshy lips. The cigar's sexual symbolism was so obvious that she thought he must be aware of it. He watched her watching him.

'Both,' she said, 'though I don't have to make huge efforts to control my emotions. The control I'm talking about is keeping my head together, whatever the occasion. When I was at *Bazaar* I once got stoned at a VIP ball and spent the whole night on the dance-floor. The Governor was there. The president of AT&T was there. Rupert Murdoch was there. I didn't talk with any of them. All I did was dance. When I woke up in the morning I groaned – not because my head hurt, which it did, but because all those useful contacts had been missed.'

Jock drank some of his whisky. 'I'm lucky. I can drink pretty steadily and still keep my head screwed on. I never in my life woke up in the morning and thought: "Christ. There was an opportunity looking me in the face last night, and I was so pissed I missed it." Which reminds me: *World* is bound to cover the Senate committee's powwow on chemical sweeteners. "Will saccharin make you trim and fit or give you a shove towards the coffin?"'

Jock shrugged as he said it. He never pretended to take an interest in the merit of such arguments: it was purely incidental that his client was a sugar king and not a saccharin one.

'I want to put a big *big* sugar ad in *World*, Georgie. And I want it to be in kissing distance of the news story on the Senate committee's investigation into saccharin. Maybe on the page before the story or on the turnover page. Your advertising manager says he can't guarantee that.'

Both were silent. Georgie ran a finger around the rim of her glass. Jock looked at the dark, shining fringe skimming the fine, arched eyebrows; he thought of that little mind whirring beneath the Jap doll hair.

Georgie looked up. The tawny light from the wall lamps made her hazel eyes seem golden. Again Jock thought of a doll: the porcelain make-up, the golden eyes, and that control – together they now made her face mask-like. Somewhere under that mask she was vulnerable. How could he find the spot?

'Of course he can't guarantee it,' she said. 'The advertising copy has to be in place before we've even got half the news.'

'Sure, sure. But supposing that Senate hearing goes on for a coupla weeks. It'd be a shame if my client spent $50,000 on a sugar ad in *World* – or maybe even $90,000 on a double-page spread – and then you suddenly decided you weren't interested in writing up the hearing that week. I'd really appreciate it if you kind of kept your eye on it.'

Jock would never have held this conversation with Hugo Carroll. Hugo was so fucking honourable that you couldn't even mention his newspaper's fashion features were linked with whether the fashion house had put ads in the paper over the past six months. Well, you could mention it, but Hugo wouldn't hear you. As for any hint that news stories might sometimes be played up or played down depending on the paper's commercial interests, only an asshole would say that in front of Hugo. For it would guarantee he took the opposite line to what you wanted. Hugo Carroll didn't write in collusion with *anybody*. Not with his paper's proprietor. Not with the President of the United States. And certainly not with some wheeling-dealing lobbyist.

Georgie was different. Jock had sensed it the first time he saw her at a Washington cocktail party. And he sensed it that evening he'd been nearly boiled alive on the Eastern Shore – why in God's name anybody chose to live in that sauna he'd never know – when they'd all been sitting out on that terrace and he'd tossed his pack of cigarettes to Georgie. He could see it in the quick upthrust of her arm when she caught the pack above the heads of those two black killers. Georgie's morals were more flexible, more pragmatic than Hugo's. How much they were like Jock's he didn't yet know.

His were non-existent: he didn't think in those terms. You kept a deal not because it was the honourable thing to do but because it meant you'd get a better deal next time. He guessed Georgie had some kind of 'morals' – if he was forced to think of the word, it made more sense to him in quotes – but he bet she was primarily a trader. Takes one to know one. And you didn't have to make the same point twice with her. He changed tack.

'Do you ever think about love–hate?'

She was taken by surprise. Philosophy was not what she'd expected from Jock.

'I think about it every day,' she said, 'even if it's subconscious. Everyone I meet is locked into a love–hate relationship with *World*'s editor. When I run a story where they look good, they love me. When I pan them, they hate me – but they've got to pretend they don't hate me, because the worst thing for them would be if *World* didn't mention them at all.'

Her face had grown animated. She likes that power, she likes it a lot, Jock thought.

He was right. Yet it hadn't made Georgie pompous. The night in the front hall in Georgetown when Hugo had wanted to hit her, he'd accused her of becoming self-important. But she hadn't grown so self-important that she couldn't see how things were. She liked being a puppetmaster, yet she knew she was in a world of other puppetmasters, each waiting for an opening. Watching Jock, she knew she was looking at someone who understood all this inside out. With most people she met for a drink at the Colony, Georgie kept a reserve. With this worldly thug, she found she didn't feel like pretending things were different from what they were.

'The worst thing that could happen to them,' she repeated, 'would be if *World* stopped mentioning them. The worst thing that could happen to me would be if they stopped spilling the stuff to me. We're all locked together. Politicians and the media. Artists and the media. Sportsmen and the media. Preachers and the media.'

He relit his cigar as he watched the play of expressions on her face.

'Think of those celebrities who do sweet f.a. except be a celebrity: they're chained hand and foot to the media,' she went on. 'All of them need *World*. And *World* needs them – though I tuck them away in the entertainments section.'

'You forgot to mention your hard-working friend J. D. Liddon,' said Jock. 'He's locked into the old interdependence as tight as anybody you know.'

Georgie laughed. She looked at her watch. The specially made Cartier had already been catalogued in Jock's mind. White and gold. An image of the Dobermans' brass-studded collars came into his mind. Black and gold.

'I've got to go,' she said, already on her feet.

On his bar stool a film director, who'd met Georgie at a party the week before, was watching in the mirror beyond the bottles, judging the right moment to turn and speak when she started for the door.

'You got your car?' said Jock, getting to his own feet.

'Oh sure.'

'See you then, Georgie.'

Jock was not unaware that most men would have

155

walked to the door of the Colony with her, might even have seen her into her car. But he had more business still to do: he'd noticed the chairman of US Steel at a table ten feet behind where Georgie had been sitting. You gotta have priorities.

By the time Georgie reached the bar's entrance, exchanging chit-chat with the director who'd seized his opportunity and sidled off his stool to accompany her to the sidewalk, Jock was already leaning over the table of the chairman of US Steel.

As her driver drew the black Buick Park Avenue on to the East River Drive, Georgie looked across the brown water flowing fast in the evening tide. On the other side, reflecting the sun which hovered above Manhattan, the sleek new office tower gleamed purplish-red as it rose erect above Long Island City.

She wondered if Jock sometimes kept his clothes on and simply opened his trousers when he wanted a quick screw. Then she felt the movement deep in her loins. It surprised her. She smiled to herself: she was meant to be thinking about who would be at Ralph Kernon's dinner. But she allowed herself another image of Jock. Then she recrossed her legs and looked at her watch.

15

Michael O'Donovan glanced out his window as the 747 began its approach to Heathrow Airport. The long thin clouds came apart, and between their wispy edges he saw the crenellated ramparts of Windsor Castle. His face showed no emotion as he tried to make out whether a flag was flying from the highest turret to announce to the world that the Queen was in residence. The first-class section was half full, and the seat beside him was empty. When the clouds closed again over Windsor Castle, he looked back to the file he'd transferred to his lap after the announcement to replace tray tables and prepare for landing.

From her window in the economy section, Lisa had seen the clouds part. 'Oh,' she exclaimed with delight. This was her first visit to Britain. It was like looking at a picture in a book of fairy tales, this romantic castle standing in splendid isolation, glimpsed only for a minute before the grey clouds drifted together again. The man squashed in the middle seat beside her said: 'That's where the Queen lives sometimes. Did you know she's the richest woman in the world? And she pays no taxes,' he added.

When the last of the economy passengers reached the terminal, the first-class passengers were already at passport control. Lisa caught up with Michael in the baggage hall where he was scanning the conveyor belt as more suitcases clonked on to the revolving trolley.

'Good flight?' he asked.

Not for the first time she thought of an alien. He wasn't like one of those monster aliens in science fiction films. He was like one of the good-looking polite aliens who appear to be almost human, and who can work in alliance with humans.

Except for the vertical grooves either side of his mouth, the lean face was smooth. Yet he didn't look young. He didn't look any age, though she knew he was nearly forty. He didn't look kind. He didn't look cruel. Nothing could be read from his face. It was unmarked, like a face grafted on someone who has been badly burned and whose surgically constructed new face will never change.

Michael's face had always been like that. The eyes might reveal something about his thoughts, yet they were so pale that any change in them seemed to be only in the pupils – the black dots enlarging or, more noticeably, contracting to small points. Lisa never felt comfortable with him.

'I'll wait until yours arrives,' he said, as he lifted his suitcase off the moving belt and on to his cart.

'Don't you want to go ahead and get a taxi?' Lisa asked, anxiously watching for her own suitcase to appear.

'No. It could complicate things. I'll wait here.'

'There it comes.'

He might have said 'Good.' He said nothing. Unless there was a purpose in conversation, he saw little point in it. Yet his manner was rarely offensively brusque; in general it was polite in a distant way. He held doors open for women, picked up shopping lists old ladies dropped and handed them back. He simply did not go in for idle chit-chat.

The taxi-driver said their flight had arrived at the right time to miss rush-hour traffic. 'That's nice,' replied Lisa, and left it at that, intimidated by Michael's silence as he looked out his window at the dull terrain flanking the motorway. She'd heard that English taxi-drivers talk more than their American counterparts, and though she would have liked him to give a run-down on where they were going, she didn't want to annoy Michael. Thus discouraged from imparting his certainties about the state of the world, the driver divided his attention between the road and Lisa in his rear-view mirror.

When the first tower blocks were in sight and the motorway just missed running into an enchanting old church with an oddly shaped tower, she could not restrain her curiosity. 'What's that church?'

'St Peter's Hammersmith. This your first time here?' said the driver, pleased she was no longer in the thumbscrews of that cold bastard sitting beside her.

'Yes.'

'We're going almost in a straight line to your hotel,' he said as the motorway reached the top of an overpass and levelled off again into west London. Rows of nineteenth-century houses, converted into cheap hotels or bedsitters when traffic on this main artery grew tyrannical, gave no hint that just behind them the leafy, exclusive streets of Kensington began.

'What's that?' Lisa asked, looking at the aloof formality of a building clad in a chequer-board of terracotta slabs, standing in solemn symmetry on the left.

'Natural History Museum. Ever seen a dinosaur? Next door's the Victoria and Albert.'

'Oh look,' Lisa said when a red-brick dome appeared on the right, and she read the name in large, scrolled white letters. 'It's Harrods.'

Michael had purposely seated himself so he wasn't in line with the rear-view mirror. Even so, by shifting almost imperceptibly, the driver could see the unreadable face of the silent man behind him, and wondered what went on with that psychopath and the girl.

As the taxi swooped up from the underpass and into Piccadilly, the driver said: 'If you look over to the right, miss, you'll just be able to see Buckingham Palace on the other side of Green Park. In winter you can see it better.'

'I love the bright green,' Lisa said. 'In Washington the leaves are already dry and faded from the sun.' She looked at the people lying on the grass outside the shadow of lacy plane-trees. Britain was enjoying one of its warm Junes. 'It's too hot at home for people to spend their lunch-hour lying in the sun like that.'

Michael glanced uninterestedly at the Ritz Hotel, and a minute or two later the taxi turned into Albemarle Street. The doorman wearing the brown livery of Brown's Hotel stepped forward as the taxi pulled to the kerb.

When they'd registered and two porters were

preceding them to the lift, Michael said: 'I have an appointment at 7.30. But you and I should meet to map things out for tomorrow. Let's meet in the bar.' He inclined his head to a door on the right. 'See you there at 6.30.'

When the porter had left her room, Lisa went to the window and looked down on Albemarle Street three floors below. What traffic there was seemed very quiet. Though Washington was far less noisy than New York with its taxis constantly blowing their horns, even Washington was not quiet like this. London seemed to be waiting for something. She became aware of the excited sensation she got in her stomach when she was poised on the edge of something new. As soon as she'd got unpacked, she would go out for a walk. She'd ask the guy on the reception desk for a map. Maybe there'd be time to look at the outside of the Houses of Parliament.

As she hung her second suit on one of the big wooden hangers in the cupboard, she thought about Michael O'Donovan. In a way it was restful not having to talk when there was nothing significant to say. And he was always so clear when he did talk that you never had to worry about misunderstanding anything. All the same, she'd meant what she said to Hugo: there *was* something creepy about Michael. She tried to imagine him in bed. Her mind went blank. She could not imagine anything about him beyond what she could see.

Stepping from the lift into the lobby, she glanced at the moon-faced platinum watch. It was the only

161

jewellery she was wearing. Her navy linen jacket with its big white buttons edged with lime swung open as she walked, showing the lime silk tank top skimming her hip-bones in the short navy skirt. Her hair hung shining and loose to her shoulders. She was aware of the two men checking in at the desk who turned to watch her as she crossed the lobby, while the porter's eyes followed her more discreetly.

At 6.30 exactly she entered the bar, and Michael walked in behind her seconds later. Only a few tables near the door were occupied. He led her to a corner table at the far end. 'You sit so you can look out.' He put his briefcase on the empty chair beside him. 'What did you do this afternoon?'

Lisa laughed softly with surprise. This was the first time he had ever asked her about anything unconnected with work.

'I walked down to Piccadilly Circus. And then I walked to Trafalgar Square. And then I walked past two guys standing in shoeboxes who looked like outsize toy soldiers. And then I peered over a tall black iron gate into Downing Street. It's awfully small – Downing Street, I mean. And then I crossed into Parliament Square and sat on a bench under an enormous statue of Winston Churchill which makes him look like a block of cement.'

She paused.

'Do you always walk everywhere?'

'When I can. You can see so much more that way.'

'Do you want a drink?'

'Could I have some orange juice? I'm dying of thirst,' she said to the waiter who was standing at their table. Often she diverted attention from the fact that she seldom drank. 'Don't display the mechanics of your control to the other party.' No one had taught her that; she had figured it out for herself.

'And I'll have a Bloody Mary,' Michael said to the waiter. With the ghost of a smile he added to Lisa: 'Sometimes I wonder if I choose a Bloody Mary because it's named for someone who knew how to deal with overbearing Protestants in this country.' He said it with such detachment that it was a moment before she registered his resentment. 'Is your room all right?' he went on in the same disengaged voice.

'Yes. It's at the front.'

Michael's secretary had booked a suite for him – some of his appointments might be held there – and a room for Lisa, but a room with a view had been specified. Economy class on the plane was appropriate for lesser members of the staff, but once they arrived abroad, they had to be seen to be living in style. Even though Lisa was still being taught the ropes and introduced to British contacts, she was representing J. D. Liddon to potential clients. A hotel as smart as Brown's was itself a continuous potential for contacts.

'Let's talk about tomorrow,' Michael said. 'We'll need to leave the hotel by three o'clock at the latest to allow time for a traffic jam. Our plane departs for Belfast at 4.45. So I've arranged for James Arden to meet us at 12.30 in the Savoy Restaurant. You'll have to be introduced to the Savoy Grill some other time: editors and Cabinet ministers are regulars at the Grill, and Arden won't want them sitting at the next table. They're a mean breed, MPs: they don't mind being wined and dined by lobbyists, but they don't want it advertised. The Brits like to pretend they're above such vulgar considerations as money – even when they're methodically stripping their invalid mother of her fortune before dumping her in an old people's home. Give me an American congressman any day.'

Lisa saw the pupils of his colourless eyes had contracted to points that looked like pinheads. She glanced up to see if the lights had suddenly brightened, but they seemed the same as when she'd first looked around the bar. She'd noticed before that the pupils of Michael's eyes seemed to respond to something inside him rather than the light outside.

'Parliament is different in a lot of ways from Congress,' he went on. 'You know how every congressman's office has the book of lobbyists.'

When Lisa had first gone to Washington, she'd been astounded by the size of the book of lobbyists – like a telephone directory with 800 pages under different headings: Lobbyists, Foreign Agents, Consultants, Legal Advisors, Public Affairs and Government Relations Representatives. But whichever euphemism they chose to describe themselves, they were all lobbyists with the same end: influencing legislators. The only difference among the listings on those 800 pages was that those who called themselves lobbyists were saying frankly: 'I am what I am.'

Smiling, she started to remind Michael of a bumper sticker popular for a while: 'Don't tell my mother I'm a lobbyist. She thinks I'm a piano-player in a whore-house.' But she thought better of it. A sense of humour was not among Michael's most conspicuous characteristics.

'The British don't appreciate how much money it costs for American congressmen to buy television time when they're running for re-election. So the Brits get sanctimonious about our PACs system. It's typical British hypocrisy: plenty of their MPs – like James Arden – receive big consultancy fees to try and influence government policy to favour whatever industry is paying them the fee.'

'What happens if the MP becomes a Cabinet minister?' asked Lisa.

'They've got to give up their outside interests. But the rest can have as many directorships and consultancies as they like – so long as each year they register them. Occasionally a journalist discovers an MP is lobbying for something where he has a financial interest and hasn't disclosed it, and then all hell breaks loose. But mostly nobody reads the register.'

'Even so, you'd think they wouldn't take the risk of being found out,' said Lisa.

'They think it's undignified to speak on behalf of Saudi oil if everyone knows Saudi oil is paying them to do it. Anyhow, there are a hundred ways to get around the register. Star Oil has been paying James Arden for three years, but he didn't have to declare it because we paid it as school fees and in transatlantic air tickets for his family holidays. It's the same old thing, Lisa: you can bend the rules so long as you don't get found out. But with Star Oil being involved in this year's round of bidding and the refinery in

Northern Ireland soon on offer, Arden must have decided it's too risky: he's declared his consultancy in the new register. I'll bet he's glad he doesn't have to declare the size of the fee he's getting.'

Michael gave a cold smile. 'And he still doesn't call it lobbying,' he added dryly. 'Once we've worked out the refinery proposal with BritRef, Arden will talk about his deep concern that the British government should be seen to encourage investment in Ulster "for political reasons, economic reasons, and, above all, moral reasons". That sort of English bullshit.'

Lisa looked at the self-possessed Englishmen seating themselves a few tables away. Both wore immaculately tailored chalk-stripe suits. Had she been more familiar with London she would have known their shirts were made in Jermyn Street and that the patrician-looking man was wearing a Guards tie. His companion casually extracted a file from his Gucci briefcase and laid it on the table as the waiter took their drink order. Lisa played a game with herself: which was the professional lobbyist representing his client's interest, which was the politician taking money for his connections and know-how? She smiled to herself as she thought of Jock delivering one of his great reflections: 'Money is power. Knowledge is power. Each of us gains when we swap.'

'Who'll pay James Arden to talk up the refinery in Ulster?' she asked. 'Star Oil or BritRef?'

'The same as with the oilfield licence: J. D. Liddon is paying him on behalf of Star Oil. So when he shows off at lunch tomorrow about all the influence he carries with Ian Lonsdale, don't put his desire to impress you down solely to your personal charms. He needs to impress me too. His pay cheque depends on it.'

Michael looked at his watch. 'I'll see you in the morning, Lisa. Do you want to stay here? I'm going by taxi to my next appointment.'

'I'll go as far as the door with you. I want to walk up Piccadilly before I decide where I'm going to eat.'

Together they left the bar. Outside on the pavement, Lisa set off for Piccadilly. The doorman flagged down a cab for Michael.

'I want to go to a house just off Stag Place. Near Victoria Street,' he told the driver.

Ten minutes later he stood on the pavement outside a terrace house whose paint was peeling. He glanced up at the two window-boxes of geraniums and petunias outside the top-floor windows. One window was open in the humid evening air. He rang the top-floor bell.

'Yes?' The voice on the Entryphone gave nothing away.

'It's Michael.'

The lock buzzed as it was released. He heard it reclick as he started up the narrow stairway to the flat where Maureen Halloran waited.

16

'Nice to see you, sir,' said the doorman as James Arden MP stepped from his taxi.

Arden strode through the revolving door into the Savoy Hotel's imposing lobby. Nimbly descending the steps to the lounge, he scanned those having a drink at the scattered tables or more discreetly on banquettes against the walls, his self-important scrutiny suggesting these people were insignificant intruders on his territory.

At the entrance to the restaurant a grave figure in black swallow-tailed coat, his silver and black silk tie distinguishing him from other swallow-tailed figures wearing black bow-ties, came forward.

'Good afternoon, Mr Arden.'

'Good afternoon, Charles. I'm having lunch with Mr O'Donovan who is here from Washington. Has he arrived?'

'Several minutes ago, sir. Let me take you to his table. I'm extremely sorry, sir, that the window tables were already booked.'

James Arden frowned. He couldn't remember when he had been given lunch at the Savoy Restaurant at any table other than one overlooking the Thames. He never actually looked out the wall of windows to the plane-trees of the Embankment and the river flowing calmly towards Greenwich and the sea. But that wasn't the point. The point was that the window tables were the ones most sought. He felt distinctly put out.

As Arden followed the head waiter to a table standing not far from those by the windows, Michael O'Donovan got to his feet to shake hands. The two men had met half a dozen times before.

'This is the member of my staff that I mentioned, Lisa Tabor.'

Lisa's smile conveyed the impression she was honoured as she reached up to shake hands with Arden.

At the same moment, one of the figures in black bow-ties hurried over to speak to the head waiter.

'Mr O'Donovan,' the head waiter said in his sombre manner, 'we've just received a cancellation for the window table in the far corner. Would you care to have it, sir, or would you rather stay where you are?'

Before Michael could answer, Arden said: 'I'm sure, Charles, that Miss Tabor and Mr O'Donovan would enjoy the view of the river. You and I can look at it flowing by every day. Haw haw. But I expect it would give pleasure to our American visitors.' Lisa was slightly disconcerted by how much Arden sounded like a braying donkey when he made that 'haw haw' sound.

As they moved to the window table where crystal and silver sparkled in the watery English sunlight, she glanced at Michael. His pupils were pinpoints.

'That's more like it,' said Arden, gesturing munificently to Lisa and Michael to take the chairs with the best view. 'Wouldn't you like a drink to start with, my dear?' he said to Lisa, as if he were the giver rather than receiver of the hospitality.

He turned to the hovering waiter. 'The young lady

will have an orange juice. Make sure the oranges are freshly cut and squeezed. What are you having, Michael?'

'A Bloody Mary.'

'Just to remind you?' Lisa said to him softly. If this MP was what Michael had in mind when he'd sneered at English self-importance, she could see what he meant. It was the first time she felt something approaching a sense of camaraderie with Michael.

James Arden MP belonged to the school of freeloaders who think business should wait until the end of the meal. Not for him the American practice of short and to the point one-course lunches. For an hour and a quarter he devoted himself to his palate and showing off.

Michael kept charge of actually ordering their meal, but Arden was right in there giving advice. 'If I may say so, my dear boy, the smoked salmon here is not *quite* up to Le Gavroche. I think you might prefer the caviar. No one can go wrong with Beluga caviar, which is what I would like.'

Even though the wine waiter handed the wine list to Michael, Arden could barely wait to display his French accent to Lisa. 'You don't happen to have another bottle of the 1982 Romanée Conti you produced last week when I was here with the chairman of ITI?' he said to the wine waiter. 'It has a lovely nose to it,' he added to Lisa, confident she'd be flattered by his adopting the familiar tone of one wine buff talking to another, 'unlike some of the rubbish passed off as vintage Burgundy. *Trop jeune, trop jeune*, I keep telling them.'

When the waiters were removing the second-course plates, Arden's scraped clean despite an over-ample serving of beef Wellington, Lisa glanced down in her lap where she'd placed her left hand so she wouldn't be seen looking at her watch: quarter to two. Doesn't this guy ever get a square meal except when he's taken to the Savoy?

'Nothing more for me,' he said, 'though I would enjoy a cigar with my coffee, Michael.'

Michael gestured to a waiter, and then he took a small, black leather-covered notepad from inside his jacket.

'I told your secretary, James: Lisa and I are flying to Belfast this afternoon. I want to have a look at the proposed site for the oil refinery. And I'm also working on a deal involving Irish linen-mills.' He paused for only a fraction of a moment before adding: 'As well as one or two other matters. We have to leave Brown's no later than three.'

'Pity,' said Arden. 'You deprive me of an excuse to give Prime Minister's Questions a miss. Just between you and me, dear girl,' he said to Lisa, 'the Prime Minister can make even an assassination sound like a vicarage tea-party. Haw haw.'

Lisa didn't look at Michael's eyes.

'If you're not to be deprived of anything else, in what time remains you had better apply your mind to Star Oil,' Michael said coldly. 'Has BITE received the final bids for the oilfields?'

'This is *entre nous*?' asked Arden.

'Not quite,' Michael replied. 'As I'm here to represent Star Oil, I'll want to give its president some kind

171

of report. He has to be able to tell his board that its British parliamentary consultant has the access they're paying him for.'

Arden couldn't offer Star Oil financial expertise or managerial expertise. What he had was the political contact. Ordinarily Michael made minimum reference to a politician being paid *mucho* for access. But this Arden was the kind of influence-peddler who needed to be reminded he wasn't being paid just for his fucking French accent while he soaked up burgundy at £120 a bottle.

Arden beetled his brow. Then he adopted his serious man-of-the-world expression. 'Right. I have it on high authority that BITE has reached the nitty-gritty of the offshore licensing rounds. The final bids are in. There are eight of them.'

'Which British companies are involved?'

Arden listed four British companies leading consortia.

'And Oklahoma Petroleum's consortium?' asked Michael. 'What about its British partners?'

'At the last moment Anglo-North came in as Oklahoma's major British partner,' Arden replied.

Briefly Michael's eyes met Lisa's. 'We thought Oklahoma wanted to keep its consortium small.'

'Oklahoma got the message they needed more muscle. Anglo-North can get slightly better technological support if it joins up with an American company. So it suits them both to get together.'

'That's five applications,' said Michael. 'Star Oil's makes the sixth. Who are the other two?'

'Saudi. Both of them. They're not seeking to be

operators, of course, but they always like a share of the action.'

Arden tipped off a quarter-inch of ash. Holding the cigar between thumb and forefinger, he put it back to his lips, drawing on it purposefully.

'What's the betting look like?' said Michael.

'Too early to say. But you can rest assured, my dear Michael, I am doing my best to point out to those who matter the advantages of granting an exploration licence to Star Oil. Once we've tied up Star Oil's latest proposal to join forces with BritRef to build the Northern Ireland refinery, that should be a big plus with the BITE Secretary. Meanwhile, I've spoken a number of times to Senator Morley's office: I am drawing up a schedule for him to meet people in a strong position to influence officials at BITE. Excellent, if I may say so, excellent to have the good Senator paddle an oar for Star Oil. We need all the help we can get. The loss of those two rigs has not made my task easier. A lot of dead, a lot of dead,' Arden said sternly.

'The inquiry ruled out any criminal charges against Star Oil's management,' Michael said sharply. 'It's now merely a question of insurance claims. The accident could have happened under any management.'

'Yes, yes, dear boy. Of course I was delighted – and relieved, if I may say so – by the court ruling. But these things leave a tarnish all the same. You've asked me to take on something that would daunt lesser men. And in the end, of course, it's up to the BITE Secretary to decide on offshore licensing arrangements. He and I were at Oxford together. Good chap, Ian Lonsdale. D'you know him?'

'No. I'd like to meet him.'

Arden drew on his cigar. 'How long will you and Lisa be in Belfast?'

'Until tomorrow afternoon. We can be back in London by six o'clock. I'd like to get back to Washington on Friday, but if it were essential I could stay here over the weekend.'

Arden tipped the ash off his cigar. 'Today is Tuesday. My own week is murder. And I expect that as BITE Secretary, Ian has a fair bit on his own plate. But if schedules permit, I might be able to manage an introduction – for you both.'

British Cabinet ministers were grossly overworked. But they also had high status, an army of civil servants, and comfort. Otherwise they couldn't do their jobs. For junior ministers and ordinary back-benchers like James Arden, life was incomparably different: they had none of the amenities taken for granted by American congressmen. Arden's office in the House of Commons was like a cell in a Victorian prison. He shared it with another MP. As it happened, that MP was Bob Brindle, parliamentary private secretary to Ian Lonsdale. And the job of a PPS was to make sure his Minister did not lose touch with ordinary back-bench MPs in his party.

'Leave it to me,' Arden said expansively. 'I'll get a message to you at Brown's before noon on Thursday. Don't count on anything. It's damned short notice, old boy. But I'll do my best.'

He looked at Lisa. 'I shall convey to Ian, my dear, that I have a particularly charming lady whom I want him to meet.'

For a fleeting moment a look of satisfaction showed on Michael's normally inscrutable face.

17

The Ford Sierra Estate was crammed with bodies, suitcases, food, wrapped presents for Sam's eighth birthday, and three dolls from whom Nina refused to be separated for a single night let alone two. A crate of Rouge Homme Cabernet Sauvignon 1985 signified Ian was still on his Australian wine kick.

'The only way to survive owning a country cottage,' Patsy's mother said, 'is to keep duplicates there of everything you need – toothbrushes, make-up, clothes, the lot – so you don't have to keep packing twice a weekend.'

But Mrs Fawcett was better organized than her daughter. However often Patsy made a list of what needed duplication, suitcases were still required. Thank God for Greva, the Norwegian au pair. She packed the children's stuff. True, sometimes Patsy got bored having to talk with Greva. 'But on balance, dear, Greva is useful to your household,' Mrs Fawcett said when Patsy unkindly mimicked Greva's conversation. 'On balance' was an essential part of Mrs Fawcett's philosophy, which was designed to keep a complicated life as agreeable as possible.

Sam and Nina went to a private day-school where so many children belonged to families who drove to the country at weekends that on Fridays school broke up at 2.30. Rush hour for the great British weekend didn't get going in earnest until three, and Patsy was seldom more than ten minutes late in collecting Sam and Nina. One would clamber into the front seat of the already packed car, the other into the back with Greva. With luck they'd get to Pig Farm by 4.15, 4.30 at the latest unless the Ministry of Transport had decided once again to dig up the whole of the M40 just as the weekend traffic began.

Pig Farm was on the outskirts of Shurston, Ian's constituency in south Warwickshire, just over the border from Oxfordshire. The house was made of Cotswold ironstone which in sunshine turned as golden as lichen. Its four acres of land consisted of rough grass, apple trees, raspberry bushes and a spasmodic attempt at a vegetable garden. Bounded by a two-bar rail fence, Pig Farm perched on a low rise facing the dramatic ridge of Edge Hill. Each time Patsy watched the sunset turn the sky crimson over Edge Hill, she thought how lucky she was.

Even so, she sometimes grumbled over constituency demands. She could hardly complain about Shurston citizens expecting to see Ian; after all he was being paid to represent them in Parliament. And in good moods she didn't mutter about their demands on her, which indeed were few. But in bad moods, when she didn't feel like dressing up on a Saturday to open a village fête, and certainly didn't feel like addressing an evening dinner to raise funds, she said it was like being some bloody vicar's wife. Her mother pointed out that at least it wasn't like the Conservative Party in her youthful days when not only the prospective candidate but his wife as well had to appear for judgement before the selection committee. On one occasion, Mrs Fawcett said, the candidate's wife was asked by a committee member to turn around so he could view her from the back. To Patsy the committee member's impertinence was too irritating to be comic.

On this particular Friday, Ian had gone to Shurston ahead of Patsy. At 12.30 a messenger at BITE had carried in a silver tray with a sandwich and coffee so the Minister could eat something while initialling papers and signing the week's final letters before he pushed off from Victoria Street.

The official car was intended for the BITE Secretary in his ministerial capacity only. But so long as he was accompanied by one or two ministerial boxes, the minister could be driven to his home in the country. (In a few instances – as with the Sports Minister, who was famous for his idleness – the ministerial box might contain nothing more demanding than the newspapers and *Private Eye*.) Ian read the complicated departmental brief for Monday's meeting on northern textile factories, and Chris coped with the traffic. After dropping Ian at Pig Farm, Chris drove the government car back to London.

Leaving the boxes in the small study off the drawing-room, Ian went up to his and Patsy's bedroom overlooking Edge Hill, thought for the hundredth time how much he liked Pig Farm's comfortable informality, and then went out to the semi-derelict thatched barn which doubled as a garage. He climbed into a Land Rover and drove up to his constituency headquarters in Shurston's high street at three o'clock sharp.

Like any efficient MP, he packed a variety of obligations into minimum time. After dealing with seven problems brought by constituents to his 'surgery', he dropped in at three separate party members' homes, ending up at a pub where he made himself available to whoever happened to be around.

At Pig Farm shortly after 8.30 that evening, Nina came running down the stairs in her nightdress. She'd heard the crunch of the Land Rover's wheels on the rough pebbled drive. With Nina in his arms, Ian went straight to the kitchen at the back of the house. Patsy was blowing on a spoonful of boeuf bourguignon so she could taste it for seasoning.

'God it's nice to be home,' he said. 'You're looking extremely fetching in that apron.'

Patsy wrinkled her nose to convey that while she appreciated the compliment, she didn't wish to spend her life in an apron. Lacking the dedicated housewife's satisfaction in producing each meal, in London she handed over as much of that role as she decently could to Greva. In fact, apart from school holidays, in London no one was home for lunch except Patsy who would go downstairs to make herself a sandwich, returning to her room afterwards to work for a couple of hours, at her easel or at her desk, on her latest children's book. But at Pig Farm she quite liked cooking all the meals, so long as Greva washed up. Occasionally Ian made what he wryly called 'househusband' gestures, but little was expected of him in that direction as he had the relentless red boxes as well as constituents demanding his time.

When he'd said goodnight to both children, he and Patsy settled down over a drink, each in a deep armchair either side of the cheerfully crackling fire in the drawing-room. Though not yet dark, by nine even on June evenings it was often cool enough to light the fire.

'You can't imagine,' he said, 'how nice it is to be home. What time do your parents get here tomorrow?'

'As soon after 12.30 as they can. Sam wants the great celebration to be at the end of family lunch.'

'Could lunch possibly be put back a little?' Ian asked. 'It's a frightful bore, but Bob Brindle has inveigled me into letting James Arden bring a couple of Americans here for a drink at noon. They want to talk shop about BITE.'

'Yuk.' This time Patsy's nose was wrinkled in distaste. 'I can't stand James Arden. He's the kind of pompous jerk who gives MPs a bad name.'

Ian laughed. 'You know how Bob nags me about not spending enough time with back-benchers. And James Arden, however accurate your view of him, is quite an important member of two Commons select committees dealing directly with my department. He and Bob share a room at the Commons.'

'Why can't Bob invite James Arden and his American friends to his own country cottage for a pre-lunch Saturday drink?' said Patsy sourly.

The question being rhetorical, Ian said: 'I told him we had a family birthday, and that forty-five minutes would be the *absolute* outside they could stay. It would be nice, Patsy, if you felt just like saying hello. I'll look after the rest.'

As her last wish was to spoil their Friday evening together, she shrugged and tossed aside further thought of James Arden and his friends. With a collusive smile, she got up from her chair and slowly walked over to Ian's.

'That's Edge Hill,' James Arden said as he slipped the Jaguar's gear down to third. 'That's where the Cavaliers and Roundheads fought the first of their battles, my dear,' he added to Lisa who was beside him. 'An ancestor of mine was hit in the thigh with a musket-ball. Good show it wasn't ball to ball. Haw haw.'

'I'll open the gate,' Michael said from the back seat as the Jaguar stopped in front of a two-bar gate whose white paint was patently overdue for a touch-up.

The front door of the farmhouse was opened by Ian. Lisa's already acute interest soared when she saw this relaxed man in his distinctly worn twill trousers, a striped shirt unbuttoned at the throat, and a crumpled, pale-blue linen jacket.

'This is Lisa Tabor,' Arden said, 'and Michael O'Donovan.'

As they shook hands, Ian looked intently at this lilac-eyed girl with her straight blonde hair falling on to the shoulders of her simple cornflower-blue dress. He'd already noticed the slim, suntanned legs when she'd come up the front steps, her shoe-thongs looped twice around her ankles. As he led the way through the flagstoned entrance hall of the house, she noticed his slight limp and wondered why it made him more attractive.

'What can I get you to drink?' he asked. 'We can go out in the garden. James may have told you it's my son's birthday, so you must forgive me for having so little time.'

As they sat in the comfortable cane chairs around a large wooden table, Ian looked at Michael O'Donovan's face and wondered what was the girl's relationship with this reserved man.

'Michael is Jock Liddon's key man,' said Arden breezily, as if every senior British Cabinet minister must know who Jock Liddon was. But Arden was not a politician for nothing. 'J. D. Liddon International is consultant to more American industries looking to invest on this side of the pond than any other Washington consultant I can think of,' he added in a neat thumbnail sketch. 'Lisa is his aide.'

'What are you both doing in Britain?' asked Ian, addressing the question to Lisa. Perhaps her eyes were more blue than violet.

'I'm running at top speed trying to keep up with Michael,' she said. 'You'd better ask him what he's doing.'

Ian looked at Michael.

'One of the things I'm examining, sir, is the prospect of Star Oil building a refinery in Northern Ireland.'

Ian was always surprised when Americans the same age as himself called him 'sir'.

'It goes without saying,' Michael went on, 'that Star Oil would build the refinery only if it got an exploration licence for a field in the Hebrides.'

'Why a refinery in Northern Ireland?' Ian asked.

'It's close to the Hebrides. Investment costs would

be lower than a good many other places you and I can think of. And as the British government has expressed concern about unemployment in Northern Ireland, we hoped your department would be prepared to give us a generous industrial development grant – especially as the refinery would be a joint venture with British Refineries.'

'I see,' Ian said noncommittally.

Michael went on: 'And of course we'd be prepared to offer you a reciprocal investment in America, maybe in a different industry.'

Michael's directness appealed to Ian. Briefly he calculated how many jobs might be created if Star Oil and BritRef built the refinery. God knows the British government needed to generate some good-will in Ulster, and if it could be done with the Americans taking a large investment risk there were great attractions.

Looking at Michael's unreadable face, something suddenly brought an unwanted memory to the front of Ian's mind – Maureen with her legs stretched wide and her little half-yawn before she said: 'Would you like to discuss the jobs of those three hundred hard-working decent Irish lads, Minister? Or shall we talk about Patsy?' Damn Maureen. Damn that bloody motor-cycle factory. He cut off the memory.

He thought for a moment about Michael's second bait: a reciprocal trade arrangement 'maybe in a different industry'. Which American industries, he wondered, did J. D. Liddon represent? Bob Brindle could find out some of them from James Arden. Arden might be a fatuous bore, but he had his uses.

For ten minutes Ian and Michael exchanged questions and answers, Michael adding a further inducement for the BITE Secretary to consider. James Arden put in a few words which were more astute than his usual smug manner led one to expect. Occasionally Ian turned to Lisa: 'What do you think?' Her answers, he noticed, were intelligent but short. She was letting O'Donovan run the show.

And then Patsy appeared at the drawing-room door opening into the garden. Both Americans took in at a glance that this was not a comfortable, cosy little wife. James Arden had said she wrote children's books, and for some reason Lisa had expected a quaint figure in a floral dress. Instead, as Patsy came down the steps into the garden, Lisa saw a softly voluptuous woman in a silk T-shirt and thin cotton trousers, honey-coloured hair caught up in two grips, the nails of her bare feet painted a vivid coral. Something about the way she walked, unhurried, almost sashaying, conveyed a sense she could take it or leave it.

'Hullo,' Patsy said to the group in general as she got closer. Lisa saw that her eyes were green.

Ian introduced his wife and the two Americans. 'And you know James.'

She greeted James Arden in a politely detached manner. But she looked with interest at Michael O'Donovan. There was something compelling in his reserve. She'd like to do a drawing of that narrow face with the vertical lines.

She looked even more closely at Lisa. Whenever Patsy was presented with an attractive girl, she looked at the girl through two sets of eyes, her own and Ian's. She now wondered uneasily if Ian would hold to his timetable, or if lunch would be put back another half-hour.

'I shan't sit down,' she said. 'Ian may have told you it's our son's birthday. At eight this is a serious matter,' she said in a self-mocking tone to soften her message that she didn't want them to linger. 'My parents will be arriving to take part in the festivities. I hope you enjoy your time in Britain.'

She gave a friendly smile, and then sauntered back into the house. Somewhere within, a child was shouting: 'Grandpa and Gramma just drove up.'

Ten minutes later, a small boy and his younger sister ran down the steps into the garden. They were followed by a handsome couple who without touching each other gave the sense even to people who had never seen them before that they were very much a couple. Michael was surprised they weren't older, but then he remembered Patsy was probably in her early thirties, so it was not odd that this fit couple who looked in their fifties should be her parents.

Mrs Fawcett called out to Ian: 'We'll take a stroll and see you later.' The judge raised one hand and smiled. With the children they walked towards the wilder part of the garden.

'We ought to go,' Michael said, getting to his feet. No point in causing irritation. 'I'm glad you could spare the time for us to call by, sir. Could I write to you and set out one or two projects which might be of some interest to your department?'

'Certainly.'

'At BITE? Or at the House of Commons?'

Ian hesitated.

'The simplest thing would be to write to me at BITE,' he then said. 'Mark it "Personal".'

After seeing them out to their car, he walked back up the front steps wondering why he had momentarily considered telling O'Donovan to address the letter to him at the Commons. It was his ministerial decisions which concerned J. D. Liddon International, so of course any letter should be sent to him at his department. His Commons secretary dealt with his non-departmental correspondence and calls, including the personal side of his life. (Again he had to shut out an image of Maureen.) And J. D. Liddon International would certainly not be playing any part in his personal life. Would it? This time an image of Lisa Tabor flitted across his mind's eye before he went out into the garden for the start of Sam's birthday celebration.

'Does a letter marked "Personal" always reach a minister?' she asked when the road began bending away from the view of Edge Hill. She had taken the back seat for the return journey.

'It's always opened first by one of his private secretaries, my dear, so if you are intending to say anything *intime*, haw haw, you might bear that in mind. But they're bound to pass it on to him if it's marked "Personal" – unless, of course, it's a letter bomb. Haw haw.'

James Arden was in expansive mood. With that visit to Pig Farm, he'd more than earned his money's worth from J. D. Liddon. He might even be able to suggest an increase in his consultancy fee.

'Today's visit can have done our chances nothing but good,' he said. 'You and Jock might want to bear in mind that Ian Lonsdale is making an official visit to Washington soon.'

Because he was Ian's parliamentary private secretary, Bob Brindle had access to Ian's appointments. It had been natural enough for James Arden, sharing a Commons room with Brindle, to ask him when next his boss was scheduled for a trip to the United States.

Michael took out his small leather-bound notepad. 'Do you know the dates?'

'July 6th to 13th. I believe his wife is going with him. During the Washington part of the visit they'll be staying at the British Embassy. The Ambassador is hosting a dinner for them. You can expect the red carpet to be well and truly rolled out. Few subjects are higher on both countries' agenda than industry and trade and energy. You might almost say that the Foreign Secretary and the BITE Secretary have interchangeable jobs.'

Arden sat back. All this could have done him nothing but good in Michael O'Donovan's assessment of him, he was sure.

'You don't know the rest of his schedule, do you?' asked Michael.

'Of course, of course, dear boy.' Among the many things on which James Arden habitually congratulated himself, one was his ability to remember dates and programmes. 'The Minister's first three days will be in Washington. Then he'll make a foray to examine various industries in the wilds of Pittsburgh and Cleveland. Then he and his wife are having a private weekend with a close friend of Patsy Lonsdale. Do you know the editor of *World*? Georgie Chase? Her husband is Hugo Carroll. *The* Hugo Carroll of the *News*.'

'I've met him,' Michael said.

Lisa said nothing.

18

Three Eames chairs were occupied. From one an intermittent column of smoke rose.

'I picked up that Ian Lonsdale has an eye for the girls. But when it comes to running his department, he plays by the rules,' Michael O'Donovan said.

'Yeah.' Jock tipped his ash into a crystal bowl on the table beside him. 'You don't often find a Limey Cabinet minister who's corrupt. But there are more ways than one to skin a cat.'

He drew on his cheroot before he went on: 'Trade is what the T in BITE stands for, for God's sake. Lonsdale would have to be a basketcase if he didn't figure the advantages of American investment in Northern Ireland. You've already got his attention, Mike. But he'll have other things on his mind. We'll need to keep reminding him.'

Jock looked at Lisa. He could have been appraising a jewel or a piece of meat. She met his eyes without expression.

Jancis came in the door. 'Michael, I'm sorry to bother you,' she said, 'but Senator Rourke wants to speak with you.'

For several seconds Michael hesitated. 'Oh. It will be about that factory in Massachusetts,' he explained to Jock.

As Michael left the room, Jock's eyes followed him. Then he turned to Lisa and said: 'It's not like

Mike to give an explanation when none was asked for. Have you ever noticed how people do that when they feel guilty?' He lay back in his chair, the cheroot between the fleshy lips, his opaque, dark eyes fixed unseeing on the wall opposite as he brooded.

Lisa broke the silence. 'I didn't know Michael was doing a deal with Senator Rourke,' she said.

Jock looked at her steadily over his cigar smoke. 'There are lots of things you don't know about Mike,' he replied.

'Has any of it to do with Belfast?' she asked. She knew that when they'd gone to Northern Ireland, two messages from Senator Rourke had been waiting for Michael at the hotel reception desk.

Jock ignored her question.

'Did James Arden say where the Lonsdales are gonna spend the weekend with Georgie and Hugo?' he asked instead. 'New York? Washington? The moon? That godforsaken Eastern Shore?'

'He didn't know.'

Jock jabbed a button on the red box beside him. Jancis's voice replied: 'Yes?'

'I want to talk to Georgie Chase. See if you can get her at *World* or find out when she can take a call. I'll wanna speak to her on my private line.' He jabbed the button again. 'Georgie hates people calling her on the speaker.' He waved his cheroot at the flat box placed on a table within speaking distance of all the Eames chairs. 'She says they sound like they're in a fucking spaceship. Since I wanna ask a favour, I'm gonna avoid any technology that gets on her nerves.'

He tipped the ash off before he said: 'Mr Upright

Hugo Carroll is a different ball game. I don't see him and me ever doing business. He's got too many hang-ups. When we want something from him, maybe you'll have to deal with that, Lisa.'

With that remark, the meeting ended. She too left the room. As soon as Jock was alone he jabbed the red box again. 'Jancis, what are you doing out there? Playing with your tits? What's happening on my call to Georgie Chase?'

He relit his cheroot and lay back in his chair, restlessly swivelling it from side to side.

His black phone rang. 'Miss Chase can take your call now,' said Jancis. 'I'm putting you through.'

As usual, Jock skipped any chit-chat about the weather. 'I'll bet you thought I was gonna remind you that if my sugar king's ad goes in a good spot, he'll wanna fork out for another one. I'm phoning about something else that might interest you, Georgie. Is *World* gonna carry something about Ian Lonsdale's official visit here?'

'I'm thinking of building a big feature on Anglo-American trade and industry around the visit,' Georgie replied. 'Why?'

'Maybe I can help you at this end,' said Jock. 'My top guy, Michael O'Donovan, is just back from Britain. While he was there he was invited to Lonsdale's home in the country. Mike O'Donovan knows more about British industry and trade and energy in some very controversial areas – and I mean big *big* controversy – than anybody. Why don't you have one of your reporters get in touch with him? He can be reached at my office. I'll tell him to give *World* all the help he can.'

'Great.'

'And I was thinking about another thing, Georgie. Michael says I oughta meet the BITE Secretary. I hear the Lonsdales are gonna have a private weekend with you and Hugo. Are you gonna be in one of your palaces?'

'Not most people's idea of a palace. We'll be on the Eastern Shore.'

'What would you think of asking your old friend Jock to drop in for a drink? I promise I'd be on my best behaviour. I'll even smile at those two black killers.'

Georgie laughed.

'Are you and Ian Lonsdale friends? Or is it Georgie and Patsy Lonsdale?' asked Lisa.

'Much more the second. They met at Oxford and then shared an apartment until Patsy and Ian got married. But I have a lot of time for Ian as well. You'll like him.'

'Didn't I tell you I met the Lonsdales briefly when I was in Britain?'

'What!' He was piqued. He wanted to be the one to introduce Lisa to the BITE Secretary. 'How'd that come about?'

'Through some MP who's a friend of Michael O'Donovan. We stopped by at the Lonsdales' place in Warwickshire.'

Someone else returning from Britain might instantly have name-dropped a meeting with a Cabinet minister. But so ingrained was Lisa's habit of saying as little as possible about her personal life that she hadn't mentioned the Lonsdales to Hugo. She did so now only because it would come out when she and Jock turned up on the Shore for the drink Jock had fixed up with Georgie.

'What did you think of them?' Hugo asked.

'I liked them.'

'He could go right to the top one day.'

'Most people think you have to be ruthless to get to the top in politics.'

'Depends what you mean by ruthless.'

Hugo propped himself on one elbow so he could look down on Lisa's face. The anonymity of lying in a public park with the Washington Monument rising like a phallus behind them, a Madras cotton rug beneath them, the picnic hamper and wine cooler on the grass, made him feel he was a college student again, necking with the girl that all the boys desired but who'd chosen him.

She smiled up at him – her eyes were a lilac-blue this evening – and then returned her gaze to the fat little clouds, still pink-tinged at the edges by the sun just dropped from view, scudding above them as the sky deepened to indigo.

He lifted his own gaze to the iridescent white of the Jefferson Memorial across the Potomac. Against the darkening sky it seemed even more three-dimensional than usual. Hugo had experimented with mescaline when he was at the University of Virginia. His heightened tactile response this evening to the Jefferson Memorial's dome and the columns of its rotunda – he could feel it in his nerve ends – reminded him of that.

All his responses were heightened since he fell in love with Lisa. Except in the worst of the humid heat, he slept in the Georgetown house with the air-conditioner off and the windows open. Sometimes he heard an owl's cry so haunting and poignant that his flesh crawled with the thrill of it. Waking in the morning before the alarm went off, waking to the excitement of being in love with Lisa, he found the early morning light so sweetly beautiful that it merged with his desire as he fantasized her and brought himself off. When he walked down the short path to where Whitmore waited in the Lincoln to drive him to work, he was aware of the thrusting individuality of the blades of grass in the front garden which previously he had registered only in terms of whether the part-time gardener was due. Being in love with Lisa was like being on mescaline.

He was careful about being seen with her too often in restaurants. Summer made it easier: this evening was the second time he'd arranged for Whitmore to collect a lavish hamper from the Willard Hotel's kitchen – smoked salmon, lobster loosened in its shell, chicken taken from the bone and laid on buttered brown bread sliced so thin it could be eaten without crumbling, champagne or chablis packed in ice in a smart green leather container.

That very first evening when he took her to Imogene's party was the only time he had taken Lisa out with his friends. She didn't tell him she wanted to be introduced to more of his high-powered connections in other grand Washington houses, in the key political dining clubs near Capitol Hill, and one day in the White House. She knew better than to push things.

Though only a couple of weeks had passed since he'd first undressed her in front of the Sheraton mirror, it seemed longer to Hugo because of the intensity with which he looked forward to their meetings, followed by the long, slow contentment which might last several days before the lust for her began to gnaw again.

'I wish you were going to stay for a meal when you come to Rycroft Lodge instead of just having a drink,' he said, looking into the lilac-blue eyes. In their pupils he could see the clouds chasing each other. 'Will you and Jock be staying on the Shore with Hammond and Lottie Marshall again?'

'Not so far as I know.'

'It seems a long drive from Washington and back again – just for a drink,' he said.

Lisa laughed. 'Jock wants to meet Ian Lonsdale. But Jock also has a passion for tall buildings with elevators zooming up and down and plenty of traffic around. After an hour or so on the Shore, he'll be more than happy to get back to DC.'

She turned her eyes to Hugo who was still resting on his left elbow, the front bits of his straight brown hair falling across his forehead like a boy's, his right hand lying inside her half-undone silk shirt.

'What I meant by ruthless,' she said, 'is someone prepared coldly to do anything to anybody to get what they want. Do you have to be like that to get to the top in politics?'

Hugo was silent for a minute before he answered. 'Not always – though lots of people imagine you do. But you have to be merciless in the sense that if a political decision is the right one, then you don't let personal feelings stand in the way. I'd prefer to call that being tough rather than ruthless. I'd call Ian Lonsdale tough.'

'What sort of marriage does he have?'

Hugo was silent again. Almost as if he grudged it he then said, 'It's meant to be one of the happiest marriages at the top end of politics. Why?'

Lisa reached up with one hand to let her fingertips rest for a moment on his face. 'I was just wondering,' she said.

19

'Since when did we start using white bread?' Georgie said acidly. 'We're not catering specifically for the toothless,' she added, just to make crystal clear to all of them that the features editor's layout for that week's lead feature was the absolute bottom, so without character that if he didn't do better he'd be out of the loop.

Unless you were in the loop, you might as well be canned. At least that's how people in the loop felt when they worried about finding themselves out of it. Those inside it were the only ones allowed to know what was going on throughout the organization. Once you were ejected from the loop, you didn't matter. If you ever doubted that, you'd learn pronto from the way you were treated by the staff when it happened to you.

Georgie sat in the middle of one long side of the conference table, flanked by her deputy editor and executive editor. The seven other chairs around the table were occupied by the heads of the different sections of *World*. In front of each was an enlarged layout waiting its turn to be shown to the editor.

Leaning against the walls of the room stood ten editorial staff, each holding a clipboard to take notes on, senior enough to attend the run-through but not senior enough to sit at the table.

All twenty were at their places at four o'clock

sharp for Thursday's second run-through. There'd be two more run-throughs on Friday before the final paste-ups of *World*'s ninety-six pages would go to the plate-making department that turned them into photo-negatives before they went on to the printers.

The editor was wearing an expensive T-shirt and a narrow skirt which miraculously didn't crease. The five other women were dressed in tailored summer clothes of various colours; they didn't need to tell each other it would be circumspect if only the editor was dressed entirely in white. Most of the men were in shirt-sleeves, some wearing steel elastic bands to pull their cuffs high enough not to rub against the inky paste-ups, all wearing a tie, all cleanly barbered. The unadorned room was so brightly lit it would have been suitable for a third-degree session in a police station.

Most faces were tense. Two or three people standing against the walls had the expression of 'We've been through this once today already.' The executive editor, number three in the hierarchy, ruddy-faced and handsome and quick to smile, wore Brooks Brothers silk suspenders over his wide-striped shirt; his half-glasses had gold rims. The deputy editor, older than the others, wore a seersucker jacket; deadpan, he chewed gum. Twenty faces stared at the offending lead feature layout spread on the table in front of Georgie.

'It's blah enough for the *New York Times*,' she said.

A few of those standing caught one another's eye, but those at the table moved on impassively; there were a lot of pages to get through in the half-hour allotted for the run-through. In the rhythmical movement of someone turning pages for a conductor, the executive editor handed the rejected layout across the table to the thin, serious woman in charge of design, who turned it face down in front of her and simultaneously handed the national news layouts to the deputy editor who spread the first of them in front of Georgie. In silence twenty people concentrated on the lead news layout.

'It's definitely an improvement but still a problem,' Georgie said.

The executive editor handed it across the table as the deputy editor laid open the next two-page spread.

'Great layout,' said Georgie. 'How's the story coming along?'

'It's coming on well,' said one of the women standing. She was the national news section's number two.

'OK.'

The staff were never sure whether Georgie was going to be laid-back or show her teeth. She knew this kept them on their toes. But though they liked the stimulation, they would have liked a break from the strain. Knowing that week after week after week they had to produce nothing but their absolute best was not good for the ulcer.

Another spread was put before her. Apart from the blocks of type used in the mock-up to designate the size of headings and standfast of the story still to come, the right page was empty. *World*'s congressional correspondent was waiting until the last moment to file his story on the Senate committee's investigation into chemical sweeteners. Any new evidence that saccharin was bad for you would be big news in a country obsessed with health. The facing page was filled with the mock-up of two ads – one for ball-bearings, the other for Singapore Airlines. The faintest smile flickered on Georgie's face: Jock could hardly be surprised that she hadn't let him get away with murder; there were no circumstances where she would let the ad be put on the facing page to the story.

The deputy editor laid out the next spread. Photographs of the feuding White House aides were on the left page, with spaces waiting for the story. On the right was a mock-up for several ads already set in colour.

'Might have had a little more oomph,' said Georgie, looking at the left page, 'but it's not a problem. How close to being done is the story?'

'It's due to come over in an hour,' said a man who'd been leaning against a wall but suddenly stood erect.

'Great.'

Glancing at the right page, she flinched and tossed the spread aside. 'Ugly ads.'

It was on the next spread that the sugar ad appeared. The story about the First Lady's nephew was on the right page. On the left was the full-page ad for sugar – about how natural sugar is better for you than chemical substitutes. In all, two pages of *World* separated the news story on chemical sweeteners from the ad for sugar. Jock could hardly complain: readers were not so dense they couldn't keep a story in their heads long enough to turn the page twice.

When *World*'s advertising manager had brought her the list of the biggest ads for that week's issue, Georgie had half forgotten the thrust of Jock's conversation over their drink at the Colony. Hundreds of other stories had come and gone. Yet she must have been thinking of Jock when she instructed the designer: 'Let's get the sugar ad somewhere close to the story. But not so close it would look like we had a special interest in sugar.' And a bit of her brain was undeniably sending him a message which said: 'You get your client to buy a two-page spread next time, and perhaps my designer will get you on the spread immediately succeeding the story.' He was right to bet she was another trader.

With all the layouts, approved or rejected, face down in two piles, everyone got up. They all trooped out.

In the corridor Georgie said to Larry Penrose, head of the national news section: 'On Monday, the British Secretary for BITE, Ian Lonsdale, is arriving in Washington for an official visit. American papers never have much on British ministers unless it's the Prime Minister. But Ian Lonsdale could well end up in Downing Street one day. I want to introduce him to Middle America now. You'll have to come up with the angle, Larry.'

'Sure,' said Larry Penrose.

'Probably Norman ought to go to Washington Sunday night. Tell him to see Michael O'Donovan at J. D. Liddon International. O'Donovan knows a lot of stuff about the British end. Could your staff get everything the library has on Lonsdale and you give me a briefing tomorrow? What about coming into my office twenty minutes before the morning run-through so we can decide how to handle it on the ground?'

'Sure,' said Larry Penrose.

When Georgie phrased orders as if they were questions, it usually meant she was in a good mood. On the other hand, Larry had heard her use this same 'polite request' technique when she was mad as hell. But she didn't sound sarcastic now. Anyway, it was the head of features who'd got the shaft today.

At 7.30, Georgie was changed into a long-skirted suit for Brooke Astor's dinner for the newly appointed French ambassador to Washington. She liked to get back to the apartment if only for half an hour with Sarah and Jamie before going on to her evening engagements. 'Oh Mama, you look beautiful,' Sarah would say, standing beside Georgie as they both looked in the full-length mirror, watching her secure the diamond and pearl ear pendants. But Thursdays were dicey with *World* getting closer to its deadline. Tonight she would go straight from the office to the dinner.

She rang Hugo's office in case he was still there. His mood these days was unpredictable. Sometimes when he heard her voice on the phone there was a pause before he said anything, and she could sense a sullen hostility. Other times when she asked him to help her with something, he seemed almost unnaturally enthusiastic in his eagerness to do so.

This time she caught him in a good mood. When she told him she was planning a big story on Ian

Lonsdale's visit, he seemed really interested when he asked: 'Any idea what you'll be pinning it to?'

'Not yet. I'd welcome any suggestion from you.'

'OK. So long as I get my piece about him written first,' Hugo said.

They both laughed. God, it was a pleasant relief to find Hugo friendly instead of distant. The last two weekends he'd seemed distant even when they made love.

'Patsy will enjoy seeing what you and I can come up with when we put our minds to it,' she said.

Patsy remained her only close friend, except for Hugo – not counting his bad days. Georgie and Patsy kept in touch by letter and telephone, but they hadn't actually seen each other since Georgie visited London two years before. However short her stays in Britain, she always had dinner with Judge Fawcett and his wife. They remained her ideal – not that she wanted a marriage as close as theirs, but because they always made her feel so good. She was not by nature introspective or inclined to reminiscence, and the idealist in her had long been cloaked by a tough, detached approach to life. Yet the cloak of cynicism slipped a little when she was with Patsy's father and mother, and it got laid aside altogether whenever she wrote to them. She cherished letters from them.

In her car on the way to the dinner party, she mulled over how to handle the Lonsdale piece in *World*. It was lucky the timing for an American–British trade piece was spot on. She wondered what British deal Jock was pursuing. He hadn't spelled out why he wanted to meet Ian. Smiling at the thought of

Jock's endlessly revved-up energy, her mind flitted to that first evening on the terrace of Rycroft Lodge – Jock's barrel chest under the tieless shirt, the coarse hands. The image of his hands was followed by an image of Lisa on the terrace at the Shore – her lilac dress held together at the shoulders with two bows. Georgie hadn't met Lisa since then, though Hugo said he'd run into her in Washington a couple of times.

While her driver waited for the red light to change, she glanced out the window at the huge building which occupied an entire block and bore a rival's name: *Newsweek*. Was Jock Liddon this very minute, she wondered, trying to set up a different deal with *Newsweek*'s editor? If so, what would be Jock's tactics with another male? There was nothing specific she could put her finger on where Jock had approached her in any sexual sense. Yet ever since he had tossed his cigarettes over the heads of the dogs, she was aware of the sexual current between them. As her driver made his way up Madison Avenue, she found she could give herself a charge just by thinking of those blunt hands with their manicured nails.

In London on that same Thursday, the BITE Secretary made an announcement in the House of Commons:

'Honourable Members will be aware of the public debate about the question of keeping open the only motor-cycle factory in Northern Ireland. While it is difficult at the present time for Belfast to compete with imports from the Far East, the social costs of allowing the factory to close would be unacceptable in the current circumstances in Northern Ireland. I am providing investment which will enable the company to reorganize itself and become fully competitive within the next few years.'

Everyone in Westminster and Whitehall knew what this meant. But for the public who watch Parliament on television, Ian's PPS, Bob Brindle, had got a back-bencher to follow Ian's statement with a cruder use of language to say the same thing. Others, he said, had argued it would be more economic for Britain to let the Belfast factory and its three hundred workers go to the wall. But what sort of economy is it, he asked rhetorically, which puts more money into the pay packets of Japanese factory workers at the expense of the jobs of their United Kingdom counterparts? The BITE Secretary had demonstrated, his own back-bencher then concluded, that whatever atrocities were committed by the IRA, industrial partnership with decent Northern Ireland workers remained the aim of BITE.

Seldom had Ian found a decision so difficult. Normally it would have been based purely on the minister's political judgement. But in this case he had to keep asking himself: how much was his judgement coloured by personal fear – by Maureen's attempt at blackmail?

Each time he went through the argument about the motor-cycle factory, he could hear her soft lilt when it had suddenly hardened at the edges: either he would look after the livelihood of those three hundred Irishmen 'whose only fault is they're not fucking

Protestants', or she would go to Patsy. His instinctive response was to let the bloody factory close down so Maureen would know she couldn't intimidate him.

And yet. It was insane and unjust to let his angry resentment of a tough little bitch lead him to take the opposite decision to what he would have done had she not existed.

Invariably, his mind turned over the best way to make sure she didn't carry out her blackmailer's threat. If he came clean with Patsy, Maureen could tell her about their affair – he winced at the word – and it wouldn't matter. That way he'd be safe. But of course he would be asking Patsy to carry the can: she'd be the one to suffer. He could remember every word of what he'd said to her nine years before: 'What I *can* guarantee is that if ever, out of childishness or male vanity or God knows what idiotic weakness of character, I had a brief fling, it wouldn't affect us in any way.' How could he now tell her what would wound her deeply?

He decided to ride out the blackmailing risk. There'd been no word from Maureen since their Stag Place confrontation in early June. 'Confrontation' was the word he used to himself whenever he thought about their last meeting in that sitting-room with the window-boxes of geraniums and petunias outside, and the cheap carpet within. 'Confrontation' had a dryness which made his actions and hers that day seem slightly less repellent.

And in the end he let his rational judgement prevail and directed that £50 million of BITE's budget go to the Belfast motor-cycle factory. It was a fine irony, he thought more than once, that the bitch would think she was responsible for the decision which in fact he had finally made for political reasons alone.

The irony would have seemed even greater to Ian had he known what took place when Michael O'Donovan had made his own visit to Stag Place. After he had left her, Maureen slept badly, waking throughout the night to brood.

'You're obsessed with this one factory because your brothers work there,' Michael had told her, 'but even if Lonsdale keeps the factory going, hit him again. Never feel grateful to the Brits for any tidbit they throw you. Keep on frightening them, hurting them. Confuse them. Bite the hand that feeds you.' When he'd made his wordplay with 'bite', something like a smile had flickered on the narrow face.

'Does your boss know what you do for Noraid?' Maureen had asked him.

'Jock? I wouldn't discuss it with him. He's aware Pat Rourke and I are close, but he doesn't want to hear about it. Jock knows and he doesn't know.'

20

'Oh God,' said Patsy.

The unwelcome request had just been announced for the third time. 'Will Passenger Gobbledegook please come forward to the flight attendant at the front of the economy section and make himself known?'

'For once a plane is ready to leave on time, and now we're going to have to sit for four bloody hours while they take off the bloody suitcases.' She unlocked her seat-belt.

With his red pen Ian made a note in the margin of the brief he was reading, initialled it, and turned the page.

'I don't know which I'd prefer,' Patsy grumbled. 'To sit here trapped like a rat while they search for Mr Gobbledegook's bags, only to discover he didn't get on the plane because he fell asleep in the airport lounge. Or whether I'd rather they actually found he'd put a bomb in his suitcase. At least that would give a point to our turning to stone while we sit here for the next few days.'

'I think I'd prefer the first reason,' Ian said amiably before rereading the paragraphs he'd only half taken in while half listening to his wife.

Bleakly she looked out the window at Heathrow's tarmac.

At that moment, Richard Norris appeared in the aisle, smiling cheerfully.

'How the good news was brought to Ghent,' Patsy remarked, as always struck by the way Richard seemed to appear by magic.

Richard Norris was head of Ian's private office at BITE. As principal private secretary, Richard had it in his hands to make life infinitely better or infinitely worse for the Minister. The private secretary is a double agent. Already far up the civil-service ladder himself, his continuous loyalty is to the department's civil-service head, the permanent secretary. His other loyalty is to his political boss, but this is transient: ministers come and go. How the private secretary juggles these two loyalties depends on his personal feelings for his minister. Richard Norris respected Ian's grasp of the intricate problems overlapping at BITE. He liked the way Ian didn't get in a flap: he knew what he wanted to achieve at BITE and he went after it. And Ian's sense of irony appealed to Richard. All these things led him to interpret Whitehall's rules in ways which would make Ian's ministerial life a bit less constricted. No one knows better than the private office that pressure on a Cabinet minister is relentless.

Richard was accompanying the Minister on the official visit to Washington. So too was the senior civil servant who dealt with international trade. Both had seats three rows further back in the first-class section – an arrangement made by Richard so Patsy wouldn't feel the civil servants were breathing down her neck. Not long after Ian became BITE Secretary, Richard had monitored a telephone call between the Minister and his wife, and thus he was aware of

Patsy's sporadic outbursts of rage over what she saw as the proprietorial attitude of civil servants: 'They're meant to be serving you, for God's sake. What's it got to do with them if you decide to meet me for lunch without telling them?' But once Patsy had discovered that a call might be monitored, she did better at concealing her recurrent exasperation with the demands of high office. Richard knew that Ian hoped bits and pieces of the American visit could be managed so Patsy had a semi-holiday.

'The pilot says he thinks the baggage compartment can be emptied in forty minutes, Minister,' Richard said. 'With any luck we'll be under way in an hour and a half. As it's already nearly two o'clock, he's told the stewards to serve something to the first-class passengers.'

Patsy was glad the curtain was drawn behind their section, making them invisible to the business class sitting further back, not to mention economy class. She enjoyed the perks that went with Ian's job. At the same time she didn't feel proud about the VIP treatment. When the steward poured out the golden Moët Brut from a bottle half-wrapped in a white linen napkin, the last thing Patsy wanted was for those who had to wait for a drink until take-off to watch as she sipped her champagne.

With meticulous timing, the British Ambassador, Sir Martin Masters, strode gracefully across the tarmac of Dulles Airport to the steps where the ministerial party were about to disembark before the rest of the passengers trudged into the airbus.

'My wife asks you to forgive her, Mrs Lonsdale,' said Sir Martin. 'She suffers from migraine, but she is much looking forward to being able to welcome you at dinner this evening.'

Ten minutes later the ministerial party walked out the front doors of the airport into the suffocating embrace of the wet heat. The silver Rolls-Royce waiting under a no-waiting sign slid forward, and its driver jumped out. The Lonsdales and the Ambassador got in. Once the baggage came off the plane, the others would follow in the Jaguar waiting under the no-waiting sign.

Thirty-five minutes later the Rolls was in the placid grandeur of Massachusetts Avenue. 'My wife and I thought you'd be glad to have half an hour to yourselves after your journey,' Sir Martin said to Patsy as she looked out at the broad street lined with an exotic succession of architectural styles, each embassy displaying its own culture. 'Don't bother to change. It will be just ourselves, your husband's staff, and several of my staff who can give you a run-down on what lies ahead.'

Sir Martin turned back to Ian. 'If you feel like it, Minister, you and I might go through some more matters before the others join us for drinks at 7.30. Seven o'clock? I'll be in my study. After your delayed journey, I hope you'll find the evening relaxing, even though it's a semi-working dinner. At least it will be short and to the point, as the schedule drawn up for you is fairly, shall I say, strenuous.' Sir Martin chuckled. These official visits would kill anyone who lacked the stamina of an Olympic long-distance gold medal winner.

A vast red-brick building standing in symmetrical self-importance came into view, its high roofs crowned with tall chimneys. When the last great English designer of country houses, Sir Edwin Lutyens, was commissioned to draw up the plans for the British Embassy in Washington, he was already involved in designing the Viceroy's palace in New Delhi. Such viceregal splendour would have been over-the-top in Washington, and Lutyens showed some restraint. Even so, he produced the most majestic of the national advertisements which stand in Embassy Row. The Rolls turned into the crescent drive sweeping beneath a porte-cochère, where a man in black livery and white gloves came forward.

Inside the house, Patsy looked up at a great flying arch. Below it rose twin staircases. The head housekeeper led her up to the next floor where Patsy glimpsed a magnificent wood-panelled library. 'That's the Ambassador's study, madam. The reception rooms are on this floor,' said the housekeeper. She led the way to another elaborate staircase which rose beneath the gaze of an eighteen-year-old Queen Victoria painted at her coronation.

When Ian went up to the bedroom floor a few minutes later, he found Patsy lying on one of the outsize twin beds at the far end of an enormous room made inviting by floral chintz; expensive elegance combined with informality was the mark of the English country-house decorator. She had kicked off her shoes. She was reading a letter.

'It's from Georgie. It was waiting here. She's out this evening, but she says to ring her at *World* tomorrow.' Patsy laughed with pleasure. The high spot of this visit, so far as she was concerned, was seeing Georgie. 'She says Hugo is going to be in touch tomorrow morning to fix up details of our weekend with them on the Eastern Shore. And we'll see them both tomorrow night. She's coming to Washington for our dinner.'

The Ambassador would have much preferred his dinner for the Minister to be held on the patio beneath the great stone pediment, the skilfully informal garden spreading beyond, a Barbara Hepworth bronze closing the vista at the end while Elisabeth Frink's bronze horse lay contentedly in the manicured grass to one side. 'The British at their best,' Sir Martin said to himself each time he thought about his garden or indeed any other aspect of his house, which meant he said it to himself fifteen or twenty times a day. But the July heat would be too stifling. Sir Martin did wish the summer climate of America's capital was a little less like Calcutta.

The guests were invited for 7.30 and at six o'clock Patsy fell on to her bed, gazing weakly at the painting of Peggy Ashcroft dressed as Rosalind in *As You Like It*.

'Do I gather you were given a zealous tour of the nation's capital?' said Ian, who had got back to their bedroom a quarter of an hour earlier and was stretched out in an armchair, a silver tray with coffee beside him. He was making notes on some points raised in that day's meetings – first with the American Energy Secretary, next at the Hay-Adams with

Washington representatives of British industry, then with the Secretary of Commerce and his team. As soon as Ian had got back to the Embassy he began a meeting with Fergus Lansbury, the chief adviser for Ministry of Defence procurements, along with two other senior civil servants at the Embassy. Probably there had been a total of thirty minutes during the day when he had not been concentrating. Sir Martin had been present at the meetings, and Ian observed that beneath the smoothie manner favoured by the Foreign Office, Sir Martin was extremely competent indeed.

'No wonder the Ambassador's wife suffers from migraine,' said Patsy. 'Americans are so kind: they want you to see two hundred years of their history in a single day. Did you know there are fourteen museums in Washington which under no circumstances can be missed?'

'Here's some homework for this evening,' said Ian, bringing her a sheaf of pages. They contained potted biographies of the thirty guests who would be at the dinner. The British excelled in this detail of social briefing, intended to enable both the Minister and his wife to use informal conversation to maximum effect.

At 7.20 Ian was fastening the clip on his black bow-tie. Patsy was fastening the clasp on a gold bracelet. At the other end of the vast room there was a knock on the door.

'Come in,' Ian said sharply. There'd been a fair bit of toing and froing of maids bringing trays and taking them away, maids returning freshly pressed clothes, one dear little maid checking that nothing else was wanted.

This time it was Richard Norris who walked in the door, his face unusually serious.

'Things can't be that bad, Richard,' Ian said, laughing. 'It's only a dinner party still to go before you can put your feet up for a few hours.'

'I thought I should let you know, Minister, the news we've just had from London,' Richard said. 'A bomb went off half an hour ago in Lord North Street. The car belonged to George Jolliffe. It was parked in front of his house. He had walked to the House of Commons half an hour earlier.'

Richard said nothing further.

Patsy was now standing beside Ian. He said: 'Was anyone near the car when the bomb went off?'

'I'm afraid so. It was Semtex. It went off when Mrs Jolliffe went out to the car for something and slammed the door. The IRA has already rung *The Times* and claimed responsibility. No reason was given, so one can only surmise it's because George Jolliffe led back-bench opposition to further British investment in Northern Ireland.'

All three were silent.

Then Ian said: 'Anne Jolliffe? Was she killed?'

'I'm afraid so.'

21

At 7.29 precisely, the Ambassador left his library and stationed himself in the centre hall. He took it as a personal challenge: the filthy IRA were not going to spoil his dinner party.

Upstairs the Lonsdales were subdued when they left their bedroom. George Jolliffe was a fellow MP, and Ian had liked Anne Jolliffe – the late Anne Jolliffe. Patsy had met them only a few times at the House. Even so. She was not short on imagination.

The Ambassador glanced at his watch – 7.30 exactly – and looked up at the staircase with its elaborate iron balustrade spiralling beneath the varnished gaze of the young queen: his guests of honour were on their way down. He knew Richard Norris had informed them of the atrocity. He had bet himself they'd still be punctilious in coming down in time to greet the first of the guests already stepping from a car just drawn up under the porte-cochère.

Sir Martin watched with pleasure as Patsy approached the foot of the staircase. Apart from a slightly withdrawn expression he hadn't seen on her face during the previous twenty-four hours, she looked as if she'd been doing nothing more demanding all day than lounging in her room, preparing for this evening. Like many English women, her skin appeared to be poreless. Patsy also, as it happened, used more make-up than others might guess; she always found the cruellest light to scrutinize her face as she applied her little brushes. Tonight her honey-coloured hair was caught up in a shiny French pleat, wisps falling prettily on to her cheeks without hiding the ruby ear pendants which had belonged to Ian's grandmother. Her deceptively simple chiffon gown was made of layers of varying shades of aquamarine which emphasized the green eyes, fringed by their dark lashes. Sir Martin drew in a deep breath of satisfaction at the appearance of the British Cabinet minister's wife he would be presenting this evening. He *did* wish he could have said the same of the VIP's wife he'd been landed with a fortnight earlier.

He moved to the foot of the stairs to greet the Lonsdales. 'Wretched news from London, I'm afraid. But if the IRA think they can intimidate us, they'll have to think again,' Sir Martin said. He offered Patsy his arm. 'Let me take you into the drawing-room, my dear.'

Ten minutes later Ian was standing with a tumbler of whisky in one hand, talking with the President's trade representative and the chairman of America's biggest electronics firm. In a gilt frame above their heads, Lady Anstruther glowed in lavish colours bestowed by Sir Joshua Reynolds's brush; the drawing-room was designed to epitomize the eighteenth century in England. Glancing across to where Patsy was listening to the chairman of the Congressional Appropriations Committee, Ian saw his wife's face suddenly light up. She turned away from the congressman and threw her arms around the slender bare shoulders of a woman with gleaming dark hair cut like a Japanese doll's. Ian smiled. He would wait. He turned his attention back to the electronics mogul's preoccupation with tax benefits from American–British trade.

'Fancy having to come to the British Embassy in order to see my best friend,' said Georgie, laughing. Her sleeveless, white silk gown was almost austere until she walked, when its narrow skirt parted nearly to her thigh. Her hazel eyes took in Patsy's appearance from top to toe. When Georgie didn't like someone, she felt a small malicious pleasure when that person's looks were crumbling by the time she was thirty. But she hated it when after a long interval she saw someone she liked, and the person had turned into a slob. She had never imagined that could happen to Patsy, but neither had she expected her to be increasingly beautiful. For the second time, she and Patsy embraced, both laughing.

'Is a mere male allowed to join the love-in?' asked Hugo.

Before he could do so, the Ambassador glided up with Imogene Randall. 'Mrs Randall is Washington's greatest adornment,' he said to Patsy.

When Imogene had touched cheeks with Georgie and Hugo, the Ambassador said, 'Imogene, will you introduce Mrs Lonsdale and our Gallery director? I must take Georgie and Hugo away for a few moments, my dear,' he told Patsy, 'but you'll have time with them later. Georgie, I promised Senator Morley I would allow him to meet you early in the evening. And Hugo . . .' the Ambassador began.

'Wait a minute, Martin. I haven't seen your other guest of honour for two years, and then on the wing. Let me say hello to Ian.'

'And me,' said Georgie, as they both made for Ian.

Two minutes later the Ambassador resolved these social conflicts by taking Senator Chalmers Morley up to join Ian's group and meet Georgie.

Lady Masters's unpredictable migraine had retreated sufficiently for her to be present as hostess, and very handsome she looked in her ink-blue silk gown, her raven hair swept up and adorned with an Edwardian rose diamond-and-cut-steel bow. A pity the hovering migraine meant she couldn't be more active in introducing their guests, but Martin handled all that so well. She smiled benignly as the American Secretary of Commerce continued his dissertation on his last visit to London.

Hugo and Ian were absorbed in journalists' and politicians' favourite pastime wherever they get together – political gossip. In mid-sentence about the White House's private view of Britain's Prime Minister, something made Hugo glance beyond Ian. Immediately Hugo's expression changed from relaxed enjoyment to an intensity which brought two deep red patches on to his cheekbones. For a moment he seemed to forget where he was in the account he was giving Ian. When Ian turned to see what had caused this effect, he looked directly into the face of a girl he had seen somewhere before – the straight blonde hair falling on to her shoulders, the lilac-coloured eyes.

'Hullo, Hugo,' she said. Then she looked at Ian tentatively. 'You were kind enough to let James Arden bring Michael O'Donovan and me to your house in the country,' she said.

'Of course,' Ian said, wondering why he hadn't immediately realized who she was.

'This is Jock Liddon,' Lisa said. 'He's my boss.'

As Ian and Jock shook hands, Ian saw this man was a different fish from the reserved O'Donovan. Even on his best behaviour, a crude extrovert's vitality emanated from Jock.

'Hullo, Jock,' said Hugo, wondering why the hell Lisa hadn't mentioned she'd be at this dinner. Where else did she go unbeknownst to him? Instinctively glancing around to see where Georgie was, he was relieved that her back was to him as she talked with Senator Chalmers Morley. He stared again at Jock.

What the hell is going on? Ian asked himself. He saw Hugo's light-blue eyes were like ice as they watched Jock's hand holding the cigar to the curly lips. Ian too found something vaguely unpleasant about the high sheen of the nails on the stubby hands. Yet he was curious about Liddon. James Arden had said he was a pivotal figure with close connections to the Appropriations Committees in both the Senate and the House. An extraordinary energy seemed to be contained in that burly, barrel-chested figure. Why was it, Ian wondered wryly, that so many men with exceptional vitality seemed to have black curly hair? And what was it about Liddon's entirely conventional and well-cut dinner-jacket that carried a slight sense of menace?

Hugo was suddenly contrite that he'd not introduced Lisa to any of his smart friends since Imogene's party. But what was she doing here this evening? The guest list would have been drawn up with considerable care. OK, he could see why Liddon was here: Liddon had his thick fingers in so many deals that he probably had some British reciprocal trade negotiation up his sleeve. But how had he got an invitation for Lisa? He wasn't parading her as his fiancée. Was he?

The British Embassy's chief adviser for Ministry of Defence procurements, Fergus Lansbury, could have told Hugo how Jock got himself and Lisa to the dinner. Once Jock had inveigled Georgie into asking him to the Eastern Shore for a drink with the Lonsdales, he telephoned Fergus Lansbury.

'Fergus,' Jock said, leaning back in his chair and swivelling it rhythmically. 'We haven't met since I helped the MoD get its knock-down price for Southern Tennessee radar components. I'm fixing a date for lunch with a key member of the Defence Appropriations Subcommittee who has some interesting things to say. Interesting to me. Interesting to you. Wanna make it a threesome?'

'Splendid,' said Fergus Lansbury.

'I'll get my secretary to phone yours and fix up a date that'd suit everybody. She'll book my table at the Hay-Adams.'

Ten days later the congressman on the Defence Appropriations Subcommittee was strutting his stuff at Jock's table beside one of the marble fireplaces in the golden Adams Room. He was a nice man, and he felt slightly embarrassed, aware his insider knowledge would already be known to Jock. All Jock would get out of the lunch was the display of access. Even so, the congressman would do his best to burnish the conversation.

'We have to have our defence commitments hammered out before the recess,' he said. 'We're into big policy decisions – troops in Germany, bases in the Philippines, great big decisions.'

'Yeah,' said Jock, 'but we're hearing rumours that some of you guys haven't got your act together. How come you aren't taking bigger advantage of the problems in the Communist countries? Here we are, the free West, and what are we doing for our own trade advantage?'

'Why fight with these guys when their system is in chaos, Jock? Let's kiss and work with them,' said the congressman emolliently.

'That's OK so long as it's a two-way deal and not just us giving away our past-their-sell-by components to show how much we love them,' said Jock. 'And what about doing more business with our own allies?'

The congressman turned to the British adviser for defence procurements. His voice was strong, his manner frank, as he said to Fergus Lansbury: 'The Asp deal will probably go forward. Otis in New Orleans has an interest in it.' His expression then grew sombre. 'I'm not sure about the Whippet deal. You've got a public-relations problem with those tests, Fergus.' Having delivered himself of the good news and the bad news, both inconclusive, the congressman applied his mind to the lemon soufflé which had just been set before him. Then he sat back and listened to Fergus Lansbury's case for why it was in America's interest to buy Britain's Whippet.

When the three men were leaving the Hay-Adams,

Jock said he had an appointment on Massachusetts Avenue, which was a lie but made it natural to offer Fergus a lift back to the Embassy.

'I've been thinking about your public-relations problem with the Whippet deal, Fergus,' Jock began as soon as they were in his car.

By the time they'd reached the British Embassy compound, Jock had agreed to see what he could do to make Whippet's path smoother, starting with his own access to other members of the Defence Appropriations Subcommittee.

'And by the way, Fergus. I'm going over to the Eastern Shore at the tail-end of Ian Lonsdale's official visit here. Before they go back to London, the Lonsdales are having a private weekend with Georgie Chase and Hugo Carroll. I haven't met the BITE Secretary before. Georgie tells me the Ambassador is giving a dinner party for him. Do you think you could arrange an invitation for me – not to talk shop across the table, but to prepare the ground? And another thing. Lisa Tabor is my best up-and-coming lobbyist as well as my very good friend. She has access to some big *big* names among American political journalists. As I don't have a wife, do you think you could get an invitation for her to come with me? She already knows the Lonsdales. She was at their country house in Warwickshire a coupla weeks ago. It was a family lunch, but they wanted Lisa included.'

The attraction of having three round tables instead of a single long one, the Ambassador regularly observed, was that protocol became less rigid. No one appreciated better than he that protocol is essential if official life is to function smoothly, and nowhere was protocol more exactingly observed than in Washington DC. But as Imogene Randall knew – the Ambassador was devoted to Imogene; she represented the very best of the New World – as Imogene knew, having several round tables with ten or twelve guests at each allowed you to bend the stiffness of protocol into a graceful design of your own. Sir Martin was particularly fond of this image of bending a rigid inharmonious form into something more fluid and convivial.

At Lady Masters's table, Ian was placed between her and Georgie. Georgie was altogether in luck: on her other side she found Jock.

'Tell me something about Liddon,' Ian asked Georgie. 'I'm rather taken with his looks.'

'You mean he looks like someone who would be perfectly happy in the Mafia,' said Georgie, laughing. 'If I'd been commissioning an article on contrasting types in the English-speaking world, I couldn't have done better than choose you and Jock Liddon. Sitting on my left is the British gentleman-politician wielding power in Westminster and Whitehall. Sitting on my right is the American wheeler-dealer wielding power in Washington.'

'Since you left London, there's much more straightforward lobbying of MPs,' Ian said, 'though the British lobbyist is seldom the man that everyone wants to know – as seems to be the case in Washington.'

'The whole set-up here is different from Britain,' said Georgie. 'It has a lot to do with American political parties being far less disciplined than at Westminster. Here the party is more like a loose organization which every four years tries to elect a president from among its members. On day one of any new session, congressmen behave like proper party members. On day two, party discipline goes up the spout. That's a main reason why someone like Jock can influence voting the way he does.' She glanced across the table at Senator Chalmers Morley. 'The other reason, of course, is the huge sums of money needed for US congressmen to get re-elected. They need the PACs – plus "discreet contributions",' she indicated the quotes, 'which Jock can arrange.'

A rattling of bone china and cutlery spread through the dining-room as fifteen waiters in livery gathered up the soup-plates, each scraped nearly clean of the spinach soup scattered with tips of asparagus *al dente*. The prowess of the British Embassy's chef was exceeded only by the chef at the French Embassy. Turning from the senator on her other side, Lady Masters inclined her upper body forward so Ian would become aware his hostess was ready for her guests to talk with their other dinner partner.

'See you after the next course,' Georgie said to Ian, making a friendly little kiss sound with her lips before turning to Jock on her other side. 'Speak of the devil,' she said.

'Meaning?'

'I was just talking about lobbyists. How are you?'

Jock turned sideways in his chair and looked

Georgie up and down. She was disconcerted to find her face went hot.

'Are they real?' he asked.

His eyes were on the string of pearls alternating with golden topaz which hung nearly to her waist, the only decoration on her white gown. The candle-light made her hazel eyes the same colour as the topaz.

'Hugo gave it to me,' she replied.

They both laughed. If Hugo had given it to her, it had to be the real McCoy.

'Is Lisa a regular part of your life on the Washington social circuit?' asked Georgie. She noticed her own tenseness as she waited for his answer.

'Irregular,' said Jock. 'She's a good kid. You could say she's my protégée. I asked if I could bring her tonight because I knew there'd be people here she oughta meet.'

He was adroit at combining candour and selectivity: at the same time as his manner appeared frank, automatically his brain was picking out which parts of an account would be useful in this particular situation, and which parts should be overlooked – 'economical with the truth', as a distinguished British civil servant once put it. Thus he left out any mention of how he had used Georgie's name – and Hugo's, and the Lonsdales' family lunch – to pressure Fergus Lansbury into persuading the Ambassador to invite him and Lisa to this evening's dinner.

'I noticed the way you handled that sugar ad,' said Jock. 'Not so close to the news story as my client would have liked, but close enough so he only cried a little. What did you think of the picture we chose for it? Pretty classy?'

'It would have been classier if it had been a two-page spread,' said Georgie. 'Doesn't your client know when it's in his interest to dig into his pocket?'

'I told him he oughta. But he wasn't willing to spend the dough without knowing the ad would appear pretty close to the story about the investigation into chemical sweeteners. Too bad you couldn't give me an assurance in advance. Ethics are cruddy All they do is make life tougher than it already is.'

Georgie laughed. 'I'm not Hugo. I don't like ethics for their own sake – as you may have guessed,' she added. His face was deadpan, but his eyes made her think of the Dobermans when they had that intent, steady watchfulness. 'But once anyone thought the editor of *World* could be bought, that would be the end of the editor. Anyhow, I don't agree with you that ethics are always cruddy. I find on the whole they make life easier – like rules. Everybody knows where they are.'

'Sure, sure, Georgie. You got a point. But everybody also knows rules are there to be broken. Otherwise, what'd be the fun? If you tell me you don't like breaking rules, I'll tell you you're a liar.'

'Next thing you'll be telling me what fun it would be if *World* ran a rave story on another of your clients,' said Georgie laughing.

'Would I ever do anything so obvious? Crude, yes. Obvious, no. Anyway, I can think of other things with you that would be a helluva lot more fun.'

He picked up his claret glass and held it like a little

toast to her before he drank from it. Under her porcelain make-up, Georgie flushed.

Jock switched gear: 'By the way, did your reporter get some useful stuff from Michael O'Donovan?'

'O'Donovan filled out a good bit of background on decisions which Ian Lonsdale is sitting on this very minute. Thanks for lining him up.'

'Any time, any time. And I'll tell you something I was thinking about earlier, Georgie. Senator Chalmers Morley is very much in the news.' Jock jerked his thumb at the handsome butterscotch face across the table. Wearing a bow-tie rather than his normal looped black ribbon, the Senator from Texas looked marginally less like an actor than usual. 'All that stuff about the cotton lobby contributing more than the legal limit for Morley's election campaign – it made him sad. Anybody can be landed in the shit if their accountant can't keep the books straight. It's all made him pretty wary of reporters. For the past month he's refused to do an interview. But I could get him to give one to *World* – so long as you let him say something about Anglo-American deals. He's going to London soon to look into possibilities for transatlantic partnerships in energy and industry. Let me know if *World* would be interested.'

As Jock tapped his head to signify his connections were stored there, Georgie watched the blunt index finger prod the black curls.

At Sir Martin's table, conversation was all the host had hoped for. He had known he could count on Patsy to help things go well.

But at the third round table, where Imogene was

unofficially in command, there was a strain. Across from her was Hugo. On his right was Senator Morley's wife. Helen Morley was a beauty in the vivid Texas manner, slightly faded, perhaps, but none the less of a quality which demanded admiration. Edgy where her husband's reputation was concerned, she was none the less good company, known for her sharp intelligence and quick wit. She and Hugo had been placed beside each other in the expectation that they would enjoy talking together. Yet over the spinach and asparagus soup, Hugo had been almost monosyllabic in his conversation with Helen Morley. He kept sitting back in his chair, apparently reflecting on the centre-piece arrangement of yellow roses and blue daisies in a yellow and blue Ming *cloisonné* bowl. But Imogene, an expert in seeing out of the corner of the eye, knew he was waiting for the person on his other side to turn far enough in her chair so he could talk with her whether it was his turn or not.

Without losing the thread of her own conversation with NBC's president beside her, Imogene's untroubled grey eyes moved to the person Hugo was so impatient to talk with. There was no doubt that Lisa was an exceptionally beguiling girl. But there were lots of exceptionally beguiling girls in Washington. What did Hugo see in her that made him abandon his usual good manners?

Lisa could feel Hugo trying to will her to turn to him, but she had no intention of turning away from the congressman on her other side until the fish course arrived. She wanted Imogene to see she was a

reliable dinner guest. Hugo would have to wait.
Hugo, after all, was hooked.

It seemed eternity to Hugo before the shad roe,
adorned with two strips of crispy bacon and half a
lemon, was placed before each guest. Lisa turned to
him.

'Why didn't you tell me you were coming tonight?'
He kept his voice low, but it was curt.

'I wanted to surprise you,' Lisa replied.

'I hate surprises,' Hugo said sulkily.

Having longed to talk with her, he fell silent. Both
ate their shad roe until Lisa made an attempt at
neutral conversation. 'Are you going to do a piece on
Ian Lonsdale?' she asked.

'Yes. For later this week. I intend to tie it in with a
lament for the way the American government con-
ducts business, and I'll be citing the husband of the
lady on my other side,' Hugo said, keeping his voice
low. His resentment of Jock now had an outlet as he
rehearsed to Lisa what he would write about the
American lobby system: 'You might well ask: what
American government? The whole system is out of
control. At any one time there are at least sixteen
different centres of power, shifting – now you see it,
now you don't.' He stabbed at what remained of his
shad roe.

'What's that got to do with the husband of the
lady on your other side?' asked Lisa quietly, leaning
forward to check Helen Morley's back was turned
and she was talking animatedly to the museum director on her other side.

'When a foreign ambassador is trying to get something for his country, do you think he deals with the State Department?' continued Hugo angrily in his low voice, still rehearsing his next column. 'Like hell he does. He smooches with K Street lawyers who will lobby Capitol Hill for him. And Chalmers Morley is the shining example of the senator who can be bought by anyone. He epitomizes a rotten system. I intend to say so.'

'Oh Hugo.'

The lilac eyes looked into his face in entreaty. Then Lisa looked down. She had become the beautiful waif.

'What's the matter?' he asked.

'I need to talk to you about something – before you write your piece. Can we meet for coffee tomorrow afternoon?'

From the corner of her eye, Imogene Randall saw Hugo's angry face change to one of tenderness. What on earth, she wondered, could they be talking about?

When the meat course was served, Lisa turned back to the congressman. While appearing to hang on his every word, she considered how she could get into a post-dinner conversation with Ian Lonsdale. It wouldn't be easy at this kind of party where he was guest of honour. Maybe she should aim for Patsy Lonsdale instead – for the moment.

'That girl James Arden brought to Pig Farm seems quite pleasant,' Patsy said. She was standing in front of the George III mirror in the bedroom, unclipping her ruby ear pendants.

'I didn't really notice,' Ian replied, though he had

used his only opportunity to impress Lisa. She'd been among the guests the Ambassador had brought together with Ian over coffee to discuss his government's handling of the latest Middle East crisis. While seeming concentrated on answering a senator and a White House aide, Ian had framed his side of the discussion to appeal to Lisa, sometimes looking directly into those lilac eyes as if what he really wanted was to be talking with her alone.

'I hope your evening wasn't spoiled,' Ian said, 'by the news about Anne Jolliffe.'

'I tried not to think about it,' Patsy said, feeling guilty that it was not, in fact, the Jolliffe family that made her so uneasy at this moment. Watching Ian in the mirror she said: 'I wish Jock Liddon wasn't coming for drinks while we're on the Eastern Shore with Georgie and Hugo.'

'I rather took to Liddon,' Ian replied, laughing. 'It's not every ambassador's dinner party where one meets a gangster.'

'Is Miss Lilac Eyes going to be with him when he comes to the Shore?' asked Patsy.

'How would I know? Ask Georgie.'

Patsy burst into tears.

'Darling,' Ian said, putting his arms around her. 'I'm a fool to mention the Jolliffes just as we're going to bed. It was a stupid thing to do. It helps nobody – least of all them.'

'I know. But it gives me such a bad feeling.'

In a way she didn't understand, what had just happened to the Jolliffe family kept merging into a foreboding that Lisa spelled bad news for her own family. Wiping her face with Ian's handkerchief, Patsy said: 'Do you remember when once I was talking with you about how something always makes luck run out? All this evening that thought kept coming back – how the black spot is still so small on the horizon we can't see it. But when it gets closer we'll see it's coming towards us.'

Holding her against him, Ian kissed her hair, rather ashamed that at the same time a bit of his mind was thinking about Lisa.

22

World's chief reporter on trade and industry, Norman
Sharpton, arrived just before ten at the British Embassy where he learned his interview with the BITE
Secretary would take place in the Ambassador's
wood-panelled study. (Sir Martin was engaged on
matters in the Chancery.) Settling themselves on the
David Hicks sofas – not too close together, not too
far apart – the two men faced each other at a comfortable distance. Each needed the other, and both knew
the rules of the game.

Not until they were well into the interview did
Norman ask: 'Why wouldn't it be in everyone's interest if the British government went into a joint venture
with an American company able and willing to build
an oil refinery in Northern Ireland?'

Ian gave Norman a hard look of suspicion mingled
with respect. Star Oil's refinery proposal had been
outlined only in recent departmental briefs. So far as
Ian knew, there'd been no public reference to the
proposal which Michael O'Donovan had first raised
at Pig Farm that Sunday several weeks before.

'Why do you ask that?' he said.

'I've heard it discussed,' Norman replied. For a
moment he could see Michael's narrow face. O'Donovan had turned out to be an exceptionally useful
source, though something about his reserved intensity
had made Norman uncomfortable. Journalist and

politician were aware the Minister didn't really expect Norman to reveal his sources.

Norman went straight on: 'OK, so after the rigs disasters, Star Oil has to pull out all the stops if it's going to persuade you to let it buy into the new fields. Even so, the refinery seems a good idea all around. That's supposing your government is serious about wanting to invest in Ulster.'

One of Norman's techniques was to annoy the other person into an unguarded response.

'Why should you think we're anything except serious?' Irritation put a clipped edge on Ian's voice. 'We've been prepared to pay a bloody high price already in trying to keep the Irish from slaughtering each other.'

'Well,' Norman replied amiably, 'I gather your department thinks its budget wouldn't stretch to the £200 million which Star Oil and British Refineries would need from the British government. That doesn't seem to indicate too much concern for the welfare of industrial workers in Northern Ireland.'

'I don't know who you've been talking to,' Ian said sharply, 'but you might tell that person: with the best will in the world, I can't just whistle up £200 million any time I feel like it.'

Norman gave a friendly smile. 'I know that. But when you've got a good political reason for whistling it up, and Star Oil and British Refineries are prepared to invest, I should think you'd blow your whistle pretty hard to get a refinery built in Ulster. What's your own view on British forces staying there?'

'Are you asking me on or off the record? My

colleague in Northern Ireland is not going to be best pleased if I swan around the United States sounding off on whether we should withdraw our troops.'

Norman used a notebook during an interview, not just for the quotes but also to note the briefly pressed lips or the swinging foot when certain questions were asked. He used a tape recorder to fall back on if there wasn't time to jot down everything he needed. Also, tapes were quite handy when someone complained of being misquoted. He switched off his recorder.

'Off the record,' he replied, 'though I'd like to take one or two notes for background.' Under the rules of the game, the journalist could not attribute 'background' remarks to the person making them. Norman flipped to a fresh page and scribbled 'bkgd' at the top.

'My view varies,' Ian said. 'When I'm thinking about the thing purely rationally, I think we should withdraw our troops. Everything the British Army does in Northern Ireland is virtually guaranteed to play straight into the hands of the IRA.'

Norman said nothing.

After a moment, Ian continued. 'What's the point in having hundreds of off-duty young British soldiers shot in the back of the head, blown up, cornered and tortured to death – when a solution for Northern Ireland remains as elusive as ever? And what thanks does anyone in Ulster extend to the murdered British soldiers' families? Bloody none. So rationally I think we might as well pull out of Northern Ireland and let the Catholic psychopaths and the Protestant psychopaths fight it out.'

Norman still said nothing.

'But then my non-rational voice says: how can you withdraw when you know these murderers will keep sucking innocent people into the blood bath?' He reached over to the coffee-pot. 'Will you have some more?'

'No thanks.'

Then Ian said: 'Of course I'm interested in Star Oil's proposal. But the IRA make a mistake if they think I'd try harder to invest in industry in Northern Ireland if they blow up the wife of a back-bench British MP who's against further investment. All that achieves is to make me wonder if BITE's money wouldn't be better spent propping up a Welsh industry instead.'

He lapsed into silence.

Norman reached over to flick the tape recorder on again before moving to questions about Britain's current row with its EC partners over steel quotas.

At 12.30 the British Ambassador's car dropped Ian at the Willard Hotel for his working lunch with Hugo. The first twenty minutes went into gossip. They'd had little time to themselves at the Ambassador's dinner the night before. Hugo wanted to pick Ian's brain about members of the British government; Ian wanted to learn the same about the Americans. Not until half-way through their Maryland crab cakes did Hugo raise Star Oil.

'Jesus,' Ian said. 'Is there anybody in this country who doesn't take an interest in Star Oil? There actually are other things that come through my department that have more far-reaching effects on industry.'

Hugo laughed. 'Was Norman Sharpton getting on to you about Star Oil?' He was irritated. His own piece on the BITE Secretary's visit was intended for Friday's *News*, and *World* would not appear on the news-stands until Saturday. Even so, if Georgie ended up with the better story, it would rankle. Just the thought of the possibility rankled.

It was almost three when Hugo walked into the virtually empty café not far from K Street. Lisa was already there. Joining her at the corner table, he said: 'I'm sorry I was on edge last night.'

'That's all right,' she replied. 'I'm glad you could meet me today. Hugo, I need help.'

She looked down at her left hand which she'd laid on the plastic tablecloth. Slowly she turned it so the palm was up, and with the third finger of her other hand she tentatively stroked the upturned palm – little strokes, unconfident. He watched her reluctance to ask him for something. Her delicate beauty made her timidity heartbreaking.

'You can tell me,' he said gently.

She looked up into his face. 'That column you're writing about the power of lobbyists. Couldn't you use another senator to illustrate your argument about corruption?'

'Why should I? Chalmers Morley is the most recent example of the whole rotten system. The difference between him and his fellow senators is that he got careless and accepted money over the legal limit. You saw him squirm before the Senate committee last month.'

'But Senator Morley's only real crime was in being found out,' Lisa said. 'Everyone does it.'

'Why do you care what I write about Morley?' asked Hugo.

Dropping her lashes over her eyes, Lisa prodded the tablecloth with her forefinger. It was all Hugo could do not to lift her hand to his lips and kiss it to reassure her.

She looked up into his face again.

'I'm accompanying Senator Morley to London next week. He's going there to explain to influential people about why BITE should grant an offshore licence to Star Oil. Star Oil is one of Jock's clients. If you raise the question of whether Senator Morley is corrupt – even though you don't spell it out – I could lose my job at J. D. Liddon.'

She dropped her lashes again and studied her up-turned palm. Hugo's eyes followed hers. The slender hand looked so innocent, lying there vulnerable and open.

'Why should what I write affect your job?' he asked. 'What I say about Morley has to do with me, not you.'

She looked up again. Her voice close to breaking, she said: 'The British press didn't take any interest in Senator Morley's problems before that Senate committee. But if you now impugn him in your column, it'll probably be picked up in the British press, and that would make him less effective in putting Star Oil's case. Jock will blame me.'

'But that's ridiculous,' said Hugo. 'Until this minute you've never mentioned either Morley or Star Oil. And everyone knows Star Oil is bidding for a field.'

'It's more complicated than that, Hugo,' Lisa said almost with a wail. 'Star Oil has sweetened its bid: if it gets the oilfield, it will build a refinery in Northern Ireland. It would be a joint venture with British Refineries – with BITE being asked to invest in it. Invest a lot. It would mean more jobs for Northern Ireland.'

Both were silent.

Then Lisa said: 'You don't understand about Jock. He knows everything. Well, almost everything. He doesn't know about our' – she hesitated – 'private life. But he knows we have meals together from time to time. After all, we do go to restaurants together. If you dump on Senator Morley, Jock will blame me. I promise you: he'll blame me.'

She looked down again. Two minutes passed. Three. Four. She went on making the nervous little strokes on that upturned vulnerable palm.

Finally he reached across the table and closed the fingers of her hand and carrying it to his lips, kissed its fingertips before he replaced it on the table. He lifted her right hand and put it protectively over her other hand.

She looked up and gave a small waif-like smile. 'Maybe I shouldn't have told you about my difficulties,' she said.

'Of course you should have told me,' he said. 'There are only too many senators and congressmen

I could name as examples of our rotten system of government. Maybe there's no need for me to mention Morley. Let's not talk about it any more.'

Few would have felt Hugo's depression at carrying out what Lisa had asked. Other journalists seldom hesitated to protect a close friend involved in some unsavoury story which supposedly they were exposing in full. They rarely reflected consciously on their proprietor's political and personal proclivities. They self-censored their stories without a thought.

But Hugo believed in ethics. He didn't self-censor. Indeed, if the thought occurred to him that he might be pulling his punches because something was in it for him if he did, almost perversely he was more hard-hitting than the matter might warrant.

And he knew that however much you wanted to help a friend, if you bent the news to do so it was the thin end of the wedge. Although his own style of speech was less crude than that of Ben Franwell, the famous British editor, Hugo knew exactly what Franwell had meant that night nine years ago at his party on the *Aureole* when he'd told Hugo: 'People say power corrupts, money corrupts. I'll tell you what corrupts: friendship.'

Once when a friend whose daughter had just been picked up on drug charges rang Hugo to ask if he could keep it out of the *News*, Hugo replied: 'I'm sorry, Tom. If a reporter spots it on the police charge-sheet, I can't keep it out of the paper. But that precinct has so many drug charges that the reporter could easily fail to take in your daughter's name. He mightn't even drop in at that precinct. All we can do is sit tight and hope he misses it.' Whatever aberrations there might be in Hugo's private life, his honour and integrity as a journalist were as important to him as food and water.

The night after Lisa had asked him to help her, he slept badly. An owl's cry woke him, but instead of feeling exalted by its poignancy, he found it melancholy. As usual in July, he was sleeping naked, the top sheet thrown back over the footboard of the bed. After he was woken a second time by the haunting cry, he got up and shut the windows and turned the air-conditioner on, pulling the sheet up over him. Once he woke from a disagreeable dream in which Lisa's same-size lips were involved, he was sure, and Ben Franwell was saying at a party on the *Aureole*: 'People say power corrupts, money corrupts. I'll tell you what corrupts: love.'

He woke in the morning not to the intense happiness of loving Lisa, but to a heavy feeling of reluctance to begin the day. He was glad the housekeeper didn't come on Thursdays. He didn't want her there when he went down to the kitchen to make coffee. His footsteps seemed slow and heavy to him, like those of a man going to his doom.

He opened the front door to collect the neatly trussed pile of newspapers waiting on the step. Upstairs in his study, he settled in his armchair and began the regular two hours of reading the papers, occasionally cutting out passages with a small knife. Automatically he wrote the date on each passage. Weeks might pass before he had any use for them.

When he went to the bathroom to shave, he looked stonily at the face in the mirror, wondering if he would look different. But his rather formal features with the straight brown hair brushed back, some of the front strands falling forward casually, looked the same.

Going downstairs to make more coffee, his footsteps were lighter.

And by the time he sat down at the larger of the two desks in his study, his adrenalin was going. He switched on the computer and screen. He felt his own surge of power as he rested his fingers on the keyboard. The piece was already three-quarters formed in his mind. The fourth quarter would only emerge as he distilled his thoughts on to the keyboard and screen.

When he reached his final sentence, he felt satisfaction. He had adopted his magisterial tone in the piece. First he rang alarm bells about the insidious danger to America of letting the lobbyists in their Gucci shoes direct American policy. Then he moved on to the BITE Secretary's approach to deals:

'When he throws his net outside his own country, any trade and industry secretary worth his salt will keep one eye on money and the other on politics. This week Ian Lonsdale is discovering firsthand which ventures with American industry could have political gains spreading far beyond economic benefits alone.

'Star Oil, for example, is bidding for one of the newly discovered fields near the Hebrides just above Northern Ireland. Even though Star Oil was cleared of any charge of manslaughter through negligence, it has not entirely thrown off the opprobrium of losing two oil rigs with an appalling loss of life. Now it has buttressed its bid for an exploration licence with a proposal to build a refinery in Ulster. Thus are trade and politics intertwined.

'For as IRA terrorism accelerates into ever more wanton bloodshed – a back-bench MP's wife murdered because her husband is against further government investment in Ulster – the BITE Secretary needs to demonstrate his own determination to have communal *rapprochement* with civilians trapped in Ulster's brutal factionalism.

'Star Oil has made a shrewd move. Its refinery proposal meets the very purpose for which BITE was in part created. The package on offer will be hard for the BITE Secretary to resist.'

Then Hugo went on to Ian's talks with the American government.

On finishing the piece, he went downstairs to collect the mail, returning with it to his study where he now sat down at his smaller desk, the mahogany Federal one which Georgie had given him. He opened and sorted out letters his secretary should handle, those he could deal with himself, others to be set aside to discuss with Georgie at the weekend.

When he returned to his large desk to polish his piece, he didn't even notice that in his ringing paragraphs denouncing the corruption of American government by lobbyists, the suspect congressmen he named did not include Senator Chalmers Morley. And Hugo had almost forgotten that the reason he was giving Star Oil a prime plug was because it was in Lisa's interest that he did so.

She had achieved what nobody else could: she had bought his integrity. Hugo had sold out – not to suck up to power politicians, and certainly not for money: he had sold out for love. He had proved Ben Franwell right.

23

At the end of Ian's two-day official visit to Pittsburgh
and Cleveland, the Lonsdales flew back to Washington in time for a round-up working dinner with the
British Ambassador and Fergus Lansbury. (Lady
Masters, who was suffering from a migraine, sent her
apologies.) Saturday morning the Ambassador's car
took the Lonsdales to the Eastern Shore. In the back
of the Rolls, Ian was reading *World*.

Georgie had indeed made sure Middle America
became aware of him. She gave four pages to British
trade and its effects on American industry and con-
sumers, with photographs which would attract both
lots. One of her talents was punctuating a heavy
business story with human interest for the general
public.

It was when he came to Norman Sharpton's
profile-interview that Ian pressed his lips. He couldn't
know that at the same moment, Michael O'Donovan
was reading *World* in his Washington apartment, and
when he came to the part Norman had got from him,
he smiled thinly.

Norman had 'angled' his piece on Ian's background remarks about Northern Ireland. He hadn't
strayed over the ethical border agreed: he did not
attribute anything said off the record. Instead,
Norman summarized Ian's views as though they were
his own speculation.

His piece began: 'Ian Lonsdale MP is from the mould of British politicians whose decisions in government have an underlying tension. Reason directs the pragmatic approach. But honour – *noblesse oblige* – pulls the other way.

'Rationally he might well observe that keeping British troops in Northern Ireland is doomed to fail in its purpose of averting bloodshed between Catholic and Protestant. Whatever the army does in Ulster plays into the IRA's hands. Young British wives are widowed to what purpose?

'Why then doesn't the BITE Secretary wash his hands of Northern Ireland and use his budget elsewhere? Welsh industries, for example, are crying out for government investment. Yet when it comes to the crunch, Mr Lonsdale is not prepared to stand aside while the people of Ulster are slaughtered by its opposing factions. Nor will he watch its economy crumble further when a decent case can be made for him to support industry in Ulster – always supposing he can find the money.

'Last week he announced he would invest in Belfast's only motor-cycle factory, thus ensuring the jobs of its three hundred Catholic workers. Far more jobs are at stake in the decision he must soon make on whether to accept Star Oil's bid for an offshore exploration licence for a field near the Hebrides. For it is understood that Star Oil is bolstering its bid with a proposal to invest in a refinery in Ulster – a prospect that will give no pleasure to Oklahoma Petroleum which also is bidding for an oilfield licence. If Mr Lonsdale turns down Star Oil's bid, this could be seen as a slap in the face to those trying to rebuild Ulster's shattered economy.

'The deep irony underlying his decision-making is that Ulster's Catholic workers, who stand to gain most from the creation of new jobs in Northern Ireland, have strong links with the IRA, who want to get Britain out of Ulster at whatever cost.'

Norman then went on to other aspects of Ian's job.

'Damn him,' Ian grumbled to Patsy. 'Everything he says is true, but I'm sorry he has blown it up so Americans will suppose BITE's only purpose is to defy the bloody IRA.'

The driver opened his window to pay the Bay Bridge toll. Instantly wet heat pervaded the Rolls. 'Crikey,' Patsy said. Five minutes later they reached the bridge's low crest and began the slow decline to the eastern side where the tidewater terrain lay flat before them, its monotonous skyline, fringed with poplars, uninterrupted as far as the eye could see.

Just after noon they drove between the two white-painted posts and followed the dirt road through the cornfield and past the farm buildings. When they came to the large wire pen, the Dobermans flung themselves at the mesh, barking ferociously, their ebony coats gleaming in the hard, white light of July's sun.

The car's wheels crunched on to the gravel forecourt where a station-wagon was parked. The front door of the house opened and Sarah came running out, followed by Georgie and Jamie.

'The thing is to wear as few clothes as possible,'

Georgie said in greeting as the sultry air pushed down on Patsy. 'And try not to get excited about anything, because it only makes you hotter. Come inside where it's relatively cool.'

The cavernous hall had been designed for duck-hunters to eat, drink and be merry before going off to the bedrooms in the wings of the house. A huge stone fireplace was at one end of the hall where sofas and armchairs, games tables, a big oak chest heaped with books and magazines, a writing-desk, all stood in comfortable informality. Another fireplace was at the opposite end where a refectory table stretched fifteen feet, Jacobean dining-chairs with worn tapestry seats along its sides. When Hugo bought Rycroft Lodge, he bought much of the furniture that the Rycrofts had used over the years. The hall was designed to be warm in the duck-shooting season and cool in the long summer months.

In the middle of the third wall were the glass double doors, now closed against the midday heat. Patsy looked through them past the quartz terrace to the faded grass running down to the wooden pier and the narrow river. Patches of the lawn were burnt brown from the sun. The river looked so motionless it could have been in limbo.

Off the hall was a bar-room, formerly the special delight of the duck-hunters. Here Hugo was making pre-lunch drinks with Sarah in charge of the ice. Georgie returned from checking up on the terrapin soup they would have for lunch. 'It looks like mud,' she said, accurately describing the Eastern Shore's most famous delicacy.

'The best part of terrapin soup is the eggs,' Sarah said. 'They look like orange marbles floating in the mud.'

'Would you like to see the turtles that aren't yet made into soup?' Jamie asked Patsy.

Sturdily built, he was shorter than some three-year-olds, and as he marched ahead of her, Patsy smiled to herself at the erect little figure. Halfway down the cellar steps she heard the harsh scraping.

'They're in the laundry tubs,' said Jamie.

Four old-fashioned laundry tubs were half-filled with diamondback terrapins the size of cannon-balls, clattering over each other's backs, somehow more primeval than any turtles Patsy had seen before. 'Daddy kills them with an axe,' said Jamie. 'Would you like to see the dogs later? I don't like the dogs but I don't mind showing them to you.'

Over the terrapin soup, Ian asked Georgie about *World*'s feature on British trade and industry. 'Thank you for putting me on America's map. But tell me: what is the great American fascination in whether an oil refinery is built in Ulster?'

'The same as the great American fascination with most Anglo-Irish difficulties,' replied Georgie. 'Sympathy for a minority who have a sentimental place in the American culture. Didn't you ever see any of those films with Spencer Tracy playing the noble Irish priest? And Noraid keeps adding fuel to the flames. Boston and New York may be the heartlands of Irish immigrants, but in other cities there's also a sense that the British have been shits in Ireland.'

'You said it,' said Hugo. 'At the University I had a

Catholic room-mate who was normally an intelligent guy. But whenever he got drunk, he'd say if he could have his way, he'd cut out the heart of every Englishman. All because of Ireland.' Hugo laughed at the ridiculous memory.

'Well, that Senator from Massachusetts who was interviewed by *World* gave a strong impression he wouldn't mind doing the same,' said Ian.

Hugo pulled a face. 'Actually, I was surprised, Georgie, that you wanted to give so much space to a thug like Rourke.'

'That's why you're not editor of *World*, Hugo,' Georgie replied tartly. 'I'm writing for the whole country, not just for a bunch of up-market readers who look to Saint Hugo to tell them what is right and proper to think.'

Ian caught Patsy's eye across the refectory table. She glanced at Hugo and saw the flush spreading up his suntanned cheeks.

'Who is this Senator Rourke? I read that piece too,' she said, anxious to get the conversation off its unexpected track. Georgie had meant her acid words to catch Hugo on the raw, and she'd succeeded.

'He's one of the people behind Noraid,' Hugo replied matter-of-factly. He regretted giving the Lonsdales a glimpse of the tension between him and Georgie. 'Rourke may have a helluva lot of constituents to consider besides those in the wards of South Boston, but he's still one of the Irish who can't escape their past – unlike the Kennedys, who've had nothing to do with Noraid. I bumped into him not long ago at one of Imogene's parties.'

Hugo stopped. For a moment he was totally distracted by the image of Lisa's silky hair skimming the eau-de-Nil silk shift she was wearing when he took her to Imogene's house. He forced himself to focus on what he was saying. 'Even in that setting,' he went on, 'Rourke was ranting about how your government encourages its representatives in Belfast to crap all over his family there. Of course he has to say publicly that he's against blowing up Brits: otherwise he might expose himself to a conspiracy indictment. But what else is Noraid in business for?'

Everyone was silent. Patsy visualized Anne Jolliffe going out to the car parked in Lord North Street and slamming the door. Ian visualized George Jolliffe when the police drove him back from the House of Commons to what lay in front of his home.

Sarah picked up the soup-plates one by one and carried them to the end of the long table where her mother ladled out more terrapin soup from an old Worcester china tureen. 'Make sure you give Patsy the eggs,' said Jamie.

Everyone concentrated on the terrapin soup.

Two pairs of bare feet rested atop the white linen counterpane. Georgie was propped against pillows on her side of the big double bed, Patsy against the pillows on Hugo's side. He had gone over to Pierce's place.

On each bedside table was a glass of iced tea, and a jug of tea with lemon slices floating in it stood in an open ice bucket on a chest of drawers. The windows had been closed against the heat since early morning, and the wooden shutters, bowed against the afternoon sun, made the room half dark. Hugo had been insistent that air-conditioning would spoil Rycroft Lodge; its purpose, for him, was to re-create the simpler life he associated with his Southern childhood.

'Is Ian proud of your success with your children's books?' asked Georgie. 'They'll catch on in America eventually. Publishers are like a bunch of sheep. Your style doesn't fit neatly into a category, so it worries them. Jerks.'

'Yes he is,' Patsy replied. She and Georgie had at once fallen into their old habit of knowing which comments required an answer. 'And having a career of my own means I bitch less about how much time he spends at his department and that stupid House of Commons.'

'You always were a great admirer of MPs,' Georgie said dryly, smiling.

'Actually, I have a lot of respect for some of them. It's the James Ardens among them – you don't know him, lucky you – who make me puke.'

'How well do you know the one whose wife was just blown up?'

'Not very.'

They sipped their tea.

'What did you think of my little exchange with Hugo at lunch?' asked Georgie.

'What was it about?'

Georgie didn't answer immediately. What *was* it about?

'I'm not sure,' she said. 'I suppose it could be

about nothing more than being married for over eight years.'

Patsy said nothing. She and Ian had been married even longer.

'But I think it has to do with our jobs,' Georgie said. 'We're doing entirely different things – he's a star newspaper columnist, I'm editor of a weekly – yet there's some sort of rivalry between us.'

'Does he mind that he was the famous one when you met, and now you're as famous as him? Even more famous, I imagine, with some people. I can't go anywhere without seeing somebody reading *World*.'

'He certainly minds sometimes,' said Georgie. 'When we got home from a dinner party last month, we had one of our worst dust-ups. He said I was a stuck-up pain in the ass. I said he was just jealous. I could sense he wanted to hit me.'

'Hugo?' Patsy was genuinely shocked.

'I know. Funny, isn't it? But of course he didn't. The Southern gent took control again.'

They sipped their tea.

'Why did you call him Saint Hugo?'

'I shouldn't have done. He made his reputation out of being honourable and gutsy. I love the way he doesn't put up with crap. But it grates when he goes pompous like that and patronizes me for being less noble than he is. I used that interview with Pat Rourke because it touches a chord with a lot of readers. I'm not running a church gazette, for Christ's sake.'

After a few minutes of silence, Georgie swung her legs off the bed, refilled their glasses and lay down again, propping herself comfortably once more against the pillows.

'What's it like for you and Hugo living in different cities during the week?' asked Patsy.

'You mean do we screw around? No. Not so far. At least, if Hugo does, it hasn't reached my ears. And I think I'd guess just from his manner. You know what Hugo's like. He wouldn't go in for having a bit on the side: it would have to be the whole hog. It would wreck our marriage. Essentially he's a romantic. He would confuse infatuation with "love".' She drawled the word to indicate the quotes.

'And you?'

'Me?' Georgie thought about the thing. 'I've always known the difference between the two. I want to stay married to Hugo. It's not just that I love him. I *like* Hugo more than I like anyone. I'm proud to be his wife. We're interested in the same things. It's good in bed – usually – and sometimes I think that could go on longer for the very reason that we don't see each other for days and nights on end. Anyhow, I've been so tied up with *World* that there hasn't been time for something on the side.'

They sipped their tea.

Then Georgie said: 'The funny thing is that lately the thought has come into my mind. I'm sure it has something to do with the fact that the guy is almost the opposite of Hugo.'

They gazed, half-seeing, at the shutters bowed across the windows.

'I'd seen him around for some time,' Georgie continued, 'but I've only lately got to know him better. I'm thinking about having a teeny weeny affair with him – just for the hell of it. You may have noticed him at the Ambassador's dinner party. He was the one who looked like a gangster.'

'You mean Jock Liddon? But he's coming for drinks this evening.'

'That's right. Hugo hasn't said so – he thinks it would make him sound snobbish – but he can't stand Jock. Shall I tell you why Jock asked me if he could come for drinks tonight? Because he wants to be able to say he knows you and Ian – not just that you were all at the same dinner at the British Embassy, but that he was with you at Hugo's and Georgie's place on the Eastern Shore. Jock has those coarse stumpy fingers – did you notice the manicure? – in God knows how many pies where the British Secretary for BITE's name would go down a treat. "Access" is what it's called in the trade.' She laughed. 'It's Jock's unconcealed vulgarity that appeals to me.'

Patsy laughed too. 'I can imagine that.' To lessen the heat on her neck, her hair was twisted up and fixed with two butterfly clips. She played abstractedly with a honey-coloured strand which had come loose. 'How well do you know that girl he's bringing?'

'Until the Ambassador's party, I'd met her only once. Here. She and Jock were staying with a congressman who happens to be a cousin of Hugo's. They all came over for a drink.'

'Is she Jock's girlfriend?'

'Depends what you mean by girlfriend. If you mean does she accommodate him when he's horny, I expect she does. But that's not the way to Jock's heart. What gets his heart pounding is deals. If Lisa can help him with deals, great. If she can't, she will mean no more to him than one of those rubber dolls.' Georgie wrinkled her nose in distaste. 'I suppose you could make a case that the world would be a happier place if each of us had a life-size rubber girlie or a life-size rubber bloke. All the same, it's not my idea of good sex.'

Patsy said: 'I don't know if Ian screws around. I think he doesn't. For one thing, I don't know when he'd find the time. But you never know. I had an anonymous telephone call from a woman not long ago. She wanted to know if Ian was home. It gave me a bad feeling.'

'Anonymous callers are the pits. They're pathetic. Don't ever let them have the satisfaction of knowing they can upset you. I'll bet she never clapped eyes on Ian except on TV. But if he actually did whore around once in awhile, would you mind terribly? So long as it was a private episode? Whores aren't a threat. Given the time Ian spent in women's beds before he married you, I can imagine him still getting the odd itch. Who cares?'

'I do.'

'OK, it would hurt your vanity. But it wouldn't mean any more to Ian than it does to Jock. Everyone knows Ian dotes on you, Patsy. It stands out a mile. He's different from Hugo: with Ian a quick fuck would be no more important than winning a set of squash. If it affected your life, Patsy, that would be another thing. But Ian would never let that happen.'

She turned her head and looked at Patsy.

Patsy smiled. 'You sound like Ian when he was telling me pre-marriage why he couldn't give a hundred per cent guarantee he would never wander. Perhaps you should have married Ian. Do you remember what you used to say: "You shouldn't let blokes control your feelings." I wish I could feel like that.'

'No you don't,' Georgie said. 'You know – and I know – that you have highs of emotion I've never experienced.' She gave a soft smile, different from her usual bright smiles. 'The other night we talked for only a minute about your father and mother. I've been waiting for a chance to ask you properly how they are.'

'The same. I guess they always will be – this amazing capacity to be a couple above all, and at the same time not exclude me. As for Sam and Nina, you'd think a god and goddess were coming for the weekend when they're waiting for their grandparents to arrive.'

'I think about them, more than you might imagine,' said Georgie. 'I always had this feeling they were one of the very few couples where the two individuals seem to make three.' She paused to sort out her thought. 'They seemed to have all the positives and negatives of true love. I knew I was incapable of ever having a relationship like theirs, but I didn't resent their having it. Seeing them together – even when physically they were in different rooms – always gave me a good feeling.'

'I dread the day when,' Patsy faltered and then chose the euphemism, 'something happens to one of them. I don't know how the other one could deal with it.'

They both were silent.

After a time Georgie said: 'You've put all your emotional eggs in one basket. I won't suffer the way you will if one day your basket gets a hole in it. But you've never wanted to be like me – detached. Have you?'

Patsy turned her head and looked at Georgie. 'Ask me when I'm feeling down,' she said. They both laughed.

Georgie sat up so she could see the clock on her dressing-table.

'Do you want a swim? The worst of the sun is over. Near the shore the river will be a bit like the terrapin soup. But it's reasonably cool when you swim out.'

'OK. What time are Jock and Miss Lilac Eyes coming?'

'Around six.'

'I'll tell you something, Georgie. I'm curious to meet Jock properly. But I've got bad vibes about her.'

'You shouldn't, you know. She has her head screwed on even tighter than mine is. She needs a lot of doors to open for her: access is all for the lobbyist. It's not in her interest to get in your bad books – let alone mine.'

'I hope you're right.'

24

The sun hung low and hazy in the big sky, and over
the terrace lay a sodden blanket of motionless air.
The three women wore skimpy dresses; even voile
trousers would have felt too close in the humidity.
Georgie took a white Chinese fan from a glass table
and rhythmically cooled her face. Jock noticed again
how her cropped black hair matched the gleaming
coats of her two attendants, her white dress in stark
contrast. Funny how you didn't get tired of her
trademark. Maybe because it suited her. A smart
broad.

'That was a good piece you ran on British trade,
Georgie,' he said. His gin-and-tonic stood on the
table beside him, hardly tasted. He remembered
Hugo's mint julep last time: there must have been
five shots of bourbon in it, and the sugar and mint
with the crushed ice made it slip down like nectar.
Even a strong head like Jock's wouldn't work its best
after one of those juleps. 'Your reporters must have
done a helluva lot of background work.'

Georgie's mouth went up at the corners. She liked
the brashness of his coded message which really said:
'I told you your reporter would get good information
from Michael O'Donovan: good for *World*, good for
J. D. Liddon International. I helped you; you helped
me.'

Jock didn't give a shit about Catholics' unemployment in Northern Ireland. That was one of Michael's hobby-horses, and as number two he was allowed to indulge it – so long as it didn't take the shine off Jock's interests. What mattered to him was *World*'s handling of Star Oil's bid. It had been all he could ask for.

He turned to Ian. 'What did you think of Georgie's handling of your trade and industry? Neat stuff about the political mileage for Britain if you decide to give Star Oil the go-ahead.'

Ian and Patsy were sipping their mint juleps slowly. Hugo had said to Patsy: 'It packs a wallop. But unlike martinis, juleps don't make people aggressive. The worst that will happen is you'll fall over. I'll catch you. And you're meant to be having a relaxed weekend off, after all.'

'I was flattered by Georgie's attention,' Ian replied to Jock. 'Personally, I'd have preferred less hearts and flowers about British troops in Ireland. But I can't accuse her reporter of misunderstanding what I told him as background. I was sorry, though, that he led his story with it.'

'Did you bring it up, or did Norman Sharpton?' asked Hugo. He was annoyed by Norman's interview. It had been more provocative than his own.

'He did. I was surprised,' Ian replied.

Lisa turned away from him and gazed at the dogs panting beside Georgie's bare brown legs. Georgie's hazel eyes had become inscrutable. Jock reached for his gin-and-tonic, took a swallow and returned the glass to the table. All three knew Michael O'Donovan had lunched with Norman Sharpton the day before his interview with Ian.

'And I was also surprised,' Ian went on, 'by this obsession with Star Oil. Both *World* and you, Hugo, seem to think Star Oil deserves that field on a gold platter. You almost brushed aside the small matter of two of their rigs going to the bottom of the sea, taking two hundred and forty men with them – not to mention the ones who were fried.'

Patsy glanced at Ian. 'You sound as if you're feeling persecuted,' she said amiably.

He laughed. Having got his grievance off his chest, he felt better. He took another sip of his julep. 'I don't know what you put in this thing, Hugo, but it makes up for the boredom of reading about Star Oil's wonderful intentions.'

Jock dug in a hip pocket. 'Do you think this time I'd better go down to the pier to smoke the weed, Georgie? The Lonsdales may think I'm polluting the patio.'

'I can live with it,' said Patsy, laughing.

'Toss me one,' Georgie said.

To Hugo's intense irritation, the scene that followed was virtually identical to the one which got under his skin the first time Jock came to Rycroft Lodge. Jock took a cigarette for himself and then drew back an arm to throw the pack to Georgie; the Dobermans leaped to their feet and pulled back their lips in open-jawed grins of excitement and menace, tail stubs quivering; Georgie said 'Stay,' reaching up to catch the pack sailing over the ebony heads. It was as if that bastard shared some sort of private joke with Georgie.

Abruptly Hugo got to his feet. 'Do you want to

walk down to the pier?' he said to Patsy and Lisa. 'At this time of day you can see the crabs and terrapins swimming up from the riverbed for their evening prowl.' He wanted some time alone with Lisa, but it would be too conspicuous.

At the edge of the terrace, as Patsy was untying the thongs around her ankles, Lisa kicked off her own sandals.

'*Come*,' shouted Hugo imperiously.

At once the Dobermans plunged across the terrace. With his fist closed, Hugo swept one arm forward in an arc as he shouted tautly: '*Go on*.' The dogs hurtled past and raced ahead towards the pier. They were beautiful, Patsy thought, but she could see why Jamie didn't like them.

On the terrace, Jock had already changed gear. No further mention of Star Oil would pass his lips this evening. The Minister was clearly ass-full of the subject.

'I wondered,' Jock said to him, 'if you'd be interested in doing a deal with an airline I have on my books. US Dawn. As you may know, it's a medium-size company operating from the east coast. It's thinking about a flight directly into Britain – at Gatwick Airport.'

'You should take it up with the Transport Secretary, not me,' said Ian.

Georgie was surprised Jock hadn't mugged up which British minister deals with airports.

'Yeah, yeah, I know about him,' said Jock. 'But I'm talking about an interdepartmental deal which would involve BITE. Your government isn't about to give US Dawn a slot at Gatwick without a comparable benefit for Britain. But why should Britain's compensation for the deal be restricted to an exchange of landing rights? Why not think laterally?'

Georgie glanced at Ian to see how he was taking this direct pitch. A trace of a smile was on his face.

'US Dawn,' Jock continued, 'buys one helluva lot of machine parts. For a coupla years Dawn has used a Tennessee ball-bearing firm for a load of its stuff. I've been asked to come up with an alternative supplier. When Michael O'Donovan and Lisa were last in Britain, they looked into the possibility of certain concessions if Dawn bought parts from a British firm.'

'I see.' Ian drawled the words in the English noncommittal-but-I-might-be-interested manner. 'The best thing would be for you to set it out in writing and send it to me at BITE.'

'Yeah.' Jock paused. Georgie waited. It was like watching a tennis player lob to buy time to get into a better position.

'There's another thing I had in mind,' Jock went on. 'You Brits are hard to match when it comes to electronics technology. I have a client who's thinking of placing a big *big* order for British computers' – he nodded solemnly in tribute to the bigness of the order – 'and you'll understand how at this stage he doesn't wanna commit himself to writing.'

Ian and Georgie watched him with shared curiosity about what he would come up with next. Jock might look like a thug kitted out in gents' weekend gear – Brooks Brothers shirt unbuttoned at the neck, seersuckers, sneakers, though Jock drew the line at wearing cruddy old sneakers: his were new, goddammit – but he was a clued-up thug. Ian had no problem getting the message: Jock was offering some millions of dollars for British exports in exchange for Ian putting in a good word for US Dawn to get a licence for landing rights at Gatwick Airport.

'There's no way I can raise an airport licence application with my Cabinet colleague at Transport if there's nothing in writing,' Ian said.

'Oh sure,' said Jock. 'That's no problem. I'll get Dawn's chairman to write whatever you need. We're having lunch together tomorrow. He's never heard that Sunday is the day of rest.'

Ian burst out laughing. Something about Jock's crude directness appealed to him. It made a change from English reticence.

'I'll get him to organize two things in writing,' Jock said. 'One will be Dawn's application for landing rights at Gatwick Airport. Two will be a letter of intent re Dawn buying ball-bearings from a British firm. Howzat?' Without waiting for an answer, he went on: 'But the cream on the cake can't be put in writing yet. That's the big *big* electronics order. I'm still working on that.' He tapped his black curls with a thick forefinger. Georgie could have watched the performance all evening.

Jock summed up: 'I get the three deals into a package – two on paper, one verbal. Michael O'Donovan or Lisa comes to London later in the week to present you with the package. You take it from there. Whaddaya think?'

Georgie felt the hairs on the back of her neck prickle. Only three hours earlier she had brushed aside Patsy's bad vibes about Lisa.

Ian sipped his julep.

Laughing as if it were a joke, Georgie said: 'Send Michael O'Donovan, Jock. We want the BITE Secretary to keep his mind on business.'

'Details, details,' said Jock, waving one square hand airily as if dismissing a fly. 'Is it OK then, Minister, if I call your office on Monday to make a date for one of my staff to bring you these proposals later in the week?'

Ian laughed. 'Can you get the package together by then?'

'No problem,' said Jock.

The wooden shutters were open and the curtains pulled back to allow night air to cool the room. Yet even after midnight the heat pressed down. Outside the grass was ghostlike under the full white moon, and twenty million crickets rubbed their wings together. Inside the bedroom was ghostlike too in the pale light coming through the windows, no lamps lit because they added to the heat. She was still dressed in her skimpy white voile, he in his shirt and seersuckers. Something about the way she stood facing him acted as a goad to him.

'At least your mother had the taste to shack up with someone who knew how to use a knife and fork,' he said.

'Please, Hugo, give me a break from all that Southern gentleman crap,' Georgie replied languidly. 'I am not, as it happens, shacking up with Jock Liddon. But if it ever appealed to me to do so, it would be because he has better things to do with his energy than fart around worrying about etiquette.'

'Etiquette!' he mimicked savagely. 'You use your brilliant, feared, powerful *World*' – he spat out the words – 'to give plugs to a pimp's shady deals. And you call that no more than a little lapse in etiquette. Does it ever occur to you, Georgie, that as an editor you're becoming a whore?'

'You're projecting again, Hugo.' She spoke in the manner of someone talking to a tiresome child, always guaranteed to enrage him.

'God I hate that pseudo-psychology crap,' he said. His light-blue eyes looked almost demonic in the moonlight. Somewhere in the back of his mind flickered the thought that she was right. He *was* 'projecting': he was accusing her of the very thing he himself had done to help Lisa.

It was Georgie's turn to mimic. 'Does it ever occur to you, Hugo, that in your high-toned manner you too gave Star Oil a boost? Does that mean you too are shacking up, to use your charming imagery, with Jock Liddon?'

He gave a harsh snort of disgust. She saw his fists clenched at his side. It was like that night earlier in the summer in the hall of the Georgetown house when she knew he wanted to hit her in her solar plexus.

'Or are you more interested in sucking up to one of his minions?' she said, standing there, challenging him. 'Lisa Tabor looked quite fetching this evening, I agree. I was sorry to see you look so sick when she left with Jock. I wonder what they're doing now?' she added sweetly.

He didn't hit her in the solar plexus. He drew his right arm back and drove it forward hard, his hand flat as it struck the side of her face. The blow knocked her off balance, so that she reeled back on to the window-sill.

The side of her face felt on fire. And she must have bruised herself when she hit the edge of the sill. She righted herself, and stood again facing him. Lifting one hand, she placed its fingertips gracefully on where it hurt most just above her jaw.

'Tch, tch, tch,' she said, like someone reproving a naughty boy. 'Hugo mustn't behave like white trash.'

He raised his arm again: he wanted to kill her. At the split second before the forward thrust, he checked the blow. He stood there looking at her from eyes that felt hard and dry. Then he dropped his arm to his side. 'If you will excuse me,' he said acidly, 'I'll sleep elsewhere.'

He turned and walked out of their bedroom.

When at last she was lying naked on their bed, one hand resting where her face throbbed, she wondered where he was sleeping. Presumably in the one unoccupied bedroom. She began to feel a small, grudging regret that she had provoked him to behave out of character. It demeaned both of them.

The unoccupied bedroom was long and narrow. Its single bed was at the window end. The moonlight coming in the open window made the room seem to

Hugo like a cell in another place, another time. He tossed his clothes on to an armchair, threw back the cotton counterpane and top sheet, and flung himself on the bed. As he lay on his back, arms and legs akimbo, the full moon shone on him. Could you actually feel moonlight? It seemed unlikely, yet he was sure he could feel it. One night when he was a child in Richmond, he had left his bedroom to go out and lie on the lawn where it was cooler. He had fallen asleep and woken to find himself in the arms of the black woman who was the mainstay of the household. She was carrying him into the house. Her voice was angry. 'Don' never you sleep in moonlight when the moon is full. Yo' aunt Celia when she a chile, full moon come an' shine on her. Thas why yo' aunt go crazy.'

The heat woke Patsy early Sunday morning. Ian lay in a deep sleep beside her. She lifted her damp hair off her neck, spreading it over the pillow. God it was bloody sweltering, and the day had hardly begun.

She slipped off the bed and put on shorts and a T-shirt. A French window opened directly on to the parched lawn. In her bare feet she padded across the coarse grass towards the narrow river. She had noticed last night that as well as the motor boat a rowboat was moored to the pier. The wooden boards of the pier were still cool. The opposite shore shimmered in the morning mist. Despite the heavy heat, she had an almost exalted feeling – one of those Wordsworth moments of being absorbed in the universe.

She climbed down into the rowboat whose oars were already in the oarlocks, and she unlooped the rope from the pier. She felt a deep happiness as she listened to the almost soundless splash of the oars. She thought of a childhood summer holiday when her father had taught her to row soundlessly, slipping the oars into the water at an angle which made no splash at all.

The sun, just risen above the horizon, was crimson. I am the sun, the sun is me, she thought, as she rowed unhurriedly, silently, past a strip of scrubby poplars which meandered down to the twisting river's shore strewn with broken clam shells. She could understand Hugo's love for the placidity of the Eastern Shore, the sense that it had been here a long, long time. Not even a restless bird intruded into the quietude stretching infinitely over the flat land.

The shrill barking and whining tore her from her reverie. She spun around on the board seat.

Between the two rows of unstirring poplars which bordered Rycroft Lodge and Pierce's place lay a triangular wheatfield parched nearly as light as the scarecrow in its midst. A man was standing in the uncut field, his back to Patsy. She recognized Hugo's tall slim build and straight brown hair. She looked to where he must be looking, where the two Dobermans barked frantically as they tore at the scarecrow, dressed in white, straw bulging from the tears in the cloth.

Quietly Patsy trailed one oar until the boat had turned around. She wasn't wanted in that triangular field of wheat.

Silently she rowed back the way she had come. The river twisted and the wheatfield disappeared behind the scrubby poplars. Looking up at the pale sky as she noiselessly dipped her oars in the water, she tried to get back her Wordsworth reverie, but something about the torn scarecrow had broken the spell. The morning air was no longer fresh. It tasted used and stale, as if it never stirred from this nearly still river.

25

Soon after lunch the British Embassy driver returned to pick up the Lonsdales for their flight back to London. Georgie and Patsy said nothing as they put their arms around each other.

'I hate goodbyes,' Georgie said to Ian.

Half an hour later, the station-wagon also pulled out of Rycroft Lodge's forecourt, Hugo at the wheel with Georgie beside him, Sarah and Jamie in the back. Conversation was strained during the hour and a half drive back to Washington. 'Is something the matter?' Sarah asked.

'I'm just rather tired,' Georgie replied. 'I slept badly last night.'

Hugo kept his eyes on tne road.

Only Georgie caught the last shuttle from National Airport to La Guardia. Sarah's nursery school had begun its summer holiday, and she and Jamie and the nanny were spending two weeks at the Georgetown house with Hugo.

Georgie liked flying in the commuter plane at night – looking down at the glistening sea, at dark, velvety forests, at the strings of fairy lights fanning from coastal towns. What was happening to her marriage?

She had egged Hugo on until he behaved like a thug. She had seen the cold hatred in his eyes. Had she, even when he hit her, hated him? Not really. She had wanted to pull him down in his own estimation. She didn't know why. Perhaps it had to do with being married. You know so well what the other person thinks, how the other person will respond, that you have to invent ways to produce the unexpected. Perhaps that's why she had made Hugo hit her.

She didn't want her marriage to end: she couldn't imagine life without Hugo, any more than she could imagine life without her children. Yet what she had made him do in their bedroom had changed things between them for ever. It cheapened things which had been central to their relationship. Before she had liked the idea of fidelity. She had liked the fact it was Hugo, and only Hugo, who gave her that extraordinary physical pleasure. Now sexual fidelity didn't seem that important.

She looked at the moon, still so full she wasn't sure it had begun to wane. Might God be out there after all? Certainly something out there had a trick up its sleeve you couldn't see in advance. For she hadn't foreseen the consequences of making Hugo hit her. Now she knew.

As the pain of her realization deepened, Georgie began automatically to detach herself. 'It doesn't matter,' she whispered as she looked at the white moon. 'It won't make any real difference. We'll still have all the other things in common that made our marriage good.'

By the time the lights of La Guardia appeared below, her pain was receding. At the same time she recognized a feeling inside her which she hadn't been aware of for a long while. She remembered the first time she'd noticed it, when she was parted from her father. 'It won't make any real difference,' she'd said to him, and she hadn't cried; she had stopped the pain. That's when she had first noticed what was the opposite to a real feeling, like a hole somewhere inside her.

Ordinarily conference at the start of the week was relaxed. This Monday it was tense. The proprietor had dropped in unexpectedly. Ralph Kernon enjoyed giving his employees little surprises. Hell, what was the point of being a publishing emperor if you couldn't catch these payroll smart-asses with their trousers down – or skirt up. Just because Georgie was queen of the press was no reason for her to get cocky. He sat on her right in the middle of one side of the conference table.

'OK,' the hoarse voice rapped out, his conversation taking its normal form of dialogue with himself, 'the British trade feature was A-1. There was something for everybody: the guy on his farm in Missouri, Mr Big in the chairman's seat at Oil Inc., east-coast Wasps whose eyes mist up when you talk of Britain, the consumer who in the end is what makes the world go round.' As everyone else at the table knew Kernon was oblivious having made a play on 'world', no one gave any sign of recognizing the pun. Kernon wasn't interested in word games. What mattered was making words pay. 'You even had something for the Irish. What the hell went wrong with the ads?'

As usual he'd allowed not even a token pause between praise and attack. Nor did his question expect answer or comment. He went straight on: 'Everybody on my payroll seems to think I don't notice these things. *Newsweek* had five more full-page ads than *World* did. Who do you think is paying for you to sit around this table?'

The hoarse voice abruptly stopped. Everyone looked at Georgie.

Beneath her light suntan, the colour had drained from her face. Only her hazel eyes showed any expression; her deputy thought of a lion's eyes. She turned to look directly at Kernon.

'I pay the others at this table – because I think they're doing their jobs better than anyone else could.' Her voice showed no emotion. 'You pay me. It's for you to say whether someone else could do my job better.'

Kernon looked at her steadily. 'Hurm.'

'You want the ads to put up the profits,' said Georgie. 'So do we all. The previous three weeks, *World* led the field in advertising revenue. It would be courteous if you mentioned those weeks as well as the last one when we let you down.'

'Hurm.'

For half a minute no one spoke. Then, without transition, Kernon said: 'Editors think death is a turn-off. I think they're wrong. A lot of people in Middle America are right this minute wondering whether they'll be allowed to meet their maker when they want to. I'll tell you what they're saying: "I don't want to be like that Karen Whatsit. If I turn into a goddamn vegetable, I don't want to stick around." OK, you got LA with people arranging for their heads to be frozen for the next coming. But that's LA. Most *World* readers want to be buried with their heads on. How about doing a big feature on that, Georgie?'

Georgie put her hands either side of her bobbed hair. 'Just checking it's there,' she said, smiling. She turned to the head of advertising: 'You could even give an alert to the undertakers that they might want to take out full-page ads that week.'

The deputy editor's mouth twitched at one corner, but the rest of Georgie's staff remained poker-face. At the best of times, Kernon's sense of humour was not one of his conspicuous traits.

After Kernon left the building, Georgie phoned through to the head of advertising: 'You'd better come in.'

A minute later he was in her office.

'What *did* happen last week?' she said sharply.

He explained.

'Well, this week I expect us to have more ads than *Newsweek*. How you manage that is your concern.'

She picked up a file on her desk and opened it to start the next thing on her agenda. The head of advertising turned around and left her room. She never looked up. He would have preferred it if she had told him off. When Georgie gave you the freeze treatment, it was the pits.

Twenty minutes later her secretary rang through to ask if she wanted to take a call from Jock Liddon.

'We haven't met for at least thirty-six hours,' said

Jock. 'What about having dinner one night? So long as we can have it in air-conditioned Manhattan. You got a nice place on that Eastern Shore, but I can't sweat through my tongue like those Baskervilles of yours. I gotta have twenty degrees less heat if I'm to concentrate right. And I got some things you might be interested in.'

'Personally or professionally?' she said archly.

Jock grunted and undid his fly.

'I meant the second,' he said, slipping his hand in his trousers, 'but now that you mention it, I'll try to come up with something that would interest you personally as well. Whaddaya say?'

Georgie laughed and said: 'I'm free for dinner next Monday.'

Her driver had the Buick's door open for her when she left the building soon after six. She'd allowed time to go back to the apartment to have a bath before setting out for the Mayor's dinner at Gracie Mansion for Barbara Walters. She looked unseeing at the rush-hour traffic, wishing Hugo was going to be at the apartment when she got there. It was one thing for him to be in Washington when everything was going right in New York. It was another thing when she was worried about her job. Ralph Kernon had dented her confidence. With everyone except Hugo and Patsy, Georgie kept up a front. With Hugo she could admit she'd been shaken by Kernon. Though he'd seemed friendly enough at the end, he had hired her fast, and he could fire her fast. Once she told Hugo, the fear would be exorcized, and she'd be confident again.

And telling him about Kernon would be a way of breaking the ice. Whatever had happened in their bedroom on Saturday night, she wanted to restore some sort of relations with Hugo, even though they wouldn't be like before. In forty-eight hours she had recovered, at least in part, from a hurt which would have shattered Patsy for a lifetime. As soon as she got back to her apartment, she would call Hugo.

Sarah answered the phone at the Georgetown house. 'Daddy said he had to work late this evening,' she told Georgie, 'but I'll leave him a message saying you called.'

Much later that evening when Hugo got home and saw Sarah's message, he looked at his watch. It was past midnight. Georgie would be asleep.

He was glad of an excuse not to return her call: only twenty minutes earlier he had dropped Lisa at the group house in Cleveland Park. He preferred to go to bed tonight thinking about the day he and Lisa had just shared at Rycroft Lodge. Crumpling the message, he threw it in the waste-basket.

26

He had taken off the whole of Monday. As soon as he'd put Georgie on the Sunday evening shuttle, he realized he was desperate to phone Lisa. He had to return to Rycroft Lodge with Lisa: he had to exorcize the brute ugliness which had burst from his core on Saturday night. He was deeply ashamed of what he had done in the bedroom. He resented Georgie for inflaming a part of his nature which he didn't want to recognize. He felt only Lisa's innocence could cleanse and wash away the memory and make Rycroft Lodge unspoiled again.

She had left a message for Dawn to pick up on the office answering machine first thing in the morning: 'I will not be in the office Monday as I have an important job outside Washington. I'll be in at 7.30 Tuesday morning to check there's nothing else to go to London.' She wasn't worried her absence might irritate Jock: after his Sunday work lunch with the chairman of US Dawn, Jock had met Lisa at his office and together they had gone through the proposals she was to take to London on Tuesday. Apart from Jock and Michael O'Donovan, Lisa was the only person who already knew she alone would be presenting the package of deals to BITE.

When Hugo arrived at the group house just before nine, she was sitting on the front steps, wearing sandals, her tanned legs crossed casually. Her hair was in bunches, held with lime-green ribbons matching her T-shirt and skirt. He had said she might want sneakers to walk through the field, and they were in a bag beside her. She looked like a schoolgirl.

When the car reached the crest of the Bay Bridge and the calm terrain spread before them, Hugo took one hand off the wheel and put it over Lisa's hand. 'When I first see it, I always have the feeling I'm coming home,' he said. 'My uncle had a shooting-lodge on the Eastern Shore. I can still remember the excitement of driving up from Richmond and beginning that long ascent of the bridge – and then starting down this side.'

Just after 10.30 he drove between the two white-painted posts. 'My uncle's lodge was not much different from Rycroft Lodge,' Hugo said as again he put his hand over the schoolgirl hand.

The dirt road was powdery from the sun, and even this early in the day the station-wagon raised dry clouds as it wound past the cornfield. When it approached the pen, the Dobermans flung themselves against the wire. Hugo opened his window: 'I'll see you two later,' he called to them. 'When we're not here,' he said to Lisa, 'Pierce takes the dogs over to his place. He has a pen there. I told him to bring them back for today. We can take them out later.'

He pulled up in front of the house, and they jumped out into the heavy heat. From the back of the car he took the hamper that had been waiting when he called in at the Willard before picking up Lisa. They stepped from the still, sultry air into the cool, darkened house. Only the glass double doors were unshuttered, and from across the big room Lisa could look straight out to the terrace where they all had sat only two days before. Hugo carried the hamper out to the kitchen, and together they unpacked it.

'What's that noise?' Lisa asked.

Hugo burst out laughing with the joy of having her alone with him in his domain. 'I'll show you,' he said, leading the way down the stairs to the cellar where the terrapins in the laundry tubs sounded like armour crashing against armour as they climbed over one another's backs.

'How long do you keep them there?' she asked.

'Until we're ready to cook them. Pierce comes in and feeds them during the week. Sometimes I kill them. Most of the time Pierce does. His wife cooks them, and then puts the jars of soup in the freezer.' He was amused by Lisa's concerned face staring fascinated as the giant diamondbacks clattered over each other. 'They rarely stay in the tubs for more than a week or two after they've been caught,' he reassured her as they went back upstairs. 'I'll take them some meat later. I told Pierce I wanted some peace and quiet, so neither he nor his wife will be coming in. Would you like to go down to the river and swim before it gets too hot?'

'Yes,' Lisa said. The pale gold hair tied in bunches made Hugo's heart move with tenderness as well as desire.

'Come put your things in my room,' he said, not noticing how he referred to the bedroom he shared with his wife.

Its shutters bowed, the darkened room was almost cool. He glanced at the double bed waiting beneath its snow-white counterpane. Lisa walked past him and into the bathroom, closing the door behind her. No one understood better the importance to Hugo of her shy innocence. It would be inappropriate, this first time in Georgie's bedroom, to behave too casually, let alone proprietorially. In the bathroom, she slipped out of her clothes. Climbing into a tank suit cut in a chic parody of a schoolgirl's navy-blue bathing suit, she looked at herself in the plate-glass mirror over the tub. She untied the two ribbons which held her hair back in bunches, and it tumbled on to her shoulders. She smiled at her reflection.

Opening the bathroom door, she saw Hugo too had retained a sense of decorum in the setting of his marital bedroom: he had changed into his swimming-trunks in her absence, his shirt and seersuckers laid over the back of an armchair. 'Shall I take one of the towels from the bathroom?' she asked.

For a moment he didn't answer, instead savouring the pleasure of seeing his golden-skinned nymph standing gracefully in her modesty. No need to rush: time was theirs today. 'Bring one for each of us. And bring your sneakers. You'll want them in the wheat-field. We can exercise the dogs before it gets too hot.'

Under its top dust, the dirt road felt hard under their bare feet as they walked back to the pen where the barking grew more clamorous. Hugo's proprietorial satisfaction swelled. He wanted to show Lisa everything at Rycroft Lodge. Washington power politics were far far away. He wanted her to see this other part of him, the man who loved the tidewater country with its cornfields and wheatfields, and poplars going down to the unhurried river. He would return here with her when the duck season opened, and he would show her his skill in bringing down the mallards. For now, he would show her his skill in handling dogs who, in lesser hands, could turn into killers.

'Wait here,' he said to her, unlocking the pen. '*Down*,' he said curtly to the leaping Dobermans as he stepped through the gate and closed it behind him. Reluctantly they settled on to their wide haunches, cropped tails quivering, lips pulled back in something like a grin, yammering as they waited to be released into activity. From a peg he took down the two thick, black plaited leashes and fastened one to each studded collar. 'All right,' he said, and they bounded to their feet, straining at the leashes. 'I'll let them run free after they've got used to you,' he told Lisa when they started back up the dirt road to the forecourt.

On the other side of the house, the parched grass was pleasantly rough against their bare feet as they walked down to the lawn's edge where the pier began, its first posts sunk in the strip of sand, other posts visible through water not yet muddied. They could see the clam and oyster shells carpeting the riverbed. Hugo picked up two large half-shells, bleached nearly white. 'You'll cut your feet if you wade out,' he said to Lisa as he unfastened the leashes. 'Stay,' he commanded the dogs.

Following him, Lisa climbed on to the pier, its

boards hot but not yet blistering as they'd be in another hour, her navy tank suit already darkened by sweat. Hugo stood at the edge of the pier and drew back one arm. On the strip of sand below, the dogs whined, their ears pricked. He flung the shells in a high arc over the lawn, and the two blunt black muzzles followed the arc. '*Get it!*' he shouted. The powerful hind legs thrust forward, and the Dobermans leaped on to the lawn and raced for their quarry, each snapping up a white shell and tossing it in the air, seizing it and tossing it again.

'Come on,' Hugo shouted. Each dog bore a white shell back to the pier where they clambered up the steps, their shining talons skittering over the wood. Hugo took the shells and stroked the panting muzzles. Then he swept one arm in a long curve towards the poplar trees bordering the lawn. 'Go on,' he said amiably. The dogs bounded over the narrow strip of sand and raced towards the poplars.

'How do you know they won't run away?' asked Lisa.

'They've been trained not to go beyond the boundaries of my place or Pierce's place – except when one of us is with them. Unless I call for them to come back, we'll probably find them in the wheatfield just beyond those poplars.'

He turned and walked towards the other end of the pier, passing the rowboat moored half way, and dived into the river. Watching his lean body flash through the air and then disappear, Lisa waited for him to surface. Treading water, he threw back his head and with one hand brushed the straight brown hair out of his eyes, laughing. She looked at him with pleasure. A man's physique was not one of her priorities. All the same it was nice when as well as possessing the things she valued – influence, access to worlds she couldn't reach on her own – he was as good-looking as Hugo: it was like a bonus. She dived into the river.

Fifteen minutes later when they climbed out again, she said: 'Before it's too hot, I wish you'd take me on a tour in the rowboat.'

'I'll get out the motor boat.'

'I'd rather go in the rowboat. It's quieter. I'm hoping to see some of those ducks contentedly growing up without any idea that come the fall, they're doomed.'

He reached out a hand and ran his finger gently down her throat where water from her hair trickled to her breasts. 'Unlike the ducks, we have all the time in the world,' he said.

Pulling the oars in the slow-running tide was effortless, yet sweat poured down his body as the white sun mounted in the sky. Already Lisa's hair was nearly dry, but its tips grew wet afresh where they rested against her throat gleaming with sweat. The shore opposite shimmered in the mist.

He didn't want to row as far as Pierce's place. Pierce and his wife were close-mouthed, and Hugo had not specified whether he was coming alone or with friends. Even so, why invite comment? He would go only as far as the uncut wheatfield between the two strips of poplars.

When they neared the first scrubby trees two ducks

rose, quacking irritably. Lisa watched with delight as, wings flapping unhurriedly, they crossed over the narrow river. Once past the first wood, Hugo dragged the oars and the boat moved towards the shore. She heard the high-pitched barking and whining.

'You'll want something on your feet,' he said.

The sneakers stuck to her skin as she struggled to pull them on. Finally she jumped out of the boat on to the shell-strewn sand. Together she and Hugo walked towards the middle of the field where the dogs were savaging the scarecrow, pouncing on it, snatching away more cloth and straw, racing twenty yards and then circling and catapulting back to tear at it again.

Hugo gave a sharp whistle. The dogs relinquished their prey, their eyes bulging, shoulder muscles rippling, straw still in the jaws of one, a strip of white cloth in the jaws of the other.

As he and Lisa approached them, he called out a command. Lisa noticed the metallic edge in his voice. Whining, the Dobermans lowered their sweat-streaked haunches. When the only sound was their panting, Hugo swept one arm in a large curve. 'Go on!' They leaped up and raced back to the scrubby poplars bordering Rycroft Lodge.

Soaked as she was with sweat, Lisa shivered. She sensed the same thing Patsy had: something about the scarecrow, its straw bulging from the tears in the white cloth, gave her a deep unease. It made her aware of her own frailty.

Yet Lisa could not permit frailty in herself. She shook off the feeling.

27

'M. O'Donovan.' In his small neat handwriting, Michael had signed across each seal on the thick envelope. 'Keep it with your hand luggage,' he told Lisa. 'When you get to Claridge's, ask for the manager. He knows it's coming. That's the end of your responsibility for it. Someone will pick it up from him.' The envelope was one of those outsize strong ones which lawyers use for documents, though it felt bulkier than most documents. It was addressed in the same meticulous handwriting: 'To be collected and signed for by M. Halloran.'

Only late on Monday, or so he had told Senator Chalmers Morley, had Michael discovered he'd have to bow out from accompanying the Senator and Lisa on the flight to London. 'If the truth be known, my dear,' said Senator Morley, reaching over to Lisa's seat and giving an avuncular pat to her knee, 'I have always shared the view that two is company, three's a crowd.'

Her role as companion and coordinator of the Senator's three days of discreet lobbying meant J. D. Liddon International had to elevate her own travel status: this time she went Concorde. She welcomed the roar of the engines: the Senator wouldn't expect her to converse for the next few hours. She needn't have worried. After he had enjoyed three tumblers of Old Turkey in rapid succession, he reached into his hip-pocket and took out the little curved Georgian silver box which Helen had found in the Burlington Arcade in Piccadilly. Helen was always trying to encourage him to use saccharin in his coffee. A pity she couldn't be with him on this trip, but Jock had drawn the line there. Patting his midriff with the pride of a middle-aged man who has kept a paunch at bay, the Senator took two small white tablets of percodan from the pretty box and slipped them under his tongue. He always found bourbon combined with a couple of opium-based downers made air travel positively agreeable. When Lisa glanced in his direction not long afterwards, he was in a happy dream of his own.

This time she didn't need the taxi-driver to identify the Natural History Museum or the Victoria and Albert. The evening rush-hour traffic was over, and it was not quite nine when they turned off Park Lane into Upper Brook Street, passed the American Embassy with marines flanking its north door, crossed Grosvenor Square, and pulled up at the awning outside Claridge's. The doorman in his top hat and Parker Ink navy-blue overcoat stepped forward to open the taxi door.

'Good evening, my good man,' Senator Morley said grandiloquently, as Lisa gave instructions for their luggage.

While she did the checking-in, the Senator surveyed the mostly empty plush armchairs at the back of the lobby, like a noble statesman expecting to find friends and admirers wherever he travelled. The concierge handed Lisa a message left a few hours earlier: 'James Arden MP will ring at 10 pm to confirm arrangements.'

'I'd like to speak with the manager,' Lisa said. 'He's expecting me to leave a letter with him.'

'He won't return until 9.30, madam. Would you care to leave the letter with me?'

'No thank you. Could you have him phone my room as soon as he comes back?'

Her room was on the third floor, the Senator's on the fourth. 'After I've talked with James Arden, I'll phone you,' she said when the lift door opened at her floor, 'and we can take it from there.' Senator Morley raised one of her hands to his lips in a courtly kiss as his porter impassively held the lift door open.

When her own porter had left room 313, closing the door behind him, Lisa took out the documents she was carrying and put them on the writing-table. Two of the three deals which Jock had raised with Ian at Rycroft Lodge were now set out formally in a smart red file. Beside it she laid the bulky sealed envelope addressed in Michael's handwriting to M. Halloran.

Lisa crossed to the windows which looked across Brook's Mews: one fat pigeon sat stolidly on the cornice opposite, enjoying the last of the long day's twilight. She turned around and surveyed the handsome room: it was a long way from hicksville. Fastidiously she unpacked her bags, hanging up her suits and shirts, putting everything else away in drawers. Not only was she naturally orderly: she wanted to have a sense of being able to live at Claridge's for ever.

And there was another, almost subconscious, thought: it was second nature to Lisa to keep her options open, and you never knew when someone might be coming back with you to your room unexpectedly; you didn't want him to find you'd turned the place into a pigsty.

Just after 9.30 the manager rang, and Lisa took the sealed envelope to the lobby to hand it directly to him.

Back in her room she kicked off her shoes and gave a little dance across the carpet, watching her reflection in the big mirror above the dressing-table. It was half a dance of triumph, half a dance of seduction. When she looked out the window again the pigeon had gone and night was closing in. Her phone rang.

A plummy voice said: 'James Arden here. To quote one of our better known playwrights: Welcome to this scepter'd isle, this happy breed of men, this teeming womb of royal kings. Haw haw. Even I can't improve on the Bard.'

Only when he got down to business was Arden's competence evident. He had arranged nothing for Wednesday morning so the Senator's inner clock could adjust, but starting at 12.30 a tight schedule for the next three days began. Morley was to lunch or give dinner to two or three carefully chosen MPs, an ex-Cabinet minister, a senior Party adviser, a member of the Number Ten think-tank. He was to dine at the House of Lords with a senior Government supporter, call on the managing director of British Refineries, and have talks with senior officials at BITE.

At these meetings, the Senator would be accompanied by Arden or Lisa who could supply any factual detail required on Star Oil's proposals. There was no need to remind the Senator he had to earn the various 'comforts' that Star Oil was providing. Like Arden, when Morley applied himself he was an effective advocate.

'I shall give you the full schedule when you and I meet for pre-dinner drinks tomorrow in the Harcourt Room at the Commons,' Arden continued, 'but here are the details you'll want now.' As Lisa scribbled on a large notepad, he said: 'Make sure, my dear, that Senator Morley gets to the House of Commons by 12.30 tomorrow. He should come to St Stephen's Entrance. I'll be waiting for him in the Central Lobby. While he and I are lunching a senior figure on the 1922 Committee, you, my dear, will be employed in even greater things.'

Arden waited a moment so his information would sink in at once: 'You and the BITE Secretary are scheduled to meet for lunch at one o'clock.'

Instantly Lisa felt her heart pumping. A steel band seemed to tighten around her head as her excitement mounted, yet coolly she said: 'I thought Michael and I had been scheduled to call on Ian Lonsdale at his department tomorrow afternoon.'

'You were, you were. Then late yesterday Michael telephoned the private office at BITE to say he was held up in Washington and you would be coming to BITE alone with Jock's package of proposals. Lo, I then received a message to ring the private office.'

Again Arden paused. Like most politicians, he

relished dramatic effect and held a high opinion of his talents in that direction.

'The Minister had decided, his private office informed me, to rearrange part of his schedule for tomorrow. Instead of having a working lunch at his desk as he'd intended, he thought it made better sense to meet with you over lunch: that would give more time to discuss the deals you'll be presenting. I understand from Michael that only two deals are on paper, and the third is verbal. I booked a table for two in Claridge's restaurant in your name. Much will rest on your lissom shoulders, my dear. Indeed. Indeed.'

When the conversation with Arden had ended, Lisa rang through to the front desk: how long must be allowed for a taxi to reach the House of Commons at 12.25? Next she rang Senator Morley's room to advise him to be ready to leave the front door of the hotel the next day at 12.05 sharp. Then she rang the restaurant to confirm her table for two: 'As I'll be having a confidential business discussion with the BITE Secretary, can you make sure we're not too close to other tables?' She was almost a hundred per cent certain James Arden would have let the restaurant manager know she would be giving lunch to the Minister, but she was taking no chances on getting anything less than the best.

Lying in the long bath, she studied her reflection in the mirror on the surrounding wall. Her straight hair fell loose, and its tips lay wet on her shoulders. As she would wash it in the morning, she didn't care that the bath oil got on it. She slipped down still deeper in the tub so that her hair floated alongside her face and only her nipples protruded from the water. After a while she moved up higher again so she could see all of her breasts in the mirrored wall. She remembered Hugo's delight when he first saw her breasts in the Sheraton mirror at the Georgetown house. The thought that Ian Lonsdale might soon be looking at them made her laugh out loud with excitement.

At exactly five minutes past noon on Wednesday, Lisa saw Senator Morley out to the taxi summoned by the doorman. Then she returned to her room. She was so revved-up she was certain she could actually feel the adrenalin surging through her. Once more she picked up the red file and carried it to a chair by the window. Three plump pigeons occupied the cornice across Brook's Mews. For half an hour Lisa restudied the pages in the file, occasionally glancing at her moon-faced platinum watch, rehearsing out loud some of the arguments she would put to the Minister. The reciprocal trade proposal – Jock's big *big* electronics order – was the one not committed to paper except for its working title.

When the lapis lazuli hands of her watch moved to 12.45, she closed the file and went into her bathroom. Ten minutes later she smiled at the unquestionably enchanting figure in the lift mirror, the simple, navy-blue linen double-breasted suit which might or might not have a blouse underneath, the red file held under one arm, the blonde hair pulled back with two tortoiseshell combs to emphasize that this was a businesswoman, and yet a sexiness pervading the image. She stepped out into the lobby with four minutes to spare and seated herself near the reception desk.

Just after one o'clock he walked in. Again Lisa wondered why the slight limp made him even more attractive. Under the flat gaze of flunkies in their blue livery she got up, her file under one arm, and went forward to meet him.

What happened next had a dreamlike character for Lisa, for Ian the pleasures of the chase. He was confident his decisions on the new trade deals which Jock was offering would be unaffected by a flirtation with the messenger. For 'flirtation' was how Ian saw his desire to get Lisa into bed. There was no question of a 'relationship'. She was here today, gone tomorrow, though with luck, she might return to London from time to time. But that was not what Ian dignified with the term 'relationship'. She was an exceedingly attractive young career woman who knew what she was about. Unlike Hugo, Ian had no misconceptions about Lisa being a vulnerable innocent.

Ian wasn't interested in the sexual conquest of innocents. What he liked was the game and the risk. But he wasn't a fool: had he imagined Maureen was even a fraction the danger she'd turned out to be, he would never have touched her. Now, when he and Lisa first sat down at their table amidst the candyfloss-pink pillars and mirrored walls of the restaurant, they talked about their recent meetings at the British Embassy in Washington and Rycroft Lodge. He tried a little probing about Jock, about Hugo's and

Georgie's marriage, even about Michael O'Donovan whose reserved intelligence and narrow face had imprinted themselves on Ian that Sunday when O'Donovan – and Lisa – had been brought to Pig Farm by James Arden. Lisa responded with amusing anecdotes and sharp observations about all four, but Ian found he learned nothing about any of them that he didn't already know. He liked that. She was discreet. Nor did it surprise him: he had guessed that inside that pretty head was a tough mind.

'Do you hate talking shop while you eat?' she asked after their salmon *feuilleté* was set before them.

'Not when you're the person across the counter,' he replied.

He was keenly interested in the contents of that red file she now laid alongside her plate: it involved millions of dollars for British exports. He looked forward to seeing how she handled her argument. If J. D. Liddon entrusted the US Dawn airline reciprocal deals to Lisa, Ian knew she had to be both competent and skilful.

He was not disappointed in either expectation.

As they hadn't wanted a second course, it was only two o'clock when they started their coffee. 'Right,' he said to Lisa, signalling that business talk was to be closed. 'Thank you very much. I have no further questions. Have you?'

'Not for the moment,' she replied. She shut the file and handed it to him: 'You'll take this with you.'

Neither of them said anything further as they drank their coffee, but Ian's eyes watched her with that particular, intent concentration of sexual lust. As she signed for the bill he said: 'Actually, I do have another question, perhaps two. What's your room like?'

The lilac eyes revealed no emotion. 'It's nice. I have varying numbers of plump neighbours perched on the roof opposite my window, cleaning their feathers.'

'Question two then: would you regard it as an unpleasant intrusion if I invited myself to your room? Normally this wouldn't occur to me after a working lunch. But ever since you walked up the steps at Pig Farm, with those ribbons looped twice around your ankles, I've dreamed of undoing the ribbons – or whatever else you happened to be wearing.'

Lisa tilted her face to one side very slightly as she looked at him. Slowly the corners of her mouth turned up.

In the lobby he said: 'You go ahead. I'll make a telephone call and then come up. What's your room number?' Neither of them needed to spell out that he didn't want to risk being seen going up in the lift with her.

Killing time, he strode along to the men's room. From where she sat in one of the comfortable plush armchairs at the back of the lobby, Maureen Halloran noted the slight limp and smiled dryly. Dressed in a dark tailored suit, she could have been any guest reading a newspaper while waiting for some appointment or other. The sealed envelope she had collected from the manager was not in sight: she had put it in the small satchel beside her.

Five minutes later Ian reappeared and crossed the lobby to the lift. When its doors closed behind him, Maureen looked at her watch: 2.15.

'I love the way you make love,' she said as she moved from on top of him and lay beside him. He opened his eyes and turned his face to hers, reaching over to touch the pale gold hair which had been hanging above him before and now was spread loose on the pillow.

'May I return the compliment, lovely Lisa?' he said with self-mocking courtliness, slipping an arm beneath her. Both of them gazed over the foot of the bed to the window and the two pigeons beyond, tilting and retilting their heads as they sunned themselves on the cornice.

After a few minutes Lisa said: 'Does lying here with me in your arms make you more or less interested in J. D. Liddon's proposals?'

'Which one? His interest in what I decide about Star Oil or the distinctly attractive sweeteners he has sent in that red file?'

'Both,' she replied. 'But if you asked me which were the more important to J. D. Liddon – and therefore to me – I'd have to say Star Oil's application for that field.' She paused. 'Does it have a chance?'

Ian burst out laughing and kissed her lightly. 'Wherever I went in America I found myself pursued by people whose greatest interest seemed to be Star Oil. Now I find myself in the bed of an enchantress at Claridge's, and what are we discussing? Star Oil.'

Drawing out his arm from under her, he propped

himself on an elbow and looked down into her face. 'It's a tough decision to make. Which are more delectable? The lilac eyes or those lips the same size?'

Lisa said nothing.

Then Ian said: 'The bidding for the licence arrangements will close on Friday. I'll want to get the bloody thing decided and over with before Parliament rises for the summer recess. I can't tell you how it will come out. But it would give me much pleasure if it turned out to be what you want. That's not the answer you had hoped for, I know. But it's the best I can give you.'

When he had stripped off his clothes earlier, he'd put his watch on her dressing-table. Now he rested his arm on her breasts while he reached for her wrist and turned it so he could read her watch: 3.05. 'I must go, lovely Lisa.'

'We're not flying back to Washington until Saturday,' she said. 'Will I see you again before I go?'

Ian's hesitation was scarcely perceptible. Then he replied: 'I like to keep Thursday lunches free: one's never certain when Cabinet will end. But with luck I could be away from Number Ten before one o'clock.'

'What do you think?' Lisa asked, reaching up with one hand to let her fingertips rest on his face.

'It would give me a chance to reach a decision between the lilac eyes and the same-size lips,' he said, laughing as he stroked both lips before getting off the bed. 'But it would also mean your having to be somewhere I could ring you after Cabinet. I thought you had to be the Senator's minder.'

'I do. But James Arden is looking after him at a Commons lunch this very minute. James could probably also manage tomorrow's lunch without me. I could leave you a message first thing tomorrow morning to confirm it, but why don't we plan on my getting back to this room by 12.30?'

Again Ian's hesitation was only fractional. 'Let me give you my secretary's number at the House of Commons. It's best to leave personal messages there. If you say lunch is on for you, then I'll ring you here as soon as Cabinet is over – and tell you I'm on my way. You might even feel like ordering lunch from room service. A picnic with Lisa in room 313 has a distinct charm.'

In the armchair at the back of the lobby, Maureen was still reading her newspaper when the lift door opened at 3.20. She watched Ian as he crossed the lobby and stepped out the front door of Claridge's. Ten minutes later she laid her newspaper aside, picked up the small satchel and went out the same door into Brook Street. She walked up to Bond Street before hailing a taxi and directing the driver to take her to Stag Place. By the time she reached her flat, it would be eleven in the morning in Washington: she should be able to reach Michael in his office.

When the regular telephone rang in the study just after 10.30 that night, Ian asked Patsy if she'd mind dealing with it. He had just got back from the House. Contentedly she crossed the room and picked up the phone. 'Hullo?'

'Is Ian there?'

Patsy recognized the soft lilt.

'He's just got home. Who is it?'

'It's a friend of his. Maureen. Could I speak with him?'

Patsy put the receiver on the table. She could hear her voice shaking when she said: 'Maureen wants to speak with you.'

For a second, Ian's lips pressed tight. Then his face became expressionless. He picked up the phone. 'Yes?'

'I haven't had a chance to thank you for reprieving the motor-cycle factory,' Maureen said.

Ian hesitated. Patsy had returned to the armchair across from his. When the phone had rung, she had just started drinking a whisky-and-soda with him. Now she picked up her glass again and held it two inches from her face, looking over the brim at him.

'It was not a personal decision,' he said.

'I'm sorry to hear that,' Maureen replied. 'I need to discuss something else with you. We could meet at Claridge's for lunch. I might even be staying in room 313.'

Watching his wife watching him, Ian wondered if his face had blanched.

'My appointments diary is with my private office,' he said coldly.

'Then you would be wise to have your private office ring me tomorrow morning,' Maureen replied.

'I'll speak to them,' Ian said and put down the telephone. Laconically he picked up his drink.

Patsy still watched him over the brim of her glass.

Finally she said: 'At least this time she was courteous enough to tell me her name.'

Ian saw how to play it. 'What do you mean "this time"?'

'You know exactly what I mean. What was it you told me before?' she said acidly. 'Oh yes. All that crap about' – she mimicked his drawl – '"bored strangers ringing numbers late at night to deliver messages which are totally meaningless". Maureen, as we now can call her, didn't appear to be delivering a meaningless message tonight.' She could hear her voice shaking again.

Ian said: 'If I'd guessed she was the one who rang before – and there must be a fair number of people who have Irish accents – I would have told you about madwoman Maureen. She claims to have brothers who are worried about their jobs in Belfast, and she persecutes any British minister who she thinks can help them. My private office is used to fending off these people who are clearly a bit off their head. I'm sorry, Patsy, that she's got it into her head to ring me at home.'

Every sentence but one was true, even though the truths hid lies.

There was nothing Patsy could reply. What he said sounded feasible enough. If she charged him with lying, it would bring a new dimension into their marriage. A piece of her warned her she might regret that. Anyhow, she couldn't prove he was lying. Perhaps he wasn't lying. She didn't want to think he was lying. But in her heart she knew he was.

28

Chris cut the engine as he drew up in front of the Pimlico house at 9.10 sharp. The Minister was going straight from home to Thursday's Cabinet Committee. It would take less than ten minutes to reach Downing Street.

Ian's study door was closed. He was on the telephone to his House of Commons secretary. 'You'll probably be getting a call this morning from J. D. Liddon's representative who's in London for a few days. Lisa Tabor. T-A-B-O-R. Tell her that today has become absolutely impossible, and I shan't be able to see her. Make all the right noises about being sorry, perhaps another time, and so on. I'm extremely interested in the proposals she has brought for BITE, so we don't want to irritate her unduly.'

When he put down the telephone, he lay back in his armchair, once again going through the possibilities. Again he ruled out the idea of Maureen and Lisa working in collusion: it made no sense. Again he ended up with the belief that Maureen must have seen them at Claridge's by chance. If she had known Lisa's name, it wouldn't have been too difficult to discover her room number. But how did she know Lisa's name?

He gave a small dry smile as he thought of the pigeons on the cornice. Maureen couldn't actually manifest herself as a bloody bird, could she?

After Patsy had stonily gone to bed on Wednesday night, he had managed to concentrate on the brief for today's Cabinet Committee. Lisa's pillow appeal for Star Oil could not possibly influence him, he was certain: he was eminently capable of separating work and play. Who more so? In any case, his views had been set out in his Cabinet brief before he went to room 313 at Claridge's. Even so, it gave him an odd feeling that his own inclination to grant Star Oil's application happened to be what Lisa wanted. He picked up the file, put it in the red box and turned the key.

He went up to the next floor and looked down the corridor to Patsy's room where she wrote and painted. Ordinarily she didn't start her work there until later in the morning, but today she'd gone there early. The door was shut.

'Goodbye,' he called. 'I hope to be back by eight tonight. I'll ring you.'

'Goodbye,' she called back without opening her door. Her voice was toneless.

The twenty-two red leather chairs around the coffin-shaped table were identical, except that the Prime Minister's chair had arms. He sat in the middle of one side of the Cabinet table, and the BITE Secretary sat opposite. At one end of the room, its panelled walls and cornices painted white, stood a pair of Corinthian columns, like sentinels. At the other end were the windows of shatterproof glass, overlooking the garden where the mortar bomb had exploded in the IRA's second attempt to murder the Cabinet.

Had that bomb landed ten feet nearer, the shatter-proof glass would have been as irrelevant as tissue-paper. From above the grey marble fireplace the portrait of Sir Robert Walpole in a horsehair wig looked down.

Ian was near the end of his argument:

'The final estimates will be completed next week. Until then, I am unable to tell my colleagues how the balance will come out between financial and political considerations. As BITE exists in part to encourage cooperation between Northern Ireland and the main-land, inevitably that must loom large in any decision I take.

'I was in the United States last week, as you know, but some of you attended Anne Jolliffe's funeral. Since her murder by the IRA was directly connected with George Jolliffe's opposition to further invest-ment in Northern Ireland, there is a temptation to wash our hands of anything more to do with Ulster. Yet if we did that, we would be playing into the IRA's hands.

'Therefore, I must tell my colleagues that though the final balance has not yet been made, I hope it will favour my supporting Star Oil's bid which would guarantee a refinery was built in Northern Ireland.'

He sat back in his chair.

Because the Anglo-Irish argument was so emotive, other members of the Cabinet Committee held strong views. Half an hour of debate ensued until the Prime Minister said briskly: 'We must now wait for the BITE Secretary to bring us his final proposals.'

The hands of the clock on the marble mantelpiece were at 11.29. In a minute the door would open for other ministers to come in for the full Cabinet. Ian pressed his lips. More than an hour still to go.

At a quarter to one, government drivers looked up when the door of Number Ten opened. Ian strolled over to his car and handed the red box to Chris: 'I'll walk to lunch, Chris. And I'll make my own way back to the department afterwards. I want some exercise.'

Buckling his seat-belt, Chris looked at his card with the Minister's engagements for that day. Nothing was written in for lunch.

Walking past the policemen at the iron gates, Ian turned south in Whitehall. Ten minutes later he pressed the top-floor bell of a peeling house with window-boxes in Stag Place.

'Yes?'

'It's Ian.' The words nearly stuck in his gullet: the familiarity they demonstrated made him angry and sick.

The lock buzzed as it was released.

She was wearing her pink trousers and pink T-shirt, the auburn curls falling on to her shoulders, her high heels clacking as she led the way into the sitting-room he knew so well. At first glance, she looked like a mistress receiving her lover.

'What would you care to drink, Minister?' she asked in the musical lilt.

'Nothing.'

He sat down in a chair facing the sofa where Maureen made herself comfortable, crossing her legs gracefully.

'I wondered why you didn't have your office ring me this morning to let me know when you would be dropping by. I was just thinking of trying you at home again,' she said.

'You know Cabinet meets on Thursdays.'

'Ah yes, so it does. Fancy my forgetting,' she said. She stretched one sandalled foot into the air, lifting the toes and studying them as if their pink nail varnish was her sole preoccupation. 'Well, as I told you yesterday evening, I wanted to express my appreciation for the help you gave that motor-cycle factory.'

'As I told you yesterday evening, my decision wasn't personal. If it had been, I would have let your brothers and the rest of those three hundred workers go to hell.'

'What a charming turn of phrase you have, Minister,' she said.

She stretched out her leg again to study the pink varnish. Ian said nothing.

'The other thing I wanted to discuss with you is this,' she said. 'I hear you're considering granting an oilfield to Star Oil providing they build a refinery in Northern Ireland.'

'How simple you make all decisions sound,' said Ian coldly.

'It is simpler than you think, Minister,' she said. 'Let me put it as clearly as I can. Obviously your job at BITE makes it right and proper that you support a new industry in Northern Ireland. It is a golden opportunity, we can all agree,' she said pleasantly, swinging her foot, 'to show you truly care about those poor Catholics who through no fault of their own are denied employment.'

She paused. Ian waited.

'And of course some men,' she went on, 'actually want to help the woman they have just fucked.' The hard edge had come into her voice. 'But the Englishman seems to think as soon as he has finished his little spasm he should punish the woman he was caressing a minute before.'

Ian waited.

'So it occurred to me, Minister, that since it would make Lisa happy if you helped Star Oil, you may decide to do just the opposite – to punish her for your own lechery. That would be sad.' The lilt had become almost singsong.

It took all his self-control not to ask how she knew what Lisa wanted from him. Yet there was no point in his laying himself open further: Maureen wouldn't give him a straight answer.

'Go to hell,' he said in an even voice.

She shrugged. 'Does Patsy know what you get up to after lunch at Claridge's?'

'Why don't you ring her and ask her yourself?' he said, getting to his feet. 'Then she too can tell you to go to hell. I've already told her all there is to tell about Stag Place and Claridge's.'

He turned on his heel and strode past the sofa towards the pinched entrance hall.

'There's more ways than one to skin a cat,' Maureen called out as if she was crooning a nursery song.

But when she heard the irregular tread as he went down to the outside door, her lips tightened into a thin line of rage.

A sense of the macabre led him to the Victoria Street pub where he had gone after Maureen's first blackmail bid. He had an hour and a half before the American Ambassador would arrive at BITE for their three o'clock meeting. Ordering a large whisky and a sandwich from the bartender, he could feel his heart still pounding.

In the mirror behind the bottles he saw his reflection – the frank grey eyes, the handsome but not too handsome face. Strangely, he looked unchanged. The shame at his own lies had made no mark on his face. He had lied to Patsy the night before. Now he had lied in an even more contemptible way: telling a vicious little tart that his wife knew all about her, when he had told Patsy nothing of the sort. The lie that breeds another lie, he thought, taking a long swallow of his whisky. Yet it had been a necessary gamble, he told himself: it was the only way to make Maureen think it pointless to ring Patsy again. Whether his gamble would pay off, he'd have to wait and see. He took another long swallow of whisky.

In the Stag Place flat, Maureen could not sit still. She paced back and forth on the cheap carpet, her mouth clenched in the line of hate. When Big Ben struck two, she got out one of her telephone cards. The landlord's practice of having pay phones for his tenants had always suited her: the numbers she phoned would not be itemized.

Just after nine in Washington, Michael was at the leather desk in his capacious office at J. D. Liddon International when the phone in his small inner room began to ring. Taking out his keys while he moved rapidly to the inner door, he unlocked it and reached the phone in time.

29

By Thursday afternoon, the pressure was bearing down hard: *World* went to the printers on Friday night. Georgie was in one of her waspish moods during the run-through which had been brought forward to two o'clock. Even the head of the national news section, Larry Penrose, began to wonder if he'd find himself out of the loop next week. As soon as she had accepted or rejected the last of the layouts spread before her on the conference table, Georgie got to her feet. 'I want to go through several things with you in my office,' she snapped at the deputy editor. Without a word to anyone else, she turned on her heel and left the room.

When he arrived in her office five minutes later, she gave instructions on what she wanted done in her absence. 'It's a pain in the ass that the President has to choose a Thursday night to give a dinner for the bloody German Chancellor,' she said, only half joking. 'I'll catch the early shuttle back in time to be here for the morning run-through. Has Larry Penrose forgotten how to present a lead story, for God's sake?'

Looking out the window as the shuttle left La Guardia and the hard afternoon sun blazoned the ugliness of the factories spread below, Georgie went over her last telephone conversation with Hugo. He hadn't phoned back on Monday evening. When she had called the Georgetown house again on Tuesday, Sarah said he was at the office, but Georgie couldn't reach him there either.

Not until Wednesday had he called her at *World*. 'Sarah said you phoned,' he said with a chilliness that had made Georgie's face flush. So much for her efforts to restore some sort of relations between them.

'I just wanted to check out Thursday evening's timetable,' she'd replied briskly.

'We ought to leave the house at 7.15,' he told her. 'I'll have Whitmore meet your plane.' She noticed he could still bring himself to say 'we', yet it did little to reassure her.

When they heard the Lincoln pull up outside, Sarah and Jamie raced each other down the stairs, Sarah exultantly leaping the last four steps so she won. Laughing and reaching out to them, Georgie forgot her unease.

But it returned as soon as Hugo got back to the Georgetown house in time to change for the White House dinner. He and Georgie could have been strangers as they moved about their bedroom, she fixing the diamond pendants to her ears, he straightening his black bow-tie. Only the children seemed to have normal responses: 'Oh Mama, you look beautiful,' said Sarah as Jamie stroked the white satin side-panels which ran from her armpits to where her long silk sheath was split.

In the back of the car, she attempted desultory conversation, but Hugo's replies were so perfunctory that she soon lapsed into silence. He had persuaded himself that his maelstrom of emotions was entirely his wife's fault. As Whitmore turned into Pennsylvania Avenue, Hugo was thinking of Lisa: it was five hours later in London. She must be asleep in her room at Claridge's. He wondered how her meeting with Ian had gone. It was only a week since Hugo had written his column to boost Star Oil – for Lisa – yet he'd managed to erase the memory of his deep repugnance at selling out his own independence. Indeed, all this week he'd had to stifle his urge to ring Ian about something, anything, and then casually bring up the case in favour of Star Oil.

Opening his window, Whitmore handed the invitation to one of the uniformed secret service who checked it against his list, while another rolled search mirrors under the car and looked inside the trunk and under the hood. When at last the locks on the gates were released, Whitmore drove up to the door beneath the great portico of the White House. Mounting the marble steps, Georgie and Hugo may have looked like a couple, but the invisible barrier between them was rigid.

Fifty guests already were assembled in the East Room, and some thirty more would follow Hugo and Georgie on to the polished oak parquet where once Teddy Roosevelt's children had roller-skated and seven presidents, four of them murdered, had lain in state.

'It could have been designed expressly for you,' said Hugo sarcastically. The East Room was decorated entirely in white except for gold damask curtains and gilt eagles supporting the Steinway grand piano, with more gilt eagles on the pier mirrors over the four fireplaces. He glanced up at the cut-glass chandeliers. 'It even has diamond ear pendants like yours,' he said in the same unpleasant voice.

'Oh Georgie,' called the wife of America's most powerful television magnate as she darted towards them, 'I was hoping you'd be here. We're giving a small dinner in New York next month for the Governor, and I'm so hoping you can come. And Hugo, too, of course,' she added.

Before either of them could answer, a slender, fine-boned woman in palest-blue chiffon glided up and touched cheeks with Georgie and Hugo. It was Imogene Randall. 'Georgie,' she said in the low voice which made you concentrate to hear her, 'we all miss you more than you know.' A burly figure appeared at Imogene's shoulder, and she half-turned to see who it was. 'Oh Pat. How nice.'

'Nice to see ya, Imogene,' said Senator Patrick Rourke. His wide face was flushed, and his champagne glass was empty. 'I wanted to say hello to Georgie. Howya doing up there in New York? *World* gets more and more on the ball.' Without giving Georgie time to speak, he said to Hugo: 'Hiya Hugo. Haven't seen you since you brought that foxy lady to Imogene's. What was she called? Lisa? I hear her boss has an interest in Star Oil getting one of those fields from the Brits. She must have been one happy little girl when she read your plug for Star Oil last week. You sure know how to please 'em, Hugo.'

For a moment Georgie stood transfixed. Imogene's smooth-browed face showed no expression as her eyes met Hugo's.

'Oh, Hugo,' said Pat Rourke with a loud chortle. 'Have I let the cat out of the bag? Sorry about that.' Triumphantly he turned his back and went off to find another drink.

At the same moment, a hush fell on the assembled guests. All eyes turned to the doorway. The President and the First Lady, who had greeted the German Chancellor and his party in the beautiful oval Blue Room, were ready to join their other guests in the East Room.

Twenty minutes later the First Lady led the way back along the Cross Hall to the State Dining Room at the other end. As they were shown to the round tables sparkling with crystal goblets and the red-bordered Reagan china service, Abraham Lincoln looking down benignly from his red velvet armchair in the painting above the marble mantel, Georgie and Hugo still had not spoken another word to each other.

She took the early shuttle back to New York on Friday, and she did not return to Washington until Saturday afternoon. The short family weekend that followed was the worst they'd ever had.

It was just after six on Monday evening when she left *World*: she wanted time to get back to Gracie Square for a leisurely bath before her date with Jock. 'It won't take much longer if we go by East River Drive,' she told her driver. She liked looking at the mud-coloured water flowing fast in the evening tide. What she'd told Patsy was accurate enough: a little fling with Jock had begun to seem a possible adornment to her marriage – her successful marriage, she had believed.

But that was before the Senator from Massachusetts blabbed. God she hated Pat Rourke. Wryly she smiled: she was turning out just like everyone else – blaming the messenger for the news he brings. Yet as soon as she thought of that jubilant chortle – his revenge for Hugo's column denouncing Noraid and, implicitly, Rourke himself – she hated Pat Rourke all over again. How *dare* he sneer at Hugo? How *dare* he wound her? Then her mind slipped back to the message he had proclaimed.

Again she gave a mockery of a smile. How complacent could she be? How could she have missed the signs that Hugo was involved with Lisa Tabor? She had actually told Patsy at Rycroft Lodge why she was confident Hugo wasn't screwing around: 'I'd know just from his manner. He would confuse infatuation and love. It would wreck our marriage.' And all the time, that's exactly what was happening. Hugo's cold hostility since the night he hit her at Rycroft Lodge, his refusal to make any comment on what Pat Rourke said – all now made plain that Georgie had been blind. She might be the powerful sharp editor, but she couldn't see the debris of her own marriage until that pig from Massachusetts pointed it out.

In the four days since the White House banquet, she had tried to detach herself from the hurt, and to a large extent she succeeded. But in walling up the pain, she seemed to have cut off other emotions as well. When Jock had rung her a week ago, the thought of their dinner tonight had given her a charge. Now she felt nothing in particular about the evening ahead.

Not until she was lying in her bath, sipping a long weak highball, gazing at her red toenails against the end of the long tub, did the stirrings of sexual desire start to return. 'I gotta have twenty degrees less heat if I'm to concentrate right,' he'd said. She touched her fingertips to one nipple. She imagined Jock concentrating on her as if she were a big *big* deal. The consummate manipulator, he would want to display his power in producing sheer erotic pleasure, manipulating her sexually with those stumpy fingers until she squirmed with desire, making her want to come back to him for more.

At five to eight her car pulled up to the heavy bronze doors of The Four Seasons. 'There's no need to hang around this evening,' she told her driver.

Inside the sparkling lobby she nodded to the Filipino woman beaming at her from the cloakroom, and went directly up the mirror-lined stairs. When she reached the top, those sitting at tables on the other side of the low glass wall spoke knowingly to one another as they watched her, some looking blasé, others not concealing that the whole point of sitting at those tables in the bar section of The Four Seasons was to be able to watch people arrive. A celebrity or a nothing? The last six people had been nothings – four Japanese businessmen and two expensively dressed American broads. Now luck had changed: not only a celebrity, but Georgie Chase. There she was in a narrow white dress that looked severe but sure made you aware of the body underneath.

The *maître d'* was scanning his big book, laid open like a Bible on a pulpit, two couples standing before him, waiting to hear their fate. The antennae of a man who has been *maître d'* for twenty years led him to look up as Georgie crossed over from the stairway. She walked with the unhurried confidence of someone who knows she'll be looked after. Immediately the *maître d'* came around to the front of his pulpit and, leaving the two couples in their limbo, went forward to greet Georgie. 'Miss Chase. I only learned five minutes ago that you were coming.'

'Good evening, Charles,' she said, offering her hand which he bowed over with inexpressible pleasure at being honoured by her friendliness. Simultaneously, his manner retained the unimpeachable dignity of the man who is unassailable ruler of his territory.

'Mr Liddon is waiting for you at his table.' The *maître d'* raised one hand imperiously and snapped his fingers. A flunky rushed forward. 'Take Miss Chase to the dining-room.' The flunky bowed, swivelled on one heel like a marionette, and led the way.

Within the perpetual twilight of the dining-room, summer manifested itself in the apple trees growing in the sunken patio at the centre. The head waiter materialized. 'Good evening, Miss Chase. Let me take you to Mr Liddon's table.'

It was next to the patio, where Jock could see and be seen. He got to his feet. 'Do you wanna face the foliage or turn your back on it?'

'I'll look at it,' Georgie replied.

'Do you know something,' Jock said after they had settled down, 'I've decided you have eyes in the back

317

of your head. I've watched you at Washington parties. It's part of your job to see who's there, but you never seem to be keeping an eye out for anybody. Yet when anybody comes over to speak to you, you know right away who they are and what you wanna say to them. I've decided you know they're coming, even before they say "Hi, Georgie" and you turn around.'

'Hi, Georgie.'

Laughing at the comedy of it, Georgie turned around. 'Hello, Donald. Why aren't you in Washington? We were talking about you just the other day. What's the good of having the Senator for New York as your own true friend if you never see him? Do you know Jock Liddon? Senator Symington.'

'Pleased to meet you, Senator. Do you wanna join us for a drink?'

'My guests will be only too delighted to get along without me for five minutes,' said the Senator, taking an empty chair at the table.

Instantly the head waiter reappeared.

'The Senator only has a coupla minutes, so we want a drink pronto. What'll you have, Senator? I'm gonna have a large bourbon on the rocks. But they got a nice line in champagne. Whaddaya want, Georgie?'

'Could I have a glass of your house champagne, Dino?' she said to the head waiter.

'I'll have the same,' said Senator Symington. 'How's Hugo?'

Georgie hesitated only a moment. 'He was fine yesterday,' she said and changed the subject. 'What's going on with the District Attorney? Everyone has gone clam.'

'He's going to be taken off the case,' the Senator replied. 'But nobody is going to say that. Instead he's going to resign next week.'

A waiter put Jock's bourbon in front of him and then poured out two glasses of champagne.

Tipping his glass to Georgie, the Senator went on: 'The best way the DA could think of to put a good face on resigning was to arrange for his wife to start dying next week.'

'You're joking,' said Georgie.

'Would I joke about a woman who is about to start dying?' said the Senator. 'I'm telling you that's what is going to be announced next week, however healthy the lady may look. Until then, everyone's to stay clam.'

'What about me?' said Georgie.

Jock watched them.

The Senator pulled down his mouth at the corners. 'Give me a buzz tomorrow. I'm taking the 2.30 shuttle back to Washington, but I'll be at my law office all morning. You've got my direct line.' He turned to Jock: 'It's surprising we haven't met before.'

'Yeah,' said Jock. 'Since Georgie will vouch for me, maybe I could ask you to have lunch one day in Washington. Or in New York, whichever you like. I've been doing a lot of work lately on munitions contracts. Maybe one of those two munitions factories upstate would like a big contract thrown their way.

Georgie watched them.

Quizzically the Senator lifted his brows. 'Phone me at my Senate office. I'd be very interested in discussing any contracts that might assist my constituents.' He finished his champagne and stood up. 'Nice to meet you,' he said to Jock. 'I'll expect your call tomorrow, Georgie.'

When the Senator was out of earshot, Georgie said to Jock: 'Every time I meet you, I learn of yet another pie you've got a finger in. Now it's munitions. How long have you been working on munitions contracts?'

Jock looked at his watch. 'Four and a half minutes.'

Georgie drank so little generally that the champagne had slightly gone to her head. She gave a peal of laughter.

'You got nice teeth,' said Jock. 'When you laugh like that, I can see your pink tongue. I gotta tell you, Georgie, I got better feelings about your tongue than I do about those Baskervilles' tongues hanging out.'

Georgie ignored this. 'What does the Senator have that you want in exchange?' she asked.

'You put things so crudely, Georgie,' he said. He liked her style. 'At the moment there isn't anything in particular he can do for me. But access is all: there'll be another day, another deal. Is he gonna let you use what he told you about the DA?'

'I won't know until I talk with him tomorrow. My guess is he'll say I can use something in *World* this week so long as his fingerprints aren't on it.' She smiled pertly. 'Especially as I mean to tell him I'm thinking of doing a feature on the state's munitions factories and the particular interest he takes in them.'

Jock's liquid-brown eyes looked at her steadily.

They had ordered only one course. Georgie had resisted the crispy duck which was better here than anywhere else in Manhattan. Her stomach had got that tight feeling low down when she'd been deciding what to wear that evening. She always wore pretty lingerie, champagne-coloured to tone with her skin during the months she dressed in white. This evening she'd chosen a lacy bra which fastened at the front. When she'd looked down at her own fingers hooking the bra together, at once she'd had an image of the coarse hands unfastening it, and she'd felt a tremor. Watching those hands across the table as Jock scanned the menu, she felt the qualms of nervous excitement return. She ordered a grilled trout.

When it arrived on the trolley and the waiter was removing the succulent flesh, Georgie saw it was exquisitely cooked, barely done near the backbone. Even so, she ate little more than half of it. The tautness in her stomach made her feel slightly sick, though she knew she wasn't going to be sick. She remembered Hugo once talking about the word 'tension' – how it meant opposite poles resisting each other, and it also meant opposite poles attracted to each other. What's going to happen tonight is Hugo's fault, she said to herself, though she only half believed it.

During dinner, they talked shop. While a minuet would not be the dance one would normally associate with Jock, there was a formal structure to their evening. In this first part, there was no overt hint of what would come next.

Over their coffee he lit a cigarette for her and a small cigar for himself. As he did so, Georgie looked at the short fleshy lips fastened on the cigar. She thought of the contrast between his hands and hers. If his too had been elegantly made, she might have found something preening in his manicured nails. It was the combination with the stumpy fingers that fascinated her. Again she wondered, as she had done in her bath, whether he would want to focus solely on her pleasure, bringing her to her climax, then exciting her again before taking his own pleasure. Perhaps he was one of those men who retain erection indefinitely while they tease and heighten their partner's desire. She didn't require love from Jock. She knew he didn't understand the word. What aroused her was the idea of his applying the same concentration to her body that he applied to his other big *big* deals.

When they were finishing their coffee, he said: 'Where's your car?'

'My driver has the evening off.'

'I'll take you home in mine.'

The two moulded leather seats in the back of the Cadillac made it easy for them to sit apart. They hardly spoke. The night had cooled the city enough to open the car windows, and Georgie held one hand spread to feel the moist air. Inside her was the delicious quivering. Jock had given no instructions to the driver that she had heard, yet she wasn't surprised when the car stopped in front of the silver, crenellated canopy of the Waldorf Astoria. As the doorman strode forward to open Georgie's door, Jock said to his driver: 'You'll be taking Miss Chase home to Gracie Square. I'll phone the car when she's on her way down.' She supposed the driver must be used to waiting for an hour or more. The thought of Jock making skilful, leisurely love to other women didn't worry her in the slightest. It aroused her more.

Inside the soaring lobby, a bellboy hurried to press a polished button in the row of ornate brass elevators. Art Deco embossments gleamed above doors which parted as Georgie and Jock approached.

While the elevator rose, he asked her about her next day's agenda at *World*. Even though the elevator boy had discreetly said no more than 'Evening, m'am, evening, sir. Hope you all had a nice evening,' they knew he knew who she was. There was nothing out of the ordinary in *World*'s editor having a drink with Jock Liddon in his suite – so long as neither of them acted as if it was out of the ordinary. But when they were again alone and walking down the twelfth-floor corridor's thick carpet, again they were silent. Georgie felt the tension tighten.

She watched his hand unlock the door. The glass-lined entrance-hall was already lit. He led the way into the living-room and flicked a switch which turned on soft, indirect lighting in a wall of plants.

'I'll get you a brandy,' he said as she sat down on a sofa.

'All right,' she said, though she rarely drank brandy.

When he returned, he was carrying two balloon

glasses, each with an inch of deep amber liquid. He was wearing a black brocade robe, the belt looped over itself with its black silk tassels hanging down where the robe was already pushed apart. She could see the condom's satin sheen.

Standing in front of her, he handed Georgie one glass and himself drank from the other. When she took a swallow, the brandy burned her throat. She took a second swallow. He reached down and took her glass and put it on the side-table, along with his own. He took her right hand and put it under the black silk tassels.

'I thought you'd like my sense of aesthetics,' he said. 'Black and white. Are your panties white too? I'd like to see them.'

The sofa was nearly four feet deep from front to back. As if hypnotized, Georgie lay back against the cushions and reached up under her silk dress. Wriggling to get them off, she pulled the champagne lace panties over her bare legs and high heels.

Jock leant over and pushed one finger into her. Then he took a cushion from the side of the sofa, and lifting Georgie's knees, he shoved the cushion beneath her buttocks. He pushed her thighs apart so he could kneel between them on the sofa. Grunting, he rammed himself into her. It hurt because there'd been no foreplay except in her own imagination. Watching his face above hers, she saw its colour drain, the black curls damp, his eyes closed. The grunts grew closer together until he gave one final lunge. He opened his eyes and got off her. On Jock's first time with a woman, he never needed any help from her in staying erect until he came.

He retied his belt which had come undone, retrieved the two balloon glasses, and threw himself back on the sofa beside her. After a minute or two he said: 'Mike O'Donovan's the guy to lay on a munitions contract for the Senator's upstate constituents. Munitions is one of Mike's specialties.' Jock looked at his watch.

Georgie took her third swallow of brandy. 'I've got an early meeting tomorrow,' she said. She picked up the tiny bundle of champagne lace. 'Where's the bathroom?'

'Through that door,' Jock replied, lifting one of the phones on the side-table. 'Miss Chase will be down in a coupla minutes,' he said to his driver.

The car was waiting immediately beyond the crenellated canopy.

'Let's go by East River Drive,' she told the driver. 'We don't all need to get where we're going in one minute flat.' Looking at the back of his cap and his neatly trimmed hairline, she thought of the black curls and the closed eyes and the grunts. She pressed her finger against her dress and felt the lace bra's front fastener, undisturbed.

Gazing across the brown water flowing out to sea, off to her right she could see, dark against the dingy sky, the sleek office tower which had seemed so phallic before. How much did she mind the gross disparity between her fantasy and reality? How much should she be offended by his complete indifference to her sexual feelings – or any other feelings she might have?

Then she smiled to herself. What had first attracted

her to Jock was the unabashed openness of his total concentration on his deals. What she'd got wrong when she had imagined this evening was whose sexual pleasure was the deal. In his way, he had behaved completely in character.

She began to laugh wildly. Even when she saw the driver look uncertainly in his rear-view mirror, Georgie couldn't stop laughing.

As she slid into her bed, glad to be in her own apartment, she realized she would sleep well tonight. The previous days had been so fraught she'd been sleeping rotten. She set her clock for 7.45 instead of seven: she would skip her workout before she dressed for the office, and the morning news, which was always on while she did her exercises, could be picked up on the car radio.

When the alarm went off, she went to the kitchen to get juice and coffee, carrying them back to the bedroom to drink while she made up her face and dressed. The telephone rang. She glanced at the bedside clock: 8.11. 'Hullo?'

'Georgie?' It was Hugo. Her heart raced. 'Are you all right?' he asked.

There was something odd about Hugo's voice.

30

Patsy loved these hours which were entirely her own. Even though Greva produced breakfast for Sam and Nina, there was a good bit of coming and going between bedrooms before the children piled into the Sierra Estate in the off-street parking bay between the pavement and the house. Like most terrace houses in Pimlico, there wasn't space for a garage. For a week or so after any new act of terrorism, Patsy would be methodical about checking under the car, and most mornings Chris had a look under the Sierra while he waited in the government car for Ian. Patsy drove Sam and Nina to school ordinarily, but today another mother was picking them up.

She liked to 'sort herself out' after they'd all gone – do half an hour of yoga, read her post, make her telephone calls before she went to her own small room overlooking the back garden. Normally it was after ten when she closed the door on the real world and entered the fantasy world of her writer's desk and painter's easel.

Since the telephone call from Maureen six nights before, Patsy had kept herself aloof from Ian when they were alone. Though neither had referred again to the telephone call, the bleak suspicion, indeed certainty, in Patsy's mind remained. But she could forget it when she picked up her pen and brush.

This morning it was later when she got going on

her current book. The previous evening she and Ian had been to a Number Ten dinner for the French President, and official social life often left her tired the next day. Then Greva had insisted on a seemingly endless conversation before finally she pushed off for a week's holiday with her own family. It was eleven before Patsy's adrenalin was humming agreeably, and she moved from the large desk to the easel.

She was working with acrylic this morning. Squeezing a bit of raw sienna, ivory black, burnt umber, vermilion on to a palette, she became the brute monster she was about to paint. The more she thought of the small figures of the girl and boy – hard to keep Nina and Sam out of her mind's eye – who in the next chapter would come to rescue their mother from the monster's sadistic embrace, the more fiendish the monster became visually. With her brushes, Patsy used line and colour so violently that they assaulted the senses, and readers looking at her illustrations would feel that only a girl and boy of determined bravery and ingenuity would be able to defeat the evil monster. Totally absorbed, she didn't hear the doorbell the first time.

Judge Fawcett pressed the bell longer the second time as he and his wife waited on the front step. A minute or so later, their daughter threw open the door. 'I didn't realize how late it was,' she said, hugging her father and mother. 'Look at me.'

Her parents looked at their honey-haired daughter in her cotton T-shirt and baggy judo trousers tied at the waist with a string, her feet bare except for coral nail varnish. Clearly she was not suitably dressed for their lunch at the elegant Ebury Street restaurant where the judge had booked a table to celebrate the Fawcetts' thirty-fifth wedding anniversary with the two people he loved most.

'Let your taxi go,' Patsy said. 'We can go in my car. My parking permit is OK in Ebury Street. Go and sit in the garden and I'll be ready in ten minutes.'

She ran back upstairs and began her quick-change act, always easier in the summer when one wore fewer clothes. At the last minute she ran back to her workroom: she'd remembered she hadn't screwed the lid back on the vermilion acrylic she'd been using when the doorbell had rung. Glancing out of the window into the garden, she smiled. Her father and mother were examining the acacia they'd given her five years before; the intense acid-green leaves adorning its graceful branches always made her think of a Chinese painting. At the same moment Patsy looked down at her parents, Georgie's words flashed through her mind: 'Seeing them together – even when physically they were in different rooms – always gave me a good feeling.'

Patsy snatched up her handbag and ran down the stairs. 'Ready,' she called out at the top of the garden steps.

They made a striking trio as they walked out of the front door – the judge erect in his pinstripe suit, Mrs Fawcett's willowy figure in a dusky rose silk, their daughter in an aquamarine cotton shift which brought out the green of her eyes.

As Patsy was unlocking the car, Mrs Fawcett was insisting her husband sit up front, and while they all three stood there, she said as she always did whenever this minor arrangement was under discussion: 'I really prefer sitting in the back seat.'

'I'm sorry to mention it, Patsy,' the judge broke in, looking back at the house, 'but you've left one of your bedroom windows wide open. It's not a good idea these days.'

'Damn,' said Patsy. She glanced at her watch: 12.30. 'I'll be right back.' Disappearing into the house again, she ran up the stairs and had just reached the bedroom door when the whole house seemed to lift as if it were inside the explosion.

She stood with one foot in the bedroom, one still in the hall, dazed by the force of the sound. Then she ran to the open window and looked out. She ran back across the bedroom and down the stairs. The front door was still open. Outside, the young writer who lived next door grabbed her. 'You can't go near it. There may be another bomb.'

She kicked him and wrenched herself free.

Clinging to a jagged piece of metal was a blackened piece of cloth which still showed dusky rose. What had been her mother was within the smoking rubble of the car. Her father had been blown on to the pavement. Gently Patsy lowered herself over the tangle of his body and laid her cheek on his until he stopped breathing. The wail of police sirens began.

Later Scotland Yard told Ian that the Semtex had been taped above the centre silencer box and would have been invisible without search mirrors unless Chris or Patsy had actually crawled under the car to check it. After Mrs Fawcett had got in the back seat, the judge must have closed her door. When it slammed, three pounds of Semtex went off.

When the bomb went off in London it was just after 7.30 in Washington. Hugo always listened to the morning news while he shaved. A few minutes before eight, the newsflash came over: 'A British Recorder of the Crown Court, Judge Nicholas Fawcett, and his wife have died in a car bomb explosion outside the Pimlico home of their daughter, who is the wife of the Secretary for the Board of Industry, Trade and Energy, Ian Lonsdale. A major purpose of Mr Lonsdale's department, known as BITE, is to encourage industrial cooperation between Northern Ireland and the British mainland. Only two weeks ago Mr and Mrs Lonsdale were on an official visit to the United States. It is understood that Mrs Lonsdale and her parents were getting in her car to drive to a restaurant to celebrate her parents' wedding anniversary. Mrs Lonsdale had to go back into the house, and during those minutes the bomb went off. It is believed that Mrs Fawcett was killed instantly and that Judge Fawcett died a few minutes later. Their daughter was uninjured. The IRA has telephoned the Press Association to claim responsibility.'

Hugo stood transfixed, his razor in his hand. Then he walked slowly into the bedroom. On a chest of drawers was a photograph of Georgie and Patsy sitting at a teak table on a balcony with Patsy's parents. All four were laughing.

A single sob wrenched from Hugo. He couldn't tell for whom he wept. Time stood still. When he next looked at his watch it was only ten past eight. Georgie would have heard the news too. A wave of compassion swept through Hugo. With a heavy sigh he picked up the telephone.

When he said 'Are you all right?' she didn't know what he meant. She only knew there was something odd about Hugo's voice.

'I think so,' she answered, falteringly. 'I'm glad you phoned.'

He didn't reply for a few moments. Then he said uncertainly: 'You've heard the morning news?'

'No.'

'Oh.'

'What is it, Hugo?'

'Well look, Georgie, it's bad news in London.' He steeled himself. 'Patsy's mother and father have been murdered. By the IRA,' he added, almost as an afterthought.

There was complete silence at Georgie's end of the line.

Then Hugo heard the dreadful wail begin. It went on and on and on, fading a little when she must have let the receiver drop on the bed beside her.

31

When the awful wailing stopped, Hugo said gently into his end of the telephone: 'Georgie. Georgie? Please pick up the phone, Georgie.'

She picked it up.

'Are you going to the office, Georgie?'

'No. I'm going to London.'

'All right. But look, I'm coming to see you first. I'll catch the 9.30 shuttle. Where will I find you?'

'Here.'

Her voice was small. When he put down the phone, Hugo knew how vulnerable she was.

Three hours later when he walked into the Gracie Square apartment, he found she had got herself together. The porcelain make-up was in place, the Japanese doll's hair shining. They stood in the hall looking at each other. Then tears began to pour down Georgie's face. Hugo had never seen her cry. He took her in his arms.

Concorde reached Heathrow in four hours, and she went straight to the house in Pimlico. Ian's dressing-room became Georgie's bedroom.

Patsy was so drained and disorientated that Sam and Nina spent much of their time with Georgie. They went in the taxi with her to the supermarket, and showed her where to find things in the kitchen. 'I'm chef and you're sous-chefs,' she told them, as they helped her prepare meals. Together they went to choose the flowers, taking a taxi to Sloane Square where Pulbrook and Gould's manager led them through the big, cool basement, flowers standing on every available surface until the staff could arrange them for delivery. Nina chose the roses, Sam the tulips, all in the same shade of dusky rose. The funeral was to be held in St George's Church in Hanover Square. 'The last time I was there was more than nine years ago – at your parents' wedding,' Georgie told the children. She didn't mention the detour needed to reach the wedding reception in Knightsbridge because a car bomb had gone off in a nearby square, killing a man and woman who were walking by.

At BITE it was business as usual. Ian issued a press statement confirming he would not be having special protection: 'BITE exists to show the IRA that their viciousness is pointless. My family and I will continue to take sensible precautions, but we do not intend to retreat behind an iron barricade. If we did that, then terrorism would have won.'

The House of Commons whips excused him from all evening votes for the rest of the week. He and Patsy were thankful for Georgie's presence: with the three of them having drinks and dinner together, it was easier to distract their thoughts for a little while. Patsy made wry jokes and laughed, though her eyes retained a lost, bruised look. Watching her, Georgie remembered an accident she had seen when a man fell from an upper window on to the pavement: he got to his feet, blood spouting from his head, and tried to walk back into the house; his eyes had that same lost, bruised look; she heard afterwards that he'd died on the way to the hospital.

In the afternoons, the two women lay for an hour or so on Patsy's big bed, propped up against the pillows as they drank tea, talking or not talking. Twice Georgie brought up what Patsy had said at Rycroft Lodge: 'I dread the day something happens to one of them. I don't know how the other one could deal with it.'

'Neither of them will ever have to,' Georgie said softly.

'I know,' said Patsy. 'I keep trying to think of that.'

One afternoon while gazing through the bedroom windows at the chimney-pots on the low houses opposite, Patsy suddenly said: 'It makes other things, which seemed the end of the world before, not particularly important.'

They sipped their tea.

'Last week,' she went on, 'Ian hurt me more than I had ever been hurt until then.'

Georgie said nothing.

'Do you remember my telling you at Rycroft Lodge about an anonymous call from a woman asking for Ian – how something about her voice gave me a bad feeling? Last Wednesday she rang again to speak with him. She said her name was Maureen. Ian said it must have been a screwball – "madwoman Maureen" – who persecutes anyone she thinks could help her brothers in Northern Ireland. I knew he was lying.'

'Did you tell him that?'

'No. But he knew I knew. I withdrew my love, as they say. It was still like that when . . .' Patsy's voice trailed off as tears filled her eyes and slowly began rolling down her face.

Georgie sucked her lips hard against her teeth, but tears started streaming down her face too. She swung her legs off the bed and went over to Ian's chest of drawers where she knew his handkerchiefs were kept. She took out two, got back on the bed, and silently handed one of the handkerchiefs to Patsy.

When both were composed again, Patsy said: 'I've never seen you cry before.'

'I know.'

They sipped their tea.

Then Patsy said: 'After Tuesday happened, it didn't seem to matter any more that Ian had lied to me. I suppose he only lied because he didn't want me hurt. Whatever he and that Irish slag had done, I don't think I really want to know now. It doesn't seem important any more. Since Tuesday happened' – she found this the best way to refer to it without breaking down – 'Ian has done everything he can to show his' – she hesitated lest she go to pieces again – 'concern for me.'

Georgie pulled in her lips against her teeth again. 'Time for a funny story. Do you remember at Rycroft Lodge when I said how Ian and Hugo were different? How if Ian ever had a quick fuck on the side, it wouldn't mean a thing to him? But how I was bound to know if Hugo was screwing around, because it would wreck our marriage? How he would confuse infatuation with love? Well, last Thursday we went to a dinner at the White House. And a thuggish senator from Massachusetts, who hates Hugo, beelined over and inquired jovially about Hugo's "foxy lady" – none other than Lisa with the lilac eyes. I told you it would be a funny story.'

Patsy had turned on her pillow, and the bruised eyes stared at Georgie. 'You're joking.'

'Actually, no. I suppose it isn't that funny a story after all,' Georgie said.

This time Patsy got up to pour them more tea before returning to her side of the bed.

'It's been awful between us,' Georgie went on. 'Really, really awful. Formal. Cold. Horrible. Last Monday I even tried out a little affair with Jock Liddon, which turned out to be the fiasco of the year. Actually, that really is a funny story. But the Hugo and me story is sad.' She turned and looked at Patsy's face, and then returned her gaze to the chimney-pots across the road. 'Hugo heard the news on Tuesday morning before I did. He phoned me. He told me. He caught the next shuttle to New York. He was like a human being again. He went with me to Kennedy and put me on the plane to London. But I don't know what it will be like when I get back.'

'You've always amazed me, Georgie. The last two days nobody would think you had anything on your mind except what's happened here.'

'In a way that's true. Since I heard about your father and mother, I haven't thought a lot about anything else. They seem more vivid – they have more reality – than anything else. It's odd.'

The funeral was on Friday. On Saturday when Ian heard Georgie's steps passing his study door, he came out and asked: 'I wonder if I could talk to you about something.'

'Sure.'

He closed the door behind them and they settled in the two armchairs, Georgie sitting in Patsy's. For several minutes he said nothing, looking down with his chin resting in one hand. She thought how immeasurably sad his face was. He sighed heavily and lay back, the frank grey eyes now fixed somewhere in the middle distance.

'You no doubt know, Georgie, that my frailties include self-indulgence – i.e., screwing around occasionally with the little Miss Sexpots of this world. Even though it happens quite rarely, you might wonder how I find time even for that. But that kind of thing doesn't take up much time – let alone much thought. At least, it didn't take up much thought until now.'

Once more he was silent.

Georgie said nothing.

Turning to her, he gave a rueful, lopsided smile and then looked away again. 'What a mess. A girl called Maureen turned out to be a blackmailer. You may have guessed from the name that she's Irish. Northern Irish, to be precise. She rang here twice. I lied about her to Patsy – obviously not to protect Maureen. Nor, so far as I can judge, was it to protect me. I lied to Patsy because I didn't want her hurt. Then after the bomb on Tuesday, Scotland Yard began the big search. I was asked if I could think of

338

anybody I knew – anybody I was even slightly acquainted with – who might have a connection with the IRA.'

It had been a nightmare of fear and guilt for Ian. Some hours after the bomb went off, Maureen came into his mind. Could she possibly have been involved? It seemed to him out of the question. He was sure she was a loner, blackmailing for a mixture of motives – concern for her brothers in that bloody motor-cycle factory, resentment of the British, simple vicious spite. Yet the word 'vicious' had associations in his mind. Perhaps she was not a vicious loner. Perhaps she was part of a vicious gang of IRA psychopaths.

He was appalled at the thought of Scotland Yard tracking down his seedy little affair. But worse, far worse, infinitely worse, was the thought that Maureen might have had something to do with the murder of Patsy's mother and father. If that turned out to be so, he would be the one who had set the whole ghastly tragedy in motion.

Since Tuesday, he had hardly allowed himself to think of the personal loss for him: Patsy's parents had taken the place of those he didn't have. Yet he knew his loss was as nothing compared to her anguish – and, in a different way, the gaping hole left in his children's lives. Now there wasn't anyone older than himself whom Ian could really look up to. Overnight he felt he had grown up. And it might be too late.

'Clearly I had to tell Scotland Yard something about Maureen,' he said. 'If I didn't, I couldn't live with myself. When she turned ugly, there were suffi-cient reasons to explain that; it never occurred to me that she might be connected with the IRA. But with the possibility raised, I had no choice. I told the detectives I'd had lunch a few times with a woman called Maureen Halloran, but when she'd become emotional about Northern Ireland, I'd stopped seeing her.'

Again he gave the lopsided, ashamed smile.

'Did they ask a lot more questions?' asked Georgie.

'Not many. It would be unusual for police to be other than respectful to a Cabinet minister. And given they were only interviewing this one because of the IRA attack on his family, it would have been doubly odd had they questioned me too closely about what was clearly a personal embarrassment.'

The understatement of the decade, he thought when he said 'personal embarrassment'. Whenever he contemplated its becoming public, he felt sick. 'I gave Scotland Yard the address in Stag Place. That's where Maureen lives. I should say "lived". When the police went there to make what they call discreet inquiries, it was as if she had never been there. Even the petunias in the window-boxes were gone. The landlord said the woman who had lived there for six months was called Mary Hanrahan. She always paid her rent in cash. She'd paid up to the end of this month. She was last seen by one of the other tenants on Sunday – carrying clothes out to a van.'

After several minutes, Georgie said: 'It still doesn't mean she was involved with the IRA.'

'I agree.' He turned again to look directly at her. 'I am almost at my wits' end. If it turns out Maureen

340

had something to do with that bomb, Patsy could never forgive me. Sam and Nina could never forgive me. I could never forgive myself.' He paused before adding: 'Yes, I know: and you would never forgive me.'

He looked away and for the second time gave a deep sigh before he said: 'Just the thought of that woman being in any way a part of what happened on Tuesday fills me with a remorse such as I have never known.'

They were silent.

Finally Georgie said quietly: 'You've got to put up with it. You certainly can't share your remorse with Patsy. Let's hope Maureen was the loner you thought she was. Until – unless – you learn otherwise, you've got to tough it out on your own. So far as I'm concerned, this conversation never took place.'

She walked over to his chair and leaned over it to rest her lips for a moment on his cheek.

After dinner on Saturday evening, Georgie and Patsy went out for a walk. Unlike Washington, late July evenings in London were cool enough to require a wrap. At ten o'clock a deep rose sky fanned over London. They talked about God. Did He exist? There must be some sort of afterlife: they'd learned in school that energy always turns into another form of energy. All that energy – the judge's energy, his wife's energy – it couldn't just turn into nothing. It had to be somewhere. And it had to be a force still entwined, at that moment they felt sure.

On their return, intending to go up to their

rooms, they found Ian's study door open. He got up from his armchair to greet them. 'Georgie, Hugo rang while you were out. He said could you ring him back? He's at Rycroft Lodge. You can use the phone here: I'm going to have a bath.' He looked uncomfortable. 'Why don't you let me make you a drink first?'

'Thanks, Ian, but I don't particularly want one.'

'Well, let me pour out a whisky in case you change your mind.' His eyes met Patsy's for a moment.

'Is something the matter?' asked Georgie. She heard the fear in her own voice.

'Everything's all right with Hugo and Sarah and Jamie. He said to tell you that. It's just something has come up that was unexpected.'

He put a large glass of neat whisky beside the phone. The size of the drink added to Georgie's alarm. She saw that Patsy, standing in the doorway, was trying to read Ian's face. Then he and Patsy left the room, closing the study door.

She heard her heart thumping as she lifted the phone.

32

Lisa had returned from London the previous weekend. When Hugo phoned, she had to tell him there was no way she could see him until Saturday. 'I've got to fly to Houston early tomorrow. I have to make a personal report to Star Oil. And after that I've got to go to LA and then some hole in New Mexico. J. D. Liddon is working on two deals out there.'

Hugo's disappointment was enormous. He had counted the days until her return from London. His only respite during the horrible weekend with Georgie had been his day-dreams about Lisa's return.

But then came Tuesday morning's newsflash when he was shaving. Its repercussions bore in constantly on the days that followed, breaking into his concentration on anything else, waking him at night, ready to confront him each morning. He tried to remember exactly when the ramifications of the newsflash had begun. Probably it was when he walked into the bedroom and saw the photograph of Georgie and Patsy laughing with Patsy's parents. At that moment he had wept within himself for a jumble of losses. As his resentment of Georgie's fame had grown, he had forgotten the jaunty, bold girl whom he'd loved so dearly, who had been the perfect partner for him. Had she disappeared forever like Patsy's mother and father? Had the Hugo who had loved her gone to some place from which he could never return?

Over and over again he remembered how time had stopped on Tuesday morning and it was only ten past eight when he picked up the telephone to call Georgie. For so long – how long? – he had felt the resentment of someone doing a duty when he phoned her, and lately his hostility had hardened into the desire to hurt her. Yet in the minutes between seeing that photograph and dialling her number, the wish to hurt her had melted into concern. Then when the heartrending wailing began, she became the wounded one he wanted to protect.

He'd been taken aback when she told him she was not going to the office: previously she had always made careful plans for *World* to be handled in her absence. Arriving at the Gracie Square apartment, he had marvelled that the porcelain face could crumple into an inconsolable little girl's. As he took her in his arms, his only thought was to try and comfort her. Neither of them had spoken of what would happen when she returned from London. They both imagined she would be back some time in the following week.

He told himself he did not love Lisa less. But she no longer was in the same perfect picture frame: she was a complication. He found he now was glad they couldn't meet until Saturday. As the days between went by, there were moments when the conflict within him stirred that deep repressed desire to punish the person causing the torment. Several times the image of the scarecrow flashed across his memory: Georgie *had* been in his mind when he set the dogs on the scarecrow, when he watched them tearing at its stuffing, ripping apart the white cloth. Of course it had been no more than a fantasy, yet he was shaken by the depth of resentment which must have lain behind it. Now he was moved by compassion instead. And he had to acknowledge something else he felt for Georgie as well: a love so deep he had forgotten it was there. Most days he phoned the Lonsdales' house, though he had thought it better not to do so on Friday: the funeral would be absorbing everyone's strength.

He welcomed each interview he held on Capitol Hill, each hour spent writing his columns. For they took his mind off brooding about Lisa. Even when he and Sarah and Jamie were playing three-sided kickball in the garden, his thoughts were shadowed by Lisa. What was he to do? What did he want to do?

Ian, he suspected, could manage to have adventures without letting them impinge on his marriage. Indeed, there was much to be said for the notion of an outside stimulant making a long marriage happier. Yet Hugo didn't feel like that when it came to himself. His love for Lisa had seemed transcendental. It had fired him, ennobled him; in a way it had consumed him. It had not made his marriage better; it had made him want to be rid of his wife. That's what the scarecrow fantasy was about, he knew. He had wanted to replace Georgie with Lisa.

Now that realization made him feel a repugnance – for himself, for Lisa. Perhaps he wouldn't feel any of that when he was actually with her. Yet the complications would remain. And how would Lisa feel if he turned his back on her? She had looked to him as a protector. How could he now hurt her? Then he thought of how he had tried to protect her, and he winced at the memory of his selling out: Pat Rourke was right to deride him for using his column for what was no more than a PR plug for Star Oil. Lisa shouldn't have asked him to do it. Hugo discovered he held a great grudge against Lisa for making him sell out.

He was to phone her at the group house on Friday evening. He woke that morning to the certainty of what he must do when they met on Saturday: he would tell her he must restore his love to his wife. He couldn't possibly say it as cornily as that, but that would be the message. But where should he tell Lisa? The answer came to him like a sudden illumination: he should take her to the Eastern Shore for the day, take her once more to Rycroft Lodge, tell her there.

He wasn't sure why he felt it was right to go to Rycroft Lodge to tell her. It might have something to do with the fact that he'd first met her there, then taken her back there as his love, made love to her in the bed which belonged to him and Georgie. Somehow it seemed the right place to end the idyll for good.

And it would be a courtesy to Lisa. Where else was he to tell her? He couldn't take her to the Georgetown house while the children were home. He was hardly in the mood for a picnic in the park. And telling her over lunch at the Willard would be too much like a PG-rated film. The drive between Washington and the Shore would give them a chance to come to terms gradually with the realization that things had changed. On the way over, she was bound to sense something was different. On the way back, there would be time to deal with loose ends, time for her to feel she wasn't being dumped instantly into the street.

When he rang her Friday night and proposed they drive to the Shore for lunch the next day, Lisa was elated: if he was taking her there so soon again, she really had him. She was not a person who often went in for self-congratulation, for she was always looking the next step ahead. But the London visit had left her less confident than usual. She didn't know whether it was Ian's work that had made him cancel their second lunch, as his secretary had claimed, or whether he had simply changed his mind about wanting to see her again.

And then when she was in Houston she'd heard the news about Patsy Lonsdale's parents. Lisa remembered them vividly from that weekend when James Arden had taken her and Michael O'Donovan to Pig Farm – when the Fawcetts had appeared in the garden and without touching each other imparted the sense of being a couple in a way Lisa had never seen. She felt no particular emotion about their murder, yet she had an uneasy feeling, hard to analyse, that in a way she couldn't discern she would be affected in consequence.

All this uncertainty made her gloat when Hugo invited her to Rycroft Lodge with him on Saturday: at least she was confident of her adroitness in handling him.

*

347

When the station-wagon started down the long decline of the Bay Bridge and the placid terrain spread under the big unbroken sky, she glanced sideways at him. She remembered what he had said the first time they'd driven together to the Eastern Shore: 'I always have the feeling I'm coming home.' And he had put his hand over hers as he said it.

This time he was silent. He had scarcely spoken since they left Washington: 'I'd better concentrate on driving.' She had rested her hand near him on the seat, but at no time had he touched it. He seemed tense. She wondered if she might have made a mistake in wearing a white sundress today. Usually he said something about her appearance, but today he had made no comment. She had worn white on a whim: why should that cow's affectations mean nobody else could wear white, for God's sake?

Dry clouds rose from the dirt road as the car wound through the cornfield. She heard the Dobermans' excited clamour before the pen came into sight.

'Did you tell Mr Pierce you were coming down for the day?' she asked.

'That's why he brought the dogs over,' Hugo replied. 'I'll get them later.'

'Please stop now, Hugo,' she said.

He braked alongside the pen as the dogs flung themselves against the wire.

'I'll get them,' she said. 'Where are the keys?'

'It's better if you don't.'

Her general uncertainty loosened her normal self-control. 'You don't trust me to be able to handle them. Only you and Mr Pierce and the wonderful Georgie are allowed to handle them.'

He looked at her, surprised. 'Don't be silly.' He drove ahead. In the gravel forecourt, they stepped out into the stifling air pressing down.

This time there was something mechanical in unloading the lunch hamper he'd picked up from the Willard. When he entered the house with Lisa, he wished the day was at an end.

'You told me last time you would take me duck-shooting,' she said.

'The season hasn't opened,' he replied shortly.

'But it would be fun to go shooting,' she said. 'I'll bet you didn't know I'm a good shot.' One of her boyfriends at college had taught her to shoot.

'All right,' Hugo replied. 'We can go target-shooting later. Look, Lisa, we ought to talk about something.'

The windows of the cavernous hall were shuttered against the heat. In the half-light, her eyes were a violet-blue. They became wary.

'I'll make us a long drink,' he said.

She stood at the glass double doors and looked out at the terrace, the parched grass beyond, the river in limbo. Returning with a Campari-soda for each of them, he said: 'Let's sit down.' He put her glass on a table beside an armchair, and sat in another chair near by, the Campari's raspberry pink reflecting in the two tumblers. He told her. The bomb that killed the Fawcetts had changed a number of lives. He had discovered his wife needed him. He could no longer go on deceiving her. He would have to give up Lisa.

349

He wondered if it was a trick of the room's shuttered light: her eyes had changed from the violet-blue to a hard, cold grey. 'But supposing I don't want to be dumped like a bag of garbage?' she said in an even voice.

'Who's talking about dumping you?' he replied, even though he knew that's precisely what they were talking about. Her directness had increased his already acute discomfort.

'You can't just go around, Hugo, picking people up and putting them down when you've finished with them.'

'I haven't finished with you,' he said. 'I want us to go on being friends. I hope we can meet and talk. What we can't go on being is lovers. If I can help you in any way, I hope you'll ask me.'

Her eyes were defiant. 'All right,' she said. 'I'm asking you to take me to Imogene Randall's party next week.'

For the first time Hugo glimpsed Lisa's hard core. It was a revelation, like scales falling from his eyes. His next reaction was to wonder what hold she had over him. Thanks to Pat Rourke, Georgie already knew.

'We can talk more about it later,' he said calmly. 'I'll go get the guns. We can use the scarecrow as the target.'

He returned with a .32 Winchester Special rifle and his Smith and Wesson .38. 'Which do you want?' he asked her.

Silently she took the rifle. Putting the revolver in his belt, he sorted out two boxes of ammunition from the store he kept in the bottom drawer of the desk.

'I'll carry mine,' she told him curtly, taking one of the boxes. When they went out the front door, the midday heat made her gasp. 'God this place is uncomfortable,' she exclaimed. All these weeks of humouring Hugo, playing the fragile flower for Hugo, were ended. There was no reason now not to show her claws. If he thought she was simply going to say: 'Of course you must go back to your precious wife, you must forget I ever existed,' he had another goddamn think coming.

He didn't answer.

The dogs' flanks were streaked with sweat as they hurled themselves against the mesh. Unlocking the gate and stepping through, he gave a short command. Reluctantly the Dobermans settled on to their haunches, tail stubs quivering, while he fastened the thick plaited leashes into the studded collars.

He was glad to have the dogs bounding ahead as far as the leashes permitted: they made a distraction from the sullen silence between him and Lisa. On the other side of the house, they stopped at the edge of the terrace while he unfastened the leashes. Although the grass was hard from the drought, she wanted to walk on it in her bare feet, and she put down the rifle and her box of cartridges to untie her white sneakers. 'Keep them on,' he said. 'You'll want them in the wheatfield.'

The Dobermans had already raced to the strip of poplars extending down to the shore. Hugo gave a high whistle and they catapulted back, careering in an arc around Hugo and Lisa, then hurtling towards the poplars and disappearing through them.

When Hugo and Lisa reached the unstirring trees she said in the same peevish voice: 'Did you bring my ammunition?'

'You were carrying it,' he replied.

'I must have left it on the terrace.'

'I'll get it,' he told her. 'Wait here.'

He turned his back to walk across the lawn, glad to be alone for a few minutes.

'Fuck him,' she said through clenched teeth, ignoring his instruction. The woods were little more than a ribbon making a boundary. Almost immediately she came out into the uncut wheatfield, the far strip of poplars marking where Pierce's place began, the narrow river at the bottom of the field misted as the high noon sun sucked up the slow-moving tidal water, the scarecrow in its torn white dress standing in the middle of the field. The Dobermans were racing round and round the scarecrow.

'I hate him. I hate her. I hate this foul, foul heat. I wish she was that scarecrow. I'd kill her.' She remembered how Hugo had commanded the dogs the last time she was at Rycroft Lodge. She gave a shrill cry: 'Get it!'

The Dobermans flung themselves on the scarecrow, ripped away more of its straw and cloth, their molten eyes bulging with desire, and then raced round it in a circle again.

'Get it!' she shouted again, brandishing the rifle over her head like a warrior about to attack. She would kill Georgie. 'Get her!'

The Dobermans widened their circle. The waving rifle and the shouting figure in the white dress increased their excitement. The powerful hind legs thrust faster as the circle widened further.

Hugo hadn't hurried about retrieving Lisa's box of ammunition. When he started back to the poplars and saw she had already gone ahead, he shrugged. His shirt dark with sweat, all he could think of was how glad he would be when today came to an end. He walked down to the pier to check the mooring on the rowboat and then started along the shell-strewn shore towards where the wheatfield would appear beyond the poplars. He heard her shout her commands. 'Damn fool,' he muttered, hurrying his pace. He was just coming to where the poplars reached the shore when the blood-chilling screams began.

For a moment he froze, suddenly cold in the searing heat. Then he rammed four cartridges into the revolver's cylinder and without waiting to fill the rest began to run.

Pierce was outside his house when he heard a woman shouting at the dogs. Afterwards he couldn't remember whether the baying and snarling grew more high-pitched before the screams began or after; everything seemed to fuse into one long, terrible cry rising higher and higher. A garden spade was in the yard, and he grabbed it as he ran towards his strip of poplars.

When he came out the other side of the trees, all he could see was the scarecrow with straw bulging from the tears in the white cloth, and beyond it the gleaming ebony backs as the dogs lunged at something in the wheatfield. Twice he shouted a command as he ran towards them, but they ignored it. Then he saw Hugo running from the bottom of the field.

Pierce swung his spade down on one of the frenzied dogs, but it hit the muscled shoulders, and the Doberman twisted off Lisa and turned to face him, its blunt muzzle covered with blood, lips pulled back in a grimace like a grin, a piece of white cloth stained red hanging from its teeth. As the Doberman leaped at Pierce, a shot rang out. A second shot followed. Then two more.

At first the silence felt louder than the shattering din had been. Under the big sky, empty except for the shimmering sun, Hugo and Pierce bent over the three bodies. A small trickle of blood had started from the limp ear of one dog. From the great muscled neck of the other, a larger trickle flowed. So much blood still welled through the torn white dress that it was hard at first to tell where the gaping flesh began. Already the red smears staining the black forelegs were drying in the sun. The lapis lazuli hands of the crushed moon-faced watch had stopped at five past noon.

33

When Hugo phoned the Lonsdales' home Saturday
evening, it was late afternoon on the Eastern Shore.
The police had taken statements from Hugo and
Pierce before Lisa's body was removed from Rycroft
Lodge. Their report and the body would go to the
county medical examiner on Sunday.

Late Sunday morning, Ian drove Georgie to Heathrow. It was not yet noon in Washington when her
plane landed at Dulles Airport. Whitmore was waiting. They drove first to the Georgetown house. Even
though she knew cameramen and reporters would be
camped outside the house, her eyes narrowed when
she saw them.

'Are you going to leave Hugo, Georgie?' 'Do you
think it was an accident, Miss Chase?' 'Look this
way for just one shot, Georgie.'

Inside the house Sarah and Jamie were sitting on
the bottom step of the wide stairway. They jumped
up and rushed to her as she closed the front door
behind her. Hugo's mother and one of his brothers
appeared from the living-room.

'I keep telling Jamie,' Sarah said, 'it wasn't Daddy's
fault what happened. She shouldn't have overexcited
the dogs.'

'I never liked the dogs,' said Jamie.

Sarah looked more closely at her mother. 'How
was Patsy?' she asked.

An hour later Georgie got back in the Lincoln for the drive to the Eastern Shore.

When Whitmore wound down his window to pay the toll, it was like opening an oven door. Shutting out the heat once more, he said to Georgie: 'It's meant to break tonight.'

As they started down the bridge's slow decline, the big uncluttered sky over the Shore began to darken. The first spatters of rain appeared on the windscreen, and she looked through the sides of the bridge to the Chesapeake Bay below. The tidal force was colossal as the vast body of water swept towards the sea. While she watched, the shifting surface of the waves began to dance from the rain pelting down. When the bridge's gentle slope at last levelled off to the highway which traversed the Shore, the late afternoon sky was black except when sheets of lightning lit up the driving rain as far as the eye could see.

'Serves them bloody right,' she muttered to Whitmore as he approached the two white-painted posts. The gate was closed, and outside it drenched cameramen and reporters huddled under umbrellas. When Whitmore got out to open the gate, someone turned an arc light on to Georgie's window while the cameras turned. Silently Whitmore got back in the car, water streaming off his cap on to his neck, drove through and then got out to fasten the gate again. When they passed the pen – 'pen sounds cheerier than cage,' she had told Sarah a thousand years ago – she flinched and looked away.

The station-wagon was in the forecourt. The shutters of the house were closed. In the seconds it took her to run from the car to the front door and get it open, the rain slicked her hair against her face, and her soaked white suit clung to her skin.

'Are you sure you don't want me to stay?' asked Whitmore, water dripping off his uniform on to the hall floor.

'We'll be all right,' she said. 'Thank you, Whitmore. We'll be in touch tomorrow.'

She heard the car's wheels crunch on the gravel, and then all she could hear was the rain beating on the roof. 'Hugo?'

She opened the shutters of the cavernous hall so the cooled air could get in. Then she opened the glass double doors and watched the rain bounce as it hit the quartz terrace, listening to it fall on the parched grass. Though it was still afternoon, the boat-house at the pier's end was nearly invisible through the downpour. She turned back into the hall. 'Hugo?'

She found him in their bedroom. There the shutters were open, and the sound of the rain falling on the grass came through the windows. He was lying on their bed, his hands folded under his head. He didn't turn to look at her.

'Shall I make us a drink?' she asked quietly.

When she returned with two Campari-sodas, she found him sitting on the edge of the bed. He looked at the drinks she had happened to choose, and their raspberry pink made a shudder pass through his body. He looked at her white dress, darkened from the rain, stuck to her skin, and again a spasm of horror went through him. He passed his hand over his eyes and then kept it there, resting his head on the elbow.

She sat down on the edge of the bed beside him.

When he at last looked up, they sipped their Camparis and watched the rain falling outside the open windows. After eight or ten minutes, Hugo spoke for the first time. His voice was without expression.

'I brought her here to tell her I wasn't going to see her any more. It seemed the right place to tell her. Even before we got here, I didn't want to see her any more. She didn't take it well. No one can blame her for that.'

They listened to the rain. Then he went on in the same dead monotone.

'She wanted to go target-shooting. I took the dogs with us. She had forgotten her ammunition. I told her to wait at the poplars. When I saw she'd gone ahead, I didn't hurry. I went down to the pier and checked the rowboat. I was walking along the shore towards the wheatfield when I heard the screams. Pierce got there first.'

He was silent again. Then he continued:

'I didn't set the dogs on her, but you could say I might as well have done.'

Each of them slowly took a long swallow of Campari.

After a while Georgie said: 'Supposing a bit of your mind wished at that moment she was dead. When somebody makes a problem for me, I often wish they were dead. But it doesn't mean anything. It wouldn't have made any difference to what happened in the wheatfield.' Like him, she couldn't bear to speak of the horror itself, only of 'what happened in the wheatfield'. She paused, then went on: 'There's no point in tormenting yourself with "if only". What happened in the wheatfield happened by chance. That's the point about accidents.'

The rain beat steadily on the roof as they sat side by side in the half dark.

'There's something else,' he said.

She waited.

'That Sunday morning after I hit you, I woke up early. I couldn't sleep. I took the dogs to the wheatfield. I set them on the scarecrow. While I was watching them attack it, I thought of you in your white clothes.' She knew what he was going to say before he went on: 'I let them go on doing it.'

She drew in a long breath.

After some minutes, she reached over for his hand and took it in hers. 'I've had some pretty odd fantasies in my time too,' she said. 'The whole point of fantasies is they have nothing to do with reality.'

They listened to the rain falling on the grass.

Early Monday morning they left Rycroft Lodge. Pierce had come over from his place to help at the gate, opening it just before the station-wagon reached it. Behind their closed windows, Hugo and Georgie gave an impersonal wave to the cameramen and reporters before heading back to the Bay Bridge. Pierce refastened the gate and walked up the winding dirt road towards the empty pen.

That evening Hugo drove Georgie to National Airport to catch the last shuttle to New York so she could be in *World* early the next morning.

34

Towards the end of Tuesday's Question Time in the House of Commons, James Arden MP strolled to his seat halfway up the government back benches. At 3.30 the BITE Secretary would be making his statement on the oilfield licences.

At 3.25 Ian appeared from behind the Speaker's Chair and sat down beside the Prime Minister. Five minutes later he stepped to the dispatch-box.

Honourable Members of the House would know, he said, that the applications under the current round had been considered in every respect. Obviously the long-term benefits to Britain remained paramount. He had decided it was in the national interest for three of the fields to go to British-led consortia.

'One particularly promising field remains,' he said, and here James Arden leaned forward tensely. 'That will go to an American company which, along with a British partner, has given an undertaking to build a refinery in Northern Ireland. My purpose in this instance is to support an industrial partnership which will create many more jobs for the people of Northern Ireland.

'Some Honourable Members have argued that each move we make to strengthen the frail strand of trust between the British and Irish people has been followed by some new act of violence as the IRA attempts to shred that trust.'

He paused for a moment, and the House waited in total silence. It was only a week since the latest atrocity had been perpetrated against the Minister's own family.

Then he went on: 'In granting an exploration licence to a company which is prepared to build a new industry in Northern Ireland, I am telling the IRA it cannot win.'

James Arden sat back, beaming.

'However,' Ian went on, 'two such ventures were under consideration. Star Oil was the first to give an undertaking to build a refinery with its partner, British Refineries. Just before the deadline, Oklahoma Petroleum gave a similar undertaking: if its bid for a field was accepted by me, it too would invest in a refinery in Northern Ireland with its partner, Anglo-North.

'Both these applications were supported by adequate assets.

'Both carried the spin-off undertaking in line with Britain's determination to achieve a communal rapprochement with Northern Ireland.

'Both stipulated that, in line with government policy, BITE would be expected to invest in the new refinery.

'In determining which of the joint ventures I should support, both offering equal benefits for the United Kingdom, the deciding factor was the safety record of the oil industries involved. Star Oil's safety record was sadly blemished by two rig disasters in the North Sea. Since then, Star Oil has improved its safety procedures which, according to independent safety inspectors, are entirely in line with our requirements.

'Nonetheless, with the two bids equal in every other respect, it seemed to me common sense to let the existing records tip the balance. Star Oil was cleared of the charge of criminal negligence. But claims against its management on other charges are still unsettled. Oklahoma Petroleum has an unblemished safety record. Therefore I have granted the remaining exploration licence to Oklahoma Petroleum.'

Ian sat down.

James Arden's ruddy face drained to grey.

His footsteps sounded heavy and wooden on the stone steps of the Commons as he returned to the room he shared with Ian's parliamentary private secretary, Bob Brindle. Arden did not look forward to telephoning J. D. Liddon International. Through his teeth he said to Brindle: 'Lonsdale's decision against Star Oil is bloody rough. Like repunishing a man who has already paid for causing an accident inadvertently.'

'That's not quite fair, James. Claims against Star Oil are still unsettled,' Bob Brindle replied.

What he didn't add was that Ian had told him: 'With the benefits to Britain roughly the same between the two applications, in the end I made my decision on a gut feeling. Too many people interested in Star Oil have turned out to be bad news.'

Two Eames chairs were occupied. A column of smoke rose from one.

'You better have a fucking good explanation,' said Jock.

'I can give you a rational explanation and an irrational one,' Michael replied.

'Jesus. I lose one of my biggest accounts, and now I gotta listen to some psych distinction about how some guy's mind works.' Jock slammed his thick shoulder-blades back against the leather cushions of the chair, making it rock jerkily on its swivel.

'Oklahoma played its cards closer to the chest than we did,' Michael said.

'Whaddaya mean "we"? You're the one I put in charge of the operation, goddammit.'

'I couldn't guess that Oklahoma and Anglo-North were going to slip in an undertaking to match ours just before the final bidding closed.'

'And Arden? What are we paying him for? Do you mean to tell me he couldn't of heard anything on the grapevine? Jesus Christ, Britain is the size of a stamp. It wouldn't have been that hard for him to discover what Anglo-North was up to.'

'His consultancy has been terminated,' Michael said coldly.

'Yeah.' Jock left a threat in the air.

'What we'll never know is whether Lonsdale turned against Star Oil because of the reason he gave or because of something else,' Michael said.

'Like finding Lisa one moment on her back at Claridge's, trying to sell him Star Oil, and the next minute he hears she's been pulled apart by two slobbering killers? I knew they were bad news the first time I saw them. Are you saying Lonsdale maybe was put off having anything more to do with Star Oil just because it reminded him of Lisa?'

Michael stayed silent as he thought of Maureen raising Star Oil with Ian the last time they met in Stag Place. She'd been carrying out Michael's instructions: 'Keep on frightening them, hurting them. Confuse them. Bite the hand that feeds you.'

Then he answered Jock's question: 'It's entirely possible some such consideration influenced Lonsdale.'

Jock rocked back and forth, his cheroot clamped between the short curly lips. He took it from his mouth.

'I gotta tell you something, Mike. I got a feeling that somewhere along the line, you misjudged the quarry. I got a feeling when you went to Britain to sell Star Oil, you let your mind wander to other things. I don't wanna hear about 'em. But I gotta tell you: I can't have somebody working for me who can't keep his mind on what I'm paying him for. Maybe you oughta work full-time for Pat Rourke's little sideline.'

The pupils of Michael's colourless eyes contracted until they were almost invisible. Then he got up and strode from the room. When he closed Jock's brass-studded navy baize door behind him, Jancis looked up from her desk. Starting to speak to him, she thought better of it. Even Jancis was unnerved by the hatred stamped on the narrow face. Without a word between them, Michael walked past her desk and out into the coral-carpeted corridor, closing the door behind him.

That same day on the Eastern Shore of Maryland, the State's Attorney took his decision on whether criminal charges should be filed following the death of Lisa Tabor. He had the police report. He had the county medical examiner's report stating the cause of Lisa Tabor's death was shock and loss of blood resulting from the severing of an artery in her neck while being savaged by two Dobermans.

The State's Attorney concluded there were no charges to file against Hugo Carroll.

When Georgie got back to the editor's office after the afternoon run-through, her secretary said: 'Can you ring Hugo straight away? He's at the *News*.'

The first thing he told Georgie was that no charges were being filed. Then he said: 'What are you doing when you finish at *World* this evening?'

'I still haven't got through the stuff that piled up while I was away last week. I was going to stay here late.'

'I want to talk to you. I was thinking of catching the 6.15 shuttle after I've finished my column.'

She hesitated. She wasn't sure she could take any more knocks for a bit.

'All right,' she said. 'I'll be back at the apartment by eight.'

They got there at almost the same time. Apart from a small black smudge of printer's ink on her white skirt, Georgie looked immaculate. Hugo's straight brown hair was brushed back, yet he had a dishevelled air.

'Let's go in the living-room,' he said. 'Do you mind keeping the answering machine on so we won't be interrupted?'

'I may die if I don't have some strong tea,' she said.

'While you're making it I'll get myself a drink.' The strain in his voice added to her apprehension.

Returning with her tea as dark as peat, she took a chair near where he sat on the sofa. Her stomach was taut.

'I'd wondered about going back to London for a few months,' he began without preamble. 'You already know that our bureau chief there is having some kind of breakdown. All this week I've been thinking that if I took over the London bureau of the *News* for six months, you and I could go back there together with Sarah and Jamie and . . .' He hesitated before saying: 'We could start all over again.'

Georgie sipped her tea.

'But even when I thought that,' Hugo went on, 'I knew it wasn't right. You couldn't leave *World* for that long without throwing in the job altogether. All I would be doing was asking you to make the sacrifice. So then I thought about the *News* main office.'

He took a large swallow of his whisky before going on. 'You know how much I love the Washington bureau. I never thought anything could make me ask to go back to the main office with all its incestuous office politics – men acting like they're still in kindergarten. But if I worked in New York, you and I – and Sarah and Jamie – could be under the same roof. I think we need to spend more time together. I'd like that. Would you?'

'This is ridiculous,' said Georgie, referring to the

tears which had come into her eyes. 'I don't suppose you have a handkerchief?'

He dug into his trouser pocket. After Georgie had blown her nose she said: 'You always told me one of the best things about your success in journalism was being able to call the shots – work where you wanted to work. You hate the main office. Let's just think.'

She finished her tea. 'I might join you in a drink after all. Perhaps even a large one.'

When Hugo returned with two large whiskies and sat down again on the sofa, she said: 'Why can't we work out a compromise? The shuttle doesn't take any longer than lots of people spend driving to work. Why don't you stay at the Washington bureau but come to New York for a night or two with me during the week? And when that isn't possible, I could take the shuttle to Washington and have a night or two with you during the week.' She paused before adding quietly: 'I'd like that, Hugo.'

'It sounds an awful lot of toing and froing,' he said. 'But if we didn't have Rycroft Lodge, I suppose that would make quite a difference to all the charging about.'

Georgie waited, tense.

'You always said you didn't want a third home with all that suitcase-packing,' he went on. 'This afternoon I rang the real estate office. I told them to put Rycroft Lodge on the market.'

He knew he would break down if he spoke of the real reason they couldn't go back to Rycroft Lodge. What happened in the wheatfield would always remain too horrific to be spelled out by either of them. Instead he gave another reason. 'I know. I thought it would be a place to return to the simpler pleasures of childhood. I was wrong.'

Imogene's party was the following Monday. Halfway through that afternoon Georgie stepped into the black Buick waiting outside *World* and soon was back on the shuttle going to Washington again. When she came out the front doors of National Airport, at first Whitmore didn't recognize her.

Ten minutes away from the *News*, he picked up his car phone.

'Don't call him, Whitmore,' Georgie said. 'I'd like to go up to the bureau for a sec anyhow. You hold the car and we'll be down in a few minutes.'

When she walked out of the elevator at the top floor, at first the receptionist behind the sleek Art Deco-style desk didn't recognize her.

'Don't bother to phone him,' Georgie said. 'I'll just go through.'

In his office with its glass wall separating it from the main room of journalists, Hugo had just shut off his computer and walked over to the Edwardian roll-top desk. When he turned around and saw her standing there, at first he didn't recognize her. Then he said: 'It's the same yellow you were wearing that night on the *Aureole*.'

Both of them stood absolutely still for a few moments, Georgie just inside the door, Hugo across the room. He tried to think what it was in her expression that he'd never seen before. Then he realized it was a sudden shyness; she had let down her guard. Ignoring the fact that they were visible to the journalists on the other side of the glass wall, he walked over to her and putting one hand under her chin to raise her face, he kissed her mouth, lightly, several times. He stood back for a moment looking at her, and then moved closer again. Slowly he rubbed his cheek back and forth against hers.

They sat close to each other in the Lincoln. The back of Whitmore's cap and his broad-shouldered uniform gave no hint he might be overhearing them.

'I had a feeling,' Georgie said, 'that Ralph Kernon might baulk at buying me a new Buick Park Avenue just because I've got slightly bored with black. So I'm ordering a respray. What colour do you think would be nice?'

In answer, Hugo took her hand.

'I suppose a yellow car would be just too vulgar,' she said. 'What about racing green?'

'Perfect.'

They both laughed.

The piece of silk edging still hung loose from one of the Regency elbow chairs in Imogene's serene centre hall. On the satinwood Regency tea-table, its hinged leaf now kept closed, two eighteenth-century *famille rose* ginger jars stood in place of the shattered Wedgwood urns.

In the library, Imogene turned unhurriedly from the group around the Secretary of State, moving towards Georgie and Hugo as if she had all the time in the world. 'You look even more dazzling than usual, Georgie. I didn't realize how becoming yellow could be.'

A quarter of an hour later, Georgie felt the presence of his vitality even before she turned and looked directly into Jock's heavy-jowled face. He removed the cheroot from his mouth.

'Listen, Georgie, we oughta get together for a drink,' he said. 'I got something that would interest *World*. Remember that electronics order I offered Ian Lonsdale as part of a package if he put in a word for US Dawn to get landing rights at Gatwick? I've just heard from BITE. They're interested. Very – very – interested.' He drew out the words and nodded his head to make plain how interested BITE was. 'It's a big *big* deal. You gonna be at *World* tomorrow?'

'First thing,' Georgie said, laughing at the unchanged crude directness.

'I'll call you in the morning,' he said. 'And by the way, what's with the yellow dress?'

Georgie caught Hugo's eye. 'It's the new me.'

Discover more about our forthcoming books through Penguin's FREE newspaper...

Penguin
Quarterly

It's packed with:

- exciting features
- author interviews
- previews & reviews
- books from your favourite films & TV series
- exclusive competitions & much, much more...

Write off for your free copy today to:
Dept JC
Penguin Books Ltd
FREEPOST
West Drayton
Middlesex
UB7 0BR
NO STAMP REQUIRED

FOR THE BEST IN PAPERBACKS, LOOK FOR THE

In every corner of the world, on every subject under the sun, Penguin represents quality and variety – the very best in publishing today.

For complete information about books available from Penguin – including Puffins, Penguin Classics and Arkana – and how to order them, write to us at the appropriate address below. Please note that for copyright reasons the selection of books varies from country to country.

In the United Kingdom: Please write to *Dept JC, Penguin Books Ltd, FREEPOST, West Drayton, Middlesex, UB7 0BR.*

If you have any difficulty in obtaining a title, please send your order with the correct money, plus ten per cent for postage and packaging, to *PO Box No 11, West Drayton, Middlesex*

In the United States: Please write to *Dept BA, Penguin, 299 Murray Hill Parkway, East Rutherford, New Jersey 07073*

In Canada: Please write to *Penguin Books Canada Ltd, 2801 John Street, Markham, Ontario L3R 1B4*

In Australia: Please write to the *Marketing Department, Penguin Books Australia Ltd, P.O. Box 257, Ringwood, Victoria 3134*

In New Zealand: Please write to the *Marketing Department, Penguin Books (NZ) Ltd, Private Bag, Takapuna, Auckland 9*

In India: Please write to *Penguin Overseas Ltd, 706 Eros Apartments, 56 Nehru Place, New Delhi, 110019*

In the Netherlands: Please write to *Penguin Books Netherlands B.V., Postbus 3507, NL–1001 AH, Amsterdam*

In West Germany: Please write to *Penguin Books Ltd, Friedrichstrasse 10–12, D–6000 Frankfurt/Main 1*

In Spain: Please write to *Alhambra Longman S.A., Fernandez de la Hoz 9, E–28010 Madrid*

In Italy: Please write to *Penguin Italia s.r.l., Via Como 4, I-20096 Pioltello (Milano)*

In France: Please write to *Penguin France S.A., 17 rue Lejeune, F-31000 Toulouse*

In Japan: Please write to *Longman Penguin Japan Co Ltd, Yamaguchi Building, 2–12–9 Kanda Jimbocho, Chiyoda-Ku, Tokyo 101*

A CHOICE OF PENGUIN FICTION

London Fields Martin Amis

'*London Fields* is more complex and affecting than its predecessor, *Money* ... It is a state-of-England novel that also examines the state of the writer ... He gives us a true story, a murder story, a love story, and a thriller bursting with humour, sex, and often dazzling language' – *Independent*

Sweet Desserts Lucy Ellmann

'A wild book ... interrupted by excerpts from cook books, authoritarian healthy-eating guides, pretentious theses on modern art, officious radio sex-advice shows, diaries, suicide notes...' – *Observer*. 'An enchanting, enchanted book' – Fay Weldon. 'Lucy Ellmann is an original' – *Guardian*

The Lost Language of Cranes David Leavitt

Owen Benjamin has a job, a wife, a son, a steady and well-ordered life, except for one small detail – Owen has spent nearly every Sunday of his married life in a gay porno movie theatre. 'An astonishingly mature and accomplished writer' – *Listener*

The Accidental Tourist Anne Tyler

How does a man addicted to routine – a man who flosses his teeth before love-making – cope with the chaos of everyday life? 'Now poignant, now funny ... Anne Tyler is brilliant' – *The New York Times Book Review*

March Violets Philip Kerr

Berlin, 1936, was full of March Violets, late converts to National Social-ism. For Bernie Gunther business was booming, especially in the missing-persons field. So when Hermann Six hired him to find the murderers of his daughter and son-in-law, Gunther was glad for the variety... 'Different, distinctive and well worth your while' – *Literary Review*

A CHOICE OF PENGUIN FICTION

Have the Men Had Enough?   Margaret Forster

'Mercilessly exact and unsentimental about the desolation of old age and the barnacles of family life ... It is a moving love story, a condemnation of the way we treat our old friends and loves, a rage against the dying of the light' – Philip Howard in *The Times*

Titmuss Regained   John Mortimer

Leslie Titmuss, the abrasive high-flyer who rose from poverty to power in *Paradise Postponed*, is now Secretary of State at H.E.A.P., the Ministry of Housing, Ecological Affairs and Planning. But market forces are sweeping up the Rapstone Valley. *Titmuss Regained* tells what happens when these seismic movements shake the Secretary of State's back garden. 'Richly entertaining' – *Sunday Times*

Passing On   Penelope Lively

'Start reading this absorbing novel and I promise you the toast will burn and the kettle boil dry' – *Daily Mail*. 'Helen and Edward Glover, fifty-two and forty-nine respectively ... have never left home, or not for very long ... What will they do now that mother has gone? ... That is what *Passing On* is about' – *The Times*

The Message to the Planet   Iris Murdoch

For years Alfred Ludens has pursued mathematician and philosopher Marcus Vallar in the belief that he possesses a profound metaphysical formula, a missing link of great significance to mankind. Ludens's friends are more sceptical. 'As highly wrought a work of art as Dame Iris has yet given us' – *Spectator*

Gabriel's Lament   Paul Bailey

'The best novel yet by one of the most careful fiction craftsmen of his generation' – *Guardian*. 'A magnificent novel, moving, eccentric and unforgettable. He has a rare feeling for language and an understanding of character which few can rival' – *Daily Telegraph*

A CHOICE OF PENGUIN FICTION

The House of Stairs Barbara Vine

'A masterly and hypnotic synthesis of past, present and terrifying future ... both compelling and disturbing' – *Sunday Times*. 'Not only ... a quietly smouldering suspense novel but also ... an accurately atmospheric portrayal of London in the heady '60s. Literally unputdownable' – *Time Out*

Summer People Marge Piercy

Every summer the noisy city people migrate to Cape Cod, disrupting the peace of its permanent community. Dinah grits her teeth until the woods are hers again. Willie shrugs and takes on their carpentry jobs. Only Susan envies their glamour and excitement – and her envy swells to obsession... 'A brilliant and demanding novel' – *Cosmopolitan*

The Trick of It Michael Frayn

'This short and delightful book is pure pleasure ... This is a book about who owns the livingness of the living writer; it is funny, moving, intricately constructed and done with an observant wisdom' – Malcolm Bradbury. 'Brilliantly funny, perceptive and, at the death, chilling' – *Sunday Telegraph*

Your Lover Just Called John Updike

Stories of Joan and Richard Maple – a couple multiplied by love and divided by lovers. Here is a portrait of a modern American marriage in all its mundane moments as only John Updike could draw it.

The Best of Roald Dahl

Twenty perfect bedtime stories for those who relish sleepless nights, chosen from his bestsellers – *Over to You*, *Someone Like You*, *Kiss Kiss* and *Switch Bitch*.

A CHOICE OF PENGUIN FICTION

Money Martin Amis

Savage, audacious and demonically witty – a story of urban excess. 'Terribly, terminally funny: laughter in the dark, if ever I heard it' – *Guardian*

The Vision of Elena Silves Nicholas Shakespeare

'A story of love and insurrection brilliantly told' – *Sunday Times*. 'An Englishman's novel of magic realism, flavoured with the more traditional English spices such as a thriller and torchsong, and a touch of Anglo-Saxon irony … A fine literary novel … and exciting to read' – *The Times*

John Dollar Marianne Wiggins

'One of the most disturbing novels I've read in years' – *The New York Times Book Review*. 'Utterly compelling … *Robinson Crusoe* is rewritten by way of Conrad and *Lord of the Flies*, Lévi-Strauss and Freud, but with female leading roles … The result is a vision of hell that's rare in modern fiction' – *Listener*

Killshot Elmore Leonard

'I shoot people,' the Blackbird said. 'Sometimes for money, sometimes for nothing.' 'The best Elmore Leonard yet … this is naturalism carried out with a high degree of art' – *Independent*. 'A grip that seems casual at first and then tightens like a python' – *Daily Telegraph*

A Clockwork Orange Anthony Burgess

'There was me, that is Alex, and my three droogs, that is Pete, Georgie, and Dim, Dim being really dim, and we sat in the Korova Milkbar making up our rassoodocks what to do with the evening...' Horror farce? Social prophecy? Penetrating study of human choice between good and evil? *A Clockwork Orange* is, dazzlingly, all three.

A CHOICE OF PENGUIN FICTION

A Far Cry From Kensington   Muriel Spark

'Pure delight' – Claire Tomalin in the *Independent*. 'A 1950s Kensington of shabby-genteel bedsitters, espresso bars and A-line dresses ... irradiated with sudden glows of lyricism she can so beautifully effect' – Peter Kemp in the *Sunday Times*

Love in the Time of Cholera   Gabriel García Márquez

The Number One international bestseller. 'Admirers of *One Hundred Years of Solitude* may find it hard to believe that García Márquez can have written an even better novel. But that's what he's done' – *Newsweek*

Enchantment   Monica Dickens

The need to escape, play games, fantasize, is universal. But for some people it is everything. To this compassionate story of real lives Monica Dickens brings her unparalleled warmth, insight and perception. 'One of the tenderest souls in English fiction' – *Sunday Times*

My Secret History   Paul Theroux

'André Parent saunters into the book, aged fifteen ... a creature of naked and unquenchable ego, greedy for sex, money, experience, *another life* ... read it warily; read it twice, and more; it is darker and deeper than it looks' – *Observer*. 'On his best form since *The Mosquito Coast*' – *Time Out*

Decline and Fall   Evelyn Waugh

A comic yet curiously touching account of an innocent plunged into the sham, brittle world of high society. Evelyn Waugh's first novel brought him immediate public acclaim and remains a classic of its kind.